Praise for *Proud Legions:*

"In *Proud Legions,* John Antal's rapid-fire novel of Americans at war, the expertise stemming from the author's decades as an army officer provides a truly gripping story of tank combat in Korea as it might be next time."

—W.E.B. Griffin, author of *The Brotherhood of War,*
The Corps, and *Badge of Honor*

"Antal . . . invests his battle scenes with authoritative detail . . . rawly realistic . . . An inside view of the machinations of two armies at war." —*Publishers Weekly*

"A marvelous yarn by an author whose literary sensibilities perfectly complement his expert knowledge of warfare in general and armor combat in particular."

—Rick Atkinson, author of *The Long Gray Line*
and *Crusade: The Untold Story of the Persian Gulf*

"Excellent, exciting, and frightening novel of modern warfare. . . . This is a relentless story, frightening in its realism, fascinating in its technical detail, and thought-provoking. Readers of Tom Clancy, W.E.B. Griffin, and other military novelists will love this novel. For the rest who are interested in a relentless novel of geopolitics, high-tech warfare, and suspense, this is an excellent choice." —*ForeWord*

"Excels in detailing ground combat, in which no superweapon can make the fighting other than brutally hard on minds and bodies, and far from bloodless. Subtle touches of characterization . . . also contribute to making this a darn good read for thriller readers and military buffs alike."

—*Booklist*

"A gifted storyteller."
—Harold Coyle, author of *Team Yankee,*
Bright Star, and *Look Away*

continued on next page . . .

Praise for John Antal's previous books:

"Undeniably enjoyable . . . [*Combat Team*] is a great departure point for examining the way our army should fight at the most critical level—the company—in tough terrain. Shows intimately how old lessons learned the hard way still apply to our high-tech battlefield. This, I think, is the book's greatest strength: the way Antal gets the reader quickly thinking by placing him in the decision-making hot seat, and then leaves his stimulated mind with plenty of food for thought for further contemplation and discussion. Plus, it's just plain fun to read."   —*ARMOR Magazine*

"An extremely clever, curious, and innovative fictional form that is part tactical decision game (TDG), part combat adventure page-turner, and part *The Defense of Duffer's Drift.* One can only hope that the book's subtitle, *The Tank Platoon,* indicates there will be more to follow, in units of different size and type."   —*Marine Corps Gazette*

"This ingenious book . . . is at once entertaining, gripping, and instructive. . . . Strongly recommended for professionals and war-gamers."   —*Tank Magazine*

A NOVEL OF AMERICA'S NEXT WAR

Proud Legions

John F. Antal

JOVE BOOKS, NEW YORK

PROUD LEGIONS

A Jove Book / published by arrangement with
Presidio Press

PRINTING HISTORY
Presidio Press edition published 1999
Jove edition / April 2000

All rights reserved.
Copyright © 1999 by John F. Antal.
Author photo courtesy of author's private collection.
This book may not be reproduced in whole or part,
by mimeograph or any other means, without permission.
For information address: Presidio Press,
505 B San Marin Drive, Suite 300, Novato, CA 94945-1340.

The Penguin Putnam Inc. World Wide Web site address is
http://www.penguinputnam.com

ISBN: 0-515-12784-1

A JOVE BOOK®
Jove Books are published by The Berkley Publishing Group,
a division of Penguin Putnam Inc.,
375 Hudson Street, New York, New York 10014.
JOVE and the "J" design
are trademarks belonging to Penguin Putnam Inc.

PRINTED IN THE UNITED STATES OF AMERICA

10 9 8 7 6 5 4 3 2 1

To my love . . . my wife . . . my life . . . Uncha

Acknowledgments

The views expressed in this book are my own and do not reflect the position or policies of the Department of Defense, the United States Army, or anyone else. The characters in this book are fictional, and any resemblance to any other person, living or dead, is pure coincidence.

I want to thank many people who helped me complete this work: Col. Henry Duran, Lt. Col. Kevin Benson, Lt. Col. David Clark, Capt. Ken Webb, Capt. David Astin, SSgt. Stephen Krivitsky, Dale Lynn, and Professor Jim Hanlon—good friends and comrades—for reviewing the manuscript and offering their insights. Thanks to Bob Kane, Richard Kane, E. J. McCarthy, and the entire crew at Presidio Press for their outstanding support. Also, to T. R. Fehrenbach for writing *This Kind of War: A Study in Unpreparedness* (New York, New York: Macmillan Company, 1963), one of the most stirring and thought-provoking books on war that I know. Introductory quotes for all chapters are taken from this work.

Last, and most important, I want to express my sincere thanks to my wife, Uncha. Chaucer once said, "What is better than wisdom? Woman. And what is better than a good woman? Nothing." In this regard, I am extremely blessed. Without my wife's deep love, support, encouragement, patience, and understanding, this book would not have been written.

"Dragon Force"
Task Force 2-72

CDR: Lt. Col. Mike Rodriguez
XO: Maj. Dave Lucas
S3: Maj. Tony Bradford
CSM: SGM Zeke Dougan

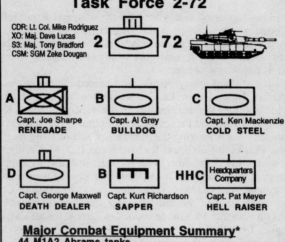

Capt. Joe Sharpe
RENEGADE

Capt. Al Grey
BULLDOG

Capt. Ken Mackenzie
COLD STEEL

Capt. George Maxwell
DEATH DEALER

Capt. Kurt Richardson
SAPPER

Capt. Pat Meyer
HELL RAISER

Major Combat Equipment Summary*
44 M1A2 Abrams tanks
14 M2A2 Bradley fighting vehicles
 6 M121 120mm mortars
 2 Grizzly armored breaching vehicles
 2 Wolverine heavy assault bridges
 1 Volcano automatic mine dispenser [truck mounted]
 3 armored earthmovers [ACE]
 7 M577 armored command post vehicles
 4 fire support vehicles [APC]
 2 combat observation lazing teams [COLTs]
 2 ground surveillance radar teams [APCs]
13 engineer squad armored personnel carriers [APCs]
10 scout HMMWVs
 6 M88A1E1 Hercules recovery vehicles
15 M113 armored personnel carriers [APCs]

*This list does not include the HMMWVs and trucks in the Headquarters Company

List of Major Characters

United States

Major Tony Bradford, operations officer (S3), Task Force 2-72. His radio call sign is Dragon Three. Bradford's tank is named *Defiant.*

Major Jim Cooper, assistant intelligence officer (G2) for Lieutenant Colonel Steve Wallace, 2d Infantry Division.

Captain Audrey Devens, intelligence officer 1st Brigade (S2).

Command Sergeant Major Zeke Dougan, command sergeant major, Task Force 2-72.

Captain Charlie Drake, assistant operations officer, Task Force 2-72.

Private Jamie Emerson, loader on tank C-34, Team Steel, Task Force 2-72.

Captain Al Grey, commander of Bravo Company (Bulldogs), Task Force 2-72. His radio call sign is Bulldog Six. Bravo Company is the reserve company for Task Force 2-72.

Alice Hamilton, civilian television news reporter.

Sergeant First Class Nathaniel Hardee, tank commander of tank C-34, Team Steel, Task Force 2-72. Hardee's radio call sign is Blue Four.

Private First Class Emilio Hernandez, driver of tank C-34, Team Steel, Task Force 2-72.

Colonel Sam Jakes, commander, 1st Brigade, 2d Infantry Division. His radio call sign is Iron Six.

Major Dave Lucas, executive officer (XO), Task Force 2-72. His radio call sign is Dragon Five.

Captain Ken Mackenzie, commander, Team Steel (Steel), Task Force 2-72. The name of his tank is *Conan.* Mackenzie's radio call sign is Steel Six. Team Steel is the primary obstacle breaching team for Task Force 2-72.

Captain George Maxwell, commander, Team Dealer (Death Dealers), Task Force 2-72. Maxwell's radio call sign is Dealer Six. Team Dealer is the Task Force advance guard team.

Captain Pat Meyer, headquarters company commander, Task Force 2-72.

Staff Sergeant Steve Obrisky, (called Ski by his crew) gunner on tank Headquarters 66 *Firebreather. Firebreather* is Lieutenant Colonel Rodriguez's M1A2 Abrams tank.

Captain Kurt Richardson, Task Force 2-72 engineer company commander.

Lieutenant Colonel Michael Rodriguez, commander of Task Force 2-72, the Dragon Force. Rodriguez's tank is named *Firebreather.* Rodriguez's radio call sign is Dragon Six.

Paul Schaefer, Alice Hamilton's cameraman and friend.

Major General George Schmidt, commander of the 2d Infantry Division.

Lieutenant Colonel Steve Wallace, division intelligence officer (G2), 2d Infantry Division.

Corporal Kye-Wan Oh, KATUSA (Korean Augmentation to the U.S. Army) Gunner on tank C-34.

South Korea

Sergeant Kim, 2d Lieutenant Sung-Joo's platoon sergeant.

2d Lieutenant Ri Sung-Joo, Republic of Korea Army (ROK) infantry platoon leader.

North Korea

Admiral Bae, deputy commander of the North Korean navy.

Lieutenant Colonel Byung Chae Do, commander, Fighter Bomber Squadron 214, which consists of twelve twin engine, SU-25 fighter bombers.

Major Chun Yong-ho, commander of the 136th Howitzer Battalion.

Admiral Gung, commander of the ROK navy and the People's Militia. Kim Seung-Hee's nemesis.

General Hyon Chol Hae, commander of 3d Corps.

Major General Kang Sung-Yil, Marshal Kim Seung-Hee's Chief of Staff of the 1st Army Group.

Marshal Kim Seung-Hee, marshal of the North Korean People's Army. His nickname is the Wolf.

Major General Park Chi-won, commander of the 820th Tank Corps.

Colonel So Hyun Jun, personal aide to Marshal Kim Seung-Hee.

Colonel Yi Sung-Chul, commander, 1st Brigade, 820th Corps.

Major General Yim, a commander in the People's Militia.

Captain Yu Sum-Chul, recently promoted to command a BMP company.

Author's Note

In 1979 the M1 Abrams series main battle tank was introduced and a legend was born. This remarkable new weapon system, with its combination of speed and quickness, firepower, and advanced armor, was the culmination of years of exhaustive research. The M1 could withstand a hit from any current antitank projectile, direct lethal firepower with pinpoint accuracy, and negotiate virtually any terrain with the quickness and agility of a vehicle a fraction its size. The ability to fight, "fightability," had now been elevated to new levels, another step closer to the warrior's dream—the ultimate fighting machine.

The legacy of armor continues today with the emergence of the M1A2 main battle tank—a weapon system offering dramatic improvements in system supportability, survivability, and fightability. The M1A2 main battle tank is equipped with improved armor, increased lethality, high agility, and a low silhouette.

The armor protection of the M1A2 is superb. Experience from Operation Desert Storm and continued live-fire testing assures that armor protection is not an empty claim. Unlike all previous U.S. tanks, the M1 is built completely from armor plate (a sandwich of special Chobham armor and ceramic blocks, depleted uranium mesh, and rolled homogenous armor plate) instead of a cast hull and turret. This armor protection, combined with outstanding quickness and mobility, nuclear-biological-chemical protection, automatic-fire suppression, and ammunition compartmentalization, establishes the M1A2 as today's most formidable main battle tank. In addition, the M1A2's suite of advanced displays, controls, and survivability enhancements as well as addition of data and power management systems elevates the fightability of the main battle tank to new levels.

The most innovative feature of the M1A2 system is the core vetronics system; which is to the close combat weapon system what avionics is to the jet fighter. Instead of separate, hard wiring components, all controls are lined through two electronic buses, one controlling power, the other data. In an integrated weapon system, all elements must be both tolerant and reliable—not only on their own, but in concert with the system as a whole.

The M1A2's vetronic system not only improves combat operations through the integration of faster, more accurate, target acquisition systems; it also improves supportability through inherently reliable digital electronics and critical component redundancy. Integrated within the M1A2 are a number of exceptional subsystems that function together as a whole, enabling the soldier to perform much more effectively on the battlefield. In addition, the commander, gunner, and driver can analyze most problems through a testing mechanism embedded in the system.

One of the primary increases in combat effectiveness that the M1A2 offers is target acquisition for hunter-killer teams. That capability is centered around a key M1A2 component—the commander's independent thermal viewer or CITV. The CITV enables the commander to view the entire battlefield, separate from the gunner, while still directing the firing of the main gun. The hunter-killer capability provides the M1A2 main battle tank with a decisive advantage in the heat of close combat.

Because the M1A2 system is fully integrated, mutual position navigation on the battlefield is now a reality. Each commander is provided with position information on his tank, the tanks in his command network, and fixed enemy positions. This permits designated battlefield synchronization of all platoon and company assets.

The CITV image and position navigation information are displayed at the commander's integrated display. Position information can be instantaneously transmitted to other command elements through the SINCGARS radio system (single channel ground-air radio system). SINCGARS is a frequency-hopping radio system that is difficult to jam or intercept.

Steer-to navigation data along with system status is transmitted to the driver through the driver's integrated display. This unit combines the operation of three panels into one line replaceable unit.

The tank commander's view of the battlefield is enhanced

through an entirely redesigned tank commander's weapon station (TCWS). The improved TCWS offers the tank commander a dramatic increase of his field of view.

The M1A2's primary sight employs a dual axis stabilized head, enabling the gunner to effectively track evasive ground and air targets. Algorithms in the core system calculate target motion and permit the gunner to engage and destroy evasive targets.

The gunner's control and display panel has automated ballistic solutions of both ground and air targets. It also has the capability to accommodate smart munitions that are currently in development.

Today, fightability is the culmination of the weapon's system availability to help the soldier make the most effective, best informed decision—in the least amount of time. The performance of the M1A2 tanks, and the tankers that crew them, defines that term.

A further note: An extensive glossary is located in the back of the book.

Prologue

Associated Press news story: North Korea threatened today to use its new rocket system for military use. The United States considered the launch a bold demonstration of North Korea's growing missile technology. North Korea reportedly is trying to develop ballistic missiles with enough range to hit Hawaii and Alaska. . . .

Reuters news story: North Korea has stepped up its "blitzkrieg" war plan against the South by deploying aircraft capable of reaching Seoul in about six minutes. North Korea has doubled its number of long-range artillery and small-sized submarines, and deployed 120 tactical fighter jets at bases near the front line. . . .

Associated Press news story: North Korea believes the United States would abandon the Korean peninsula in less than a month if an opening rocket and artillery barrage could inflict at least 20,000 American casualties, a North Korean defector told a congressional panel. Choi Joo-Hwai, who was a colonel in the North Korean People's Army, said if war breaks out on the Korean peninsula, the north's main target will be the U.S. forces based in the south and in Japan. . . .

1

REVENGE

For every time a nation or a people commits its sons to combat, it inevitably commits its full prestige, its hopes for the future, and the continuance of its way of life, whatever it may be.

—T. R. FEHRENBACH

4:00 P.M., 22 February 1968, South Korea, one kilometer south of the demilitarized zone. He stared at the cold, snow-covered field with the eyes of a practiced predator. He sensed victory. Now and then, he recognized, there is a sharp moment in time when you see something and realize that it can go either way. The vision shimmers in and out. In one possibility you seize the opportunity and win; in the other, your enemies grind you to dust.

This was one of those moments.

The major lay in the cold snow, listening, waiting, oblivious to the frigid ground. He concentrated his thoughts, his entire being, on one purpose—revenge. He rolled the feeling over in his heart, and it kept him warm.

He considered his next move.

The major wore white camouflage—a white parka, white field trousers, and white gloves. His men wore the same camouflage; even the stocks of their PPSH submachine guns were white. Only the steel-blue barrel of the major's Marakov pistol and the small red star fixed in the center of his white fur hat clashed with the snow. His men moved eagerly across the snowy field·like a pack of hungry wolves closing in for the kill.

The sinking sun cast long shadows on the barren South Korean field as a flock of magpies landed a hundred meters away. The birds disregarded the heavily armed North Korean patrol and pecked at the dry rice stalks sticking out of the snow. Then, suddenly aware and startled, the magpies flew off to the mountains to the east.

The major smiled slightly as he thought of himself as a wolf on the hunt. His fifteen-man patrol had slipped through the barbed wire and minefields of the demilitarized zone (DMZ) and infiltrated past the American outposts in the cold darkness of the early morning. It had taken the patrol most of the day to carefully work its way to the ambush site. The plan was simple. The Americans—notoriously sloppy with security—would simply drive down the road and fall into his trap.

The major scanned the line of fir trees that paralleled the road directly in front of him. He did not have to be here, risking himself like a common soldier. There were dozens of other experienced fighters who could have accomplished this mission. But that was not his way. His aggressive leadership and his reputation for ruthlessness had already marked him as one of the rising stars in a military hierarchy dominated by other tough, relentless, hard-hearted wolves.

But it was more than ruthlessness. The major was a hunter who loved the hunt. He always went forward, leading from the front. It was positive and effective; pushing from the rear was defeatist and impotent. These were the tenets he lived by and would always follow. No, he did not have to be here. He wanted to be here, if for no other reason than to get another crack at the Americans.

He waved his right arm, signaling for his men to move forward. They obeyed without hesitation. They ran swiftly across the fallow rice field to the line of trees, their weapons at the ready. He heard the muffled sounds of heavy boots crunching through the crusty snow as the wolves ran forward.

The major dashed to the trees, and then plopped to the ground near the road. Two soldiers positioned a Russian-made RPK machine gun to his right. The rest of the pack—most carrying 7.62mm PPSh-41 burp guns with heavy seventy-one-round magazines—lay to the left and right. Silence covered the ground again as the hunters waited.

The hills in the distance were scarred and devoid of trees. The emptiness of the frozen rice paddy was blanketed with anticipation. A biting wind blew from the east, and he felt the temperature drop a few more degrees.

He pulled the slide of his automatic pistol to the rear and flicked the safety to the fire position. As he waited for the enemy to arrive, the rustle of the cold wind across the barren land triggered his memories. War had been his life as long as he could remember. He had learned to fight—and hate—when he was only a boy of twelve. During the 1950–53 Korean War, his mother, two brothers, and a sister were killed as they slept when American aircraft dropped a wave of high-explosive bombs on his village. He had been away that evening visiting his father's grave on a nearby mountaintop, a trip he made every week without fail. Returning to find the devastation, he felt as though his world was destroyed. As he sat in the ashes of his home and waited to die, a North Korean patrol arrived to look for survivors. The soldiers gave him some water and a handful of rice. He didn't know how many days he had been sitting there. They took him with them. Since that day, he had served in the Inmun Gun, the North Korean People's Army (NKPA).

At first he acted as an ammunition carrier. Then, when they discovered that he could read and write, he became a message runner. Finally, when his zeal to kill was acknowledged, they gave him a rifle. He became a sniper. He kept score of the enemies he had killed by cutting notches on the stock of his rifle. When the war became stationary, with both sides operating from dug-in trench lines that crossed the width of the Korean peninsula, his killing talent became legendary. As the war drew to a close, he often went out alone to snipe at the enemy and didn't return until he had a confirmed kill. He didn't make many friends, but he did kill many South Koreans and Americans. In recognition of his deadly skill, his fellow soldiers gave him his nom de guerre, the Wolf.

The Americans formed the nucleus of the hatred that burned in his belly. These arrogant devils—the *mee-gook-nom*—with their affluence and sophisticated war machines, had killed his family and divided his country. To him, the Americans were not men but merely targets; they deserved nothing less than extermination for preserving the agony of Korea's civil war. He relished the moment when an American was in his rifle sights.

The minutes ticked by as the hunters waited silently in ambush, stone statues lying prone against the cold earth. The major had drilled his handpicked team into a perfect killing machine, having rehearsed each mission a dozen times before. The price of admission into this select group was complete discipline and absolute personal loyalty to him. All the men were willing to suffer any hardship, including death, for their cause and their leader.

The sky changed from gray to deep violet. The major glanced at his watch, angered that the Americans were late. Previous patrols had reported that an American jeep transported mail from Uijonbu to the American camp on the DMZ each day at 4 P.M. Time is everything in war.

"Comrade Major," whispered the soldier to his right. "There."

The major smiled and looked down the icy road to the south. A jeep was moving at a steady pace, the tire chains clanging against the wheel well. There was no escort vehicle, just a lone jeep on a routine jaunt down a deserted road.

The machine gunner aimed at the enemy, then glanced at his leader for permission to fire. The Wolf shook his head. Time seemed to move in slow motion as his heart thumped loudly in his chest. He pulled a stick grenade from the right side of his belt and checked the pin. Then, as he had experienced a dozen times before, a strange, callous calm came over him.

The last rays of the sun sank below the horizon. The jeep rolled forward like a lamb to the slaughter, skidding on patches of ice but moving ever closer to the wolves. The machine-gun team was ready to fire, the gunner barely breathing as the jeep approached from only a hundred meters away. The major pulled the pin on his grenade and snapped back the string in the base of the stick in a sharp jerk. The grenade fuse smoldered. The soldier to his left pulled back the charging handle on his burp gun. Fifty meters . . . thirty.

When the major could clearly see the faces of the driver and passenger in the front seat, he lobbed the grenade toward the center of the road. It bounced on the ice, slid in front of the advancing jeep, and exploded. In a wild turn, the vehicle careened into the frozen rice paddy to the right of the road.

The blast from the grenade resonated in the empty Korean hills. For a few seconds nothing happened, then the door of the jeep opened and a South Korean soldier staggered out, shocked and confused.

"Fire," the Wolf yelled. The North Korean machine gun opened up on the stunned survivor with a quick, short, killing burst. The high-pitched, tearing sound of the Russian-made RPK machine gun echoed across the frozen valley. The bullets ripped into the driver's chest and he fell to the ground, splattering crimson over the white snow.

"Take them," the major commanded. He stood up and rushed the jeep as the rest of his soldiers sprang forward. "I want the rest alive."

Three of the men sprinted across the road, tore open the canvas doors of the jeep, and pulled two dazed survivors from the wreck. Other North Koreans formed a security perimeter around the vehicle.

They shoved the two Americans facedown into the snow. Both men wore well-made olive drab fatigues, field jackets, and black leather gloves. The tall, dark-haired man, who wore the chevrons of a sergeant first class, was bleeding from the forehead.

A North Korean captain kicked the short, curly-haired private, who screamed in terror. Another North Korean pressed the barrel of his burp gun to the man's head. The captain searched the American's pockets and took a pack of cigarettes and a lighter, wallet, and wristwatch. He stuffed the loot in his own pocket, then placed the watch on his wrist.

The captain moved to the sergeant, who arched up in opposition. The captain deftly delivered a stroke to the captive's back with the wooden butt of his burp gun. The American crumpled to the ground, and his captors savagely kicked him.

"That's enough," the major commanded in Korean.

The kicking stopped and the sergeant lay still, gasping for breath and spitting up blood. The captain searched the sergeant and removed some papers and a gold cigarette case from the man's fatigue jacket. Then he dutifully handed the cigarette case over to the major.

"Pathetic, aren't they?" the Wolf said in clear English, calculated to taunt his captives. Holding the cigarette case in his left hand, he glanced at his watch, then switched back to Korean. "It's getting too late for prisoners."

The North Koreans forced the two Americans to kneel in front of the major.

"No, no," the younger, curly-haired American screamed. "Don't kill me. I'll tell you whatever you want."

"Shut up, Jenkins," the sergeant ordered. "You tell 'em nothing."

"No . . . please," the boy said as he kneeled, sobbing, in the snow.

The Wolf tucked his pistol in his belt. He held the cigarette case and admired the flat, gold rectangle as if it were a prized trophy. Pushing a button on the case's side, he opened the top, revealing ten American cigarettes. He removed one and lit it with the pilfered lighter, then, in the light of his burning cigarette, he slowly translated the English inscription engraved on the inside of the case.

He smiled and closed the case with a snap. The American sergeant watched in silence as the major puffed slowly on the cigarette. It burned to the end, extinguishing its purpose. The Wolf threw it into the snow and watched the glowing butt turn cold and dark.

"Don't kill me," repeated Jenkins as he continued to sob.

The major stepped over to the private. With all the emotion of a man dropping a piece of rubbish in a trash can, he put his Makarov pistol to the boy's head and pulled the trigger. Blood and pieces of Jenkins's skull splattered the sergeant. He turned away as the body jerked, muscles reflexing from the shock of death. The North Koreans plopped the private in front of the American sergeant. The ghastly caricature that had once been Jenkins's face stared back at him.

A roar broke the silence as a helicopter flew low overhead, moving at maximum speed only twenty feet above the ground. The North Koreans immediately dispersed, then raised their rifles and fired.

The major stood and looked up as his men shot at the helicopter. Although it was unarmed, it would have a radio and would report their presence, the major thought. He knew that he would have to withdraw quickly to the safety of his own lines a few miles north across the demilitarized zone.

With a mighty lunge, the tall American took advantage of the confusion and grabbed the major. Before he could react, the big American slammed him into the jagged bumper of the crashed vehicle. The North Korean screamed like a wild animal as the sharp, serrated metal bumper gouged the left side of his face.

A long flash of machine-gun tracers chased off the helicopter. At the same time, three North Koreans pounced on the American sergeant, threw him to the ground, and butt-stroked him with their burp guns. The sergeant doubled over in pain.

"Stop," the Wolf ordered as he struggled to his feet. He rose from the front of the jeep and faced the sergeant. Shaking with pain, he took a 9mm pistol from his belt and cocked the hammer.

A cold breeze blew over the frozen field as the North Koreans forced the sergeant to his knees. The major dropped his blood-covered white glove and revealed the terrible gash in his left eye. The American, kneeling and battered, his face also bleeding from repeated blows, faced his executioner.

The major couldn't see through his left eye. He knew, as clearly as he knew that the American sergeant was about to die, that he had lost his eye.

Trembling in pain, the major pointed the pistol at the sergeant's head and looked into his eyes. In spite of the sergeant's predicament, his face revealed proud defiance. The look enraged the major.

"Fuck you," the American sergeant mumbled, his jaw broken and bloody.

The Wolf fired, and the sergeant collapsed in the snow.

The major holstered his pistol and picked up the gold cigarette case lying at his feet.

2

PREPARATION FOR COMBAT

While civilizations live, they may still aspire, and hope—as long
as their legions can hold the far frontier.   —T. R. FEHRENBACH

**Present day, 6:00 P.M., 25 September, Osan Air Force Base,
South Korea.** "All passengers will now exit the aircraft," a
well-rehearsed female voice directed over the Boeing 747's intercom system. "Please remember to check for all carry-on
baggage. The crew of Flight 008 and Tower Airlines thank you
for your patronage and hope you have a pleasant stay in
Korea."

"Sounds like we're tourists or something," a young soldier
with one stripe on his green army uniform said with a laugh.

"Yeah, you're gonna see all the sights," another soldier ban-
tered. "Just don't forget to send postcards."

Private Jamie Emerson smiled and picked up a small black
canvas backpack. He moved through the line of soldiers waiting to depart, then stepped off the airplane onto a stairway that
led to the Osan Air Base tarmac.

The overcast sky was heavy with the promise of more rain.
Puddles of water speckled the runway.

"So this is the Land of the Morning Calm," someone said.

Emerson heard the comment and wondered why everyone

used that description for Korea. All he knew with any certainty was that it wasn't anything like Kentucky.

"This way, keep moving," a soldier with an armband that read "Port Reception" announced. "Follow the yellow line."

Private Emerson moved with the other passengers of the chartered aircraft and followed the line of soldiers into the terminal building. The slight, drizzling rain that sprayed him with moisture failed to dampen his spirits.

For him, the long journey from Fort Knox, Kentucky, to Osan, Korea, was the beginning of a great adventure. Before today, he had never set foot outside Kentucky. Serving in the army in Korea sounded exciting. Visions of strange places, beautiful almond-eyed girls, and exotic food had filled his dreams; now the great adventure was about to begin.

"Welcome to Korea and the Eighth United States Army," announced a hard-looking black sergeant in heavily starched U.S. Army battle dress fatigues. "Hold on to your bags and move in a line to the processing stations to your left," he said as the new arrivals entered the airport terminal building. "Once you arrive at the first station, have your orders and ID card ready."

Emerson and the others obeyed as a few nervous jokes were quietly bandied back and forth. The soldiers moved slowly through the queue, showing their papers to a series of unsmiling clerks and dour South Korean customs officials, until they finally arrived at the baggage pickup point. Heavy green duffel bags were piled unceremoniously in a huge mound. Emerson searched for his bag and finally discovered the one with his name and serial number stenciled in tan letters on its side. He joined another line to board a bus marked "2d Infantry Division Only." In minutes three buses, packed to overflowing with replacements and their baggage, headed out.

Emerson's bus raced north along Highway 3, jinking in and out of the clogged traffic like a prizefighter bobbing and weaving in the ring. Emerson could not believe how many cars there were in Korea. To make the ride more hair-raising, each car, bus, and truck on the road appeared to have the right-of-way. Emerson watched as the nonchalant Korean bus driver, who seemed oblivious to the danger at every turn, cut in and out of traffic as if he were driving a Maserati sports car.

Emerson smiled to himself, thinking that this ride looked like something out of a scene from a grade B movie he had once seen: *Death Race 2000*. If there were any traffic regulations in this country, Emerson thought, this bus driver must be exempt. After a two-hour ride, he sighed with relief as the bus slowed down and entered a U.S. military installation. The harrowing traffic gauntlet was over. A well-lit sign over the front gate read "Camp Casey Replacement Center."

A South Korean security guard wearing a brown uniform and a white armband with the large letters SP lifted a barber-striped pole that blocked the entrance and waved the bus through the gate. The bus drove inside and came to an abrupt halt seconds later. A sergeant entered the bus and barked some curt instructions. Then the tired soldiers, surrounded by duffel bags and suitcases, formed a human chain to empty the bus.

Exhausted after the eighteen-hour plane ride, Emerson staggered out of the bus and lined up with the rest of the replacements. After a short greeting by the sergeant in charge of the detachment, the weary men hurried through a linen issue and were assigned to bunk beds arrayed in an open-bay barracks. The soldiers made their beds quickly, stowed their gear under their bunks, and collapsed on the thin mattresses, happy for the opportunity to rest.

Emerson spent his first two days in Korea in a place affectionately named, and unofficially titled, the Turtle Farm. It was the replacement center for the 2d Infantry Division. At the Turtle Farm each soldier who entered the division was billeted in an ancient Quonset hut, issued a Kevlar helmet and several bags of essential combat gear, and briefed on subjects from hemorrhagic fever to venereal disease—typical army horror stories of ghastly illnesses that were contracted from contact with everything from bugs to sex. Then the men were processed through finance, dental, and hospital administration sections and assigned to a battalion. All of this was conducted with an efficiency that impressed Emerson.

He learned that the Turtle Farm was Camp Casey's eternal joke on all new replacements. In the old days, so the story went, soldiers could not leave Korea until they grew their own replacement. The joke was that it took twelve months to move from the reception to the departure station, as slow as the speed of a turtle. New soldiers were christened turtles; they were hatched at the Turtle Farm and were destined to return only after their twelve-month journey, when more turtles would arrive to replace them. After the Turtle Farm, tankers went to one of the two tank battalions or the division cavalry squadron. On his second day in-country—or was it still the first? Emerson was too tired to know—he received assignment orders. He and five other new 19-kilos—the military occupational specialty (MOS) code for an M1A2 tanker—were assigned to the 2d Battalion, 72d Armor.

"You six nineteen-kilos, get over here," a sergeant shouted. "Y'all belong to me now. Y'all are joining the Dragon Force, the best fucking outfit in the army. My outfit. Any questions?"

Emerson remained silent. At basic training he had learned that sergeants were the nearest thing to God on earth. The last thing he wanted to do was piss off one of them on his first day. The rest of the new soldiers must have felt the same way. No one asked any questions.

"Now, quit standing there being useless and hop into the back of my Humvee," the sergeant bellowed, obviously amused at the confusion on the soldiers' faces. "Assholes and elbows, gentlemen. We haven't got all day."

The sergeant pointed to the back of his truck, and Emerson and his mates responded immediately. They quickly threw in their baggage and climbed aboard.

The overcrowded Humvee, a half-ton utility truck identified by the unpronounceable acronym HMMWV, for high-mobility multipurpose wheeled vehicle, rolled slowly out the gate of the Turtle Farm and up the hill to the 2d Tank Battalion headquarters building. The soldiers sat in silence on the short ride as they took in the sights of their new home. After the truck jerked to a stop, the sergeant ordered the men to dismount and grab their gear.

"Hanson," the sergeant yelled to his driver, "tell the PAC that the latest batch of turtles has arrived."

A minute later the door opened to the battalion's Personnel Action Center (PAC). Three sergeants, one carrying a clipboard with a stack of papers, approached the truck.

"Welcome to the Dragon Force, 2d Battalion, 72d Armor," a thin, serious sergeant said as the replacements stood in a semicircle in front of the unloaded Humvee. The other two sergeants stood quietly by his side. "I'm Sergeant First Class Sterling. If you know what's good for you, you'll listen up."

The replacements circled closer to the sergeant, waiting for the word.

"You're in the big black patch division now, called the Indianhead Division. It's the only army unit still operating in the Land Before Time. This ain't Kansas and you aren't at Auntie Em's anymore. You can click your heels all you want, but for the next twelve months you'll still be right here."

The soldiers chuckled.

Sterling smiled. "Now listen and maybe you'll stay out of the shit for a while. This ain't Fort Carson and this ain't Fort Hood. You can't own a car and you can't go home to momma at night. You'll live in a barracks, when you're not in the field, and you'll soldier hard. Those of you thinking about an early drop—going home early—forget it. You won't get one."

The smiles evaporated, but Sterling was moving into high gear. A pair of Blackhawk helicopters flew low over the hills to the west, close enough to draw the attention of the replacements. Sergeant Sterling paused to let the noise pass before continuing his speech.

"This place, Camp Casey, will be your home for the next twelve months. We're located twenty kilometers northeast of Seoul, the capital of ROK. Seoul is just thirty klicks from the DMZ. For you turtles, that's the demilitarized zone that separates North and South Korea. Although the friggin' Korean War ended in 1953, the Reds never signed a peace treaty, and the United States is still technically at war with North Korea. North of us about fifteen klicks are about a million screaming motherfucking communists who want to mount your heads on spikes."

Sterling paused, obviously proud of his presentation, and waited for his words to sink in. "Here in the Dragon Force, we have to be ready to fight within two hours. Do you understand what I'm saying?"

"Yes, Sergeant," was the jumbled reply.

"Here we train for war," Sterling continued. "Since we're only fifteen kilometers from the DMZ, we're well within range of North Korean artillery. In the 2d Infantry Division, you'll live under the range of the enemy's guns every day. Any questions?"

"Sergeant, how long will everyone call us turtles?" asked a thin black soldier to Emerson's left.

The men laughed.

"That all depends on you, soldier," Sterling answered with a smile, then looked down at his clipboard. He handed a paper copy of military assignment orders to the two sergeants standing by his side, Sergeant Webster and Sergeant First Class Hardee.

"Okay, Sergeant Hardee, these three are yours—Emerson, Champion, and Marlet." Sterling pointed to Emerson and two soldiers standing next to him. "Sergeant Webster, Delta Company gets Strain, Elting, and Weinberg."

"Okay, any more questions?" Sterling said, raising his left eyebrow.

"What are our barracks like?" a young soldier, Private Champion, asked.

"You'll find out soon enough," Sterling replied. "It ain't called a hardship tour for nothing."

"Sergeant," Private Marlet said in a confident voice, "where's the nightlife around here?"

Sterling laughed, shook his head, and looked at Sergeants Webster and Hardee, who grinned. "Take good care of them. We won't be getting any more replacements for a while. And Hardee, make sure you show your turtles some of our nightlife."

Hardee laughed. "They'll get an education tomorrow."

Sterling snickered at the inside joke and turned toward the building. Sergeant Webster motioned for his three soldiers to follow him. The replacements bound for Delta Company walked away.

Emerson, Champion, and Marlet stood in front of Sergeant Hardee. The sergeant was a big NCO, powerfully built, with thick, strong arms. His weathered face was serious. His dark complexion and bushy, dark eyebrows created an air of ferocity.

He eyed the replacements with disdain. "All right, you turtles. Pick up your shit and follow me. You're all part of C Company now."

Emerson, Champion, and Marlet followed Hardee like lambs to the slaughter. Each man carried two overstuffed duffel bags and a bulging sack of combat gear—helmet, gas mask, pistol belt, poncho, and sleeping bag—the tools of the trade. Struggling with their heavy bags, they made their way to the Charlie Company orderly room.

"Wait here," Hardee ordered.

The three new soldiers dropped their heavy, unwieldy bags in a heap and dutifully stood outside the room while the sergeant went inside. A few seconds later another sergeant emerged wearing the chevrons and diamond of a first sergeant.

Emerson knew about first sergeants. Reverently called "top" by veteran soldiers, first sergeants ran the army. They were responsible to the company commander, a captain, for discipline and individual training. A first sergeant was the man in charge and the nearest thing to God in a tank company.

"So, Hardee tells me you're interested in our nightlife. Well, you've arrived just in time for the fun," 1st Sgt. Dennis Spurr said as the privates listened quietly. Spurr, a thin black man, looked each man over in an intense, head-to-toe inspection.

Emerson and the other two soldiers stood still, wondering nervously what would happen next.

"Welcome to Team Cold Steel, better known as Steel, the best company in the Dragon Force," said Spurr. "Champion and Marlet, you're assigned to 1st Platoon. Emerson, you go to 3d Platoon, tank three-four. Sergeant Hardee is your platoon sergeant and your tank commander. He'll take you to your billet. You two will come with me."

"What about tomorrow, Top?" Hardee asked. "You want them to come along or stay here and in-process?"

"The field is the perfect introduction for these fine young men to learn about our off-duty hours recreational program," Spurr said with a wide grin. Then he turned to the replacements, the smile leaving his face. "We leave tomorrow morning at oh-six-hundred for a four-week tank gunnery training exercise. I'll see you at formation at oh-four-hundred. Sergeant Hardee will get you settled tonight, after you get your field gear ready. Just remember one thing and you'll never have any trouble from me: Nobody in Cold Steel ever quits."

2:00 A.M., 28 September, Marshal Kim Seung-Hee's bunker, northeast of Pyongyang, North Korea. The old man gently rubbed his black eye patch while he contemplated his next move. Cigarette smoke fouled the air of the dimly lit conference room as four senior army generals, an air force general, and an admiral—each personally selected by Marshal Kim Seung-Hee, the Wolf—sat in leather chairs around a large three-dimensional model of the northern half of South Korea. A large screen adorned the wall opposite the officers.

"Each of you has been invited here to share a proposal that I intend to present to our Great Leader, Kim Jong II," Kim Seung-Hee explained. "Each of you has sworn secrecy about these discussions. General Kang Sung-Yul, the chief of staff of the 1st Army Group, who planned Operation Daring Thrust, will brief us first. Then we will have time for a short discussion."

"Phase one of Daring Thrust has been executed according to plan," General Kang said proudly, pointing to a set of colorful briefing slides on the screen. "All the prescribed units are in their designated underground shelters. All report unit readiness status one in maintenance, logistics, and training."

The briefing room grew silent as Kang waited for his master to speak. The air seemed heavy. The significance of the meeting was not lost on the audience, particularly in these troubled times.

Kim Seung-Hee puffed smoke rings into the air and watched them float across space to the ceiling. He enjoyed the dramatic effect of the silence. His headaches, which were frequent, diminished when he smoked. When this failed, he found some relief in the painkillers his doctor had prescribed. He hadn't taken any of the little white pills for several hours.

"The Daring Thrust plan calls for a shock battle campaign of twenty-five elite divisions," Kim announced. "These divisions will attack with thunderclap surprise, emerging from their protected underground facilities before the enemy can mobilize. The goal of this attack is to dramatically reverse the political-economic situation on the peninsula in a campaign of only ten days."

The gray-haired marshal with the black eye patch smiled cynically. He knew the plan well. The men in this room were his trusted senior leaders. The officers commanding the twenty-five divisions designated for the attack had been hand-picked by Kim. The sequence of events that would propel the plan into action, however, was known by only a few.

"The objective of Daring Thrust is the surrender of the South Korean government and the withdrawal of all foreign forces from Korea," General Kang continued. "We all know that we do not have the strength for a long war. Instead we will aim at penetrating the border in several specific strike sectors. Strategic and tactical surprise is critical. Once our infantry forces have penetrated the enemy's initial defenses, the highly mobile 1st Army Group will smash its way south and isolate Seoul. We will then propose a cease-fire. If the South Koreans do not agree we will threaten to bombard Seoul with nerve gas."

General Kang paused to let this point sink in. Everyone in the audience understood the tremendous political significance of this bold plan.

"Why should the fascists negotiate with us?" a white-haired admiral interjected. "Won't they just fight until more Americans arrive?"

"Admiral Bae, you fear the Americans too much," Marshal Kim Seung-Hee said with a sneer. "The Americans are cowards and fear war; they will do anything to avoid it. The South Korean government has the same disease and is composed of weak politicians and fat businessmen who care only about their mistresses and their bank accounts."

The generals laughed. Admiral Bae did not.

"The Americans expect their technology to allow them to fight at a safe distance," Kim jeered. "They believe that wars can be fought with minimal casualties. They have no stomach for the deadly, close combat that we intend to wage against them."

Cigarette smoke hung in thick clouds near the bright lamps above the terrain model. The rest of the room was conspicuously dark. Kim glanced at the six armed guards standing at rigid attention against the walls, their well-oiled AK-47 assault rifles glistening in the dim light.

General Kang saw his cue and continued. "Comrades, here are the details of Daring Thrust. Prior to the attack, special operations units will infiltrate the second front—the enemy's rear areas—by land, tunnel, sea, and air to attack critical targets. They will attempt to destroy all airports and air bases, Seoul's communications centers, American military garrisons, vital bridges, military ammunition dumps, storage facilities, and seaports. In the first hours of the attack, a massive wave of Nodong rockets will pulverize Kimpo, Osan, Suwon, and other air bases to cripple the enemy's air forces and inhibit reinforcement. Air attacks will follow these missile launches. After a massive artillery barrage on the enemy's first line of defense, our infantry assault divisions will infiltrate by air, sea, and tunnel to attack select breakthrough sectors along the DMZ."

"This attack will coincide with the replacement of the enemy forces along the Demarcation Line with new formations," Kim Seung-Hee interjected with a broad grin. "Our agents in Seoul have confirmed that they are sending their veteran formations home this week to coincide with local political elections. A significant portion of the enemy's defensive line will be manned by new, poorly trained recruits. Kang, continue."

Kang bowed slightly, then pointed to several critical places along the demilitarized zone on the terrain map. "Most of the ROK Army is deployed in a linear defense of the border. As our artillery stuns and disrupts their border defenses, the infantry will puncture their lines in several places. Once holes in the enemy defense are created, our mobile forces will emerge from their underground shelters and exploit these penetrations.

"To add to the enemy's confusion, we have invested in some technologies that will provide short-term solutions to disrupt the enemy's command and control. These tactics will throw the South Koreans off balance long enough for us to deliver the goal of our bold strike: the envelopment of Seoul. We will crush Uijonbu, a key city ten kilometers north of Seoul, in three to five days. Once we demonstrate to the fascists what happens to cities that do not surrender, we will be ready for the final phase. The mass of our artillery will move within range of Seoul and threaten the destruction of the city and its stunned citizens. Our armored formations will move forward and around Seoul, cutting off the enemy's retreat. With their army smashed on the border and Seoul in danger of destruction, the civilian government will capitulate. In less than ten days the fascists will collapse and we will institute a new order in Korea."

"The enemy will have to choose between surrendering or witnessing his largest city turned into a graveyard. In our attack, speed is everything. We must win the war in ten days, before the Americans can reinforce the south," Kim Seung-Hee preached slowly, gauging his audience with each word, performing like a magician casting a spell.

"This is a great risk. What about the Dear Leader? What about Admiral Gung?" Bae questioned as he searched the other men's faces for signs of support.

The Wolf studied Bae momentarily, rubbing his eye patch with his hand, trying to sense the danger in Bae's comment. Admiral Gung was the one man whom Kim hated and feared the most. The room grew ominously silent. The old men looked at one another as if asking what was supposed to happen next. Kim knew that he needed to bolster their courage. As much as he hated to admit it, he needed their support.

"I will convince Kim Il Sung and persuade his chief assistant, Admiral Gung," Kim persisted, tapping a new cigarette on his gold cigarette case. He put the cigarette to his lips and dropped the case into his breast pocket. "There is no alternative. This is our last hope. Our allies are gone, our economy is bankrupt, and time is running out. We must strike or die."

Many in the group nodded their approval of Kim's words.

"Comrade Kim is right," said an army general, Hyon Chol Hae, the commander of the 3d Corps, as he stared at the map. "Serious riots have broken out in my districts. Too often we have dispersed angry crowds rioting for rice. There are reports of cannibalism in Huichon. My jails and work camps are full. Not even our secret police will be able to hold back the collapse if we can't feed the people. If we do not risk war now, we will lose the opportunity forever. The soldiers are loyal now, but if I keep asking them to shoot their brothers and sisters, what will happen?"

"The great General Hae sees the true course," Kim said, looking straight into the eyes of the 3d Army Corps commander. "What about the rest of you? Do you have the courage to act?"

Each man nodded his agreement.

"But will Kim Jong Il and Admiral Gung agree to your bold plan? What about the People's Militia?" General Hae asked. "This is the most important question."

"Our Dear Leader will approve Daring Thrust," Kim answered. Then he stood up to leave, signaling an end to the meeting. "I know I have your complete loyalty. As for Admiral Gung and the People's Militia, they are of no consequence."

General Hae and Admiral Bae stood up and silently watched Kim Seung-Hee as if he were a panther on the prowl, a force to fear and avoid.

"If you will excuse me, then, comrades," Kim said, smiling, "I have an urgent meeting to attend."

Kim and Kang left the room, passing two guards at the door. They walked quietly down the red-carpeted hall and stopped at the duty officer's desk. A major sitting behind the desk snapped to attention as the general neared.

"I need to use your telephone, Comrade Major," the general said quietly, his lips drawn in a tight, thin line. "Phone my operations center."

The duty officer dialed the number and handed the general the receiver.

"This is Marshal Kim," the one-eyed man said into the telephone transmitter. "We will keep our appointment as planned."

Kim hung up the phone, then continued down the hallway, rubbing his left eye through the black patch. He winced in pain from the headache that racked his brain, a pain that seemed to intensify every day.

He knew he did not have much time.

10:00 A.M., 29 September, multipurpose range complex, Chorwon Valley, South Korea. For a brief instant, Lt. Col. Michael Rodriguez was lost in the moment. His attention centered on a hawk soaring high above the Korean hills, which appeared as waves of a stormy ocean captured in granite. The hawk circled the tank range, flying freely above the activity that played out on the training range below.

Rodriguez tore his gaze from the hawk. He was troubled, but he didn't know why. He believed that a person was his choices, and he wondered if he had made the right ones.

In the early hours of 28 September, the Dragon Force had moved north from Camp Casey to the tank range. The first tanks in the firing order, Team Dealer, were already shooting at the pop-up targets on the highly sophisticated, computer-controlled tank range. Training was proceeding smoothly. The tanks were moving downrange, executing the training course. In the assembly area, trucks were refueling armored vehicles while crews were conducting maintenance and fire control system checks on their tanks. To the untrained eye, all the activity appeared frantic and chaotic. To a tanker, it was just another workday.

A tank cannon boomed and Rodriguez focused his binoculars on his tanks. With a quick glance he surveyed the actions of his men. His serious hazel eyes darted from one critical point to another. He stood near the front of an M113 armored personnel carrier on a hill that overlooked the training area. Standing six feet tall and weighing 170 pounds, Michael Rodriguez was every bit the image of the professional warrior. He wore the olive drab Nomex tank suit that was the uniform of his trade. Around his waist a web belt held a pistol, an ammunition pouch, a first-aid kit, and a chemical protective mask. A pair of binoculars hung around his neck. Rodriguez often scolded his officers that a tanker was useless without his binos.

The radios inside the carrier squawked as the big, sleek M1A2 tanks clanked to positions below him. Another tank cannon thundered; the blast echoed across the rough terrain. Machine guns chattered as the M1A2 tank, with its turbine engine whining, ran down a narrow defile and shot at green plywood targets.

"Sir, the brigade commander's helicopter is inbound," a muscular command sergeant major with a shaved head said to his battalion commander. "He'll land at the upper pad."

Rodriguez nodded and turned around just in time to see the OH-58 helicopter hover precariously over the small helicopter pad on a hill above his observation post. The swirling blades of the small, four-seat aircraft revved to a high pitch, then slowed as the bird gently touched down. The brigade commander, followed by Capt. Audrey Devens, the brigade intelligence officer, stooped low as they exited the helicopter and walked down a rock-tiled stairway.

"Dragon Force, sir," Rodriguez saluted, sounding off with the battalion's motto. "Iron Brigade."

The colonel returned the salute with a nonchalant wave and a wide grin. "How's the tanking today, Mike?"

"Great, sir. The first few tank crews started shooting our new defile course about an hour ago," said Rodriguez.

He had served under many brigade commanders in the seventeen years he had been in the army, but he had never served with a better man than Col. Sam Jakes. Jakes was an impressive officer and a thoughtful mentor with a personality that a Civil War historian might have described as a blend of the best of Robert E. Lee and Ulysses S. Grant. Jakes knew how to lead and get the best from his people. He could process an immense amount of information in a short time and still keep his sense of humor. Most importantly, Jakes embraced the unorthodox, a trait that endeared him to Rodriguez.

Rodriguez nodded a friendly hello to Captain Devens and motioned toward a set of folding chairs that Sergeant Major Dougan had placed near the side of the carrier. Two captains and a sergeant, responsible for controlling the tanks as they executed the course, stood in the open hatch of the APC.

"Sir, I believe you know Captain Charlie Drake, my assistant operations officer, and Captain Rod Fletcher, my artillery fire support officer," Rodriguez announced as they all sat down. He handed Jakes a pair of binoculars, then pointed to the officers in the carrier. "They designed this new course."

The brigade commander nodded. "I hope you're keeping Dragon Six here out of trouble, Charlie."

"Yes, sir," the captain replied. "This range is running like a fine watch."

Jakes chuckled and focused the binoculars on the tank at the starting line. The captains in the carrier nodded and went back to work, issuing instructions to the tank crews by radio as the tanks executed the demanding training exercise.

"The next tank to run the defile course is starting now," Rodriguez said, pointing to the M1A2 tank at the ready line. "The objective of this course is to fight through a defended defile. Tank, armored personnel carriers, antitank teams, and troop targets are represented by wooden panels that pop up when my range crew here activates the target lifters. This course represents exactly what we'd be up against if we took on a North Korean force blocking a defile."

Colonel Jakes scanned the defile course and nodded approvingly. "My compliments to your captains. What do your tank crews think of this?"

"The crews like it, sir," Rodriguez continued. "They know that if we fight here in this restricted terrain, this is the kind of training that will keep them alive."

The tank in the defile surged forward. A target on the left side of the hill popped up, the turret of the tank swiveled rapidly, and the cannon fired as the tank continued moving down the trail. The round hit the target, and it fell immediately.

"Looks good, Mike," Jakes said. "They'll need quick shooting like that to force their way through this kind of defense."

The tank continued to progress down the narrow, winding trail as Rodriguez and Jakes watched from their high vantage point. More targets representing enemy infantry and antitank teams popped up to the left and right along the route. Never stopping, the tank dropped these with machine-gun fire. At a narrow point in the trail, the tank jerked to a halt.

"They've just come up to a simulated minefield," Rodriguez explained. "Watch this."

The tank's machine guns plastered the area with fire as a volley of smoke grenades exploded in the air ahead of the tank, masking it to the front. The tank loader, firing the 7.62mm machine gun positioned to the left of the tank commander, sprayed targets to the left. The tank commander knocked down targets to his right with the heavier .50-caliber machine gun. The gunner, hidden inside the tank, moved the turret to fire the coaxial machine gun on targets that popped up to the front. The driver, buttoned up and protected inside his compartment, dropped the mine plow attached to the tank. With all three machine guns blazing, the tank moved forward, plowed through the mines, and cleared a path for follow-on vehicles.

"Sir, as you can see, Drake and his pals have put a lot of thought and effort into this training. I think it provides you with a superior product—crews that are trained to fight here in Korea, not just the deserts of Kuwait or the open plains of Texas or Kansas."

Jakes grinned. "Mike, I hate to interrupt this fine show, but we need to talk for a few minutes. Audrey, show Colonel Rodriguez and Sergeant Major Dougan what you've got."

Captain Devens, a thin, red-haired female intelligence officer who had earned Rodriguez's confidence with her exact and competent manner, opened up a green canvas document case and pulled out a map and several reports. She handed one of the reports to Rodriguez.

He studied the report, then looked up at Jakes. "Looks like another infiltration attempt to cross the DMZ. Do you think this is an indication of bigger trouble?"

Colonel Jakes shrugged. "Lately, there have been too many of these reports along the DMZ to ignore. Let's just say I'm concerned."

Devens unfolded a plastic-covered 1:100,000 map of the northwestern zone of South Korea. Red symbols indicated the location of known North Korean units along their side of the DMZ. Red arcs dipping south past the DMZ indicated the ranges of North Korean howitzers and rocket launchers. Rodriguez immediately saw that Devens had done her homework.

"As you know, we've previously discussed the two most likely war scenarios," the brigade S2 said. "The first scenario is a surprise attack by the North Koreans, which is considered the least likely. The other is a situation in which instability, civil war, or collapse results in a confused situation that leads to hostilities."

"The reports of starvation in North Korea paint a pretty bleak picture," Jakes added. "Things seem to be getting much worse. We may be seeing the second scenario that Devens talked about. The North Korean government may be losing control of the situation, imploding from the weight of years of mismanagement and corruption. What do you think, Sergeant Major?"

"Couldn't happen to a sorrier bunch of assholes," Dougan said, his arms crossed over his chest. "Let the bastards fall apart. The sooner they collapse, the sooner we can all go home. Besides, the North is too poor to launch a war. They couldn't take the entire peninsula with the junk they've got."

"Maybe it all depends on how desperate they get," Devens interjected, laughing at the sergeant major's colorful language. "They have a huge military."

"Yes, ma'am, they're big, but their equipment is ancient. They're still using T55 and T62 tanks," Dougan continued. "Those damned things were made in the 1960s. You told us yourself that their tankers fire only a few rounds a year."

"They may be poor, but it's a mistake to think they're stupid just because we're rich," Devens answered calmly. "The North Koreans may have a third-world army, but they also have the biggest artillery force in the world and a large number of special forces units. They've spent the last twenty years preparing to fight a technologically superior force with third world means."

"Audrey's right, Sergeant Major," Jakes added. "We shouldn't underestimate them."

"Hell, sir, they must know they can't beat us," Dougan said.

"Remember the Vietnamese?" Jakes replied with a disarming smile. "They were poor too. More importantly, the choice to go to war is seldom a rational choice. The single most important reason for everything the North Koreans do is the survival of their regime. If they're going down, you can bet your boots they learned something from the collapse of Romania and the fall of East Germany."

"You think they're ready to fall apart?" Dougan asked, interested.

Jakes smiled. "Who knows? I was in Romania in 1989, at the U.S. consulate in Bucharest. We didn't think anyone could change that government. Then one day the Romanian revolution started. The people rioted at Timisoara, demanding an end to communist rule, and the Romanian security police slaughtered hundreds of them. More protests and riots ensued. Every atrocity by the security forces brought more people to the streets. They just wouldn't give up. Romanians cut holes in all the flags, tearing out the communist hammer and sickle. They seized the Communist Party headquarters, armed themselves, and built barricades in the streets. They appealed to the regular army to help them. When the secret police began shooting army officers who would not shoot at the crowd, the army quit the government and joined the people. The government of Nicolae Ceausescu fell almost overnight. They arrested Ceausescu and his wife and executed them both on Christmas Day on national television—shot them and left their bodies in the street. It all happened in ten days."

Rodriguez and Dougan listened silently.

"This is the scenario that I believe the North Korean leadership fears the most," Jakes continued. "My read is that the communists in North Korea are determined not to end up like Ceausescu. That's why the survival of the regime is the paramount reason for everything they do. They would do anything to survive, even risk war."

"But what could they hope to gain?" Dougan questioned. "All of their allies have left them. How could they win a war against us?"

"I guess it all depends on what you consider winning," Jakes continued like a teacher in school. "Maybe they figure that if they cause enough chaos, they could drive the ROKs to negotiate a more favorable situation."

"That's a pretty big 'if,' sir," Dougan said, shaking his head.

"Desperate times bring desperate solutions," Jakes answered. "But this is all speculation. Let's talk about what we actually know. S2, continue."

"The division G2 passed me a report today indicating that the North Korean Army is conducting multiple division-sized maneuvers," the brigade intelligence officer said. "There's a lot of activity going on right now. But the indicators don't point to an imminent invasion or use of force."

"No one seems concerned," Jakes said, shaking his head. "Nevertheless, it's the largest maneuvers in three years, and I wanted you to know."

"Sir, do you want me to stop training and redeploy back to Camp Casey?" Rodriguez asked.

"No. This whole thing may blow over. We have to take prudent steps without overreacting," Jakes said. "You're better off here in the field, dispersed and uploaded with fuel and ammo. Besides, this is damned good training."

"Wilco, sir," Rodriguez said with a grin.

"This is probably just another false alarm in our long and proud tradition of false alarms," Jakes said, handing the binoculars back to Rodriguez. "Well, Mike, I'll try to come back and visit you tomorrow."

Rodriguez nodded.

The colonel stood as Captain Devens folded her map. "By the way, the division chief of staff has a TV news reporter and photographer visiting. They want to see some tanks in action, so I'm sending them here to visit you."

"No problem, sir," Rodriguez lied, unhappy to be strapped with a tourist. Rodriguez was sure that this was just another attempt by Jakes to mentor his subordinate, to drive home a well-rounded education in the responsibilities of command. "I promise to take good care of them."

"I know you will," Jakes said with a wide smile. "They'll be staying with you for a few days. Arrange for their accommodations and show them around."

"I'll make sure they get a tent," Rodriguez said, trying to conceal his displeasure at being tasked to take care of a member of the press. "I hope they don't mind eating army rations."

"No special treatment," Jakes replied, smiling. "Mike, here's your chance to get your soldiers on national TV. That's always good for morale. Just give them free access to all you do. No restrictions. Consider this part of your continuing education."

As if there wasn't enough to do, Rodriguez thought. Reporters were such pushy, shortsighted people. This one would be no different, he decided. He remembered the last painful experience he had with the press. It was a humid night in Bosnia at a vital bridge that separated hostile communities. He remembered when the crowd surged forward and beat a U.S. soldier half to death with wooden clubs. His men had saved their fallen comrade and held their fire against the hysterical crowd, proving their discipline and avoiding an international incident. He felt the old anger that had consumed him as cameras were pushed into his face by an overbearing reporter—an American—who tried to take pictures of the badly wounded American soldier. Rodriguez had refused to let her take the pictures and, when she persisted, removed the film from her camera. The threat of being court-martialed for obstructing the press—Rodriguez was lucky to escape the situation with a severe ass chewing—was still fresh in his mind. But that was a long time ago and a few continents away.

Rodriguez beamed and nodded again. "Yes, sir, you can count on me. I need all the education I can get."

Colonel Jakes laughed, knowing Rodriguez's history in Bosnia. The colonel turned and walked up the stairs with Captain Devens. The helicopter revved its engines in preparation for takeoff.

"Well, Sergeant Major," Rodriguez said as he watched the colonel's helicopter fly off. "Better get ready for tomorrow's visitors."

"I know, sir. The usual dog and pony show," Dougan said with a smirk. "I'll warn Obrisky to be ready to brief. By the way, don't forget you're marching with Team Steel on their little twelve-miler tonight."

"Wouldn't miss it for the world," Rodriguez answered. "Maybe the weather will hold."

Dougan looked up at the dark clouds. "No way."

5:00 P.M., 29 September, North Korean People's Air Force airfield, twelve kilometers southeast of Kaesong, North Korea. Lieutenant Colonel Chae Do Byung sat in a large briefing room surrounded by air force officers. The room, in a huge underground facility just north of the demilitarized zone, was brightly lit by powerful overhead lights.

More than a hundred officers were crammed tightly together on wooden benches waiting for the briefing to begin. The officers talked quietly with one another, bragging about their units and sharing stories of how difficult it was to command their squadrons in this terrible time of shortages. Most of the talk was about the lack of spare parts and fuel and reduced flying hours. Only a few select squadrons had received an adequate share of resources.

Byung listened without comment. His unit was one of the fortunate ones. He knew that other commanders envied his good luck. Byung also knew that luck had nothing to do with it.

Byung commanded a special squadron of ground attack bombers. Pugnacious and warlike by nature, Byung had a reputation as a natural pilot. He was thirty-six, five feet four, and 120 pounds. He was a devoted flyer and was recognized as an expert instructor in fighter-bomber tactics. Two years ago he had been selected to command the prestigious Fighter Bomber Squadron 214, which consisted of twelve twin-engine SU-25 fighter-bombers. His men and machines represented the best-trained ground attack aircraft in the North Korean Air Force. Byung bragged that his squadron alone could defeat the South Koreans and Americans. Few who knew Byung doubted that he believed his boast.

The lights dimmed as an air force marshal walked onto the stage. His chest was decorated from his belt to his shoulder with red badges.

The officers sprang to their feet and shouted in unison, *"Nam chim."*

"Comrades, take your seats," the gray-haired air marshal commanded.

"The largest air maneuvers of the decade will begin tomorrow," he stated. A twenty-foot curtain moved aside to reveal a well-lit map behind him. Red lights formed an unbroken line that indicated the flight paths of the squadrons to their designated targets. Dotted lines depicted the path south of the DMZ.

"These are your wartime routes," the air marshal boomed. "Study them; know them by heart. If we were to launch in defense of the motherland, these objectives would be your sacred duty to accomplish or die."

Two officers moved to the stage as the air marshal sat down. The briefers used long wooden pointers to designate the critical terrain points of the attack plan. The speakers droned on for seventy minutes, detailing every aspect of the plan.

Finally the briefers stopped talking and the air marshal stood up. "Comrades, you all have been given your sealed orders."

Byung fondled the sealed envelope in his hands. The words "Top Secret" were written in red across the seal. Each officer in the room held a similar envelope.

"Now it is time to open them and learn the destiny of the motherland."

6:30 P.M., 29 September, near the multipurpose range complex, Chorwŏn Valley, South Korea. Heavy rain followed the setting sun. Private Jamie Emerson looked at his new Casio G-Shock watch, a high school graduation gift from his mother. He pushed a button to illuminate the face. It was 1830. That left only about four more hours of marching in the rain.

He rested in an inch-deep puddle of water. There was no dry place to sit, although, with the rain falling in buckets, it really didn't matter. Tired and soaked to the bone, he contemplated his fate and the sequence of events that had led him to this miserable situation. Soldiers, most of whom he did not know, were sprawled out on both sides of a narrow Korean road. Nobody talked. Each man rested, too tired to waste the energy in conversation, and waited for the word to move again.

Thunder resonated through the heavens. A late monsoon, atypical for this time of year, was battering Korea. Emerson had never seen such rain. It poured from the clouds like water rushing from a fire hose.

"Emerson."

Jamie looked up and saw his big, stern tank commander, Sergeant First Class Hardee, standing fifteen meters in front of him.

"Yes, Sergeant, on the way." Emerson tried to sit up, but the pack on his back was too heavy. He was five feet nine inches and weighed only 130 pounds, but with his rucksack, M16 rifle, and combat gear, he weighed at least 200 pounds. His legs, unaccustomed to long foot marches, felt like cement blocks. Trying to obey the summons, he rolled to his side and pushed up to his knees. The burdensome rucksack bit at his shoulders.

"Let's go, Emerson. I don't have all day."

He struggled to his feet, then waddled over to his tank commander. "Yes, Sergeant."

"Do you know what a plugger is?"

"No, Sergeant."

"Don't they teach you guys anything in basic?" Hardee answered in mock disgust. He held up a book-sized light brown plastic box. "This is a plugger—PLGR, portable lightweight GPS receiver. It gives your position in ten- or six-digit grid coordinates, and it gives the time. Do you know why the time is important?"

"No, Sergeant."

"You use the time to set our radios. Our SINCGARS radios are difficult to jam because they use frequency hopping. The transmitter and receiver are synchronized by time. If you don't have the right time, you can't communicate. Tankers are expected to shoot, move, and communicate."

"Yes, Sergeant."

"One more thing, 'cruit. Set that brand-new watch you're so proud of to plugger time," Hardee ordered, placing the plugger in front of Emerson's face.

He put his rifle between his knees and played with the dials on his watch.

"Got it?"

"Yes, Sergeant," Emerson answered, grabbing his rifle.

"Okay, let's go," Hardee shouted to the soldiers sitting on the ground. "Break's over. The sooner we get moving, the sooner we'll be done."

A collective moan arose from the eighty-three soldiers, tankers, and engineers, who made up Team Steel.

"For a tank battalion, we sure do a lot of walking," a voice in the dark shouted cynically.

"If you ever lose your tank, this may save your life," came the answer to the man's comment. "Now, let's move."

"You heard the company commander," Sergeant Hardee's stern voice bellowed in the warm night air. "What do you want, a goddamned engraved invitation? Team Steel, get your fucking asses in gear, right now."

Private Hernandez, weighed down by his pack, lay on his back on the ground like an upturned turtle. "Hey, man, give me a hand," he pleaded.

Emerson, newly assigned as the loader on tank C-34, reached for the soldier's hand and pulled Hernandez to his feet. The momentum of the move almost knocked Emerson over, but he caught his balance just in time.

"Let's go," the voice of authority said. "Move out, Team Steel. Pick up a five-meter interval."

Emerson walked on the right side of the road. He could feel the blisters growing on his feet. The rain poured down, soaking his uniform and filling his boots. The deluge was so constant that half an inch of running water covered the concrete. Emerson waited as the 1st and 2d Platoons walked by.

Steel was the nickname, motto, and radio call sign of C Company. Tonight, soaked steel might be more appropriate, Emerson thought, chuckling to himself as he tightened the strap to his rucksack. He ached from head to foot. He was barely over his jet lag, and he definitely was not ready for a twelve-mile foot march.

No one had told him that tankers did foot marches. Suddenly the reality of hard soldiering in the Land of the Morning Calm was registering on his tired mind. As one of the newest members of Team Steel, he remembered the first sergeant's words and quietly swore that he would not quit.

"But I never signed up to be an infantryman," Emerson said aloud. "I wish I was back in Kentucky." He was thinking about his friends in basic training, the high school he attended in Owensboro, Kentucky, and the home he left.

"Hell, turtle," Pfc. Emilio Hernandez replied with a heavy Latino accent. "You ain't seen nothing yet. We've got six more miles to go."

"Man, I can march with the best of you," Emerson replied, "but it's as if we've been running most of the way. Who's setting the pace for this outfit?"

"It's the commander," Corporal Oh, one of the KATUSAs in 3d Platoon, answered in heavily accented English. "He walks fast. But we keep up."

Emerson had heard about the Korean soldiers who served in the U.S. Army in Korea. KATUSA stood for Korean Augmentation to the U.S. Army. The program was a holdover from the 1950s when Korean conscripts were assigned to U.S. units fighting during the Korean War. Since that time, KATUSAs had been an important part of the U.S. force structure in Korea. There were seven Korean soldiers in Team Steel, and forty-three in the battalion. On the positive side, the KATUSAs, who served two-year tours in the battalion, provided cohesion, Korean language interpreters, and a quick infusion of local knowledge about Korea and its people. On the negative side, the KATUSAs presented their chain of command with soldiers typically weak in English language skills and without knowledge of U.S. military technology. Most KATUSAs needed considerable training to drive a tank safely or load a 120mm tank round.

What KATUSAs lacked in skill, however, they made up for in desire. Emerson felt a fire behind Oh's words that he instantly respected.

"All right, knock it off," Sergeant Hardee replied. The 1st and 2d Platoons had already moved down the road. "The old man wants a fifty-meter interval between platoons. Let's get it in gear, Third Herd. Move out."

The weary men sparked to life and shouldered their packs. Individually they checked their M16s and assorted gear and formed up on the road. On order, the column of troops marched forward.

Lightning split the heavens, followed by the crashing volley of thunder. The celestial fireworks added emphasis to the sergeant's orders. The monsoons had come late to Korea this year. Normally they arrived in August; this year they came in September. The weather was still warm enough to move around without a jacket. When a few tankers had shown up at formation wearing their rain ponchos, First Sergeant Spurr made short work of them. "Get those damn ponchos off right now, you fools," the top sergeant had growled. "You'll be heat casualties in fifteen minutes under those sauna suits."

The thunder cracked again, followed by bright bursts of lightning striking the trees on both sides of the narrow road.

"Sheeiitt," complained a soldier with a squeaky New York accent. "Top, what if we get hit by lightning?"

"Then we'll use you as a lightbulb to guide the way, Franco," the first sergeant joked. "Don't worry about the lightning. Just keep moving. We've only got a few more miles to go."

The rain poured down in sheets. The tired soldiers, drenched and burdened with packs made heavier by the rain, trudged through the dark night. Thunder, mimicking the blast of artillery, echoed in the Korean valley. Lightning lit the dark sky in mad flashes, searching for something to touch.

Emerson's blisters grew. As Team Steel trudged on, he grew more determined to make the distance. He wasn't going to let anyone see him quit.

Lieutenant Colonel Michael Rodriguez kept pace with his soldiers. Two of them in vests with orange reflective tape marched ahead of the column, performing the role of safety guards for the company. Their job was to warn any oncoming civilian drivers that a column of dismounted tankers was walking on the side of the narrow road. Fifteen paces behind them, to the right of the route, marched the company commander and the battalion commander. Rodriguez walked right behind Capt. Ken Mackenzie, the commander of Team Steel.

"Sir, don't you ever get tired of carrying that grease gun?" chided the captain in front of Rodriguez.

Rodriguez carried his favorite weapon, an M3 submachine gun. It was an ancient relic, used in World War II, Korea, and Vietnam, but there were still two of them authorized in the battalion for M88 tank recovery vehicle crewmen. If he was going to be called the "old man," he thought, he might as well carry the oldest weapon in the arsenal. In addition to the M3 submachine gun, Rodriguez carried an M1911A1 .45-caliber pistol that his father had once owned.

Rodriguez had carried the pistol since his first assignment in the army. When the army switched pistols to the 9mm Beretta, Rodriguez swore that he would still carry his trusty .45. It made him feel a link with the past. He pampered it and replaced many of the worn-out parts as the years went by, adding a new, extended slide release and special rubber grips. Using it was against every army regulation in the book, but he got away with it.

"Shit, I just like the way it fires," Rodriguez said. "By the way, Steel Six, you sure did pick a great night for a foot march. Worst weather of any night this month."

"Yes, sir. But if we have to fight in the rain someday, my boys will be ready. Can't let a little rain stop us."

"You call this a little rain?" Rodriguez said, trying to make small talk to keep his mind off his swollen feet. "You know, situational awareness is part of your leadership evaluation, Captain."

Mackenzie chuckled.

Rodriguez admired his young commander. Mackenzie was a no-nonsense tanker. He trained his men for combat harder than any of the other companies in the Dragon Force. He cared.

There were five team commanders in the Dragon Force, five captains who held the responsibility to train, prepare, and fight the soldiers whom Rodriguez commanded. Rodriguez had given his captains special roles to play in the task force combat scheme—specialties they could master. Captain George Maxwell commanded Team Dealer, the advance guard company team; Capt. Ken Mackenzie, Team Steel, the breach company team; Capt. Joe Sharpe, Team Renegade, the mechanized infantry heavy company team; Capt. Al Grey, Team Bulldog, the task force reserve. Captain Kurt Richardson, the task force engineer officer, usually deployed with the task force command group or moved to assist breaching operations with Team Steel. Each of these team leaders was expected to take his soldiers on a twelve-mile march every month.

Rodriguez joined his companies on these hikes with full gear and weapons, convinced that the marches were as important to tankers as to infantrymen. Someday, Rodriguez told his men, they might have to walk. These twelve-milers made sure they would be prepared. Jakes had told him about this: "You don't avoid a traffic accident by closing your eyes. If you want to survive the cold equation of war, you have to prepare."

Rodriguez knew that all soldiers want to prove their mettle in front of their leaders. With men rotating out of the unit every twelve months, creating tough, disciplined combat units was a difficult challenge. Team building was an essential skill for units in Korea, and conducting dismounted foot marches was one technique that helped form cohesive teams and prepare them for Colonel Jakes's "cold equation."

A tremendous clap of thunder split the heavens. Lightning, searing out of the night sky, hit a tree on the hill to the right.

Captain Mackenzie picked up the pace. It was apparent to Rodriguez that he wanted to be sure that the colonel got his money's worth.

I'm getting too old for this, Rodriguez thought to himself. He adjusted his pack and tilted his submachine gun forward to take the weight off his side. If I'm going to keep up with these young studs, I need to practice this more often. He felt the blisters forming in his water-soaked boots.

"So, sir," the captain said, "the sergeant major tells me you're going to be on CNN tomorrow."

"Not me," Rodriguez replied, wondering just how much Dougan had told Captain Mackenzie. "The brigade commander will be there and we'll show them the defile run. You better have a tank crew ready that can shoot straight."

"Don't worry, sir, we'll maintain the honor of the battalion for national television."

"We'd better, Mac, or the brigade commander will have my scalp hanging from his teepee," Rodriguez chided. "By the way, how many men do you think will complete this foot race?"

"Sir, all of them will make it," Mackenzie answered, the pride he had in his company ringing in his words. "They'll stick together and make it, if only because they don't want you or me to see them fall out."

Rodriguez smiled as he remembered a proverb he had once read: "If you want one year of prosperity, grow rice. If you want ten years of prosperity, grow trees. If you want one hundred years of prosperity, grow people." All the teaching and mentoring was paying off, he thought. He was growing leaders.

Lightning flashed and struck a tree five hundred meters away, illuminating the valley for a moment. The sky burst with rain as the heavens growled.

8:00 P.M., 29 September, 2d Infantry Division headquarters, Uijonbu, South Korea. Lieutenant Colonel Steve Wallace removed his wire-rimmed, aviator-style glasses and slowly wiped each lens with a handkerchief from his battle dress cargo pocket. As the division intelligence officer, the G2, it was his duty to call emergency staff meetings when the situation justified it. The trick was not crying wolf too often.

"Sir, the general and the chief of staff are here," Maj. Jim Cooper announced as he opened the door to the conference room.

A tall, thin, bald-headed officer in military uniform and an even taller man in civilian clothes entered. The chief wore a starched green camouflage battle dress uniform (BDU). The commanding general, Maj. Gen. George Schmidt, who had just come from the officers' mess, wore slacks and a red polo shirt. Wallace stood up as the men walked in.

General Schmidt carried a brown pipe and a bag of Captain Black tobacco in his left hand. He placed the pipe and tobacco on the highly polished wooden table and motioned for them all to take their seats.

"Okay, Steve, you've dragged the old man in here, now

show us what you have," ordered Colonel Hassay, the chief of staff.

Wallace nodded, his face pressed with concern. He wanted to show them what was on the other side of the hill. He hoped his hunches were right.

"Steve," General Schmidt announced seriously, "if you don't have something important to tell me this time, you're fired."

Wallace looked straight ahead and blinked. "Sir . . ."

The general held up his hand and grinned. "I'm kidding. I'll always take time for you. Show me what you have that's so important."

Wallace nodded to his assistant to dim the lights. A slide of the forces along the DMZ appeared on the projection screen. The top and bottom of the slide had blue lettering that read, "SECRET (REL/ROK). DARING THRUST."

"Despite the tremendous economic burden of the past few years, the Democratic People's Republic of Korea, or North Korea, continues to spend thirty-five percent of its gross national product on defense," explained Wallace. "Their military is a mobile force of 1.2 million active-duty personnel augmented by a reserve force of 5 million men. Sixty-five percent of these forces are deployed within sixty miles of the DMZ.

"According to reports from recent NKPA defectors, the North Koreans are practicing a new attack concept called Daring Thrust. A similar idea was developed by the Soviet General Staff, or STAVKA, in the last years of the Soviet Union. This plan, according to our sources, involves an attack with speed and surprise without full mobilization. Apparently they believe that if they attack with a select group of trained and well-supplied shock divisions, they can surprise the Combined Forces Command, neutralize the ROK forces near the DMZ, disrupt ROK mobilization and U.S. reinforcement, isolate Seoul, and initiate peace negotiations within seven to ten days."

Schmidt looked carefully at the slide. It showed a map of South Korea with four arrows pointing south and enveloping Seoul. The general picked up his unlit pipe and placed it between his teeth.

Wallace continued, "Select formations from their million-man ground force, supported by thirty-five hundred tanks, four thousand armored personnel carriers, eighty-four hundred artillery pieces, twenty-four hundred multiple rocket launchers, and sixty thousand special forces soldiers would execute a combined conventional and infiltration attack. Special forces will infiltrate the ROK by land, tunnel, air, and sea to attack airfields and command and control facilities and create confusion and paralysis."

A new slide appeared on the screen. The top and bottom were labeled in bright red lettering: "TOP SECRET (U.S. ONLY)."

Wallace explained, "Sir, air force U2R reconnaissance aircraft and radio intercept reports indicate a higher than usual level of operations occurring in North Korea this week. Six divisions were identified yesterday moving into their predesignated underground facilities. Some of these UGFs can hold hundreds of tanks, in battle columns, ready to attack on order.

"Shown here are the current dispositions of U.S. and ROK forces in their armistice positions and garrisons." Wallace pointed to a map colored with blue and red military symbols. "The units in red are the North Korean combat units north of the DMZ that could affect the 2d Infantry Division's area of operations. As you can see, the North Koreans have three armored or mechanized infantry corps in assembly areas just north of the DMZ."

"Sir, I called the CFC chief of staff this evening," Colonel Hassay interjected. "He told me that the CINC is not concerned with this. The CINC views this as a routine exercise designed to raise tensions on the peninsula. The usual saber rattling."

"The ROKs have made some dangerous moves in the past ten months," Schmidt reflected. "The North Koreans understand power, but I'm not sure they understand reconciliation."

"The ROKs are tired of spending money on a war that will never be fought," Hassay acknowledged. "It's hard to argue that they're jeopardizing their security by disbanding a couple of infantry divisions while we're cutting down our own military."

"Three frontline infantry divisions, a tank brigade, and an entire artillery brigade were taken out of their active force structure this year," Schmidt replied, holding his round-bowled brown pipe as a pointer. "More units will be deactivated in the near future. The ROKs are taking a huge gamble that the North Koreans will see this as an opportunity for parallel reductions in force, and they're betting on us to make up the difference."

"The ROK's economy can't afford a big military anymore," the chief answered with his characteristic Texas accent. "They have to reduce military expenditures to revitalize their economy."

"Sir, I have two more reports today that were important enough to call this emergency meeting. The first is a satellite reconnaissance picture of a battery of Russian-made S-300 antiaircraft missile systems," Wallace announced as a slide of a North Korean manned S-300 air defense system lit up the screen. "This new version of the S-300, a mobile and highly accurate system like our Patriot, can destroy targets as low as ten meters above the ground and as far away as one hundred fifty kilometers."

The room grew silent. The jerking movement of the second hand of the electric clock seemed suddenly loud.

"Do we know how many of these systems are in North Korean hands?" Schmidt asked.

"No, sir, but the North Koreans have been trading heavily with the Russians and Japanese in the past year," Wallace said. "The S-300 missile tests have been monitored for the past six months. If the missiles are deployed in mass, coupled with the air defense systems they already have, the North Koreans have the potential to deny us the airspace over the enemy for four to five days."

"Okay, got it," the general said, leaning forward in his chair. "Anything else?"

Major Cooper, standing behind the podium, glanced at his boss. On a nod from Wallace, the major punched a button that brought up a colored satellite photograph on the screen.

"This is a picture taken ten days ago of a Nodong 2 intermediate-range ballistic missile," said Cooper. "You'll notice that the missile position is under heavy camouflage and is covered by a battery of S-300s."

"What are the specs on the Nodong?" Colonel Hassay asked.

"The Nodong 2 is an improved Scud surface-to-surface ballistic missile with a range of a thousand to fifteen hundred kilometers," Cooper explained, flashing a slide of the missile's characteristics on the screen. "It can range all of South Korea, Japan, and a significant part of China. It's four meters longer than the older Russian-made Scud B. It can carry a warhead—conventional explosives, gas, biological, or nuclear—that weighs a maximum of five hundred kilograms. The missile is probably guided by commercially purchased global positioning satellite technology. This improved missile, we believe, cannot be shot down by our Patriot air defense batteries. These missiles are primarily targeted at airfields."

"The air force won't be happy to hear that," the general replied, looking at his chief of staff.

"As you know, the Nodong 2 is capable of carrying a fifty-kiloton nuclear warhead or enough deadly VX persistent nerve agent to take out a small city," Cooper answered. "We don't believe that they have nuclear warheads for their Nodong 2s. They do, however, have chemical warheads."

Colonel Hassay shook his head. "Wallace, I don't think we need to panic. This information is old stuff, and a blurry photo of a Scud launcher and a battery of S-300s doesn't mean much."

"Yes, sir, but if you look at this enhanced view," Wallace replied as Cooper punched up another slide, "you'll see that the entire missile crew is wearing chemical protective clothing. I believe that the truck near this missile is there to load the warhead with liquid chemical agent. This could mean that some of the Nodongs are now armed with chemical warheads."

The room grew silent again. Schmidt leaned back in his seat, his pipe between his teeth.

"How long can they keep them armed with chemical agents?" Schmidt asked.

"They don't have sophisticated binary chemical munitions like we used to have," Wallace answered. "Most of their stuff is raw liquid chemical, pumped into a metal warhead. Most of it, VX for instance, is highly corrosive. The warheads can probably stay loaded for a few weeks, maybe a month, without corroding through the metal."

"So, are you saying that they're going to strike us with chemical weapons within thirty days?" the chief asked.

"I don't know the intentions of the North Koreans, but it seems prudent to believe that they wouldn't fill warheads with chemical agent just to test how long it takes the canisters to corrode."

There was a long pause as the senior officers considered this point.

"What does J2 at Combined Forces Command headquarters think?" Schmidt asked.

"The J2 told me there's nothing to worry about," Colonel Hassay said cynically as he glanced at Wallace. "We're over-reacting. These pictures are of maneuvers that have been planned for a long time. Hell, they could be putting water in that missile for all we know."

Wallace looked betrayed. It was difficult enough trying to read the goddamned North Koreans, he thought, let alone fight against his own chief of staff.

"Sir, I'm concerned," Wallace continued. "This information, coupled with recent DMZ violations, sets a dangerous pattern. If they attack now, even if they just fire their missiles at us, they couldn't pick a better time. The South Koreans are in the middle of a divisive election, the ROK economy is in trouble, they've weakened their military, and they're conducting extensive unit rotations on the DMZ."

"What unit rotations?" Colonel Hassay asked, his curiosity piqued.

"The ROKs started last week to replace seventy-five percent of their units on the DMZ with new units. The rotations will be complete by 30 September," Wallace reported.

"Well, Steve, it looks like you aren't seeing eye to eye with the J2 or the chief," the commander replied. "But don't worry. I don't pay you to tell me what everyone else thinks. I want to know what you think."

Wallace smiled in relief until he saw the glaring look of Colonel Hassay. The chief's eyes raked over him like machine-gun fire.

Quietly, a short female officer opened the back door of the

conference room. She stuck her head in and quickly walked straight to Lieutenant Colonel Wallace. She handed him a piece of paper and rapidly departed the way she had entered.

Wallace read the fax and looked up at the commanding general.

"Well, what is it?" the general asked, tiring of the suspense.

"Sir, it appears there has been another incident at the DMZ," the G2 said, offering the fax to the chief of staff. "A North Korean patrol was caught in a firefight on the south side of the DMZ by the ROKs."

"Sir, this kind of stuff happens all the time," the chief of staff interjected after he rapidly scanned the fax. "It's the usual roller coaster we ride in Korea. If we overreact and call an alert, we'll all look like idiots and risk triggering an unnecessary response from the north."

"Maybe so," Schmidt announced, tapping his unlit pipe against the table, "but Steve's got my attention. Keep on it, G2. I think I'll keep you as my intel officer, at least for the time being."

3

THE PLAN

His pride in his colors and his regiment, his training hard and thorough and coldly realistic, to fit him for what he must face, and his obedience is to his orders. As a legionary, he held the gates of civilization for the classical world; as a bluecoated horseman he swept the Indians from the Plains. . . . He does the jobs—the utterly necessary jobs—no militia is willing to do.

—T. R. FEHRENBACH

6:30 A.M., 30 September, multipurpose range complex, Chorwon Valley, South Korea. The air smelled of ozone as the cool, fresh September wind blew gently across the rain-soaked Korean hills. In the valleys, puddles of water splotched the rocky ground. The rain had thankfully stopped for the moment, but the dark clouds foretold the promise of a storm. Lieutenant Colonel Rodriguez looked up at the sky and realized that the respite would not last long.

He stood with his sergeant major in front of a HMMWV eating a not-so-tasty breakfast of MREs (meals ready to eat). Small brown foil packets of crackers, cheese, and corned beef hash lay spread out on top of the hood of the Humvee. In the distance, tank cannons boomed and machine guns rattled as the colonel's tanks negotiated a combat training course. A worn book in a plastic bag lay on the hood next to the brown packets.

The sergeant major picked up the colonel's book, scanned the title, and casually dropped it back on the hood. "The ill-leead? Never heard of it."

Rodriguez smiled. Command Sergeant Major Zeke Dougan looked like the classic top sergeant. In spite of the rain, his

Nomex tanker's uniform appeared pressed. His demeanor was tough and always sharp as a blade; he was a force to be reckoned with. He was five feet ten inches tall and weighed about two hundred pounds. A weight lifter by choice and a soldier by blood, Dougan had been a centurion for more than twenty-three years. His scalp, hidden under his Kevlar helmet, was clean shaven, dramatizing his tough, no-nonsense warrior mien.

"You might like it," Rodriguez replied with a slight trace of a smile. "Plenty of fighting, drinking, and sex."

The sergeant major's eyebrows raised and he moved the book with one finger, scanning the title again. He shook his head. "Naw, sounds too much like Greek to me. When's the last time the Greeks won a war?"

Raindrops plopped from the heavens as they munched their breakfast.

"Speaking of sex, sir," Dougan said with a wide grin, "you ever think of getting married again? Kaye has a younger sister."

Rodriguez gave Dougan a look that could have burned through.

"Okay, guess I'll drop that subject," the command sergeant major said as he scooped up a spoonful of cold corned beef hash. He looked at the sky to find a way to change the subject. "I've never been so wet in my life. Will this rain ever stop?"

"No way, Sergeant Major," Rodriguez replied with a sly smile, mimicking the reply his sergeant major had given him yesterday. "Don't worry, you won't melt."

"No, sir, I guess I won't, but in a few short weeks I'll be on a freedom bird headed home to momma, my motorcycle, and the land of the big PX. No more Korea, no more standing out in the rain, and no more lousy MREs. Once I'm gone, it can rain here in the land of Chosun all it wants."

Rodriguez's smile slowly faded. He knew he would miss the sergeant major's colorful banter. The Dragon Force was going to lose a great leader. Dougan was the life energy of the unit. In three weeks he would retire after twenty-three years of wearing the uniform.

"It will be a black day for the army," Rodriguez whispered. "My old man used to say that once the army is in your blood, once you're a member of a proud legion, you can never quit."

"Ah, bullshit . . . sir," Dougan replied. "It won't be a black day. Everybody retires someday. You'll get somebody just as good to replace me. The army's full of good people."

"Sergeant Major Dougan, you won't know what to do once you leave the army," Rodriguez continued. "There was a saying in the old British army that explained how a professional soldier was wedded to his duty: 'Married to the Brown Bess.'"

"You're a good man, sir, but you think too much," Dougan said, shaking his head in disbelief. "I don't know what a Brown Bess is, and I don't care. Just let me enjoy my breakfast."

"I tell you, Zeke," Rodriguez pressed, "you won't like being a civilian."

"What? Wear whatever I like, anytime I like. No one to tell me what to do," Dougan replied. "Sure, retirement will be pure misery."

They both laughed, but Rodriguez knew his sergeant major. A soldier's soldier, Zeke Dougan had been married to the army since he enlisted at age seventeen. Rodriguez worried for his friend, because he knew that Zeke Dougan didn't really want to shed his uniform. The two men were almost the same age: Dougan was forty-one and Rodriguez was thirty-eight. They had been together for eleven long, busy months: tank gunnery, force-on-force maneuver exercises, platoon and company training, and the endless hours of talking and leading the troops they loved so much. But now the team was breaking up. Battalion commanders spent two years in Korea in command. Everyone else left after twelve months. Rodriguez understood that building cohesive combat teams under such conditions was difficult at best. With Dougan gone, it would be harder.

"Your father was an NCO," Dougan said. "I know if he was still alive, he'd be damn proud of you when you retire. Don't give me such a hard time . . . sir."

"Okay," Rodriguez conceded. "Yeah, I bet he would. You know, I miss him a lot. I remember he loved to read to me. That's where I probably learned my love of books."

"Is he the one who taught you the riddle of the sergeant?"

Rodriguez beamed, accepting the requirement to repeat the line that had become the glue of their relationship, of their teamwork as commander and sergeant major. "That's right. What's the difference to a soldier between a sergeant and a four-star general?"

Dougan repeated the well-known mantra: "When a sergeant gives a soldier an order on the battlefield, it must have the same weight as that of a four-star general."

The two men laughed as the battalion executive officer, Maj. Dave Lucas, walked up and saluted. Rodriguez returned his salute.

"Sir, I don't mean to interrupt, but I just got word from brigade. The CNN crew will be about an hour late."

"Thanks, Dave," Rodriguez replied. David Lucas was a superb executive officer and an important part of the command team. Lucas balanced Rodriguez, often acting as the devil's advocate. What made Lucas more unique was that he was an infantry officer. In the 2d Infantry Division, tank battalions were assigned an infantry officer as executive officer, or XO in military parlance. This helped integrate combined arms in the battalions. "Want some breakfast?"

"No, thanks," Lucas replied in mock disdain at the sight of the cold hash. "I'm trying to quit. I'll bring the reporters to you when they arrive."

Lucas saluted, moved to walk away, then turned. "Oh, sir, Colonel Jakes called and said he wouldn't be out today. Weather's too bad to fly."

Rodriguez shrugged as thunder roared in the sky and rain started to fall.

9:00 A.M., 30 September, airfield twelve kilometers southeast of Kaesong, North Korea. Colonel Byung checked the latest navigation charts and scanned the most recent weather report. North Korean forces had been alerted to a state of "maximum wartime mobilization" for major nationwide military exercises. Exact calculations were essential, especially if the events unfolded as he anticipated.

He opened the large brown envelope that contained his secret orders one more time and reread the instructions. They outlined drastic action, action essential to rescue the motherland from ruin by foreign devils. The decision to institute a maximum defense posture was the leadership's response to the threats posed by recent South Korean military maneuvers, the increased U.S. armed presence in South Korea, and other foreign attempts to take advantage of North Korea's economic and agricultural disasters.

"Comrade Colonel, we've been at this for eight hours," a thin-faced major announced. "I suggest that our plan is complete; the Nodongs will clear the way. We need to rest."

"No, the MIG-23s are the key," Byung chanted out loud, taking another long drag from his cigarette. He was tired, having been up all night planning his squadron's tactical approach to his assigned objective. The ashtray was full of cigarette butts, testimony to the hours he had spent in strenuous mental effort. "The key to beating the fascists is in our air tactics. It can be done."

"There is no doubt," the younger man answered. "But now it is our duty to prepare ourselves. We must be on the ready line in less than ten hours."

Byung closed his eyes for a minute and drifted off to another world. His passion was aviation, aircraft, and engines. He reveled at solving problems. He played the deadly drill in his mind: the movement to the objective, the method to counter the enemy's interceptors, the technique to scramble their air defenses, and, finally, the execution of the target. His main priority was the destruction of the target and the welfare of his airplanes; everything else was secondary.

"Yes, but we must make one final check of the aircraft before we rest," Byung replied. "If an armored personnel carrier breaks down, the infantrymen can fight on foot with rifles, grenades, and bayonets. But our aircraft are something else. If something goes wrong with our SU-25s, we are finished."

"Of course, Comrade Colonel," the major answered. "Leave that to me. I will check the technicians and inspect each aircraft one last time."

Byung smiled. "You are a good man, Major Li. I will leave this important task in your capable hands."

The major rose and saluted. The colonel ground out his last cigarette in the ashtray, returned the salute, and headed off to his cot to sleep.

10:00 A.M., 30 September, multipurpose range complex, Chorwon Valley, South Korea. The colonel watched his crews negotiate a tank gunnery exercise from a hilltop that overlooked the tank range. Captains Drake and Fletcher stood in the open hatch of an armored personnel carrier that acted as the command post for the range exercise. The APC was stuffed with radios, each blaring instructions for some activity on the range.

"Sir, they're here," Sergeant Major Dougan announced.

Rodriguez turned around and saw Maj. Dave Lucas, his executive officer, escorting a woman and a man up the stairs to the command post.

"Ms. Hamilton, Mr. Schaefer, may I introduce Lieutenant Colonel Mike Rodriguez and Command Sergeant Major Zeke Dougan," Lucas said.

Alice Hamilton wore white jeans, a blue button-down shirt, and a khaki jacket with large pockets that made her look as though she was on safari. She stood poised, as if she was watching herself as played on the evening news. There was strength in her face that was evident at a distance, her blond hair, green eyes, and sharp features setting her aside as a pretty, lively, and ambitious woman. Her cameraman, a bearded, graying man in his late forties, was dressed in dark slacks, a white shirt, and a khaki jacket. He carried a large canvas bag, and a video camcorder rested on his shoulder. He held it so deftly that it seemed almost a part of his body. He was already filming as Rodriguez stepped forward to recognize his guests.

Hamilton stopped suddenly and eyed Rodriguez with a curious look, as if she had seen him before but couldn't remember when. She gazed at him for a long moment, then closed her eyes and nodded.

"Yes, it's me," Rodriguez answered. "Bosnia. The incident at the bridge."

Hamilton nodded to Rodriguez with a look that said she remembered.

"Paul, get some footage of those tanks before the colonel here confiscates our film."

Rodriguez bit his lip. A flood of memories came back to him: Alice Hamilton at the bridge in Bosnia. Of all the places in the world to report the news, why did she have to pick my tank range, he thought. He stood silently watching the reporter talk to her cameras, resenting her presence in his world.

Hamilton finished her sound bite and the cameraman switched his focus to a tank that was darting down a rocky trail.

Rodriguez never liked reporters in general, but this one, as he knew too well, would do anything for a story. Cold, ambitious, politically savvy, and beautiful—a dangerous combination of fire and ice. Soldiers meant nothing to her; they served merely as backdrops in a drama she hoped to put on film, with herself as the centerpiece. She was a tourist, an observer who danced above reality, playing the role of commentator.

Six hundred meters away a tank lumbered forward and fired its 120mm cannon. The blast echoed in the hills as the wooden panel target burst into splinters. The tank raced farther away under a billowing cloud of dust. Two more targets suddenly appeared far off to the northeast. In quick succession the tank fired at the nearest target—direct hit—then attacked the second. Both targets were knocked to the ground in less than fifteen seconds.

"Cut," Hamilton ordered, eyeing Rodriguez for a cold moment, then turned to Dougan. "Sergeant Major, what do you know about these tanks?"

"I've been tanking for a few years," Dougan replied with a grin. "That's Sergeant Hardee's crew moving to the firing line now. He's one of our best tank commanders."

"Please tell me about this tank," Alice said, making a motion with her hand to cue the cameraman to resume taping. "The M1A2."

"Yes, ma'am. It's the best damn tank in the world," Dougan answered, eyeing Hamilton's slim figure with a twinkle in his eyes. "Inside it's all digital. The tank commander—the TC—has a thing called the commander's independent thermal viewer, or CITV. It's that stubby cylinder on top of the turret that looks like a periscope. With the CITV the tank commander can scan for targets independent of the gunner. With the push of a button the TC can swing the gun onto a target and fire. The CITV allows the gunner and tank commander to search for targets at the same time."

"I see," Alice answered, her eyes flirting with the sergeant major. "Is that what makes this tank so good?"

"Yes, that and several other things. The tank commander has another gadget called an IVIS that allows him to send map graphics and orders without voice radio transmission. From his IVIS display the TC also knows the location of his tank and all the other M1A2s in the task force. The M1A2's POS/NAV system keeps track of where the tank is and where it came from. We also have a new thermal driver's viewing periscope that allows the driver to navigate on a pitch-black night or in dense fog. These improvements, and a crew of well-trained soldiers, make it your basic supertank."

"Supertank, huh?" Alice said with a sly, feminine purr. She pointed to the tank getting ready to fire. "Paul, get a picture of that tank on the trail."

"They're fast too," Dougan continued. "Despite their weight—almost seventy tons—the Abrams can cross level terrain at forty miles an hour, fire on the move, and hit a target at three klicks with one round."

Rodriguez couldn't keep his eyes off Hamilton, and as she turned her head their eyes locked for an instant. Ironically, in that moment, he felt strangely attracted to her. Somehow, in spite of their past, he admired her confidence and poise, and he hated himself for this weakness. He looked away and wrestled with his feelings, questioning his suicidal inclination to forever fall for fatal attractions, like a moth to a flame. He could command a tank battalion like a trained, experienced samurai, lead soldiers as if he were born to command, but when it came to romance he was always a kamikaze. Did he have a death wish when it came to women? He shook his head.

Sergeant Hardee's tank, located only a hundred meters away, fired its first shot. Hardee's tank was a lot closer than the others. The explosion of the 120mm cannon startled Hamilton and her cameraman.

"The 120mm sabot round travels at sixteen hundred and seventy meters per second. In air force terms, that's about Mach 4," Rodriguez said, noticing that the reporter had jumped from the noise of the cannon's blast.

Hamilton handed the microphone to Rodriguez with a grin, trying to regain the initiative in their contest of wills. Rodriguez hesitated, then reluctantly took the microphone and waited for her questions.

"Your tanks are good at firing at wooden panels," Alice announced, "but aren't they just big sitting ducks on a modern battlefield?"

"Fighting in the real world is complex, Ms. Hamilton," Rodriguez answered, looking straight into the green eyes of the female reporter. "Our M1 tank is a superb machine with great protective as well as offensive power, but it's the men behind the weapons that make the biggest difference."

"The men, not the machines," she nodded in mock acceptance.

"Yes. Let me give you an example. During Desert Storm an American tank got stuck in a sand pit near the Euphrates River. As you may remember, the weather was awful during the ground offensive, and it had been raining heavily. Another tank tried to pull out the mired tank, but with no luck. Since the platoon had to continue its mission, the platoon leader told the crew to sit tight and wait a couple of hours for a tank retriever to pull them out.

"While the crew waited, three Iraqi T72 tanks came over the hill. The T72 was the best tank the enemy had. Deploying on line, the Iraqi tanks attacked the stuck M1A1. The lead T72 fired a 125mm high-explosive antitank shell at the front of the M1's turret. The round exploded against the frontal armor, with no effect on the tank or crew. The crew was surprised but didn't panic. Alone, outnumbered, and immobilized, the men immediately made a courageous decision—they decided to fight.

"The gunner fired his cannon at the lead Iraqi tank and, in the blink of an eye, blew off the T72's turret. The second T72 fired a shell that also hit the M1's frontal armor but did no damage. The American tank commander laid the gun on the second target and fired. He hit the tank and transformed it into a burning inferno.

"The last Iraqi tank fired an armor-piercing round that smashed against the M1's turret but bounced off. The tank raced behind a sand dune about five hundred meters away and hid. Through his thermal sights the American gunner identified the hot exhaust gas coming from the Iraqi tank. He aimed where he thought the enemy was and fired a sabot round into the berm. The round penetrated the sand, hit the T72, and sent its turret fifty feet into the air."

"Very nice story, Colonel, but that's history," Hamilton said. "Some people say that if there ever is another war, it'll be fought with precision-guided weapons: robot fighter-bombers, rockets, and missiles. Your tanks, and your good soldiers, won't last long against those weapons."

Rodriguez offered a determined grin, then looked straight at the camera. "The point of the story is that the best equipment is effective only if the soldiers behind the weapons have the courage, group cohesion, and will to fight. You win wars through disintegration, not extermination. Firepower is always important, but it's only part of the cold equation of war. Stand-off precision weapons may punish an enemy and reduce close combat casualties, but they will not win wars by themselves. If you want to keep wars short and decisive, you must move on the enemy. Defeat by disintegration attacks the enemy's organizations by disrupting his soldiers' will, cohesion, and teamwork, incapacitating his organizations. In the end, no matter what the techno geeks may tell you, you still must physically dominate the enemy."

"Bravo, Colonel. That was quite a speech," Hamilton said in feigned praise. "But in view of the high-tech warfare you disdain, your concept seems a bit barbaric, don't you think?"

"War is a cold equation; we have to deal with it in its crudest, bloodiest sense if we want to avoid it," Rodriguez answered, holding his ground against her softhearted assault. "It's not a video game. Cheap, easy, bloodless victory is an illusion. It takes discipline, iron-hard training, and ruthless execution to fight and win wars. It takes soldiers willing to fight in close combat, move across the deadly ground, and impose their will on the enemy."

Another tank cannon boomed in the valley below. Rodriguez turned to his left just in time to see the round miss the target and fly over the hill.

"Cease-fire freeze!" Captain Drake yelled into his radio transmitter. "Charlie Three-Four, you may have fired a round out of the impact zone."

The cameraman turned his camcorder to capture Captain Drake in the process of ordering the cease-fire. Hamilton looked to Rodriguez, the trace of a sly smile on her lips. "You were talking about well-trained soldiers?"

Rodriguez remained calm, his lips tight. "Captain Drake, call the firing tank and find out what happened."

Command Sergeant Major Dougan ran to his HMMWV, sat down in the front seat, and started talking on the radio.

"What you've just witnessed, Ms. Hamilton, is a tank that probably loaded the wrong ammunition. We're here to train for war. This crew made a mistake, but they'll learn from it. We've built safety into this course to handle the possibility that a crew would fire over the hill."

"Colonel," Hamilton said, "you might be able to fool your wife with that line, but I don't buy it."

"First, Ms. Hamilton, I'm not married. Second, if you don't believe me, why not go down and talk to the tank crew yourself?"

"Not married, Colonel?" Hamilton replied. "I'm not surprised."

Rodriguez didn't answer but turned his attention to the tank that had just fired. He uncapped the covers to his binoculars and raised the glasses to his eyes to observe the action downrange. All the while, Hamilton's cameraman was filming him.

Dougan jumped out of his vehicle and walked toward his battalion commander like a bull heading for the matador. "Sir, I talked with the crew on the radio. It's just as you suspected. The loader, a new kid named Emerson, loaded the wrong round. It was a HEAT engagement and he loaded sabot. The gunner put in the superelevation for HEAT. That's why the round went over the hill. It's okay, though. It landed inside the safety fan—no harm done."

Rodriguez nodded. "Major Lucas, why don't you take my Humvee and drive Ms. Hamilton down to Charlie Three-Four's afteraction review. She can get a firsthand look at how we train our crews. Maybe even get her inside the tank and let them drive around a bit."

Lucas shot a worried glance at Rodriguez, then nodded. "Yes, sir, I'd be happy to."

"Stay with our guests and make sure they see anything they want."

"Wilco, sir," Lucas answered, and saluted.

Before the reporter could argue, the major had her and the

cameraman moving to the Humvee. In another minute they were off, bounding down the muddy trail.

"Boss, sometimes I worry about you," Dougan said as he pulled out a cigar and handed it to the battalion commander. "She got to you, didn't she?"

Rodriguez took the cigar and gave Dougan a steady gaze. "Sergeant Major, if there's one thing I've learned in my short life, it's that success is the result of working hard, playing hard, and keeping your mouth shut."

"You're right there," Dougan said with a laugh.

"So I think I'll just keep my mouth shut," Rodriguez answered as he pulled out a book of matches to light his cigar.

4:00 P.M., 30 September, Kim Jong Il's command bunker northeast of Pyongyang, North Korea. A North Korean army major observed a security display that adorned his large metal desk. Two guards with gleaming, stainless steel AK-47 assault rifles stood at the head of the corridor that marked the entrance to the command bunker. A trim-looking soldier wearing camouflage coveralls walked to the front of the security officer's desk.

The major looked up and quickly studied the colonel with the wry smile of a bureaucrat who had unquestionable authority. "How did you get in here? I didn't see you on my cameras."

The man handed the major a piece of paper.

He scanned the paper quickly. "Comrade Colonel, your orders do not grant access to the briefing room. This is a restricted area. The Dear Leader, Kim Jong Il, is—"

With the movement of a panther on the strike, the man in the coveralls pulled out a 9mm pistol and shot both guards between the eyes. The guards were flung against the wall. In the next second the man shot the startled major.

With a look of utter surprise, the dying major fell to the floor. The assassin reached into the pocket of his coveralls, removed a small electronic device, and placed it on top of the console. The device hummed and in seconds deactivated the bunker's security mechanism.

More men in camouflage coveralls arrived. Within minutes a party of fifteen commandos had secured the entrance to the bunker. While two men stood guard, the others stopped in front of the desk and unzipped their coveralls, revealing South Korean Army uniforms. The men ditched their coveralls, then pulled black ski masks over their faces.

The leader glanced at his watch. "Kill everyone."

The commandos nodded. They reached into their bags and put on their American-made night vision goggles. The lights in the compound suddenly went out. All power, except the power to the ever-present video cameras and the glow from the security console's viewing screen, was out. The inside of the bunker was pitch-black.

The commandos switched on their night vision goggles and silently moved down the dark corridor. A confused voice shouted in the dark. The lead commando blasted three frantic North Korean guards with a quick, quiet burst from his silenced submachine gun. The bodies crumpled in the dark hallway as the commandos moved on.

The group halted in front of a thick wooden door. Signals were whispered and everyone took up positions. The lead commando opened the door, tossed in a grenade, and closed the door.

The grenade exploded and the door blew open. Bodies lay all over the floor. A man crawled in the corner, only to be executed by a commando with a pistol. The large antechamber led to another door; this one was made of steel and looked like the entrance to a bank vault. Two commandos moved forward and quickly set an explosive charge on the handles of the door. In seconds the charges were armed and ignited.

"Three, two, one," the leader whispered as he looked at the luminous hands of his watch. A klaxon blared fiercely from the hallway. All the lights inside the bunker suddenly came back on.

The heavy steel doors that protected the command bunker blew open in a tremendous flash. The air filled with a choking dust. The commandos took off their goggles and entered the breach, firing as they moved. A few dazed guards scurried about as the commandos fired rapid bursts at their stunned prey. The commandos moved to each room, hunting down their victims without mercy. They killed everyone they found.

Television cameras, one in each corner of the briefing room, captured every detail of the scene. Two commandos walked by all the victims and fired at them several times to be sure they were dead. One commando moved past a large terrain map and fired four slugs into the broken body of an admiral in a white naval uniform who lay lifeless underneath the table.

The firing stopped. There was only one target left—the soft, pudgy, short body of the Dear Leader, Kim Jong Il, cowering behind a stuffed chair. A commando took aim and fired several rounds into the chair. The man fell back against the wall, then slid slowly to the floor.

The assassin walked over to the body of his dead dictator, pulled out his 9mm Beretta pistol, and fired seven times into the dead man's skull.

The cameras moved back and forth, filming every move.

5:30 P.M., 30 September, multipurpose range complex, Chorwon Valley, South Korea. The sky broke and deluged the mountains and narrow valleys with rain. It seemed to drop in sheets, layers and layers of water beating down on the soldiers, tanks, Bradley infantry fighting vehicles, armored personnel carriers, and trucks that made up Task Force 2-72.

Sergeant Major Dougan sat in the backseat of Lieutenant Colonel Rodriguez's HMMWV, watching the rain fall against the windshield. Rodriguez sat in the front passenger seat. Corporal Finley, Rodriguez's driver, sat behind the wheel, trying to stay dry.

"I ain't ever seen it rain this hard," Finley said.

No one replied. Dougan could tell that the old man was in a foul mood. He hadn't said a word for the past thirty minutes.

Dougan respected his boss. Rodriguez was a West Pointer and all army, born and trained to lead. In moments of decision, Rodriguez was in his element. In another place, at another time, however, he might have been a teacher, a physician, even a poet. His face possessed a natural dignity, and the touch of good humor at the corners of his mouth gave the impression of wisdom. In quieter times, Dougan had seen another part of Rodriguez, a part that seemed to be searching for something inside him that was missing.

The sergeant major unzipped his Gore-Tex rain jacket, opened the breast pocket of his Nomex uniform, and took out an envelope. It contained pictures of the last field exercise. He handed them to Rodriguez.

"So, you finally developed those pictures of C21," Rodriguez said with a laugh. He looked at the photos one at a time, handing them to Finley in turn.

"Man, that tank's almost off the damn cliff," Finley exclaimed.

"Yep," Dougan said with a gleam in his eye. "The bastard nearly rolled right off."

"We were running platoon tactical exercises a few months ago, before you arrived in the battalion," Rodriguez commented. "Each tank platoon had to fight down a narrow mountain road against a mock North Korean defense."

"Why on such skinny roads, sir?" Finley asked.

"We were developing the boss's defile tactics, teaching the crews how to fight in Korean terrain," Dougan interjected, pointing to a picture of tanks moving through the hills. "You use every poor excuse for a road that you can find in this country. This trail was about a tank and a half wide. One side was a steep mountain cliff and the other was a straight drop-off into nothing."

"You picked this road, Colonel?" Finley replied, staring at a picture that showed a tank on the verge of falling off a cliff.

"It was a hell of a lot wider when we started to train," Rodriguez answered, shaking his head.

"We ran the defile fight with each platoon three times," Dougan continued. "After a couple of days of this, one of our tanks drove down the road and the road gave way, just disappeared from the right side of the damned tank. The tank slid off the road and was left hanging on the side of the cliff by a few road wheels. The crew—a green-as-fresh-cut-grass second lieutenant, a sergeant, a KATUSA corporal, and a new driver—got their asses out of there. We were lucky that no one was hurt.

"I arrived on the scene with the old man just after it happened," Dougan went on, pointing at the picture of the tank at the edge of the cliff. "The colonel was as calm as a granite statue. He ordered the tank recovery section forward and told the recovery chief to pull the tank back onto the trail."

"Calm . . . hell," Rodriguez protested. "I was scared stiff we'd lose that tank."

"So, did you get it out?" Finley asked.

"Take it easy, youngster, and listen. You might learn something," Dougan replied. "Unfortunately, this tank didn't want to be rescued; it was stuck hard and we couldn't get around it because the road was too narrow. Most of it was over the other side. We moved an M88 recovery vehicle to the front of the tank, and the recovery section debated the problem for a while. They tried to drag the tank out, but no luck. We almost lost the tank. I waited, watching the ground giving way pebble by pebble, while they jack-jawed about their next move.

"Finally the maintenance chief threw his hands in the air and the recovery section said it was impossible. By now it was dark and the maintenance chief suggested to the old man that we wait until the next day when it got light. In the meantime I could hear the rocks trickling down the hill one at a time. The recovery section said that three M88s were needed, one to hold the tank in place and two to pull it back over the ledge, but they couldn't do that from the front. Then some asshole made a comment about using Chinook helicopters or digging the road down with bulldozers."

"Could a helicopter lift the tank?" Finley asked.

"No way, that was just fantasy talk. But the old man didn't want that tank hanging there overnight. So he ordered two more M88s to drive around the hill to the rear of the tank—an eight-kilometer trip—and pull it from the same direction as it went off the side. It was that or nothing."

"Sounds like a disaster," Finley said, gawking at a photo of a tank hanging on to a cliff with only one set of road wheels showing. "What happened?"

"Well, the M88s finally pulled around from the other side and got into position," Dougan explained, his arms gesturing the route of the tank retriever. "The cables were fixed. The snatch blocks were attached. We needed one hundred and forty tons of pull power. We had only one hundred and thirty-five with two M88s, but after six hours of playing with this thing we were ready to do it. The two rear eighty-eights pulled with cables while the one in front used a cable to keep tension on the tank to keep it from sliding down. Then, in the rear, the left clevis connecting the cable to the tank snapped apart.

"Now the tank was being held by only one cable in the rear

and one in front. The tank quivered but the cable held. I walked over to the tank with the old man and we reconnected the left cable with a new clevis. We were afraid that the other cable might snap and cut everyone in half who was within range of the wire. We held everyone else back and lifted the ninety-pound snatch block and reconnected the cable to the tank. We finished the job with only the taut cable to our left holding the tank. It was so tight that I could see the dirt jumping off it in the recovery lights of the eighty-eights.

"Once we moved back out of the way, the colonel gave the order to pull again. The tank groaned and creaked and began to move. The winches growled and the tank seemed to stop. Suddenly it came up over the cliff, and the back end moved close to the M88s. After a few anxious moments, we pulled the sucker to the level road."

"That's a hell of a story," Finley said with a toothy grin.

"Shit, that's the understatement of the year," said Dougan. "But the old man and I just smiled and lit up cigars. He told me that, after all, it was only a stuck tank."

"Thanks for the story, Sergeant Major," Rodriguez said with a nod. "I guess I shouldn't have had that tank on the road in the first place. That's one crisis I'd rather forget."

"I'll wager it won't be the last crisis you'll have to face in command, and I'm not so sure you're right about not trying to train there. If there's one thing I've learned from you, it's that we should always play to win."

"Dragon Six, this is Warrior Two. Your frequency. Over," the radio blared, interrupting the sergeant major's mentoring session. The two men looked at each other, surprised to have a visitor on their radio frequency.

"Speaking of bad situations, that's the G2 calling. I wonder why he's on my battalion command net," Rodriguez said to Dougan as he grabbed the radio hand mike. "Warrior Two, this is Dragon Six."

"Dragon Six, I'm flying just south of the tank range. Just thought I'd check in with you since I'm out and about. Have you seen any unusual ROK unit activity? Over."

"Negative, Warrior Two. We haven't seen any ROKs at all. Over."

"Okay, Dragon Six. Look, something may be brewing up

north," Wallace continued. "I don't have any hard intel on what's on the other side of the hill, but you may want to take extra precautions for the next few days. Consider this a personal INSTUM to a friend."

"Roger, Warrior Two. Thanks. Anything further?"

"Negative. The cloud ceiling is getting worse and we have to return to base. I'll call you if I hear anything else. Out."

"What was all that about?" Dougan asked.

"I don't know. I've known Steve Wallace ever since the academy. He's one of those brilliant guys—got straight A's at West Point, memory like a steel trap. He isn't the kind who spooks easily. If he's up in a helicopter checking out the ROKs, he's one nervous puppy."

"If anything was up, wouldn't brigade call us?" Dougan asked.

"Sure, if they knew. But let's play the G2's hunch. Assemble the commanders for me in the TOC in thirty minutes. I'm going to talk to the XO and figure out our fuel, ammunition, and class one status."

"Wilco." The muscular sergeant major snapped open the door of the HMMWV, sighed, and slowly walked through the pouring rain to the five M577 armored command vehicles that made up the battalion tactical operations center.

10:00 P.M., 30 September, South Korean defensive position, six kilometers south of the DMZ. "What a miserable night," the young South Korean lieutenant said as he shivered in the cold drizzle that blanketed his battle position. He sat on the wet ground in a four-man foxhole that was roofed with heavy timbers and sandbags. The foxhole served as his platoon command post.

"Private Chang, try again to reach the commander on the radio. I must talk to company headquarters."

Chang tried in vain for several minutes. "Sir, no one answers on any frequency."

The rain renewed its attack against the waterlogged soldiers; it fell at an angle that entered the trench line and the covered defensive positions. The fog and mist reduced visibility to about fifty meters.

Second Lieutenant Sung-Joo Ri, of the Republic of Korea

Army, knew that something strange was happening. He was new to the army, but he understood the military. Three months ago he had graduated from the Republic of Korea Military Academy. As the son of a general, he pictured himself as an old-fashioned warrior. He believed in honor and country, and he planned a life of duty and glory. Now he was responsible for the lives of fifty-three infantrymen cringing in the cold rain in their defensive trenches just south of the DMZ. He knew the military enough to know when things were really screwed up.

Lieutenant Sung-Joo and his infantrymen sat in their positions as the rain soaked into their bones. His platoon occupied a trench line commanding a road leading south into the Chorwon Valley. They were situated on the north slope of a small hill that was part of the first defensive line of the ROK Army. Their position guarded a major avenue of approach into the valley. Unfortunately, the platoon was just learning the area of operations; they had relieved a company that had occupied the position for a year. This was the platoon's first night on duty.

Sung-Joo didn't know why they were occupying the trenches so late at night. Border duty was usually boring, according to his friends. He understood that the Chorwon Valley approach was a traditional invasion route into southern Korea. He knew that for thousands of years, conquering armies from China or Japan had moved through and fought over the valley that led to the cities of Pochon and Uijonbu, only a few miles from Seoul. If the North Koreans attacked, one of their major avenues of approach would be the Chorwon Valley.

Sung-Joo also believed that the world had changed and that war between North and South Korea was unthinkable. For all their Stalinist rhetoric, the North Korean communists were still people, just like him. They wouldn't kill brother Koreans. This alert, he guessed, was the work of his overly ambitious company commander, who was probably trying to show the new battalion commander how combat ready he was.

The problem was that everyone was new. Sung-Joo's platoon had been formed only a few weeks before he joined the unit. Nevertheless, he thought with a smile, they are good men. They had marched through the night and occupied their positions like veterans. They carried their normal basic load of small-arms ammunition and a dozen 90mm recoilless rifle rounds for the two 90mm antitank rocket launchers and six antitank mines.

Sung-Joo had not been issued any special orders. No one had explained to him what was going on. Since his platoon had occupied the trenches, he hadn't heard a word from anyone.

The twenty-two-year-old lieutenant pulled up the hood on his rain poncho. Something had to be wrong. Why hadn't his commander explained what was going on? Why had the men been issued live ammunition? Why couldn't he reach his commander or the artillery observer on his radio? Had his superiors all gone to sleep? Was this some kind of test?

Sung-Joo studied his map. His position was located at the base of an inverted T. The long stem of the T was a narrow valley with a two-lane asphalt road that ran north approximately two thousand meters. His position was in a natural route for troop movement to the Chorwon Valley to the south. High ridges paralleled the road. The sides of the road were impassable to vehicles, so traffic was channeled to the road.

Four hundred meters in front of his trenches was a twelve-foot dirt wall. The road narrowed to one lane, like a sally port in a castle battlement. This opening was protected by a rock drop designed to block the road and form a choke point that would deter an advance from the north. With explosives, a few men, and a pry bar, Sung-Joo could force the large cement blocks onto the road and block the opening.

The problem was that he had no orders to do anything other than occupy his positions and defend the rock drop. His orders specifically stated that the rocks were not to be dropped into the road without direct instructions from the company commander.

Platoon Sergeant Kim entered carrying a field telephone and pulling a length of communications wire. He placed the telephone next to the lieutenant and hooked in a wire.

Sung-Joo looked up. "What do you think?"

"I've walked to each position and talked to the men," the sergeant said, squatting next to his officer. "They're all miserable and eager to head back to the barracks. I kicked them in the butt, made them dig their positions deeper, and they laid communications wire lines from each squad position to the platoon command post. I also went forward and checked the rock drop."

"Good," the lieutenant said, embarrassed that he hadn't thought to do those things. "We'll probably get the word to return to the barracks soon."

"I have spent many nights out on the fence line," the sergeant said with the confidence of a veteran soldier. "This alert is different. If the communists are coming, we will know shortly."

"Don't be silly," Sung-Joo replied. "There isn't going to be any war. This is just a test to see if we can do our jobs."

"Yes, sir," Sergeant Kim reported formally. "Many people believe that the enemy will never come. Of course, then the surprise would be greater."

Sung-Joo looked inquisitively at his sergeant. "What do you mean?"

"Sir, this is not a normal drill," the sergeant said, deliberately tilting his head. "I believe that the stinking communists have finally decided to fight. Lieutenant, I think we're going to war."

The hours ticked by as the miserable, cold, wet night wore on. The reports sent over the squad telephones were routine. Sung-Joo sat down in the cold bunker with his radio telephone operator, Private Chang. In seven hours it would be daylight and this miserable night would be over. Satisfied that he had done all he could do, he pulled a wet blanket over himself, and—in spite of the rain—immediately dozed off to sleep.

4

ALERT

A "modern" infantry may ride in sky vehicles into combat, fire and sense its weapons through instrumentation, employ devices of frightening lethality in the future—but it must also be old-fashioned enough to be iron-hard, poised for instant obedience, and prepared to die in the mud. . . . If liberal, decent societies cannot discipline themselves to do all these things, they may have nothing to offer the world. They may not last long enough.

—T. R. FEHRENBACH

12:20 A.M., 1 October, American embassy, Seoul, South Korea.
A cold, persistent drizzle fell on the city of Seoul as typhoon Angela battered South Korea and Japan. The city lights glistened on the wet streets. Although Seoul never slept, tonight it seemed only half awake.

United States Marine Corps staff sergeant Michael Chatworth sat at his desk scanning a row of TV surveillance monitors and fighting off boredom. He was on the graveyard shift, from 2300 to 0500, when the time ticked away as slowly as cold maple syrup dripping from a bottle. Nothing exciting ever happened on this shift. Rainy nights were especially slow.

The guard station that Chatworth manned was the central security post at the entrance to the U.S. embassy. Four marines and five Korean nationals provided security for the embassy compound. The bulletproof glass that Chatworth sat behind and the MP5 submachine gun fastened by clamps underneath his desk were a reminder of the seriousness of his job.

Chatworth poured himself another cup of coffee from the shiny stainless steel thermos decorated with a large Marine Corps globe and anchor emblem. Embassy duty was good duty, he thought. As a marine, Chatworth had experienced his share of being cold, wet, tired, and hungry. On a night like tonight it was good to enjoy the comforts of a warm building and hot coffee.

His mind wandered as he sipped the warm, dark brew.

Prior to his posting to the embassy, he had served six years in the Fleet Marine Force, or FMF, as the jargon went. Sailing in amphibious troop transports all over the Pacific and Indian Oceans, he had seen the world, at least that part of it where marines were needed. His time in the FMF was exciting but lonely. On "float" for six months at a time, traveling from port to port, he seemed destined to remain a bachelor forever. His assignment to the U.S. Marine security detachment at the embassy in Seoul, however, had changed all that.

From his seat at post number 1, he could observe six television cameras with a glance. The cameras covered every angle of the embassy. He glanced at the ever-present screens but didn't notice anything unusual. This night was routine. As on other nights, he expected to get off at 0500, run his usual five miles, then get some rest for his big date tomorrow.

"Post one, this is QRF," the hand-held Motorola radio squeaked, interrupting his thoughts. "We'll be in java one for the next fifteen. Over."

"Roger, QRF," Chatworth answered with a sly grin. The QRF was a quick reaction force of two marines armed with submachine guns. Sergeant Russell, in charge of the QRF, was in the break room drinking coffee with Corporal Doughty. Java 1 was the code word for the break room.

As Chatworth shuffled through a stack of duty reports from the past week, he thought about his fiancée. He smiled as her memory filled his soul. Chang Wa was beautiful, a dream come true. He had met her only eleven months ago at the U.S. Marine Corps ball, but it seemed that he had never had a life before her. As usual with Chatworth, it had been a case of lust at first sight, and then it suddenly and rapidly turned into something more substantial. He knew now that he was hopelessly, madly in love.

The Marine Corps ball is the social event that every marine looks forward to every year. Chang Wa's father, a distinguished Republic of Korea marine general, had brought her to the ball and proudly displayed his favorite daughter to all the marines and dignitaries as if she was a prize of priceless value.

Chang Wa was indeed a prize, as Chatworth quickly discovered. As they danced, he learned that she had graduated from Seoul University and majored in English. She loved American music and movies. She wanted to visit America and see the Grand Canyon, New York City, and the Golden Gate Bridge.

They danced all evening, almost without stop. Before the night was over, Chatworth had her telephone number. After several formal invitations to her home, he gained her father's respect. Within three months he and Chang Wa were lovers.

The rain picked up, falling in buckets outside the embassy building where the sergeant was planning his campaign for matrimony. He didn't see the camera record the infiltrator in a black uniform sneaking over the compound wall. He wasn't watching the TV when the man placed an explosive charge on the back of the heavy metal embassy gate.

"Gate two to post one," the radio transmitter blared.

It's Corporal Ghent at post 2, Chatworth thought, putting down the picture of his future bride. Ghent's going to be a great marine someday. Does everything by the book. A future Chesty Puller. "Post two, this is post one."

"Post one, there's a truck at the bottom of the hill with its engine running. Two occupants. It's been there about fifteen minutes. There should be an ROK policeman down there, but I can't see him. It looks suspicious. Suggest you notify the—"

The corporal didn't have time to finish his sentence. A huge blast blew the heavy metal doors of post 2 thirty feet into the air.

The force of the explosion tossed Chatworth to the floor. The foundation of the building rocked as if an earthquake was tearing at the ground. An automatic siren, set off by the electronic security system, wailed in the embassy compound.

"What the hell?" Chatworth cursed. He struggled back up to view the console. Four of the six TV cameras were blank. The other two were showing nothing but rain and darkness. The central embassy security station was blind.

"Post two, Corporal Ghent. Report."

There was no answer. Chatworth heard the burst of an automatic weapon outside.

"All gates, intruder alert!" Chatworth screamed over the radio. He reached under his desk and grabbed the MP5 submachine gun. He tapped the magazine, then pulled back the charging handle. With his left hand he snatched his walkie-talkie radio off the desk and shouted into the transmitter. "Lock all security doors. Sergeant Russell, get the quick reaction squad in here."

Outside his station Chatworth heard the sound of a truck engine revving at high revolutions per minute. He stared at the heavy steel doors ten feet in front of his desk.

"Shit . . ." The last thing that Staff Sergeant Chatworth saw was a truck smashing through the embassy doors. It would detonate a thousand pounds of explosives directly in front of him.

12:30 A.M., 1 October, radio message sent to all commands of the North Korean Army. Martial music played on every station of the North Korean radio and television spectrum. Large red banners and North Korean flags paraded in a pretaped recording on the television screen. The image dissolved and changed to the somber face of Marshal Kim Seung-Hee. Kim sat at his desk wearing a dress uniform bedecked with ornate medals. A large North Korean flag hung on the wall behind him.

"Soldiers of the Inmun Gun and people of the Democratic People's Republic of Korea. The hour of our greatest challenge lies before us. The cursed South Korean fascists have murdered our Dear Leader in an insane attempt to destroy us. The Dear Leader has died, but his spirit to crush our enemies lives on. His death must be avenged."

Kim looked directly into the camera as the screen narrowed in a close-up view of his stern face. With passion he thumped the desk, emphasizing his next line.

"Our great hour has arrived. Large attacking armies are moving against the southern psychophants and their warmongering imperialist fascist allies. We will crush these bloody killers who have killed our Dear Leader.

"I am now in command of the military and the government. I expect all commanders to remain loyal to me and our cause. Those in our ranks who may have supported this assassination will be found out and eliminated. Together we will win. We will have our revenge."

The camera moved back, ending the close-up. The screen displayed Kim and the flag.

"Each of you has a sacred duty to sacrifice everything to achieve victory. Steel your hearts and show no mercy to the hated enemy. Avenge the death of our Dear Leader, Kim Jong Il. Make the enemy pay for their heinous attack on our beloved leader. We attack to free our brothers and sisters who are living in slavery under the boot heel of the southern capitalists. Do not hesitate in your attack. Forward, to victory. *Nam chim.*"

12:45 A.M., 1 October, intelligence collection office, G2 section, 2d Infantry Division command bunker. "Sir, our satellite imagery went off-line three hours ago. Some kind of software problem," Major Cooper reported.

"That's never happened before," Wallace said. "How many are down?"

Major Cooper read the report in his right hand. A concerned look came over his face. "That's funny. They're all down."

Wallace closed his tired eyes and tried to put the pieces of the puzzle together. What the boss wants, he thought, is a clear indication of an attack. What he really wants is the enemy's intentions.

Somehow Wallace sensed that he was running out of time. His fifth cup of coffee wasn't rallying him in his battle against exhaustion. He felt that he was on the edge of a great revelation, but he wasn't able to get the kind of information that would convince the decision makers. Are we so used to denying any possibility of a North Korean attack that we can't see reality? he wondered.

"I'm worried, Jim. I think I can see what's happening on the other side of the hill, but I can't prove it. If this Daring Thrust operation is only an exercise, I'll eat my hat."

"Maybe the guys in Seoul are right," Cooper said as he got up and walked over to Wallace's desk. He deposited the one-page report. "Maybe we're seeing ghosts. The satellite problem could be a fluke. The latest intel reports could be read both ways. This radio intercept on Daring Thrust, for instance, says that phase one is complete. Phase two is probably the order to stand down and return to garrisons."

Wallace studied the report for a few moments, then he took

out a yellow highlighter and marked several lines of the trans-·
lated intercept. The· message ordered an unknown number of
North Korean combat units to execute phase 2 of Daring
Thrust.

"No. I·can't believe that phase two is the order to stand
down. We'd have seen more activity. Phase two must be something else. Something big is about to happen. Let's look at the
facts. First, the ROKs are shuffling divisions on the DMZ, creating a window of vulnerability. Second, the loading of Nodong
missiles with chemical weapons and the deployment of the
S-300 air defense weapon system. Third, this damn Daring
Thrust exercise. Fourth, the weather is lousy; rain and heavy
fog are predicted for the next six days—perfect attack weather.
Fifth, we've just lost all of our intel satellites. We're blind."

Wallace put down the report and reached for his coffee cup.
He brought it to his lips and noticed that there was nothing but
cold grounds in the bottom of the cup. Cooper, standing next to
his boss's desk, walked a few paces to the coffee stand near the
wall and returned with a half-full decanter of coffee. He poured
the warm black liquid into Wallace's waiting mug.

"What about U2 reports?" Wallace suggested.

"The U2s were grounded this morning because of typhoon
Angela."

"Well, this will add to the paranoia," Wallace declared with a
smile, handing Cooper two pictures he had been studying. "The
first photo shows units of the 820th Corps moving south. The
second photo, taken the next day, shows the road clear. Where
did they go?"

"UGFs?"

"That's my guess. They're all snug as bugs in their
bombproof bunkers waiting for the word to attack. What about
North Korean air activity?" Wallace questioned. "Any idea on
the positioning of their AN-2s?"

The AN-2 Colts were ancient, single-engine, propeller-
driven biplanes that could carry a squad of heavily armed commandos all the way to Pusan. Because they were made mostly
of wood and cloth, they were difficult to detect. The north had
about 270 Colts. Wallace tracked their movements routinely by
studying satellite photos of their home airfields and counting
them on the runways. Two weeks ago they had mysteriously

moved closer to the DMZ and hadn't been picked up in any satellite imagery.

Either we've missed their return flights or they're hiding somewhere, ready to pounce on us, Wallace thought.

"Sir, there's nothing new on the AN-2s. I don't expect to get much more now that the satellites are down," Cooper said quietly, showing genuine concern for the boss he admired. "It's late. We all need rest. You haven't slept much in the past two days."

"No time," Wallace said, sipping his coffee. "Time is the one thing I don't have, Jim. We have to unravel this puzzle before morning. Get me all you can on the AN-2 Colts."

The door to Wallace's office opened. A female captain stuck her head into the room. "Sir, I'm transferring a secure call to you from the CFC G2."

"Thanks, Mary," Wallace answered.

Wallace and Cooper looked at each other. The secure telephone rang. Wallace picked up the receiver. "Lieutenant Colonel Wallace here. This line is secure."

"This is Colonel Griffin. Steve, you may be right. Something big is happening. There's speculation of a coup or something up north. Pyongyang radio and TV are broadcasting patriotic songs and martial themes over all stations. All our prehostility indicators have lit up like a goddamned Christmas tree."

Wallace's eyes narrowed. How much time do we have before the ax falls? he thought.

"Steve, we've got reports of enemy units infiltrating all over the place, not just along the DMZ. ROK police are reporting incidents as far south as Pusan. CFC is calling a full alert. The CINC should be on the phone with your commander now. He's alerting the 2d Infantry Division and ordering all units to their local dispersal areas."

Wallace could hear the confusion in the speaker's voice. If the CINC, the commander in chief of the Combined Forces Command, was on the secure phone with General Schmidt at this late hour, the situation was really serious.

"We don't know much else," the colonel said nervously. "Most of the strategic stuff is down—some kind of technical glitch with the software. The satellite connections are all scrambled. We're getting nothing but lines of computer code and no pictures. This may be a deliberate attack on our information systems, but we're not sure. . . . Hold on."

Wallace waited tensely as he tried to discern what the colonel was talking about in the background.

"Shit, we've got a confirmed Scud launch. Steve, I gotta go. I'll get back to you."

The phone went silent. Wallace slowly put down the receiver. Major Cooper stood frozen in front of his boss and waited nervously for instructions.

Wallace looked up at Cooper with resignation and shook his head. "The North just launched a Nodong missile. CFC is on alert. We're too damned late."

A blaring siren screamed in the night, signaling that an alert was in progress. The piercing alarm echoed from several sirens inside the bunker.

"Jim, get everyone in full battle gear and man all our intel stations."

The screaming sirens got louder, wailing the call to war.

"I'll contact the brigades and find out what they know," Cooper said. He brought his hand to his forehead in a nervous gesture of concern. "There'll be hell to pay. We're not ready. The ROKs aren't ready. It'll take the ROKs a week to nine days to mobilize the entire army."

"We can't do anything about that now. I'll have to brief the CG soon. Get everything we've got on Daring Thrust, especially enemy troop deployments, UGF positions, and artillery locations. We're the intel guys. Let's figure out what the guy on the other side of the hill is going to do next."

Cooper nodded. As he turned to leave, a huge explosion shook the ground, and the lights dimmed for a second. Cooper fell against the side of the desk. "What the hell was that? Artillery?"

"We're under attack," Wallace shouted, yelling over the blare of the sirens that had gone off inside the bunker. He moved over to the safe in his office and dialed the combination. He opened the door and pulled out two 9mm pistols and three magazines of ammunition. "Get everyone moving. You know the drill. I'll head outside to find out what's going on."

Wallace handed the second pistol and one magazine to Cooper, then ran down the hallway toward the heavy metal blast doors guarding the entrance to the command bunker. A young corporal stood in a small room protected by bulletproof glass, like a desk clerk at an all-night hotel. The guard controlled the electronic locks to the entrance to the command bunker with the flick of a switch.

"Sentry, are you armed?" Wallace questioned, sticking his face up to the glass. The bewildered guard didn't respond. "Soldier, I asked you a question. Do you have a weapon?"

"No, sir," the guard said, looking as though he had been asked a question in a foreign language. "We never carry weapons on duty. My M16 is locked up in the arms room."

"Don't open the door to this hallway for anyone other than an American MP or me. Do you understand?" Wallace growled forcefully. "I'm going outside to find out what's happening. I'll be back in a few minutes."

The guard nodded. His shocked face seemed to ask a dozen questions. Wallace didn't have time to give him any answers.

The screaming sirens wailed in the dark, wet night.

Wallace moved through a short exit tunnel and walked up several concrete steps. The command bunker was on a hill that provided a clear view of the camp. Floodlights illuminated the road to the entrance and filled the area with alternating light and shadow. The constant drizzle covered the road with a slick sheet of water.

Wallace looked toward the main camp entrance, below him about a kilometer from the bunker, and saw the source of the explosion. The buildings near the gate were blazing with jagged orange and yellow flames. The ruins of a large civilian truck lay upside down near the entrance to the compound. Smoke billowed from several other locations in the camp, bearing witness to the work of enemy commando teams.

The siren continued to shriek. Pistol shots and shouts added to the cacophony. Suddenly a tremendous screaming sound, as if the air was ripping apart, blasted overhead. Wallace ducked instinctively. He looked up just in time to see the bright, glowing flames of the engines of jet aircraft thundering south.

The sky was suddenly dotted with sparks of machine-gun fire. Antiaircraft positions from ROK military bases surrounding Uijonbu shot trails of red tracers into the sky.

"Goddamnit, those must be MIGs. The bastards have launched a full-scale attack."

Suddenly the floodlights flickered. Wallace looked up to see a man silhouetted against the bright lights about thirty feet away. Instantly Wallace crouched against a concrete wall. Taut with alarm, he charged his Beretta. "Halt, who's there?"

The figure immediately turned and fired a burst of automatic rifle fire at Wallace. Wallace ducked, but he smashed his shoulder into the wall with the violence of his maneuver. Rifle rounds ricocheted against the wall. Dust and splinters of concrete fell on him. Thinking quickly, he rolled down the steps and crawled into a dark corner of the bunker entrance.

The firing stopped. He heard Korean voices and breathed heavily as he steadied the Beretta in his right hand. Distant explosions and the sound of aircraft screeching overhead filled the air. Wallace lay perfectly still on the cold, wet concrete, his pistol at the ready. He knew he didn't stand a chance of fighting his attackers on even terms. They had rifles. He only had a pistol with fifteen rounds and an extra magazine in his pocket. He couldn't run and he couldn't hide. He lay like a snake on his belly, ready to shoot the first thing that entered the bunker.

He could feel the pistol, its rubber grip slick from sweat, quivering in his hand. His left shoulder hurt and he couldn't move his left arm. He wanted to check his shoulder with his good right hand, but he was afraid to move the pistol away from the opening of the bunker.

Two men came into view, carefully moving into the opening of the tunnel that led to the bunker's entrance. Each was carrying a rifle. One man crouched forward, pointing his rifle at the entrance to the bunker. The other moved quietly behind, searching for the man who had yelled at them. Both men carried heavy packs.

The men were now less than fifteen feet away. Wallace waited. His heart pounded so fast he thought it would leap from his chest. One of the intruders turned toward him.

A bright explosion outside the tunnel lit up the entranceway. The two men looked up, distracted by the fireworks. Wallace held his breath and fired.

The two figures fell in a heap to the ground. Wallace stopped pulling the trigger.

One of the figures quivered for a few seconds, then lay still. After a few moments Wallace realized that his pistol was empty. In a panic he laid it down and grasped the extra magazine with his right hand. Cradling the pistol against his body, he fumbled with the magazine release, dropped the empty magazine, and inserted the full magazine into the pistol. Anxiously, he released the slide forward and chambered a round.

Nothing stirred. The two corpses lay in front of him, their lifeblood draining onto the concrete walkway. Wallace waited. After several minutes he staggered to a crouch, pushed his body against the concrete wall for support, and stood up.

His shoulder throbbed with pain. He tried to move his left arm, but it was numb. *I must have dislocated my shoulder in the fall,* he brooded. *What a hell of a way to start a war.*

A flickering red light shimmered against the wet concrete wall as a HMMWV rolled up to the bunker's entrance. The vehicle, with a soldier manning the .50-caliber machine gun mounted in the pedestal on the roof, stopped a few feet in front of Wallace.

"Over here," Wallace shouted, waving his pistol.

A soldier with a white-lettered military police armband jumped out of the HMMWV, his pistol at the ready. The MP standing in the opening in the roof pointed the big machine gun at Wallace. The soldier who approached Wallace pulled out a flashlight. He shone the light at Wallace, then walked over to the bodies.

"Man, you sure got these guys," the soldier said with a whistle as he shone the flashlight on the corpses. He kicked the North Koreans over to their sides to make sure they were dead. "Shot this one through the head three times, if you can call what's left of his head a head."

Wallace leaned back against the wall and stared down at his handiwork. He started to shiver, exhausted from his brief, sharp encounter with death. He felt sick. The last thing he wanted to do was vomit in front of the sergeant.

He looked away, out at the flickering city. The night sky was a confused cascade of dancing lights and glimmering reflections. Portions of Uijonbu were on fire. An arc of red tracers from an antiaircraft machine gun filled the sky like the long tail of a kite. Sirens continued to wail in the night. Another explosion echoed in the distance, foretelling the completion of the deadly task of another infiltrator. *The world has gone mad,* Wallace thought. *Now there's nothing left to do but count our dead and fight.*

"Good job, sir," the MP said in a voice reminiscent of someone congratulating a quarterback on a successful high school football game. "No tellin' what these assholes would've done if they'd made it inside. There are enough goddamned explosives in their packs to send us all to hell."

The MP dragged the two bodies to the side and took their weapons and explosives. More military police vehicles arrived. In a few minutes three squads of soldiers armed with machine guns and rifles secured the perimeter guarding the entrance to the bunker.

"A car bomb blew up the front gate," the MP told Wallace. "Took out about six of our guys. It looks like we're fucking at war, Colonel."

"Here, Sergeant, clear this for me," Wallace said as he handed the sergeant his pistol. The sergeant pulled back the slide and a bullet fell to the ground. He dropped the magazine and turned the pistol sideways to make sure it was clear. Satisfied, he handed it and the magazine back to the colonel.

Wallace took the pistol and stuck it and the magazine in his right BDU pants cargo pocket. "I'm Lieutenant Colonel Wallace, the G2. Who are you?"

"Sergeant Fitzpatrick, 1st Platoon, 2d MP Company."

"Okay, Sergeant Fitzpatrick, you're in charge here. Guard this entrance and the top of the hill. Don't let anyone inside you can't identify. No matter what happens, you and your men don't leave this post. Do you understand?"

"Loud and clear, sir."

The streetlights and building lights had gone out all over Uijonbu, leaving the city wrapped in an eerie darkness punctuated by fire. Several burning houses exploded, shooting angry red and yellow flames high into the sky.

The sergeant stooped down and picked up the fallen 9mm round. "Here, sir, you may need this before the night is over."

Wallace nodded grimly. He had pushed his luck to the limit and far beyond. So far, it was still holding. Exhausted and sore, he staggered into the bunker.

1:58 A.M., 1 October, hardened artillery site on the North Korean side of the DMZ. Artillery was the god of war, and Maj. Chun Yong-ho, the commander of the 136th North Korean Peo-

ple's Army howitzer battalion, was one of the god's greatest
disciples. He had trained for this day all his life. Now that it was
about to happen, he felt great excitement and an unlimited en-
thusiasm for the fight.

"No artillery in the world, and not even the finest air force,
could reach us in our bunker defenses," the major said, looking
out through the thicket bulletproof glass. His preparations were
complete. His splendid 2S3 152mm self-propelled howitzers
were combat loaded. The crews that manned his howitzers were
trained and ready. The firing doors of the hardened artillery site
were open.

The major's howitzers were the newest Russian-made howitzers in the Inmun Gun and the best in the North Korean Army.
Each carried a crew of five men along with forty-six rounds of
high-explosive shells. The major could launch his shells a distance of 17,230 meters. With rocket-assisted projectile (RAP)
charges, his range was 21,880 meters. Right now, his guns were
preparing to fire RAP rounds on the unsuspecting fascists. He
hoped that the artillery would kill them all.

Major Chun Yong-ho looked at his watch. It was 0159.

The largest artillery army on earth was about to unleash its
fury. To the major's left and right, all along the DMZ, hundreds of
batteries of 122mm, 130mm, 152mm, huge 170mm KOKSAN
self-propelled guns, and 122mm and 240mm multiple rocket
launchers (MRLs)—almost eight thousand cannons, howitzers,
and MRLs—waited to fire on carefully preplanned targets in
the south. Hundreds of tons of artillery shells of all calibers had
been prestocked for this great day. More than a hundred artillery battalions and eighty-two rocket battalions would blast
the South Korean and American fascists from the face of the
earth. Rocket battalions firing Frog and Scud missiles would
destroy the enemy's airfields and cities. The artillery would
launch ten thousand rounds a minute. The firestorm that would
result from this wave of devastation would create the conditions for the breakthrough.

Chun had studied at the artillery school at Sunchon and
earned a reputation as the best artillery battery commander in
the Inmun Gun. He knew that the massed artillery of a thousand
guns would smash the South Korean forces manning the demilitarized zone. Massive artillery fire strikes would kill the South

Koreans in their barracks before they could deploy to their bunkers and trench defensive positions. More artillery would destroy the enemy's tanks and armored personnel carriers as they were parked in their motor pools. The artillery would win the war, Chun thought smugly. Nothing on earth can withstand the wrath of our guns. We will kill all the enemy.

Once the artillery had stunned and destroyed the enemy, the infantry would infiltrate into the depths of the enemy's positions. The panic that this infiltration would cause, coupled with the devastating fire of the artillery, would enable the infantry to open huge gaps in the enemy's defenses. Once holes were punched through the first defensive line, the tanks and mechanized infantry would race through the gaps. The tanks would move forward as far and as fast as possible while the mobile, self-propelled artillery followed close behind. If the tank attack was blocked by a stubborn enemy defense, the infantry would dismount and attempt another infiltration attack. Once the self-propelled artillery was in position to support the infantry attack, the sequence would start again.

Everything depended, therefore, on the artillery.

Major Chun Yong-ho looked again at his watch. It was 0200. "Fire," he shouted. "Fire all guns."

His eighteen 152mm howitzers belched their deadly rounds at their targets. Rapid fire, they sent two rounds a minute into the air.

Everything was going as planned, he thought. The sky along the entire length of the DMZ seemed to burst in a simultaneous explosion. The North Korean multiple rocket launchers and the heavy NKPA artillery exploded along the 208-mile front. The sky lit up as if someone had set off a thousand flashbulbs. Such power, he thought. The sound of the firing built up his confidence. Within minutes, the lead elements of twenty-five crack NKPA divisions with twenty-five hundred tanks would attack south. The Inmun Gun was on the march again. This time, Chun knew, they would destroy their enemies completely.

"We will fire from these positions for another twenty minutes, then move back into the safety of our firing tunnel," Chun announced to a captain who manned the radio in the dimly lit bunker.

There was no return fire from the enemy. Apparently, Chun thought, we have taken the fascists by complete surprise.

Chun's face was exuberant. His howitzers belched another volley. He could hear the rumble of the guns all across the front. Never, he thought, had so much artillery been fired across the width of the Korean peninsula. The fascists would pay dearly for their subjugation of Korea. The liberation of the motherland, he was confident, was close at hand.

"Captain, next week we will celebrate our victory in Seoul."

The captain looked up, proud and ready for anything. "It is a great honor to serve with you tonight, in this historic moment, Comrade Major."

Chun smiled. It appeared that the sky was on fire. The sound of the firing was deafening. Never before had he been so proud. The firing was continuous—a roar that ebbed in strength but never let up. He looked out from his bunker observation post on the hills above his gun tunnels. The sky glowed red in the south with secondary explosions and fires, grim testimony to the awesome firepower of his army's cannon.

"Execute target six-zero-two-three," Chun shouted into his radio transmitter. "High explosive."

His guns moved with the precision of a single mind. The cannons shifted to the new target. Rounds were rammed up the heavy metal breeches. Then, in rapid volley, 162 rounds, nine rounds per gun, were fired in less than four minutes.

Chun's orders were to deploy his howitzers forward after firing this mission. His mission was to keep his battalion behind the breakthrough battalions but close enough to use the seventeen-kilometer range of the 152mm howitzer to support their attack. The high volume of fire that he was shooting would change once his battalion was on the move. Right now his guns had the luxury of fighting from their excellent tunnel positions. As the war moved south, he would carry his ammunition and fuel in the battalion's support truck company.

Chun knew that two mechanized corps, the 806th and 815th, and the 820th Armored Corps had been secretly moved forward over the past six months to huge underground facilities near the DMZ. Chun also knew that their main objective was to drive deep behind enemy lines and cut off the withdrawing or reinforcing enemy forces. The goal of the entire campaign was to destroy enemy forces north of Seoul and enable the NKPA to commit its operational exploitation forces. Once this occurred, the war would be over. The United States could negotiate peace terms in Tokyo, because South Korea would surrender rather than face annihilation.

As Chun surveyed the skyline with his binoculars, the door to the bunker opened. A lieutenant from the communications center entered. "Comrade Major, a sealed message for you from Marshal Kim Seung-Hee himself."

Chun signed for the message, took the envelope, and opened it. His hungry eyes devoured his new instructions. A wide grin formed on his face, and his eyes grew narrow as slits as he foresaw the future. He placed the message in his shirt pocket.

"Now the red god of war is truly invincible."

2:00 A.M., 1 October, multipurpose range complex, Chorwon Valley, South Korea. "What the hell?" Lieutenant Colonel Rodriguez shouted as three jet aircraft hurtled past them directly overhead. He opened the door to the range tower and stepped outside to look up into the rain-filled sky.

The operations officer, Maj. Tony Bradford, stumbled out into the dark, trying to determine what kind of aircraft had just shot by. Captain Drake, the task force assistant operations officer, trailed close behind Bradford.

"That guy needs his pilot's license revoked," Drake announced. "Doesn't he know this is a tank range?"

Another jet aircraft, an SU-25, flew fast and low toward the south.

"Holy Christ," Bradford shouted. "Those guys are out of their minds."

A rumble emanated from the north like a tremendous thunderstorm. Then the sky lit up in bursts of light and noise.

"Oh, my God," Bradford muttered, looking at Rodriguez. "They're attacking. The North Koreans . . . the stupid bastards are actually attacking."

Rodriguez seemed dazed for a moment. He studied the northern sky and listened to the explosions. The skyline flashed with the strikes of hundreds of shells. Suddenly Rodriguez understood the situation. He turned to his S3 and placed his arms on Bradford's shoulders. "Tony, get down to the bivouac area.

Get everyone to man his vehicle as fast as you can. Full alert. Move everyone into a tight perimeter against the south side of the mountain."

Major Bradford nodded and ran down the hill toward his HMMWV.

"Sir, this can't be happening," Drake said. The captain seemed stunned, unable to comprehend what was going on. The look in his young eyes registered sheer terror. "Maybe it's some kind of ROK exercise."

"No way, Charlie. This is the real thing," Rodriguez answered, looking toward the pulsating lights to the north. "That barrage sounds like it's moving south. We're in range of their bigger guns. If they're coming across the border, we may be in range of their mobile artillery. We have to protect our force."

"Roger, sir," Drake gasped, the excitement forcing out his words in rapid fire. "What do you want me to do?"

"Get on the radio and report to brigade. Tell them we're observing artillery fire and this ain't a simulation. Get me when you reach them. Help Bradford tell the companies to man every vehicle and move to the south side of this hill. The camp area is a target just waiting to happen."

"Yes, sir." The captain saluted and ran back into the tower to send a message to the task force's subordinate units over the FM radios.

Rodriguez shuddered. As much as he'd trained for this moment, as hard as he worked to be ready, he wasn't prepared. He never thought his battalion would really go to war, especially while deployed on a training exercise. His task force was all alone on one of the traditional major avenues of attack—the Chorwon Valley. That put his men closer to the DMZ than any other element in the brigade.

A jolt of fear ran up his spine. He realized that he was scared. And if he was scared, he knew that his soldiers were too. He would have to set an example tonight. He would have to generate the kind of leadership that would kindle the courage of his men. Tonight their courage would have to be reborn.

He hoped he could do it.

Men were running down the hill to the parked vehicles. Rodriguez imagined the confusion that would break out among his men in the camp, some of whom were sound asleep, lying side by side in twenty-man tents.

A soldier ran up the stairs and faced the commander.

"What do you want me to do, sir?" Corporal Finley asked, panting from his run up the concrete steps to the top of the hill.

"Stay calm, Finley. Get the Humvee ready to move off this hill," Rodriguez said in a steady voice. "Any orders from brigade? Any contact?"

"No, sir. I did hear a call from a 407 Cav unit on our brigade net. I tried to answer them, but they couldn't hear me."

"All right. Captain Drake will work the communications with brigade. Get the Humvee ready to go, listen to the radio, and put that box of forty-five slugs that we have in the backseat into my extra magazines."

"Yes, sir," the young soldier said, wide eyed, standing next to his colonel as if he expected something more.

"Okay, that's it," said Rodriguez, who was listening as more explosions resonated in the hills, these detonations sounding much closer. "Get going."

Finley ran off to his HMMWV.

The ground trembled as if to acknowledge the seriousness of the conversation. Artillery began falling several kilometers to the north. Artillery rounds whistled high overhead.

"Goddamnit," Rodriguez cursed. He felt helpless as he watched the storm of fire erupt on the northern horizon.

2:15 A.M., 1 October, thirty kilometers north of the DMZ. Horrible flying weather, the North Korean fighter-bomber pilot thought as he glanced at his flight radar. Visibility was barely two kilometers.

The pilot knew how important surprise was to achieving his goal. The potential cost to the Inmun Gun of a frontal slugging match without surprise in the narrow valleys south of the DMZ was prohibitive. The pilot's survival, and the victory of the motherland, depended on surprise. To win and maintain the initiative, the enemy's airpower had to be neutralized for at least six to ten days.

The aircraft crossed the DMZ. Now the pilot was in South Korean airspace.

Lieutenant Colonel Byung Chae Do glanced down to view

the illuminated display of the radar on his aircraft's instrument panel. It took his complete concentration to avoid the jagged mountains that crisscrossed his low-level approach to the target. The clouds covered the mountains in a dense mist that made flying a challenge. Patches of rain filled the dark night sky.

His aircraft darted quickly out of the clouds and across fog-covered rice paddies toward his objective. Luckily the unwary South Koreans still illuminated their towns and highways with bright white lights. Navigation, in spite of the bad weather, was aided by the enemy's unpreparedness.

In a few minutes Byung's aircraft squadron would put their experience and training to the test. The first barrage of Nodong missiles would be launching now to pulverize the enemy's airfields. Byung was convinced that his twelve twin-engine SU-25 fighter-bombers would destroy any of the fascists who survived the missile attack.

His Sukhoi SU-25 was a Russian-built aircraft, like most of the planes in the North Korean inventory. Like the American A-10 Thunderbolt, it was designed specifically for ground support. Piloted by one man, the SU-25 could carry a 4,000-kilogram bomb load and fly 345 miles without refueling. It wasn't the newest aircraft in the world, but it was the most effective ground attack bomber in the North Korean inventory. Flying low, evading enemy radars, the SU-25 could badly damage an airfield, and that's exactly what Byung intended to do.

Byung felt an exhilaration, an exaggerated sense of awareness that he had never felt before. He knew the importance of his task. His squadron hurtled forward. Everything was going just as they had planned. The Nodong missiles had already launched to destroy the enemy's airfields. His squadron would follow up these strikes. Four of his aircraft were destined for Kimpo airfield. Two were attacking a smaller South Korean Air Force airfield just south of the DMZ. The other six, led by Byung himself, headed toward the hardest target—the Americans at Osan Air Base. Osan had the greatest number of American aircraft. Once the strikes on Osan were executed, the Americans would be forced to move their aircraft south. This would reduce their access to the battlefield and gain precious time for the North Korean ground forces.

Byung knew that in war, time was everything.

He also knew that his squadron was not the only force conducting the attack. The North Korean deep attack plan called for a coordinated assault by six hundred aircraft and more than three hundred special forces teams. In addition, special units from North Korea's special forces, many of whom had infiltrated south days before, were already attacking their targets: enemy air bases, command and control facilities, and other key installations in Korea and Japan. These dedicated commandos, who were willing to give their lives to destroy their targets, provided a human counterpoint to the enemy's vaunted technology.

So what if Byung's aircraft were not as new as the South Korean or American planes? He was sure that his countrymen would win the battle for the air through cunning, shrewdness, and surprise. Discipline and will would counter the enemy's technology.

Byung's SU-25 Frogfoot fighter-bomber raced from mountaintop to mountaintop at six hundred miles an hour. He carried four huge cluster bombs under his wings. He listened carefully to the beeps of his radar, trying desperately to detect the telltale launch of an enemy air defense missile. So far, the enemy had not reacted.

Byung mentally ticked off the critical points of the attack plan. By now the special forces attacks would be in full swing. The teams had orders to attack the enemy's strip-alert aircraft and hangars. The enemy would be in a panic, fighting infiltrators and wrapped in confusion.

Two IL-28 Beagle aircraft flew high overhead, conducting electronic countermeasure attacks to jam enemy radars—a suicide run but a necessary sacrifice to make the mission successful. As an added precaution, a special squadron of twelve MIG-23 Flogger aircraft preceded the advance of Byung's seven SU-25s by fifteen minutes. The MIG-23s had the mission to provide aerial preparation, clearing a safe corridor for the SU-25s to make it to their target. The fascists would scramble every available aircraft to intercept the attack by the MIG-23s. The Floggers would clear the skies of enemy aircraft by drawing ROK and American fighters away from the SU-25s. Byung knew the pilots of the MIG-23s. He had practiced with them for this mission countless times in the past year. He knew that the MIG-23s, which were no match for the enemy's F-16s, were also expendable.

The fighter-bombers flew on. Byung felt the gentle rumble of the engines. His attack plan called for his Frogfoots to attack in pairs. One pair flew in front of him and one pair flew behind. All of his planes flew as low as possible to avoid enemy radar and missiles. Flying low, his SU-25s were to slip underneath the enemy's air cover to release their bombs on the American hangars and fuel storage sites at Osan Air Base. With luck, the rest of the enemy aircraft would be lined up on the runway waiting for takeoff, offering perfect targets for his cluster bombs.

The colonel smiled. He sensed the exhilaration of the hunt and eagerly awaited the kill. Everything was going as planned. His aircraft buffeted when it hit heavy air as he entered another dense cloud bank. He held his flight control stick tightly in his right hand, watched his instruments, and kept to his prescribed attack vector.

An automatic warning beeper suddenly screeched in his helmet's earpiece. He quickly scanned the small radar screen in the center of his cockpit display. It was illuminated with a dozen small white triangles, each one representing an enemy aircraft. Apparently the Americans and the ROKs were not totally surprised.

"Frogfoot Flight, decrease altitude, same attack vector."

"Frogfoot Commander, this is Flogger Lead. Contact. Enemy aircraft, six o'clock. We are engaging."

Damn the bastards, Byung thought. They have their fighters up in spite of the weather. How did they get them up so fast? Enemy contact had not been predicted so soon.

"Frogfoot Commander, this is Flogger Lead. Enemy aircraft have lock-on," a tense voice said over the radio. "They are firing missiles."

Byung shot a nervous glance at his flight instruments. The lower his planes flew, the safer they were from enemy fire but the greater the danger of crashing into a mountain. He squirmed against the straps of his uncomfortable seat, arching his back to look out the top of his canopy.

He saw explosions at three o'clock high.

"Frogfoot Commander, this is Flogger Lead," a surprised voice announced. "I've lost two aircraft."

Beads of sweat fell from his forehead. One after another, the blips that represented friendly MIG-23s were dropping from his screen.

"Frogfoot Commander," the voice of Byung's young wingman pleaded. "The enemy is closing fast behind us. Do we change attack vector?"

"Negative. Fire flares now and stick with the plan," Byung shouted. It was, after all, the only thing he could do. If he deviated from his plan and returned safely to North Korea, he could be shot for disobeying orders. Every son of the Inmun Gun was expected to obey orders precisely. Initiative meant making the plan work, not changing the plan. No one had the authority to change a plan.

"Continue with the plan. Use maximum speed. Fire flares again two minutes out from the target. We will avenge the deaths of our dear comrades."

Electronic countermeasures by the defenders suddenly added to Byung's problems. His squadron worked through its antijamming drill, changing frequencies every two minutes. In the switch, Byung lost radio contact with the MIG-23s.

He glanced again at his instruments. His greatest fear now was missing the precise point where he was to pop up, gain altitude, and find the airfield below him. If that happened, he would have to circle until he found the airfield, alerting the enemy's air defenses and losing the element of surprise.

"Two minutes to target," the lead Frogfoot pilot announced over the squadron frequency. Byung heard the distinctive tone of an enemy radar in his earphones.

"Frogfoot Flight, check initial target points. Prepare for attack run."

"Incoming missiles," the voice of the trailing SU-25 pilot shouted over the radio. "I'm locked on."

"Frogfoot Commander, this is Frogfoot Four. My wingman has been hit. Continuing evasive maneuvers," a frantic voice reported. "Request permission to drop my bombs and evade enemy aircraft."

"Negative," Byung shouted. "Continue your mission. Do your duty."

"Frogfoot Commander, I have missile—" The trail pilot was suddenly cut off in midsentence.

Byung flew evasive maneuvers. Enemy radars locked onto his planes. One by one Byung was losing his squadron. The plan was unraveling fast.

We're almost there, he said to himself as he unlocked the arming controls and armed his cluster bomb release mechanism. Suddenly his automatic aircraft defensive systems sounded a screeching alert. He was locked onto by an air-to-air missile. Immediately he fired flares and took evasive maneuvers. His SU-25 was almost at the designated target—the hangars and parked aircraft at Osan Air Base.

"Frogfoot Commander, this is Frogfoot One. One minute to target," a cold, mechanical voice from the pilot of the squadron's lead aircraft reported. "I have taken over the lead. One, two, and three are down."

Byung grimaced. He had lost three aircraft. No time for regrets now, he thought. Concentrate on the mission. Stick to the plan.

Ahead, Byung saw the final major landmark, a highway near Osan that designated his high-angle attack point, brightly lit by street lamps. Cars were speeding down the road, oblivious to the conflict above them. He verified his position with his radar. His watch read 0235. The target appeared on his small radar screen as a flashing red box. As soon as the box stopped flashing, he would press the bomb release and send all four canisters onto the runway below.

The air defense warning radar screeched again, louder than before.

Byung wasn't afraid. There was little time for fear. He was too busy. Flying an attack mission at night, at high speed and a hundred feet above the ground, didn't leave much time for reflection or fear. One slip and his jet would crash and burn, smashed over ten acres. It took a deft, calm hand to bomb a ground target. He had to concentrate on the task at hand.

Electronic warning systems were screaming in his earphones while he monitored the radar screens and tried to issue orders to his wingman. Sitting in his dark cockpit, Byung faced all the anxieties of war alone. Still, there was just too much to do to be afraid.

"Enemy missile launch, take immediate evasive maneuvers," his wingman warned. "Fifteen seconds to target lock-on."

A bright explosion erupted to Byung's right. Frogfoot Five, his wingman, had been incinerated by an enemy missile.

"Damn them," Byung shouted. His hand moved forward to release the bombs. He heard the distinctive *beep-beep* warning of an incoming enemy missile.

"Steady, steady," he said out loud. His words reassured him, just as they had in countless training missions. "I'm too low to be hit. They will never get me. Almost there. Just as we rehearsed. Time to pop up."

"Frogfoot Commander, this is Frogfoot One. We are with you."

"Good flying, One," Byung shouted, making his final run to the target. He pulled up on his stick and gained altitude. "Engaging target now."

Byung pushed the bomb release. Although he couldn't see the bombs, he visualized the Russian-made cluster canisters flying in a tight arc and landing on top of a line of American aircraft parked on the tarmac and preparing for takeoff. He smiled, then quickly jerked the stick to the right to return home.

In the next second his SU-25 disintegrated in a bright ball of flame and burning metal as an antiaircraft missile detonated inside the aircraft's starboard engine.

2:30 A.M., 1 October, multipurpose range complex, Chorwon Valley, South Korea. Alice Hamilton shivered in the dark, cold armored personnel carrier. She held on tight, white knuckled, as the APC bounced across a rough dirt road at high speed. The engine screamed, sounding like an out-of-balance washing machine.

"Paul, do you still have charged batteries for the camera?" she quizzed, a look of deep concern on her face. "If we don't have batteries, we'll miss some great shots."

Paul sat next to her with his arm around her shoulder. He looked at her in sad disbelief. "Let's not worry about that now, Alice. The story can wait a few hours."

"Do you have the cellular phone?" she cried hysterically.

"Yes. Now just relax for a few minutes," Paul said with the

tone of a friend who was trying to shelter someone he cared about. "You've been through a bad time. Just hold on."

Alice looked down. Her mind was racing; everything seemed a blur. She struggled to remember what she had just experienced. She remembered sleeping in a tent. She'd hoped to talk to Lieutenant Colonel Rodriguez, at least to be civil, but he was too busy with his damned tanks, so she had gone to bed early.

The armored personnel carrier's engine growled as the vehicle made a sharp right turn. Alice held on to the web strap dangling from the aluminum ceiling and struggled not to fall out of her seat.

Slowly she remembered. She was wearing her running suit, a habit she had learned when living in the bush. It was a particularly bright idea when the only female bathroom facilities were two hundred paces from her tent. She remembered the loud sound of explosions. When they began she quickly threw on her jacket and ran out of the tent. A few seconds later Paul found her, and she told him to get the camera equipment and start filming. Then the artillery shells fell on the camp.

Shells crashed into the ground like a rolling wave of thunder. Time suddenly moved in slow motion as tents were shredded with flying steel. Sergeants and officers shouted orders as soldiers ducked for cover.

Alice ran. A soldier grabbed her by the arm and asked her where she was going. All she could remember was how silly his question seemed. She stood staring at him as an artillery shell exploded. There was a tremendous flash, and she was swept off her feet and slammed hard to the ground.

After a couple of seconds—or minutes, she wasn't sure—she became aware of her surroundings. Her ears were ringing, but somehow she understood that the shelling had stopped. The scene she witnessed was sheer pandemonium. To her left a tent was on fire; a shell had torn it to pieces. A man walked out of the wreckage, stunned from the blast. He stumbled, his clothes hanging like strings on his blackened, scorched body.

A voice screamed, "Medic, medic, over here."

Two men lay on the ground, not moving. Alice pushed herself to a sitting position. Out of the corner of her eye, she saw something staring at her. The object was only a few feet away from her right side. In the poor light she couldn't make it out. She inched closer and reached for the flashlight in the pocket of her jacket. Her mouth immediately opened and her chin dropped as she realized what it was. She wanted to scream, but no air came out of her lungs.

It was a head—the head of a young soldier, severed neatly at the neck. She looked down, turned on her flashlight, and saw that her jacket was covered with blood and slime. The shell had showered her with the remains of the young man's body.

Suddenly her lungs kicked in and she breathed. She screamed and backed away in panic, kicking with her feet at the rocky ground. She tore off her bloody jacket, exposing her running suit top. Somehow, in the confusion, Paul found her and led her to the open ramp of an armored personnel carrier. She was inside the protection of the APC when she realized that she was still screaming.

"It's okay, Alice," Paul said soothingly. "You're all right. Stop screaming." The moments took on a fluid, surreal quality. She tried to focus her mind, to remember what happened next. She listened to herself asking if they had batteries for the camera—a silly question, she thought, but the words just tumbled out of her mouth. She looked up at the plastic intravenous solution bag dangling from a hook in the roof of the APC. A plastic tube from the bag trailed down to her arm.

A soldier sitting across from her adjusted the tube. She looked at him as if he were from another world—a world she didn't understand, a world she didn't belong in. She stared at the young soldier and shivered in the cold.

The armored vehicle's engine roared loudly and the vehicle tilted as it climbed steep ground.

"You're going to be all right, ma'am. I'm a medic. This is just an IV of saline solution. You haven't been hit," the soldier said. He handed her a Gore-Tex jacket. "Take this. You need to keep warm."

She wanted to take the jacket, but she couldn't seem to move. She was suddenly tired. She wished she could just close her eyes and make it all go away.

"Thanks," Paul said as he took the jacket from the medic. He unfolded it, draped it over her shoulders, and gently placed the hood over her wet hair.

The APC jerked to the left, swaying the passengers in their seats.

"Don't worry," the medic said, not very convincingly. "We'll be all right. Everything's going to be all right."

He doesn't believe that, she thought as she closed her eyes. Words . . . words without meaning. How could everything be all right? The world was insane. She thought about the dead soldier's open eyes staring at her from a severed head. How could everything ever be all right again?

5

THE ATTACK

But air [power] over a country like Korea could never be in itself
decisive. The country was too broken and the NKPA was . . . very
good at camouflage and at night movement. —T. R. FEHRENBACH

**3:00 A.M., 1 October, South Korean defensive position, six
kilometers south of the DMZ.** Lieutenant Sung-Joo Ri shivered
in the dank air as he listened to the shells fall to the south. He
couldn't stop shivering. He felt as if the cold, dark night held a
premonition of the future—a damp, chilling future that was
drawing the very warmth from his soul. Peering at the sky, the
young lieutenant rubbed his tired eyes as the rain splashed
against his face.

The water was ankle deep in the trenches. The men close to
the command bunker fidgeted nervously in the mud.

The rumble of the artillery intensified. Sung-Joo looked to
his left and right. "Private Chang, try to get the company commander on the radio again."

Chang obeyed with resignation at the futility of the task. The
radio operator transmitted, listened, and transmitted again. He
fussed with the PRC-77 radio, changing frequencies, checking
the antenna and battery connections. He repeated these actions
several times, then shrugged and raised his hands as if to say,
what can I do?

Fear was in the air. It slowly enveloped Sung-Joo's mind just

as the fog had enveloped his battle position. The explosions resonated closer, creating an overwhelming sense of doom.

The field phone rang.

"One-Six, this is One-One. Over," an excited squad leader,
Sergeant Woo, announced over his squad telephone to the platoon leader.

"This is One-Six. Send it. Over," Sung-Joo replied.

"What is happening?" the squad leader asked.

A series of distinct explosions abut a kilometer to the west
answered that question with certainty.

"I don't know," Sung-Joo said, sounding anxious. He picked
up his field telephone transmitter. "Sergeant Kim, this is Lieutenant Sung-Joo. Do you see anything?"

"Nothing. What does the company commander say?" Kim
replied.

"I still can't reach headquarters."

"Have you checked to see if your radio is working?"

"Of course. That's not the problem."

"So we are on our own," Sergeant Kim answered stoically.
"What are your instructions, sir?"

The rumble of the explosions pulsated in the young officer's
head. Years of academy training and lectures on tactics seemed
suddenly inadequate. Sung-Joo saw a vision of his father, the
general, looking sternly down on him in this moment of crisis.
He strained to think, attempting to block out his fears. The
flashes to the west were still several kilometers away. Whatever
was going on, he thought, everything seemed to be happening
somewhere else. How can I use this time to accomplish our
mission?

"Our orders are clear: Defend this position. So take a squad
and place the antitank mines in the narrow approach of the road
and on the near side of the rock drop," Sung-Joo ordered.
"Leave two men to guard the mines so no friendly forces enter."

"Yes, sir," Kim answered with the pride of a professional
warrior. "I also suggest that I take the demolitions team with me
and place the explosives at the rock drop. We should be ready,
just in case."

"Yes, of course, but I cannot detonate the explosives at the
rock drop without orders from the company commander," the
lieutenant answered, embarrassed that he had not thought of

preparing the demolitions and more embarrassed that his company commander had not trusted him with orders to destroy the rock drop if necessary. "Call me when you have completed the tasks."

The sky to the west lit up with the eerie glow of artillery flares. Sergeant Kim moved forward as Sung-Joo scanned to the north with his night vision goggles. Tense seconds became anxious minutes. Private fears grew as the fifty-three men in the platoon, each lost in his personal thoughts, waited for the enemy.

After only thirty-five minutes Sergeant Kim and his men returned from their tasks. Two soldiers brought the blasting machine for the demolitions to the lieutenant's bunker.

"I placed three antitank mines to the left and right of the road on our side of the rock drop," Kim reported on the field telephone. "The explosives are ready."

"Good. Connect the wires to the detonator in my bunker now," Sung-Joo replied.

A flight of aircraft screamed overhead, flying low over Sung-Joo's position. He couldn't see them in the fog, but he heard the horrible screech of the engines as the planes hurtled to the south. In a few seconds he heard the unmistakable noise of the detonation of a large cluster bomb.

"By God, we are at war," Sung-Joo muttered. "They're coming for us. Was that our air force or theirs?"

The men cringed, their shoulders shrugged and tense, behind the dirt protection of their trench. The two soldiers guarding the minefield shouted that they were coming back to enter the trenches. As Sung-Joo crouched within the protection of his bunker, he heard the sharp sound of exploding grenades and the crack of machine guns off to the east and west.

As the minutes passed, the steady drumbeat of the shelling increased. The rhythm of the artillery changed as shell fire fell closer to their position. The orange and yellow explosions burst on the other side of the rock drop. From a distance they were almost beautiful. The ground quivered as the rounds hit the small ridge of the rock drop and shook Sung-Joo out of his thoughts.

The field phone rang again. It was Corporal Woo. "I hear something. I think it's the sound of tanks moving just north of us, coming toward us. The sound gets louder every minute. Are our tanks coming to help us?"

"I don't know of any friendly tanks forward of our position," Sung-Joo commented, shaking his head. He knew the battalion defensive plans for this sector. All the South Korean tanks were to the south, far to the rear of his position. "Can you tell how many there are? Can you see them?"

"No, Lieutenant, not in this fog. But they are north of us and getting closer by the minute."

Sung-Joo thought a moment. He tried his FM radio again but was unable to make contact with any station. Why can't I reach the company commander? he wondered. He looked to his left and right and realized how alone, how exposed, his men were on the forward slope of the hill.

Abruptly his mind kicked into gear. He remembered his training: Expect an artillery attack to be followed by a direct ground assault by infantry supported by tanks. The enemy's objective is to rapidly penetrate our forward defenses. A successful penetration employs the element of surprise and strong firepower. Stop the enemy's rapid penetration and you defeat his plan. Somehow the words seemed little consolation right now. Could he stop the enemy tanks?

He placed the field phone down and brought his night vision goggles to his eyes. He focused the goggles on the rock drop, barely visible in the fog. He stood up and shouted. "Everyone lock and load weapons. Take cover."

The sound of artillery fire shifted to the west of his defensive line. Curiously, no shells had landed near his positions. The temperature dropped a few degrees as the rain increased. The wind picked up and the fog dissipated slightly; it was rolling in and out of the engagement area in front of the rock drop. Sung-Joo strained to see what was coming at them.

Now it's up to my infantrymen and me, Sung-Joo thought. There is no one else. He handed the radio hand mike back to Private Chang and crouched to get out of his bunker. He stood up, so that some of his men could see him, and shouted, "The North Koreans have attacked. It is our duty to defend this place. They must not get through that rock drop. Get ready."

The crash of distant explosions continued, sounding like the strike of a huge hammer pounding the earth. The men waited.

Sung-Joo returned to his bunker and peered through the rain with his night vision goggles. Through his green-tinted goggles he saw large black shadows moving like ghosts in the distance. The enemy was advancing on his position. The shadows moved confidently, as if they were on parade in Pyongyang.

"The tanks to our front are North Korean," Sung-Joo screamed to the 90mm recoilless rocket gunners in positions to the left and right. "I will pop the illumination flares as soon as we see a target. Don't fire until the enemy enters the mine-field."

His men murmured nervously in their foxholes. The tension of men experiencing their first combat filled the trench line.

"Two tanks," he whispered quietly over his platoon phone. He opened a parachute flare from its metal tube. Crouching outside the bunker, he peered through the fog and transmitted another command: "Don't fire until I give the order."

The two tanks moved forward, rumbling down the road toward the rock drop, each with a cluster of infantry riding on top. The tanks seemed to be the embodiment of power, thought Sung-Joo. How could mere mortals endure against such a tremendous force? He swore he would learn the answer to that question.

"Are the explosives ready?" Sung-Joo questioned, turning to his radio operator, Private Chang.

"Yes, sir," the private replied nervously, pointing to the demolition blasting machine at his feet.

The tanks were now arrogantly close together in the rock drop. How could they be so bold? thought Sung-Joo. Do they expect to just take our country without a fight?

A tank entered the rock drop. Sung-Joo waited until it entered the narrowest point, then smashed the bottom of a parachute flare against the open palm of his left hand. The rocket shot upward, igniting directly over the rock drop. In spite of the fog, Sung-Joo saw clumps of soldiers jump off the tank and run forward along the sides of the rock drop.

"There they are," Sung-Joo screamed, pointing to the advancing tanks. They stopped abruptly as the infantry dismounted. "Fire."

A volley of small-arms fire pelted the enemy soldiers in the confined space of the rock drop. Tracers cut through the night and sparked off the steel sides of the tank. The North Korean riflemen who had been riding on top fell to the ground and hugged the rear of the advancing tank.

The lead tank jerked forward, its engine whining above the noise of the small arms.

"Fire at the lead tank," Sung-Joo shouted to the 90mm rocket gunner standing in a firing position a few meters to his left. The private manning the 90mm recoilless rifle nodded.

The rocket fired, sending exhaust smoke, flame, and debris to the rear of his position. The rocket hit the turret of the North Korean M1985 light tank. It stopped, its commander's cupola hatch opening with a clang. A burst of white-hot flame shot through the top hatches, illuminating the rock drop.

"I hit him," the 90mm rocket gunner yelled in exultation.

Sergeant Kim's machine gun opened up and cut down the infantrymen near the burning tank. Caught in the fusillade, trapped inside the rock drop, with nowhere to hide, the North Koreans fell in bunches to Kim's fire.

The second enemy tank fired its 76mm gun at the defenders and pushed forward, discharging smoke grenades to cover its advance. Two stunned North Korean infantrymen were crushed against the hard sides of the rock drop by the charging tank.

The enemy tank fire sailed harmlessly over Sung-Joo's bunker. Another 90mm recoilless rocket struck the wall of the rock drop near the second tank, exploding among the infantry. Bodies fell in a tangled mass.

The wind, blowing from the north, rolled the smoke from the burning tank toward Sung-Joo's positions. The tank, undaunted, jerked forward, determined to push through. The 90mm recoilless rocket gunner fired his third round. This rocket missed also, exploding against the rocks in a white-orange splash.

The tank raised its cannon to maximum elevation and pressed against the wrecked tank that blocked its path. Slowly, its engine roaring like a tortured beast, it pushed the burning tank through to the south side of the rock drop. The tank's tracks ground to the left and churned as the tank jostled the flaming wreck out of the way.

All alone, the tank surged forward, its machine guns blazing defiantly at its opponents. In a blast of fire, dirt, and black smoke, the beast staggered as a searing shot of flame tore through its soft underbelly. The force of ten and a half pounds of explosives from an M21 antitank mine ruptured the bottom of the tank and transformed the fighting compartment into a glowing hunk of burning steel. Seconds later the tank's ammunition exploded, sending hatches and pieces of metal into the air.

Sung-Joo smiled a cold, cruel smile. Slowly the ROKs stopped firing. The battlefield grew suddenly quiet, except for the crackling of the two burning tanks and the moans of dying North Korean soldiers.

4:15 A.M., 1 October, multipurpose range complex, Chorwon Valley, South Korea. The clamor of artillery shells echoed in the mountains as a cold drizzle and thick fog cut visibility to a few hundred meters. The reduced visibility and the rain made everything difficult.

The American armored task force formed an arc against the tall mountain that formed the backdrop of the tank range. The tanks and Bradleys formed the outer perimeter; their cannon and machine guns, manned by nervous crews, bristled out from the circle. The lightly armored APCs and soft-skinned trucks and HMMWVs occupied the center of the circle.

Rodriguez sensed that the worst of the enemy's barrage was over. The fire had been unobserved fire—deadly if you were unlucky enough to be in the strike zone but nonlethal if you got behind a hill. Repositioning the task force to hug the south side of the largest mountain in the tank range had prevented further casualties. After their move, about fifty shells fell in the tent area without causing any harm. Other angry rounds detonated harmlessly against the north side of the mountain.

Rodriguez climbed down from his tank and picked his way across the broken ground to the task force command post. Five M577 armored command vehicles served as his tactical operations center. He ran up to the open ramp of an M577. The executive officer (XO), operations officer (S3), and scout platoon leader were standing in the dark as ten men from the headquarters section struggled to erect the command post's expandable shelter tent.

"Did you reach brigade?" Rodriguez asked as he got within voice range of the three figures.

"No, sir. We can't talk to anyone outside the task force," Major Bradford commented. "FM retrans is not responding and the mobile subscriber telephone is dead. Even the civilian telephone lines are down. We've tried everything."

"Find a way to communicate with brigade," Rodriguez ordered, rubbing the stubble of his beard with his right hand. "What's our strength?"

"Our status is forty-four tanks and nineteen Bradleys. The engineer company has three operational ACEs, one Grizzly, two Wolverines, and a fully loaded Volcano. We're green across the board," the S3 reported efficiently, ticking off the unit's strength like an accountant counting money. "The total vehicle count is two hundred and thirty-five, including sixteen M113 armored personnel carriers, six 120mm mortar carriers, eight M577 armored command post vehicles, eight M88 armored tank retrievers, and one hundred and fifteen assorted trucks and Humvees."

Rodriguez had a powerful combined-arms task force at his command. The main combat power of the force was forty-four M1A2 tanks and fourteen Bradley fighting vehicles and their infantry squads. The other pieces of the task force, however, were just as important. He had an air defense platoon equipped with Bradley Stinger vehicles that could attack enemy aircraft and enemy infantry. His engineer company rounded out the task force. In addition to three sapper squads, which were mounted in M113 armored personnel carriers, the engineer company possessed three ACE armored bulldozers for digging tank fighting positions, one Grizzly armored combat engineer breaching vehicle equipped with a bulldozer blade and a separate power-driven excavating arm for reducing obstacles, and one Volcano mine-laying carrier. The Volcano was designed to discharge an antitank minefield in minutes, creating an effective and deadly means to block the movement of enemy armored vehicles. The two Wolverine bridge-laying vehicles rounded out his force.

"We lost six men, all hit in the first salvo that struck the tent area," Major Lucas, the tall, thin executive officer added quietly. "Five more are wounded. I had the dead and wounded brought to the battalion aid station against the south side of the hill.

"Doc says only one of the wounded, Specialist Wilson, is critical. We need to evacuate him ASAP. The other four are mostly concussion and splinter injuries, all from Bravo Company."

Rodriguez bit his lip. Wallace had warned him that something was up, but how could he have guessed that they would be at war this morning? Rodriguez thought about the 850 men in his command. The casualties had been light, considering the amount of artillery that had showered the area, but he couldn't tell that to the men who had died. How many more would he lose before this mess was over?

Thunder hammered and boomed along with the sound of distant guns. The skies opened up and poured rain on the dazed and shaken American tankers hiding against the side of the tall hill. The thunder crashed as if the heavens were joining the battle.

"Look, Dave, we're lucky, damn lucky," Rodriguez said as he tilted his Kevlar helmet back on his head and looked at his executive officer. "We'll have to do all we can for the wounded right here. We can't risk an evacuation until we know the situation better."

"Sir, maybe you didn't hear me," Lucas said, his voice showing the strain they all felt. "Doc says that Wilson will die in the next few hours if we don't get him to a hospital. We have to do something."

"I heard you quite clearly," Rodriguez answered, emphasizing his last two words.

"We have a duty to protect this force," Lucas preached, cocking his head slightly to the right. "I don't think the brigade will be coming out here. We need to get the hell back to them."

"I'm not going anywhere half-cocked in this fog until I know more about what's going on," the commander said. He stopped stroking his chin and paused for a moment. His eyes squinted, as if he were trying to see the answer to a distant problem.

He looked back at Lieutenant Whitman, his red-haired, eager scout platoon leader, and grabbed him by the arm. The young officer had backed off a bit, obviously embarrassed to be in the middle of an argument between the commander and the executive officer.

"First thing we must do is get your scouts out," Rodriguez said as he pulled a small red-filtered flashlight from his Nomex shoulder pocket and held his folded map in front of the three men. He shone his light on several locations on the map. "Red, I want you to deploy your platoon to establish early warning in the two valleys to our flanks, both east and west."

"Roger, sir," Lt. Red Whitman answered, standing with his hands on his hips.

Rodriguez smiled a tired smile, trying to exude confidence. In the dark he didn't know if it was working, but he knew Whitman's caliber. He trusted Red implicitly to do the right thing. Everything about the young platoon leader radiated competence.

"We're ready to go anywhere, sir. We know this ground like the back of our hands. I can be set within an hour."

Rodriguez put his hand on the young scout's shoulder. "Red, you're the best I've got. Don't get excited out there and get into a fight. Remember, you're my eyes and ears. The tanks and the infantry do the fighting; scouts provide reconnaissance and surveillance."

The three men moved out of the way as the final section of the TOC shelter was set up.

"Wilco, sir. I understand," Red answered, sounding brave.

"Okay. Keep your head down and call us when you're set in position," the commander ordered. "Dave, Tony, let's move inside. We've got some planning to do."

The scout platoon leader ran off to his platoon.

Rodriguez and his two majors moved into the newly constructed command post. A generator hummed in the distance as the headquarters soldiers connected lights inside the shelter. A table and folding chairs were placed in the center of the TOC under the bright white light, and the three officers sat down. Rodriguez sat in the center, his left hand on his chin, and his majors sat to the right and left.

"We have ROK units all around us, but we can't talk to them because we don't know the radio frequency and codes of this defensive sector," he announced. "We can't talk to brigade because we're out of range. The way I see it, we're all alone, a tank-heavy task force in the middle of the forward defenses of the South Korean Army, right between two major enemy avenues of attack."

"Sir, this valley may be swarming with North Koreans in the morning," Major Lucas persisted. "Our medical support and supplies of fuel, ammunition, and spare parts are back there with the brigade. Don't you think we should head south and link up with the brigade?"

Rodriguez shook his head and looked at the map. With his finger he tapped an area that was a few kilometers north of the multipurpose range complex (MPRC), then traced the outline on the map of the DMZ. He saw the highways that led into the Chorwon Valley and the two major avenues of attack that his task force was now astride.

"You're right, Dave. Fuel will be our biggest problem. Are all the fuel HEMMTs full?"

"Yes, sir, as you ordered yesterday," Lucas answered.

"Then the task force has twenty HEMMT fuel trucks, each with twenty-five hundred gallons of JP8, but that will provide only enough fuel for two refills. That means we have about thirty hours of fuel if we run the tanks nonstop."

Rodriguez knew the magnitude of the supply problem. Modern war demanded a huge consumption of supplies. Each M1A2 tank carried about five hundred gallons of JP8 diesel fuel. Each M978 HEMMT fuel tanker truck carried twenty-five hundred gallons, enough for five M1A2s. The tanks guzzled gas fast, operating for ten hours without refueling. To extend their capability, each tank was equipped with an auxiliary power unit (APU), a generator that ran all the electrical functions of the tank without running the engine. With so many vehicles, and stretching his fuel to the maximum extent possible, Rodriguez could operate for two days.

"The ammunition situation is better, sir," Bradford interjected. "We have two of the new STAFF rounds on each tank as part of our forty-round basic load. In addition, there's plenty of training ammunition that we stockpiled for our tank gunnery training."

"I'm eager to see how the STAFF rounds work. Put out the word that I don't want any fired unless I give permission," the commander said. "On the other hand, let's hope we don't have to find out if a 120mm training sabot round will destroy a North Korean tank or an armored personnel carrier."

"The task force has enough food and water for five days," Lucas added. "In a pinch this could be stretched, but I don't like it."

"So the major problem is fuel," Rodriguez concluded. "Lack of fuel could bring us to our knees."

"There are two gas stations just down the road," Lucas offered. "If you tell Captain Grey and Team Bravo to secure them, we might be able to suck some gas out of those storage tanks."

"That's a good idea," Rodriguez answered, nodding. "Get right on it, Dave. Tell me as soon as Captain Grey moves."

"Sir, what about the reporters?" Major Bradford asked. "How will we get them back?"

Rodriguez shrugged. "Are they okay?"

"They were with Bravo Company when the artillery hit the camp," Bradford explained, "but both are unharmed."

"Hell, I'd forgotten all about them," Rodriguez replied. "Dave, please see to it that they're taken care of."

Lucas nodded. "I got Hamilton and the cameraman away from Bravo Company and put them with the medics. I told her not to take any pictures unless you said it was all right."

A sergeant ran up to Major Bradford and handed him a small black bag. "One more thing, sir," said Bradford as he unzipped the bag and took out a small civilian cellular telephone. The bantam-sized battalion operations officer looked up at Rodriguez with a smile as wide as his Kevlar chin strap. "I took this from her. Spoils of war. It's worth a try, sir."

"Hell, she'll probably sue me for this after it's all over," Rodriguez joked.

6:20 A.M., 1 October, South Korean defensive position six kilometers south of the DMZ. Balls of orange flame erupted in front of the South Korean platoon, signaling the beginning of another assault.

"Here it comes. Take cover," Sung-Joo screamed, diving for the bottom of his fighting position.

A wave of noise and accurate fire rolled over the defense line. Artillery shells smashed into the trenches, throwing dirt and rocks into the air. The shock waves from each strike jolted the ground. Mortar shells exploded overhead, sending showers of hot fragments onto the roofs of the defenders' bunkers. Shell splinters whizzed through the air.

Sung-Joo hugged the cold, rocky floor of his bunker as the world trembled. He didn't think he would survive the shelling. His mind raced as he grasped for options to help his men survive the annihilation that seemed imminent.

"Sir, Sergeant Kim reports that the enemy is in the engagement area," Private Chang shouted. He had just received the report over the field phone.

The report gave Sung-Joo new courage. The lieutenant's ears were ringing so badly that he could barely hear. He moved to kneel in front of his firing aperture and could see more tanks moving north of the rock drop. At the same time, enemy infantry appeared on top of the ridge. Sung-Joo guessed that they were trying to disarm the explosives that would drop the rocks to seal the pass.

The lieutenant brought his M16 rifle to the firing parapet and fired a full magazine of 5.56mm bullets at the enemy soldiers. Red tracers ricocheted off the rocks. Several attackers fell but more stepped forward. The North Koreans moved in small groups. They ran forward a few yards, then dove for cover, supported by the deadly bursts of several 12.7mm machine guns firing in support of their attack.

Sergeant Kim's machine gun blazed. The enemy infantry rushed forward, falling in heaps. At the same time, the South Korean trenches were splattered with fire.

Sung-Joo ducked to the bottom of his trench as the bullets zinged overhead. He quickly dropped his empty magazine, grabbed a fresh one from his ammo pouch, and reloaded.

The field phone rang. Sergeant Kim's telephone operator screamed on the other end that another tank was coming toward the rock drop. The lieutenant looked to his left and saw that the 90mm gunner was dead. He looked to his right and saw the surviving gunner. "Is your recoilless rifle loaded?"

"This is our last round, sir," the soldier said, crouching behind the bunker.

"A tank is in the rock drop. Destroy it," Sung-Joo ordered.

The soldier nodded, took a deep breath, and stood up to fire his antitank weapon. He was cut down before he could put the weapon on his shoulder. He slid down inside the trench, his chest torn apart.

"Damnit," Sung-Joo cursed. He ran over to the dead man, crouching low behind the trench line. He pried the launcher from the dead private's fingers and placed it on his shoulder. He knew he had only a few seconds and would get only one shot.

Machine-gun bullets smashed into the sandbags near the platoon headquarters. Sung-Joo waited for them to stop, then stood up and twisted his body toward the enemy. The tank was in the center of the rock drop. Quickly he placed his eye to the sight and fired.

The rocket whooshed out of the tube. A heat wave rolled down his back. The rocket flew true, showering sparks and flame as it raced forward. The warhead detonated against the front glacis of the tank, making a huge splash. The T55 stopped in its tracks. Smoke trickled from inside its turret. The hatches opened.

Sung-Joo quickly tossed the 90mm tube over the trench, stepped over the dead soldier's body, and raced back to his bunker. Safely inside, he cautiously lifted his head to the line of sandbags and peered into the black smoke billowing from the tank. The dead tank smoldered at the south end of the rock drop next to the two tanks that his men had destroyed in the first attack. To his dismay he saw another T55 moving forward to push aside the damaged tank. He had seen how they had pushed a damaged tank through the rock drop the first time. In seconds they would do the same thing again. The rock drop would be clear and the enemy would be through the gap. Sung-Joo looked at the blasting device again.

Sergeant Kim's machine gun barked a steady *rat-a-tat-tat* at the rock drop.

Sung-Joo knew he had to do something, but his options were rapidly evaporating. It was all happening so fast. If the rock drop wasn't detonated, the enemy tanks would break through like water through a cracked dam, then race south. He looked at the blasting device and remembered his company commander's last words: "You cannot destroy the rock drop without my direct orders."

"Call company headquarters on the radio again!" Sung-Joo screamed to his radio operator. "I need permission to execute the obstacle."

"I can't reach them, sir," Chang replied, frustrated at his inability to improve the situation.

Sung-Joo slammed his fists against the sandbag. Four years of training at the ROK Army Military Academy had taught him the value of obedience. It was the highest virtue. He looked at the big, gold, academy ring on his left ring finger. He should be inspired by the knowledge that his sacrifice might be part of the bigger plan.

Bullshit, he thought. In this situation, shouldn't he think for himself? Did he have time to wait for a commander's orders that would never come?

"Damnit," he cursed amidst the crackling gunfire. The T55's engine growled as the tank struggled to push the dead tank through the rock drop. He could see a dozen North Korean infantrymen crouched behind the T55, following it for protection. He cupped his hand to his mouth. "Fire all weapons at the enemy in the rock drop."

The young lieutenant kneeled at the aperture of his bunker. He looked down and eyed the blasting device carefully. "Only on order of the company commander," he fumed.

A few rifles began a desultory fire from all along the trench line, but most of the South Koreans were silent, dead or ducking from the fire tearing away at their sandbagged positions. A machine gun opened up on the enemy tank, the fire coming from Sergeant Kim's position. Dependable Sergeant Kim, Sung-Joo thought as he saw the rounds bounce off the T55's tough armor. If only the entire army had such fierce fighters.

The lieutenant, feeling impotent, whirled about in the trench, looking for a weapon to fire at the enemy. He spied Private Chang's M203 grenade launcher and grabbed the weapon from the frightened soldier.

"Hand me a grenade, quick," Sung-Joo screamed as he moved to the side of the bunker. Chang fumbled with his ammunition bandolier, produced an HE grenade, and handed it to the lieutenant. Sung-Joo quickly pushed forward on the grenade cylinder, placed the 40mm high-explosive round in the cylinder, then slammed it to the rear, seating the grenade. He aimed the M203 carefully at the advancing tank and pulled the trigger, hoping that his 40mm grenade might stop the snarling beast.

With a hollow *thunk,* the grenade lobbed through the air and exploded against the tank's turret. For a moment the tank stopped, embroiled in sparks and fire. Sung-Joo shouted in exhilaration. His hopes fell as the tank resumed its struggle to push the dead T55 forward, seemingly contemptuous of this minor harassment.

Bursts of machine-gun fire swept the top of the trench line. Sung-Joo couldn't stop the tank with grenades, and he was out of 90mm rounds for the antitank rocket launcher. For a moment he anguished over the decision. He did not have authority to drop the rocks. Disobeying orders was a court-martial offense, but so was letting the enemy break through. He knew that the only hope was to blow the rock drop.

"Sir, they're breaking through," a voice shouted.

Sung-Joo hesitated. He could not disobey orders. He disconnected the wires to the blaster.

Private Chang looked up at his lieutenant with wide-eyed disbelief. He saw the angry return look in his lieutenant's face and turned his head away.

The T55 tank moved inside the rock drop, blazing away at the South Korean defenders with its cannon and machine guns. In front of it were the burning remains of two M1985 light tanks and a T55. Unsure of what lay ahead, the tank loitered at the opening, firing in support of the infantry attack.

A yell rose from the north side of the rock drop. North Korean infantry jumped up all along the ridge and rushed forward and through the rock drop. Sergeant Kim, whose bunker was outside the T55's arc of fire, shot the enemy infantry as they stormed forward. They fell in batches to the fury of his machine gun, turning the area in front of the rock drop into a slaughter pen. After a few minutes of this, even the bravest attacker had second thoughts, and the enemy tank and the surviving infantry melted back to the north side of the ridge.

The smell of death hung heavy in the air. A strange silence fell over the battlefield as the sun rose above the eastern hills. Sung-Joo could hear the cries of the wounded and the dying.

For the time being, he thought, we have done our duty. We have obeyed our orders. But he knew that the silence wouldn't last long.

8:30 A.M., 1 October, 2d Infantry Division command bunker.
The 2d Infantry Division command bunker was a frenzy of nervous action. Soldiers rushed around the operations room, sending messages, making telephone calls, and posting maps. Communications were a shambles. Telephone lines and radio antennas had been cut by enemy commandos. To make matters more difficult, most of the officers on the division staff were new to their jobs. The G3 had been killed in the initial attacks, and the chief of staff was seriously wounded. Major Beady, the assistant G3, had arrived in Korea only a few weeks ago. As the senior ranking officer on the staff, Wallace was in charge. Having such a new team made the demands of running a division staff appear overwhelming.

The confusion inside the bunker, Wallace thought, was a reflection of the unbridled chaos that was occurring outside. In the early-morning hours, the compound came under artillery shelling and sniper fire. Fifteen to twenty enemy attackers seemed determined to get within range of the command bunker. The military police, reinforced by anyone who could fire a rifle, eventually fought this attack to a standstill.

American casualties were heavy. Besides the G3, at least forty-three other Americans and twenty ROKs had been killed inside the compound. A makeshift aid station was operating in the bunker to handle the ever-increasing number of wounded. By 0900 a battalion of ROK infantry had arrived and brought the enemy sniper attacks to a halt.

It was a black day for the U.S. Army and the 2d Infantry Division. Overwhelmed by the surprise and fury of the assault, the Americans defended their base camps against terrorists, snipers, and car bombers. Scud missiles and heavy artillery fell on them in their garrisons like avalanches. Several units were shattered by the fury and mass of the North Korean attack. Some small units located closest to the DMZ were cut off and isolated by the enemy's attack. Several of these held on and fought bravely, but too many were never heard from again.

The ROKs were also hard pressed. Stunned by the surprise attack, they reacted slowly to the Inmun Gun's massive blow. The carefully constructed defensive front was disintegrating. The Combined Forces Command, with its satellite imagery gone and its communications disrupted, was unable to do much to change the situation. When a U.S. attack helicopter battalion counterattacked near Munsan, the AH-64 Apache helicopters were knocked out of the sky by North Korean S-300s. Twelve of the sophisticated attack birds were destroyed in a few minutes by the highly effective S-300 air defense systems. Without helicopter or close air support, the ROK front cracked under the North Korean ground attacks.

"Sir . . . Colonel Wallace," a staff officer said frantically. "I've got a colonel on the line who says he's calling us from a mobile telephone."

Wallace moved quickly through a maze of computers and desks to get to the telephone. He carefully guarded his left arm, now cradled in a sling tied around his neck.

"This is Wallace, division G2. Who am I talking to?"

"Steve, this is Mike Rodriguez."

"Mike, where the hell are you? Remember, this line isn't secure. The North Koreans may be listening."

"Steve, I've got my element positioned . . . near that place you called me at yesterday. Do you remember?"

"Roger, Mike. I understand. What's your strength?"

"I'm green across the board and I have all my friends who are supposed to be with me. I've got five wounded, one of them critical."

Wallace closed his eyes for a moment. Rodriguez had the entire Dragon Force, a task force of three tank companies, one mechanized infantry company, and an engineer company just south of the advancing enemy. Green meant that he was at 90 percent or higher on personnel, ammunition, fuel, and equipment. The G2 looked at the large situation map on his right. A staff captain had just posted the latest information on the enemy advance. The red arrows were about eight kilometers north of the battalion position. There were no effective ROK units in the enemy's path.

"You're in a special place, my friend. Very dangerous. The enemy is just a few kilometers north of you. It looks like elements of a reinforced infantry division are attacking along both avenues, followed by several tank brigades. They're busting through all over. We estimate that the enemy's lead divisions are at seventy percent strength."

"Roger, Steve. Tell the CG that we've watched the ROKs

take a pounding all morning. The situation up here is pretty lousy. The ROKs could sure use some help."

"The ROKs are moving south," Wallace replied. "You've got the critical sector, Mike, the cork in the bottle. We also have a report that one of our Gary Owen troops is somewhere to your front."

"I understand. Look, Steve, I can't reach my brigade. I need to know what the CG wants me to do—stay and fight or head south."

Wallace understood. "Mike, you need to—"

The line suddenly went dead.

"Damnit," said Wallace as pain shot through his shoulder. There hadn't been any time to take care of it other than to put it in a makeshift sling. He handed the phone to Major Cooper.

"Jim, try to get him back on the line. I'll be right back."

The assistant G2 nodded and took the telephone. Wallace walked quickly into the situation room. Two majors stood in front of Major General Schmidt. One major, talking in a low, hushed voice, briefed the general concerning the unfolding situation.

"Sir, we've got to pull everything back now," the young major pleaded. "The counterfire fight has failed. The 1st and 2d Brigades have been hit hard by special forces teams. Most of our attack helicopters were destroyed on the ground by commandos. The enemy knew just where to hit us."

Wallace could smell disaster in the air.

"What are our casualties?" General Schmidt asked, holding a stack of reports in his hand. "I need an accurate assessment of the situation, not hysteria."

"The reports are still coming in," the staff officer answered as a look of defeat flashed across his face. "The reports are all bad. Heavy casualties."

Schmidt put his hand on the major's shoulder. "Son, first reports are always bad. We have good people out there and they need our help. Let's start unraveling the mystery. I need the facts."

"Sir, the enemy has penetrated the ROK's first line of defense at several places along the DMZ," the major offered. "Some North Korean units are reported ten kilometers south of the DMZ. If the enemy keeps moving this fast, many of the division's battalions will be cut off. We must pull back and regroup."

"He's right, sir," a second major added.

"No," Schmidt decided, pulling a pipe from his pocket and putting the stem between his lips. He smiled slightly to ease the tension. "You guys are my planners. Take a deep breath, sort out the situation, and figure out a way for us to get into the fight."

"Sir, I've just talked with 2-72 Armor," Wallace reported, interrupting the doomsayers. "The task force is at the MPRC at full strength."

General Schmidt looked up, his tired and red eyes flashing. He raised his pipe in the air, silencing the crowd that surrounded him. "Where?"

Wallace drew the positions on the situation map as Rodriguez had explained them to him. The blue circles that depicted Rodriguez's force were a few kilometers south of an ROK infantry division.

The general smiled for the first time in six hours. "He's set up to block the enemy's advance into the Chorwon Valley. They might gain us the time we need, and maybe it will gain us enough time to help the ROKs to withdraw before they're surrounded."

Wallace nodded. "My latest read from Combined Forces Command is that the ROK Corps commander north of Rodriguez's force is attempting to do just that."

"How did you get in touch with Rodriguez?" the general asked.

"Civilian cellular telephone," Wallace announced. "He called us."

The general shook his head. "Millions of dollars spent on information-age gadgets and we're communicating over a civilian cellular phone. Do they have enough ammunition? Any artillery support?"

"He reports that he has ammo and is ready to fight," Wallace answered. "I don't know about any artillery."

Schmidt folded his arms and stared at the map. "If I know Rodriguez, he'll fight as long as he can. Get in touch with him and tell him he's under my direct control. I want him to block the enemy on both avenues of approach until I tell him to pull back. The ROKs are counting on us. Don't forget, we're part of a coalition."

"Sir, I lost contact with him on the cellular before I could give any instructions. Major Cooper is trying to reestablish communications."

Major Cooper entered, looking perplexed and frustrated. "No dice, sir. I can't regain contact. All cellular services are out, permanently."

Wallace nodded.

"Well, we're busy enough just trying to stay alive right now," the general said, wiping his face with his right hand. "Now it's up to Lieutenant Colonel Rodriguez."

9:00 A.M., 1 October, fifteen kilometers north of the DMZ, at the exit to the 820th Armored Corps' underground facility. The road was filled with tanks and armored personnel carriers moving south. Vehicles seemed to come out of the ground as rows of tanks emerged from the protection of their bunkers. Three North Korean BTR-60 armored personnel carriers were parked side by side next to a muddy crossroads. Each of the BTRs had five radio antennas sticking out of its roof, showing it to be the mobile command post of the corps commander.

Major General Park Chi-won, the commander of the 820th Tank Corps, stood in the open hatch in the back of his BTR-60 command vehicle. He was a tall man for a North Korean tanker, standing almost five feet nine inches; he weighed 145 pounds. His left hand was bandaged from an accident with the heavy metal hatch of his BTR. The hatch, weighing about twenty pounds, had pinched his left hand when the BTR jolted across rugged ground. Luckily the wound was more embarrassing than serious. Nevertheless, it throbbed painfully as he watched the tanks pass the vital crossroads north of the DMZ.

This scene appeared out of place, General Park mused. He imagined the groan made by hundreds of tank engines and the quake of hundreds of tank tracks as the roar of angry dragons. The dragons were leaving their caves, eager to hunt down and kill their enemies. Moving like one continuous serpent, his column of armored beasts, bristling with machine guns and anti-aircraft weapons, clanged south. The echo of artillery, the low-hanging fog, and the drizzling rain added to his impression of a primeval scene, gigantic and overwhelming.

A tank corps is an awesome force, the general thought. It was the instrument of decision, the force that would win the war. Park mentally assessed his strength. His corps, a reinforced division by Western standards, was a powerful force of tactical exploitation consisting of five tank brigades and six supporting artillery brigades. He commanded a total of more than fifteen hundred armored vehicles.

An awesome force indeed, he thought with a smile. Each armored brigade consisted of ninety-three T62 tanks, forty-six M1985 light tanks, fifty-nine VTT323 armored personnel carriers with infantry squads, eighteen 152mm self-propelled howitzers, eighteen 122mm self-propelled howitzers, and four BLG-60 armored vehicle–launched bridges. In addition, he could count on the support of a truck-mounted infantry division.

The 1st Armored Brigade was the spearhead of General Park's corps. Its commander, Col. Yi Sung-Chul, was the most aggressive and talented brigade commander in the 820th Corps. Park felt that nothing could stop Yi's determined assault. Park watched in silent satisfaction as his lead brigade moved down the road. The raw power of this formation and the discipline of their march made him swell with pride.

He yearned for the moment when his corps would cross into South Korea. Park's mission was clear: Exploit the penetration made by the forward units and move east and south of Seoul, the enemy's capital. Their direction of attack was the eastern Chorwon Valley, with Uijonbu—a major city at a vital crossroads—as their immediate objective. There was no doubt in General Park's mind that he would take his objective, then plant the red-starred flag on the South Korean National Assembly building in Seoul.

Park looked up at the clouds that hung low in the sky. He knew that the chance of an enemy air attack was slim. The combination of bad weather and damaging air and commando attacks had negated the enemy's airpower, at least temporarily. The rainy weather and the heavy, low cloud ceiling would hide his attack and work against the enemy's close air support.

If I believed in the gods, I would swear they are on our side, Park thought with a grin. Even so, he took comfort in the fact that each brigade had twenty-four twin 57mm self-propelled antiaircraft guns, dozens of SA-16 shoulder-fired antiaircraft missiles spread out along the line of march, and several batteries of the new S-300 air defense system to counter the enemy's attack aircraft.

A colonel, General Park's chief of staff, walked over to the commander's vehicle and handed him a stack of battle reports.

"Good news, Comrade General," the chief of staff announced, standing near the general's BTR. "The enemy is crumbling. The forward echelon divisions are heavily engaged, but a breakthrough is expected in the next twenty-four hours in the eastern Chorwon Valley. Here are the latest reports."

Park's eyes flashed. He grabbed the reports with his good right hand and scanned them eagerly. Five infantry divisions supported with tanks and heavy artillery were fighting to the south along his planned direction of attack. Although the South Korean resistance was still determined, and a few local counterattacks were mounted with ferocity, there were growing signs of disarray in the ROK defenses. The attacking divisions in front of Park's corps were executing small encirclements of their own, isolating the defenders and disrupting their tardy attempts to counterattack. As soon as these divisions created the breakthrough, Park's 820th Corps would exploit the gap and drive deep into enemy lines to seize his objective. His corps would drive a wedge into the South Korean defenses that would shatter their resolve and end the war.

"Comrade General," announced a major, one of the officers assigned to Park's personal staff as a radio operator in his BTR, "the lead elements of the 1st Brigade report that they have cleared their assembly area and are moving south at fifteen kilometers per hour. All is going according to plan."

General Park grunted and nodded with approval. The plan was all important. No matter what, he was expected to stick to it. And keeping to the timetable was essential. Hundreds of vehicles had to move swiftly down narrow roads, so any variation in the road march table would cause costly delays. He had specific time lines to meet. He knew that his success depended on crushing all opposition in his path, moving rapidly south, and maintaining the attack schedule. If he was delayed and deviated from the planned schedule, the artillery would not be able to move forward, and the synchronization of the attack would be disrupted. He knew that the artillery would fire as scheduled. If he expected to take advantage of the shock created by the artillery fire strike, he would have to bypass enemy resistance and advance without hesitation. Any delay would be unacceptable.

Right now the artillery fired from prepared, hardened sites. After his tanks exploited the breakthrough in the South Korean lines, he would create the space necessary for the artillery to move forward to support the continued advance.

The all-important objective was the large city of Uijonbu, a crucial road junction northeast of Seoul. Its loss would be a humiliation for the fascist government and its destruction a lesson.

Park knew that his superiors considered him a ruthless, by-the-regulations commander who got results no matter what the cost. The exercise of troop control in the 820th Armored Corps was considered to be the most efficient in the entire army. Park knew, however, that his early promotion and select posting to command the most prestigious armored unit in the North Korean Army was due to the personal intervention of his mentor, Marshal Kim Seung-Hee.

Park was one of Kim's strongest supporters and a major force behind the Daring Thrust attack plan. Park knew that speed was critical, so he ordered his soldiers not to take prisoners. Nothing must impede the march tables. Attack south, kill them all, and keep moving. Seize Uijonbu quickly. Prisoners would only get in the way.

A column of T62 tanks, the 2d Brigade, churned past the general's command car. Each tank was carefully camouflaged with pine boughs tied on the top and sides. The brigade commander, a young, aggressive tank colonel whom Park had personally picked for command, stood in the turret of his tank and saluted.

Park returned the salute and watched as the T62s moved rapidly south. Then he lowered his right hand and cradled his damaged left hand in front of his chest. With such men, he thought, we will march all the way to Pusan.

The column moved at fifteen kilometers per hour with a distance of twenty-five meters between vehicles. Even with this extremely tight march column formation, Park's lead tank brigade was eight kilometers long. To move faster, he was moving his brigades on three separate roads. From east to west his brigades attacked south: 3d Brigade and two brigades of artillery attacked down Highway 47; 1st and 2d Brigades, followed by another brigade of artillery, moved in a column along

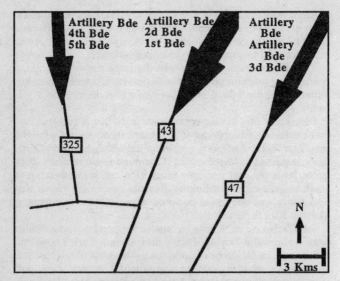

NKPA 820th Armor Corps Attack Plan

the main axis of attack, Highway 43; and 4th and 5th Brigades
conducted a supporting attack down Highway 325.

A column of 152mm howitzers moved forward, following
the 2d Tank Brigade. Behind them came a truck-mounted
BM-21 multiple rocket launcher battery. Each of its forty launch
tubes carried a 122mm rocket that could shoot a high-explosive
fragmentation warhead a distance of twenty kilometers.

A motorcycle raced through the mud, slipping madly across
the track-worn road. It stopped abruptly in front of the general's
command car. A thin, tall soldier quickly parked his cycle and
sprang off the seat to hand the general a sealed envelope.

General Park opened the envelope and read its contents eagerly. After a few seconds he looked up and smiled. Park's chief
of staff was waiting, anxious to share the message.

"We have penetrated the enemy's lines," General Park said
fiercely, holding the letter in his clenched fist. "The southern
fascists are on the run. Now we must attack with great speed."

Thunder crashed in the morning sky. The rain began again, falling gently at first and then picking up force.

"Keep them moving, Colonel," the general shouted to his chief of staff over the sound of the rain and moving armored vehicles. "I want nothing to stop us. We must take Uijonbu."

"Nam chim." The colonel saluted and returned to his BTR-60.

The general sat down in his seat and carefully closed the top hatch of the APC. Cradling his bandaged left hand on his lap, he connected his vehicle radio and intercom headset. Two officers were inside the well-lit compartment of the command vehicle, listening to the radio and posting the latest unit locations on the operations maps fixed to the wall of the vehicle. Park noted the forward line of the red arrow drawn on the 1:50,000 scale map that the officers placed in front of him. Along Highway 47 the arrow was twelve kilometers south of the DMZ. Along Highway 43, where the opposition had been more stubborn, it was only six kilometers south.

"Sir, ready to move at your command," the BTR driver shouted smartly over the vehicle intercom system.

"Move out," Park ordered. "We have an objective to take."

9:30 A.M., 1 October, South Korean defensive position, six kilometers south of the DMZ. Sung-Joo peered from the trench line. He gazed sadly at the bodies of several of his men who were sprawled across his defensive position. There were now more dead than living. He was down to about a dozen men defending a position that was designed for fifty. His men were almost out of ammunition. There were no more grenades. The situation was impossible.

He looked at the few men he could see. The fortunate survivors crouched low against the side of the trench, afraid to raise their heads above the line of sandbags that marked the top of their firing pits. One rifleman sat with his back to the dirt wall, his head sunk low over his chest, his arms at his side.

Sung-Joo stared at the man as a few enemy mortar shells whistled overhead. As he crawled closer and yelled to him to see if he needed attention, he saw that the soldier was dead. A portion of his face was torn off, exposing the muscle and cheekbone. Sung-Joo shuddered and crawled slowly back to his bunker.

A sudden wave of mortar fire swept over the South Korean positions like a stampede of angry elephants. The barrage was getting more accurate. This time several mortar rounds scored direct hits on Sung-Joo's fighting positions. He was consumed with fear and anger. *The platoon is being pulverized by enemy fire,* he reflected despondently. *I must do something.*

The enemy fire lasted for fifteen minutes, then stopped abruptly. White smoke billowed from the rock drop.

"Medic, medic," someone called out.

"Squad leaders, report," Sergeant Kim screamed.

One by one the survivors shouted in their report. Sung-Joo sat in his bunker and pressed the field telephone hand mike to his ear to reach his platoon sergeant.

"Lieutenant, here is my report," the steady voice of Sergeant Kim came over the field phone. "Twenty-four men are dead, twelve wounded, and three unaccounted for. We have lost all the squad leaders. We are almost out of ammunition. We have only a few men, but we still have plenty of fight left."

"Hold your position and aim at the rock drop," Sung-Joo ordered, trying to match his sergeant's courage. "Fix bayonets. Out."

Lieutenant Sung-Joo put down the telephone. The enemy had made several attempts to take the choke point with infantry. Each attempt had failed due to Sergeant Kim's accurate machine-gun fire. To hide their latest attempt, the North Koreans were lighting smoke pots in the rock drop, adding clouds of white smoke to the thinning fog.

Sung-Joo looked over to Kim's bunker and shook his head. A proud smile formed on his face as he saw an eight-by-eleven-inch South Korean flag flying defiantly over the bunker. His sergeant had single-handedly held the key to the choke point, Sung-Joo thought with pride. The platoon had rallied around tough Sergeant Kim. With him as the center they had kept the North Koreans away from the vital crossroads and slowed their attack into the homeland. The enemy's tank attack had failed, and so had six consecutive infantry assaults.

Sung-Joo knew that Kim would never surrender. He wondered if he had as much courage.

"Sir, I got through to someone at regiment on the radio," Chang yelled. "They've pulled back. All of our units have been surrounded by enemy infantry. Everyone is being shot to hell. The enemy is everywhere. We're on our own."

"Enemy infantry behind us?" Sung-Joo questioned. A puzzled look streaked across his tired face. The enemy must have infiltrated behind us and attacked the battalion, he thought. Did they come through one of the tunnels he had heard so much about? Why have they left us alone?

He grabbed the hand mike from Private Chang. "Battalion, this is 1st Platoon. I request permission to destroy rock drop one-eight. Over."

"Here they come again," Chang yelled.

A storm of fire exploded over the defenders. Enemy machine-gun fire raked the top of Sung-Joo's bunker. Several of the defenders fell, their bodies thrown violently against the side of the bunker. Flying metal filled the air, whizzing past at high speed in a terrible trajectory of death. Sung-Joo ducked low behind the cold earth protection of his bunker.

He dropped the hand mike and fired his M16 at the advancing enemy. He fired single, controlled shots, but they were not enough to stem the enemy infantry. A dozen attackers climbed over the steep ridge and raced across the open field to the platoon's left. "They've flanked us," exclaimed a terrified voice near Sung-Joo.

As enemy automatic weapons fire scoured the top of the trench line, mortar rounds exploded in midair. The sweeping fire from the enemy's machine guns hissed overhead, driving the defenders to cover, forcing them down into the wet, red mud of the trench line. Soon, no one was firing at the North Koreans.

We can't win, thought Sung-Joo. We've held off the North Koreans for almost seven hours without support, artillery, or resupply. We have obeyed our orders.

A wave of machine-gun bullets struck the bunker. Both men ducked. Chang cowered low in the hole next to his platoon leader as lead splinters ricocheted against the roof of the bunker. The radio operator strained to hear the radio by pressing the receiver hard against his ear.

"Sir, the radio's been hit," Chang cried, pointing to a bullet hole in the set. "We must leave."

"I'm out of ammunition!" a tired, desperate voice screamed to Sung-Joo.

North Korean infantry fired at them from the left side of the position, sending deadly enfilade down the trench line. Grenades exploded somewhere to the far left. Two more of Sung-Joo's men fell to the strike of the enemy's assault fire.

"Sir, the enemy is all over the place," Private Chang cried, looking frantic in the artificial light. "We should pull out."

Sung-Joo stared at the frightened soldier and shook his head. "Hand me the telephone."

Chang handed the telephone to the platoon leader. An explosion detonated overhead, sending dust down on top of them. Sung-Joo tilted his steel helmet to hear the report.

"Sir, we cannot hold this position," Kim's voice shouted in desperation through the receiver of the telephone. "We're out of machine-gun ammunition."

Sung-Joo knew that his men couldn't hold, but he knew it was his duty to defend. There was no one to ask for permission. He had to decide.

The sound of Kim's machine gun sputtered, then suddenly quit. Enemy tank fire blasted away at the trench line. To Sung-Joo's left a wounded man screamed in agony. The sound of enemy rifle fire increased on the left flank. No one was returning fire from the South Korean lines. The platoon is finished if we stay here, thought Sung-Joo.

"Withdraw to the southwest," ordered Sung-Joo, his voice cracking from the dust and fear. "All squads, take the wounded and withdraw."

The sound of the telephone was quickly replaced by another blast of tank fire. The ground in front of Sung-Joo trembled as the shells exploded all around. Enemy fire ripped through the roof of his position. Sung-Joo ducked to the bottom of his hole and waited for the fire to slacken.

He looked at the demolitions blaster, then leaped over Chang and quickly reconnected the wires to the firing device.

"To hell with my orders," Sung-Joo shouted to Private Chang. "They can't court-martial a dead man."

Chang looked back at the lieutenant and smiled a brave, proud smile.

Holding the blaster in his lap, Sung-Joo twisted the T handle on the device. Nothing happened.

He quickly checked the wires. In the excitement, one wire

had slipped out of its post. The lieutenant put the wire in his mouth, stripped off some of the plastic coating with his teeth, and reinserted the wire in the post. Gripping the T handle with all his force, he twisted it again.

The demolitions exploded. Flame and smoke accompanied the roar of the TNT, engulfing the valley in confusion for a brief moment.

After several seconds the haze cleared. Sung-Joo could see that the heavy rocks had dropped into the choke point, blocking the route. He smiled at Chang.

"Let's go. Everyone out," Sung-Joo ordered, shouting as loud as he could. He pulled the pin on a white smoke grenade and threw it in front of their bunker to cover their withdrawal.

The white smoke billowed. Sung-Joo and Chang crawled out from the trench and ran up the hill in short, quick rushes. Machine-gun bullets whizzed all around them. Everyone ran. A soldier to Sung-Joo's left was dropped in midstride as 7.62mm machine-gun rounds riddled his midsection.

Chang raced ahead of the lieutenant until a burst of fire punched him like the blow from an invisible boxer, causing him to stop and arch backward. Sung-Joo kept running and dove for cover behind the body of his stricken radio operator. An enemy machine gun plastered the area where Chang lay dying. Bullets from several enemy weapons sliced into the dirt in front of Sung-Joo, striking Chang's body.

Sung-Joo felt for a pulse on the young man's neck. Chang was dead. At the same time the lone survivor of the 2d Squad stood up and ran to Sung-Joo's right.

"No, no," the lieutenant screamed, trying to warn his soldier to get down. The soldier ran a few feet before the bullets hit him and threw his lifeless body to the ground as if he were a broken doll.

He struggled to breathe. The only South Koreans that Sung-Joo could see were dead. As far as he knew, his entire platoon— all fifty-three men—were either dead or captured.

A trail of machine-gun bullets marched toward Sung-Joo in small geysers of spurting reddish mud. His heart pounded as he crawled away, bullets zinging over his head. After several agonizing minutes he inched rearward on his belly, then slowly rose and ran away in the fog.

11:00 A.M., 1 October, multipurpose range complex, Chorwon Valley, South Korea. "Al's moving out now," Major Lucas announced as he entered the command post. "He had to make two three-man crews."

Rodriguez nodded. All but two of the dead and wounded had come from Bravo Company. Captain Grey, Bulldog Six, had to rearrange his crews to make sure that at least three men were in each tank. This meant that two M1A2s would fight without gunners. The tank commander would have to fight, aim, and fire the main cannon and coaxial-mounted 7.62mm machine gun from his position. That was one of the reasons he picked the Bulldogs for the gas station mission. It was better to get them moving, doing something positive, rather than let them sit around and think about their dead friends.

"Sir, I finally got someone on brigade frequency," an excited radio operator shouted to Rodriguez.

Rodriguez took the hand mike as the radio operator turned up the volume.

"Any station, this is Saber One-Six. Over."

Rodriguez checked the radio operator's call sign chart. Saber One-Six was the troop commander of A Troop, 4-7 Cavalry.

"This is Dragon Six, Saber One-Six. Send your message."

"Man, am I glad to hear from you," the voice answered. "Where are you located?"

Rodriguez recognized the voice of the Alpha Troop commander, Capt. Rick Pelham, whom he had worked with on an exercise a few months before. "We're at the MPRC. Where are you? Over."

"We were training with an ROK unit near the DMZ when all hell broke loose. We got hammered a few hours ago by mortar fire and engaged with enemy infantry. I've got fifteen wounded and twelve dead. I'm seven kilometers northeast of you on Highway 47. I'm under orders to fall back, but I have a platoon somewhere north of you on Highway 43 that could really use your help."

"Roger, Saber One-Six. Do you have radio contact with them?"

"Now and then, Dragon Six," the cavalryman answered. "My last report from them is two hours old. They were attacked

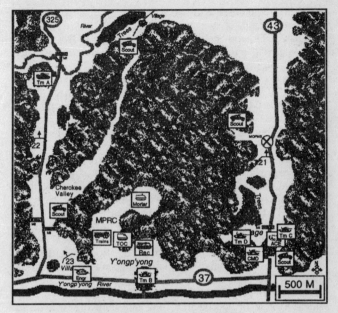

Dragon Force at MPRC

by snipers and lost their platoon leader. They are supposed to be heading your way."

"I'll keep an eye out for them," Rodriguez replied. "I don't have contact with my brigade. What's the situation?"

"Things are a mess along Highway 47. The ROKs are withdrawing south, but if somebody doesn't hold the North Koreans on Highway 43, this withdrawal will turn into a disaster. My orders are to head south with the ROKs and cross over to Highway 43, but I can't leave my 1st Platoon up there all by themselves."

"Got it, Saber One-Six. We'll hold the bastards until you get away, and I'll do what I can for your platoon. I'm going to pass you over to my assistant S3. Confirm your platoon locations and radio frequencies with him. I promise you we won't abandon your platoon."

"Thanks, Dragon Six. I'll call you when the ROKs pass and we're ready to pull out," a grateful voice answered over the radio. "I owe you one."

"Sir, you can't be serious," Lucas said to Rodriguez, shaking his head. "If the cav's pulling back, we should pull back. There are only two M1A2 task forces in Korea. We're too important to stay here."

"What's gotten into you?" said Rodriguez. "If we leave, the gap we create will offer the enemy a clear route to the south. If the North Koreans blow through here, they could crack the whole front wide open." Rodriguez was irritated by his XO's consistent questioning of his orders. He handed the hand mike to the radio operator and turned to his S3.

"Front?" Lucas questioned. "What front? You heard yourself, the ROKs were running. If they're not going to stand, what's the point?"

"Maybe it's time the running stopped," Rodriguez decided, looking down at his map. The tank range was situated in the middle of two high-speed avenues of approach. A high mountain range, impassable to vehicles, blocked the center. The widest avenue of approach, a four-lane highway, was in the east.

"Tony, I want to block both valleys," Rodriguez said calmly, tapping the map with his right index finger. "I want Delta and Charlie in the east to block Highway 43. Team Charlie is the main effort and gets all our countermobility engineer assets in support. Put the infantry heavy team, Team Alpha, in the west to block Highway 325. Assign the Volcano minelayer to backstop Team Alpha, just in case. I'll use Team Bravo as my reserve to counterattack in the east or west as needed."

"That will spread us out quite a bit," Major Lucas offered. "We'll have our flanks exposed to his infantry. We can't cover all those hills."

"Dave," Rodriguez said with a smile, putting his right hand on his executive officer's shoulder, "an armored force is always in the desperate situation of having exposed flanks. We'll just have to get used to it."

"Is this worth the risk?" Lucas asked, his left hand touching his lip. "We don't know how many ROK units are still fighting. Wouldn't Colonel Jakes expect us to fight our way south to link up with him?"

"No. I think he'd be the first to say we never leave any of our own behind," Rodriguez said with finality. "Okay, that's it. We'll fight here. We won't leave the cav and we won't abandon our allies."

"Wilco, sir," Lucas replied with a nod. "I just wanted you to see all sides. You told me a long time ago that it's my job to state the options."

Rodriguez nodded. "The day you always agree with me will be the day one of us is not thinking. Now, everybody fights, nobody quits."

A soldier walked over to the executive officer and handed him a slip of paper. "This is a note from the aide station. Specialist Wilson just died."

1:00 P.M., 1 October, Marshal Kim Seung-Hee's office, 1st Army Group command bunker near Kaesong, North Korea. An ashtray sat on the big oak desk, adorned with six dead cigarette butts. The air in the room was thick with the smell of burning tobacco.

The general sat in a big leather chair staring at a twenty-four-inch Hitachi color television set. He opened his gold cigarette case, retrieved another cigarette, and lit it. His office, deep in the same bunker that had seen the murders of the ruling elite of North Korea, was large and comfortable. It was the one place the general could collect his thoughts and make decisions without being interrupted by events. He leaned back in his chair and puffed on the strong, American-made cigarette.

Admiral Bae stood alongside his chair, watching the screen intently.

The television picture suddenly attracted Kim's attention. He turned up the sound. The character in the picture, a uniformed member of the Public Information Department, looked solemn and grief stricken as he explained the murder of Kim Jong Il at the hands of South Korean terrorists. Martial music played in the background as the commentator agitated for the maximum effort in the war against the imperialist aggressors.

"Admiral Bae, it was lucky that you and I were not with the

Dear Leader when this dastardly attack took place," said Marshal Kim. His mind raced as he studied Bae's reaction. He looked back at the television screen, the slight trace of a smile on his lips. "Comrades, we will avenge you."

"Yes, how fortunate, that all of the senior leaders of Daring Thrust were also absent," Bae said in a voice heavy with skepticism. "It is also unfortunate that all of the South Korean assassins who perpetrated this dastardly deed were killed before we could find out how they were able to penetrate our security so effectively."

"Yes, that was unlucky," Kim answered, not too convincingly, "but they would not surrender."

The television flashed a scene of the brutal assassination. There, on the color screen, was a South Korean commando with his pistol in hand executing the leadership of North Korea. The body of the Dear Leader and the mangled, unrecognizable body of his chief executive agent, Admiral Gung, lay tumbled about like broken dolls in a smashed playhouse.

The evidence was obvious, the camera angle superb. A better performance could not have been arranged. Kim frowned for a moment as he studied the body of Admiral Gung. "Did anyone escape the attack?"

"No," Admiral Bae replied. "Every leader in the room was killed."

"I promise you that they will pay for this," Kim announced in a steady tone as he rubbed the side of his head. "In a few days this heinous act will be avenged by the complete capitulation of our enemies."

"Yes, I am pleased at how quickly our forces have reacted," replied Bae. "Your Daring Thrust is achieving remarkable success. My staff tells me that you even sabotaged the enemy's satellite systems."

"Yes, it is amazing what money can buy in this modern age," Kim commented. He reached into his pocket, pulled out a small white pill, and placed it in his mouth. He reached for the glass of water on his desk and took a gulp.

Bae nodded. "And there is talk about the purchase of special weapons from Russia."

"My stratagem is paradoxical and asymmetrical, as in our game of *paduk*," Kim answered, setting down the glass and avoiding the question. "The Americans think only in terms of concentration. I have thought in different terms. I have already blinded their satellites. Now I must use the ultimate stratagem. Since I cannot completely destroy their power, I must immobilize and negate it."

"How?" Bae asked. "I understand that you have issued special instructions to one of my submarines, orders that even I am not permitted to see. The submarine left this morning with a full crew of your security police."

"Yes, it is time that I let you in on this part of the plan," Kim smiled, enjoying the role he was playing, as if he were a puppeteer manipulating marionettes. "The operation is called North Wind. It provides a decisive means to negate the Americans."

Kim reached over to an intercom box and flicked the switch. "Colonel So, come in here immediately."

Seconds later there was a knock at the door.

"Come," Marshal Kim answered.

Two guards opened the door, and Colonel So Hyun Jun entered and saluted.

"How much longer until North Wind is in position?" Kim asked as he reached into his top desk drawer and retrieved the gold cigarette case.

"Eight hours, Comrade Marshal," Colonel So answered.

"Is the other package ready for transport?" Kim questioned.

"Yes, Comrade Marshal."

"Excellent," Kim said as he flicked open the gold case and picked out a cigarette. For a moment he stared at the inscription on the side of the case, then put it in his breast pocket. "Prepare my helicopter. I want to be at 1st Army Group headquarters in the morning. I look forward to teaching our enemies a lesson in war that they will never forget."

6

THE DRIVE SOUTH

A great and continuous weakness of the United States Army fighting in Asia was its tactical and psychological dependence on continuous battle lines, such as had been known in Europe. In Asia, terrain and Communist tactics made such lines rare—Communist armies tended to flow like the sea, washing around strong points, breaking through places where the dams are weak.

—T. R. FEHRENBACH

2:15 A.M., 2 October, four kilometers southwest of the demilitarized zone, near Munsan, South Korea. "Face it, Willows, we're lost," the truck driver announced defiantly. The driver's blond hair, just a bit longer than regulation length, protruded from underneath her Kevlar helmet. "We can't be going the right way. I've driven these roads for three months and I've never come this way before."

The sergeant on the right side of the seat didn't answer. He fumbled with his map and flashlight, searching for answers to their dilemma.

The rain pounded against the windshield as the large supply truck stood motionless in snarled traffic. The rhythmic sound of the wiper blades added to the dissonance from outside the truck's cab—civilian drivers cursing in Korean, the grinding of transmissions, and the honking of horns. A stream of automobiles and trucks jammed the two-lane concrete road. Hundreds of refugees were traveling south, away from the fighting, hoping to find safety. The narrow secondary road was illuminated only by headlights. Vehicles, which were lined up bumper to bumper, crawled along the road one halting inch at a time.

The world has gone crazy, the truck driver thought as she inched forward. Private First Class Jessica Patterson had joined the army thirteen months before to be a computer operator. The army had trained her as a repair parts clerk. True to army efficiency, after arriving in Korea she was assigned as a truck driver. Now she was running away from a shooting war, a possibility she had never quite imagined when she negotiated her army assignment with her recruiting sergeant.

Both sides of the narrow road were hemmed in by rain-swollen rice paddies. A few vehicles that had stalled had already been pushed off the road by panicked drivers. Those people too unlucky to have a vehicle hitched rides in trucks and buses or walked precariously along the side of the road.

Everyone is trying to get south, away from the fighting, Patterson thought. The withdrawal of civilians from the battlefield was supposed to be controlled by the ROK military police. A few sporadic checkpoints had kept the traffic moving. But something was wrong. She hadn't seen any ROK military police for quite a while.

The civilian car in front of her moved a few inches and stopped.

Patterson slowed the five-ton truck to a halt. She saw that the cars to her front were full of frightened families—old men, women, and children—packed six or seven to a car. How cruel, she thought, that these innocent civilians were paying the price of war. The sergeant in the front seat looked nervously at Patterson. The road was blocked by a truck three vehicles ahead of them that had stopped on a one-lane concrete bridge. There were no side walls or guardrails, typical of the small bridges that spanned gaps in the rice paddy irrigation system.

The starter of the stalled truck sputtered, then the headlights dimmed. Dozens of horns honked as startled drivers tried in vain to move the truck with their protests. The road is completely blocked, thought Patterson. We'll never get out of here unless they push that son of a bitch over the side.

"Damnit," the sergeant yelled at Private Patterson in a voice filled with fear. "We've got to get around this mess. I know that the turn is somewhere up ahead."

"Calm down, Sergeant Willows," the female driver said in

frustration. "What do you want me to do? In this traffic I can't go forward and I can't go back."

"Patterson, don't tell me to calm down," Willows said sanctimoniously. "You just keep going straight ahead as soon as the traffic gets moving. The main road to Seoul should be another kilometer or so to our left. As long as we're headed south, we'll be okay."

"But we were supposed to be going north to Munsan," Patterson protested, "not Seoul. What about the repair parts we're supposed to be taking to Camp Gary Owen?"

"You heard those explosions," Sergeant Willows said, looking at Patterson with wide eyes as if she were crazy. "We're getting the snot kicked out of us. Hell, our guys are probably all dead at Gary Owen. We may be the only ones left. We've got to get to Seoul."

Patterson shook her head and held the steering wheel tightly. Willows had panicked, pure and simple, she thought. Her supply sergeant boss wasn't the warrior type, and now she was painfully aware of his lack of courage and poor judgment. He had ordered her to turn the truck around at the first sound of gunfire. Now they were who knows where, stuck in an exodus of terrified civilians trying to flee the battlefield.

Patterson watched as a car tried to pass the stalled truck on the bridge. She saw from the glare of the headlights that there wasn't enough room for two vehicles. That was the driver's fatal mistake. Patterson watched helplessly as the passenger car drove off the bridge, flipped over on its side, and fell upside down into the rice paddy. If the occupants didn't get out, they would drown in the cold, shallow water.

The rain increased, smashing into the windshield more cruelly than before. Patterson shifted the truck into neutral and pulled up on the emergency brake. "We have to help those people."

"Do you want to end up like that?" the sergeant shouted hysterically, holding her shoulder with his left hand. "Not while I'm in charge here. I order you not to leave this truck."

"We should help them, Sergeant," Patterson shouted, eyeing her boss with disdain. "If you won't, I will." She shrugged off his grip and opened her door.

KARRUMMP! The night sky flashed as a barrage of mortar

shells slammed into the road a kilometer in front of the truck. For a brief moment, the night turned to day in a fiery flash of orange and white.

"Sarge, we gotta get out of this truck," Patterson howled.

The sergeant looked straight ahead. Patterson could see that he was paralyzed with fear. A car had been hit and exploded; it flew fifty feet into the air and landed upside down on a small truck. A crowded bus was splattered with shrapnel, which filled the inside with smoke. Huge gaps were torn in the queue of stalled cars and civilian trucks. Patterson could hear people screaming above the roar of the explosions. The mortar fire grew more accurate. The cars and trucks exploded in line, one after another. The flaming debris of shell-shattered buses, trucks, and cars, along with their passengers, flew through the air in a frenzy of destruction.

KARRUMMP! KARRUMMP! Patterson opened the cab door, dismounted the truck, and ran along the side to the back. The light of the explosions flickered against the side of the truck as she quickly unfastened the chain that locked the tailgate.

"Patterson," a female voice screamed inside the back of the five-ton. "What's happening?"

"Holley, Jefferson—out of the truck, right now," Patterson shouted. "Leave everything but what you can carry."

One female and one male soldier climbed out of the truck carrying their helmets, NBC masks, and M16 rifles. They crouched at the rear of the truck.

"What are we going to do?" Holley cried.

"Head for that hill, over there," Patterson yelled, pointing to the southeast.

Vehicles continued to explode in front of them. The line of explosions continued as more shells fell on the crammed column.

"Where's Sergeant Willows?" Private Jefferson, the male soldier, shouted above the roar.

"I'll get him. You run for cover that way," Patterson ordered, taking charge. "I'll meet you as soon as I get him."

The two soldiers crouched lower as the car to the front of the truck exploded. Then they quickly climbed down from the road and ran along a rice paddy embankment.

Patterson rushed to the left front of the truck and opened the driver's door. "Willows, get out."

Mortar fire fell on both sides of the road. A couple of mortar flares ignited overhead. Patterson could see the road littered with broken vehicles, burning cars, and screaming refugees. Willows was in the driver's seat.

"No, I'm not leaving this truck," the dazed sergeant yelled. The fire from the burning cars was mirrored in his wide, fear-crazed eyes.

"Sergeant," she yelled, "goddamnit, get the hell out of this truck, now." With one hand she held her rifle and with the other she pulled at Willow's left arm with all her might. The sergeant fought back, holding on to the steering wheel, gripping it in fear. With a violent push he knocked her off balance. Patterson fell into the rice paddy, landing on her back.

She felt the cold, stinking water cover her. She struggled to lift her head, gasping for air. Resting on her elbows, she looked up from the muddy water. Her helmet and rifle were somewhere in the muck.

Suddenly the truck exploded. The heat from the explosion forced her to turn away. She felt the blast wave cover her and then reside. Pieces of metal and debris showered the rice paddy.

Her ears were ringing. Stunned, she struggled to her feet but stumbled and fell back into the water. My ankle, she thought, I must have twisted it in the fall. She fumbled in the foul water, looking for her rifle and her helmet. Her blond hair reflected the fire on the road above.

"Patterson, are you okay?" Private Jefferson said as he rushed to the aid of his friend. He pulled her up and glanced at the cab of their truck.

"Oh, my God. Look at Willows," Private Holley screamed.

Patterson turned back to look at her sergeant. The truck burned brightly. Inside the cab she could see the macabre outline of Willows, slumped against the wheel, burning like a dried-out Christmas tree. The flames raged out of control, billowing black smoke into the rainy, dark sky.

3:50 A.M., 2 October, Chorwon Valley, South Korea. Second Lieutenant Sung-Joo, of the Republic of Korea Army, moved quietly south, grieving for the loss of his men and dishonored by the thought that he was the lone survivor of his platoon. He walked, dispirited and ashamed, along a narrow trail that followed a jagged, tree-covered ridge.

He didn't think about where he was going. He was moving on automatic pilot, one step at a time, seeking a means to escape the sound of the gunfire.

He was tired, a bone-weary tiredness that made each step a struggle. Below, in the mist-shrouded valleys, he heard the continuous roll of man-made thunder as the North Korean guns fired to the south. The sharp crack of their shells burst along the mountain crests south of the DMZ.

Sung-Joo arrived at an opening in the trees. Looking down to the valley below, he stopped to watch an uneven battle as a North Korean division assaulted a weakened South Korean infantry battalion.

Artillery shells screamed through the trees and sprayed vicious fragments of steel onto the defenders. The rounds filled the foggy sky with fire. Hundreds of North Korean infantrymen bounded up the hills toward the South Korean defensive line.

There was a frantic shrill of whistles and the yell of officers and sergeants as the North Koreans made a mad rush up the hill. The machine guns of the defenders blazed in fury. The communists fell to the defenders' weapons in batches, cut down like rice from a mowing-machine blade. Although Sung-Joo's countrymen staunchly defended, the enemy attacks never faltered. More North Koreans stormed forward, and the defenders' fire slackened with each successive attack.

Soon the first signs of disintegration in the ROK defenses became apparent as they were bombarded with massed concentrations of artillery and attacked by wave after wave of infantry. The dark shadows of the communist line moved steadily uphill. The fire from the defenders, now desultory and weak, could not stop the advancing onslaught. The enemy seemed to grow right out of the ground as the savage close-range fight with rifles, machine guns, and grenades continued.

Tears filled Sung-Joo's eyes. The soldiers were just youngsters, he thought, fulfilling their obligation of service in the army. One out of a thousand might stay in the army; everyone else hoped to go to the university or work in offices in Seoul. The society respected education. Even before the military leaders who had run South Korea had been discredited in scandals and retribution from their stint as dictators, the thought of military service was anathema to most South Koreans. No one wanted to believe there would ever be a war.

A group of North Koreans raced forward, the astonishing stutter of their assault rifles plastering the defenders with fire. The last few ROK defenders answered with a ragged volley of rifle fire. Grenades detonated in bursts of yellow flame. A Claymore mine exploded, showering the enemy with pellets, and several of the attackers fell, only to be replaced by more. The *tchug* of enemy mortars, firing behind the attacking squads, was soon replaced by the blast of mortar bombs as they exploded in the defenders' trench lines. The ROK guns slowly went silent. This heroic defense would not last much longer.

Sung-Joo clenched his fists in anger. He screamed and hurled insults at the attackers, as if that would somehow slow them down and stop their attack. He wanted to strike back, to help turn the tide, but he was without a weapon, high above the fight, out of reach.

With a sibilant hiss and then a roar, the brilliant geysers of the North Korean flamethrower teams splashed against the opening of the defenders' pillboxes. Sung-Joo watched as sheets of flame poured through embrasures or smothered the outside of the bunkers in burning oil and phosphorus. Burning men ran screaming into the night, trying to beat off flames that would not extinguish, until finally the macabre human torches lay still, glowing on the side of the hill. In the light of the flares, Sung-Joo observed other attackers throwing satchel charges. The dark figures raced toward the bunkers, pushing explosives through machine-gun slits. Thundering detonations shook the steel and concrete forts with bright flashes of fire.

The exchange of fire was now completely one-sided. By flame, explosive charge, machine-gun fire, and hand-to-hand combat, the battle raged. One after another, the ROK bunkers fell silent. Shocked and confused, the defenders, mostly two-year draftees who had never wanted to join the army, were the only force blocking the gateways to Seoul. One by one, the South Korean positions died in agony before the determined assault. The noise of the fighting slackened, and Sung-Joo heard the familiar, sickening growl of armored vehicles and the crack of 100mm cannons, announcing the arrival of the enemy's tank support. The tanks moved forward, engines roaring, guns blasting the next set of defensive positions.

Sung-Joo saw the whole battlefield turn into one huge graveyard. Alongside the silent South Korean dead he saw wounded men stumble out of bunkers. Several men, appallingly injured, were crying out in pain. The North Koreans shot them one by one. The single cracks of their rifles, dispatching one wounded or captured ROK soldier after another, hit Sung-Joo's heart like arrows. He watched until the last ROK soldier was dragged to a trench and executed. The North Koreans laughed.

It was madness, Sung-Joo thought, and murder. Murder in the truest definition of the word. Warriors fought with honor; they did not execute their prisoners like cattle in slaughter pens.

The battlefield turned silent except for the squeak of the tank tracks and the noise of the engines as the tanks roared south. Sung-Joo gradually came out of shock, like a person waking from a nightmare. He turned his head and suddenly realized what he had to do. He had to get south and join up with another unit. "I will avenge their deaths," he said aloud, thinking of Sergeant Kim and Private Chang and the other men of his platoon.

Sung-Joo turned away and walked south, following the ridge. After an hour he saw a large, square object blocking the narrow trail. Slowly, cautiously, he crawled up to the object. It was an American jeep, the big, square kind called a Humvee. It was turned over on the narrow mountain trail.

Sung-Joo moved around to the driver's side and stumbled. His hand caught something soft—the goo of a blood-soaked body—jammed underneath the side of the vehicle. He recoiled in horror and stared at the body. He regained his composure and slowly searched the body and the vehicle for weapons, water, and food.

The driver was obviously an American. He was dead, with a gaping wound in his head that had apparently been caused by a large piece of shrapnel. Most of the American's face was gone.

Sung-Joo shuddered. No man should die like this, far from home and friends, he thought. He reached for the identification tag around the man's neck and, with a brisk movement, snapped the chain. He put the tag in his pocket and continued his search. Another man lay dead on the other side of the vehicle. His battle dress uniform was soaked with blood. On his left sleeve was the Indianhead patch of the U.S. 2d Infantry Division.

In Sung-Joo's search he discovered a flashlight, an M16 rifle with one magazine, a 9mm pistol without ammunition, a pair of binoculars, a water bottle, a pack with several rations, and a SINCGARS backpack radio. He examined the radio carefully. He had never used a portable radio like this before, but he knew that it might come in handy. If these Americans are here, he thought, maybe there are more nearby.

The explosion and splash of artillery shells racked the hill six hundred meters to the east. Sung-Joo ducked.

"The artillery must have gotten you, my friend," Sung-Joo said to the dead man in heavily accented English. "If a communist had killed you, he would have taken your weapons and this radio."

Sung-Joo put the pack on his back and ran off to the southwest, following the narrow path on the ridge.

8:30 A.M., 2 October, 1st Army Group headquarters near Kaesong, North Korea. "Surprise is the decisive factor in attaining success. In spite of the enemy's modern electronic surveillance means, we have surprised them," Maj. Gen. Kang Sung-Yul said to the junior officer staring at the battle map. "Now we must drive on ruthlessly until the enemy surrenders. Everything depends on keeping the armored spearheads moving south—always south—never stopping."

The junior officer nodded, handed a report to Kang, and withdrew through the door, leaving the general by himself.

Kang stared at the map as if he were foreseeing the future. He seemed to see the red forces push south, overwhelming the resistance, driving the attack to the heart of the enemy.

Kang was the perfect organizer, a man who relished a difficult military problem. Brilliant and ruthlessly efficient, he had been handpicked to mastermind Daring Thrust for Marshal Kim Seung-Hee. As the chief of staff of 1st Army Group, Kang also knew that Daring Thrust was a gamble that was the last desperate hope of a dying nation.

Kang was proud of his work. In the past two years he had

created a specially designed briefing room with reinforced steel and concrete walls in the command bunker to act as the forward command post of the NKPA. His efforts to train his staff as the forward headquarters for the army had gained him recognition and promotion.

The briefing room was large and impressive. A mammoth red and white North Korean flag decorated the back wall. Bright lights hanging from the twenty-foot ceiling illuminated the front wall, which held at 1:25,000 scale situation map of Korea. With the exception of the massive eight-foot steel blast door, the bunker appeared to be designed like an extravagant movie theater.

This situation map was a work of art, beautifully depicted in bright fluorescent colors. The most up-to-date Japanese maps had been used. Behind the special glass wall, a complete operations staff worked to update the map with the latest information. Red and blue unit symbols depicting the attacking and defending units displayed the most current information on the fighting. The staff operators wrote backward on their side of the map to make the words and symbols appear correctly in the briefing room.

The thin major general smiled at the ingeniousness and absolute boldness of the plan. He was confident that his Daring Thrust would bring decisive victory to North Korea. The plan was succeeding, but not as smoothly as he had hoped. The situation maps at 1st Army Group North Korean headquarters on the morning of 2 October showed that the forward attacking corps—the 4th, 2d, 5th, and 1st—were decisively engaged from left to right along the DMZ. The South Koreans, defending stubbornly, were pinned to their fixed fortifications. The 1st Army Group, the center of Daring Thrust, had penetrated and bypassed the defenders and driven deeply into enemy lines.

The NKPA attacks had achieved surprise on the first day. Battles raged along the entire DMZ, with the air force, special forces, infantry, artillery, and tanks acting in concert, but the Inmun Gun massed its main attacks at selected points. Once the enemy defenses were punctured at chosen points, the exploitation forces would storm forward with tanks, mechanized infantry, and tremendous artillery support.

The thick fog helped mask the infantry as they infiltrated

gaps in the first South Korean defensive line. Some South Korean units had surrendered without much of a fight. Other enemy units had fought like tigers, delaying the North Korean advance.

Kang knew that it was the nature of war that operations seldom go as planned. The natural friction of war impedes movement. Kang believed, however, that surprise, mass, and planning would alleviate this friction. His job was to keep the mass moving and maintain the momentum of the assault. It all boiled down to a matter of mass and momentum.

Kang also knew that he must keep bad news away from the good ears of Marshal Kim Seung-Hee. The Heroic Leader, as Kim was now demanding to be called, was in personal command of the 1st Army Group. Kim Seung-Hee had repeatedly demonstrated to Kang that he trusted no one. Commanding from the front and micromanaging every detail was the Heroic Leader's style.

Kang silently recited Kim Seung-Hee's tenets, which had been drilled into the chief of staff through constant repetition: "Combat leadership is conducted from the front. Leadership from the front is positive and effective; pushing from the rear is defeatist and impotent."

Six armed guards abruptly entered the room and took up positions at the doorway, relieving Kang's bunker guards. Kang looked nervously at the guards. He straightened his tunic and glanced back at the situation map. He was annoyed by this offense to his authority but understood the futility of protest. The men were the handpicked bodyguards of Kim Seung-Hee. Kang was clever enough to know that he must never displease his master.

Kim Seung-Hee's personal aide, Col. So Hyun Jun, entered and shouted the call to attention. Kang stood stiffly in front of the map and watched as the new leader of North Korea walked to an overstuffed chair. Kim stood opposite the situation map for a few seconds rubbing his patch-covered eye with his left hand, studying the situation. Abruptly he sat down and looked up expectantly at General Kang. "Begin," he said.

"Everything is going exactly as planned," the short, gray-haired Kang said as he faced his distinguished guest. "Our shock divisions have penetrated the DMZ and destroyed a significant portion of the enemy's forward forces. We will complete the destruction of enemy forces in the first line of defense today, probably just after midnight. I expect that the exploitation forces can be launched after zero-one-hundred hours."

"All units must drive forward and take advantage of the surprise and chaos," Kim replied, eyeing his chief of staff carefully. "Every minute is precious. The exploitation phase of Daring Thrust must proceed without hesitation."

General Kang nodded. "The forward corps conducting the initial attacks have fixed or destroyed the equivalent of six fascist divisions along the border. We have used thirty-seven invasion tunnels to infiltrate behind the enemy lines. Our artillery has flattened their mobile forces and stunned their bunker garrisons. We captured a large force of Americans and South Koreans in the Joint Security Area near Panmunjom. We've executed the South Koreans and are keeping about forty of the surviving Americans alive; you may want to use them as hostages later."

Kim Seung-Hee nodded his approval.

"Our forces have driven the enemy back all along the front," Kang continued. "We have achieved a great surprise."

Kang paused and surveyed the map. The 1st Army Group plan called for an assault that resembled a clenched fist with a projecting index finger. The fist was formed by the west-wing corps, locked in close combat with the ROKs, directly north of Seoul, along the Kaesong-Munsan avenue of approach. Another corps was stopped north of the town of Chongok, along Highway 3, on the western Chorwon Valley approach. The index finger was made up of the divisions attacking along the eastern Chorwon Valley on Highways 43 and 47. The crooked finger was displayed in dashed red lines moving south along these routes, showing the planned penetration. The finger pointed to a town along the eastern Chorwon Valley approach, then to Uijonbu, which commanded the major road junction northeast of Seoul. Uijonbu was the initial objective of the Daring Thrust attack.

Kang studied Kim Seung-Hee, the Heroic Leader of North Korea, who had once been called the Wolf. The marshal stared at the map. Officers updating the situation map removed another blue symbol, an ROK infantry unit overwhelmed by the red tide of battle in the western Chorwon Valley.

"Sir, as you can see, we surprised the enemy before he could mobilize. Our special forces units are disrupting the enemy's mobilization and destroying his airfields and fuel and ammunition depots. We made the farthest advances into the enemy's lines here," the chief of staff said, pointing to Highway 43. "We are pushing forward. Our casualties—"

". . . are irrelevant," Marshal Kim finished the sentence. "Maintain the momentum of the attack. I don't care if you have to commit every man to meet the time line. Do you understand? We will execute the plan."

Kang hesitated; he knew that the attack was already running behind schedule. This was real war, Kang thought, not war on paper. He had seen the reports from the front and had listened to the radio broadcasts of the forward units. He knew how tough the fighting had been and how heavy the casualties were. Even though he was confined to a safe bunker watching red and blue symbols on a map, he still understood the confusion and chaos of war.

"Yes, of course, Comrade Marshal," Kang answered. "We expect to make the immediate corps objectives before noon tomorrow. This will make up for today's delays. Then we will send forward the infantry again, at night, to secure the penetration."

"We should be eight kilometers farther south along Highway 43," Kim mentioned quietly, looking at his watch. "The lead division is four hours behind the time schedule."

Kang shifted nervously in front of Marshal Kim. The one-eyed general obviously had better vision than might be anticipated. "A momentary setback, Comrade Marshal. The enemy has many more minefields and road obstacles than we expected. He has blocked most of the routes to the south and destroyed many bridges. His defensive positions were strong."

The marshal stood up, then moved to face Kang. The two men were separated by only a few inches. "Any defensive system, no matter how strong, whether based on natural or artificial barriers, can be penetrated with mass and determination. No more delays."

"Nam chim," Kang replied with conviction. "I have spoken

with General Park this morning. The exploitation forces are moving forward."

Kim grunted, turned toward the map again, and continued his contemplation of the situation. Officers behind the huge glass map posted the latest round of information. The red markers moved south a few more inches.

"Additional infantry and mechanized units will be thrown into the fight to force a breakthrough," Kang added. "The greatest difficulty . . ."

Kim silenced Kang with a wave of his hand. Kang bristled and braced himself for another rebuke. He struggled to control his reactions, even the slightest of which might be seen as an act of insolence.

"Use whatever it takes to maintain the timetable," Kim demanded. "Tell General Park to seize the crossroads of Highways 43 and 325 before noon or I will have his lead brigade commanders shot as an example of what happens to cowards who cannot conform to the expectations of the plan. I will accept no excuses."

Kang bowed as a vassal to a medieval warlord, signifying his complete compliance. Now I know the penalty for bad news, Kang thought. Marshal Kim Seung-Hee, our Heroic Leader, will hear only good news from now on.

10:50 A.M., 2 October, small shed southeast of Munsan, South Korea. Private First Class Patterson jolted awake. She was lying on her back on a rotting board in the dilapidated field house that they had crawled into during the night. Her ankle ached unbearably.

She heard voices.

"Jefferson, did you hear that?" she whispered. "There's someone outside talking in Korean."

Patterson looked frantically for her rifle, then remembered that she had lost it in the muddy rice paddy when the truck had exploded. Jefferson, who was supposed to be on guard, was sleeping in a corner of the ramshackle hut.

"Jefferson," Patterson cried loudly.

Private Jefferson recoiled as if he had been startled by a snake. He grabbed his rifle and moved toward the flimsy wooden door that blocked the entrance. He pulled back the bolt to his M16 rifle and chambered a round.

Private Holley looked at Patterson in panic, frozen with fear, unable to move. Holley's rifle was just a few feet out of Patterson's reach.

Patterson swung her body sideways to grab Holley's rifle. Pain shot through her ankle as her bad leg hit the cold floor.

Jefferson moved to open the door. Before he touched the handle, a volley of bullets fired through the wood. Jefferson stumbled to the side of the room, then fell face first onto the dirty wooden floor.

Patterson rolled to the floor as splinters and metal fragments filled the air. Jefferson gasped for air for a few moments, then didn't move.

"Oh, my God," Holley screamed. "My God."

The door burst open. A North Korean special forces soldier, wearing a brown cap and a red collar insignia on a brown uniform, pointed his AK-47 rifle at the two American women.

Patterson lunged for Holley's rifle. The North Korean jumped forward and kicked it out of her reach. Two more North Korean soldiers, each wearing web harnesses with American-style grenades hanging off their web straps, entered the shack.

Private Holley screamed. She backed up against the wall of the shack and raised her arms to surrender. The second North Korean who entered the shack gave her an emotionless stare, then fired four bullets from his automatic rifle into her body. She crumpled against the wall with a faint whimper. A surging crimson pool formed on the floor at her side.

"You bastards," Patterson screamed, raising herself up to attack the men who had just killed her two friends.

The first Korean to enter the room struck her across the face with his rifle. She recoiled from the blow, falling back onto her makeshift wooden bed.

She opened her eyes to find the North Korean on top of her and saw the grenade strapped to his web harness. She reached up with both hands, grabbed the grenade, and pulled out the pin. She held him tight as he struggled to tear her and the grenade away.

She closed her eyes. The last thing Pvt. Jessica Patterson

heard was the detonation of the grenade against the North Korean's chest.

12:50 P.M., 2 October, along Highway 43 in the Chorwon Valley, South Korea. Colonel Yi Sung-Chul, the commander of the 1st Brigade of the 820th Corps, cursed as he waited for the road to be cleared. The narrow choke point blocked the movement of Colonel Yi's armored brigade. Orders from his commander were to keep moving at all costs.

This was a bad omen. The time line was disrupted by the restricted ground, the stubborn defense of the enemy, and a hundred other excuses. Yi knew that General Park, the commander of the 820th Corps, would not accept excuses. Yi also knew, as a man knows his inner soul, that death in battle was preferable to humiliation, and maybe even execution, at the hands of General Park.

Scores of Yi's armored vehicles were lined up along the muddy roads, waiting for the roadblock to be cleared. The constant rain had washed away portions of the roads and produced deep mud puddles, which held the vehicles fast. The weather had also turned the infantry assaults upon the forested hills into a misery of slow-moving advances uphill against an enemy concealed in well-designed pillboxes that dominated every avenue of approach.

Seventeen dazed South Korean prisoners sat with their hands on their heads next to the double-lane road that led south. The battlefield they had defended still smelled of cordite from the detonation of grenades and the firing of machine guns. The bodies of North and South Korean soldiers lay around the road, a grim testimony to the fierceness of the struggle.

Six North Korean guards in full combat gear held their weapons pointed at the despondent group of South Korean prisoners. The North Koreans wore steel helmets, brown fatigues, nylon combat webbing, and good-quality boots—standard issue in the NKPA. Each soldier carried an AK-47 assault rifle.

On both sides of the road, hundreds of North Korean infantrymen were trudging south. The 45th Infantry Division of the North Korean People's Army, approximately 12,800 men strong, was on the attack, moving as fast as the men could walk.

South Korean resistance was crumbling. Nothing was slowing down the advance of the infantry.

Colonel Yi's tank brigade was another matter. He needed the road to move his tanks, armored personnel carriers, and howitzers. The road south was blocked. At a narrow point in the road a concrete wall had been constructed, and specially designed concrete blocks had been placed on the top. These rock drops were carefully sited by the South Koreans, who had executed the obstacles with skill. The defenders had fought for several hours, but superior numbers won the day and they were overwhelmed. The few survivors were herded into a tight circle on the north side of the obstacle.

The colonel watched as North Korean engineers toiled feverishly in the drizzling rain to clear the narrow passage in the Chorwon Valley road. Using explosives, they were clearing the obstacles away one by one. Yi knew that most of the avenues of attack in South Korea were guarded by such obstacles.

Colonel Yi stood by the side of his T62 tank and smoked a cigarette in the drizzling rain. His deputy commander, a young lieutenant colonel, stood at his side. Without warning, as if Yi didn't have enough trouble, the corps commander's BTR armored car drove up to the side of the colonel's tank. The six-wheeled APC splashed up next to Yi. Standing in the open hatch was General Park, a white bandage wrapped around his left hand.

"I want no mistakes," the harsh voice of General Park, the commander of the 820th Armored Corps of the North Korean People's Army, shouted from the top of the BTR. "We are behind the time line. We must break through Highway 43 and drive south. You will not stop until you reach Uijonbu."

"Nam chim." Colonel Yi and his deputy commander saluted. Yi knew that General Park, always a short-tempered man, was irritated. He knew that Park would stop at nothing to secure his objective. Everything and everyone was expendable to achieve the brigade's objective. Already, rumors were circulating in command channels of the executions of several commanders unable to achieve their objectives on time.

WHAM! A huge explosion signaled the destruction of the first hexagonal rock in the rock drop by the engineers.

"Sir, it will be done," the colonel answered, ducking at the sound of the explosion. "The infantry is moving now. I will have the tanks moving again in a few minutes."

"I expect you to capture these rock drops before they are detonated," the general replied curtly. "You cannot waste time with these cheap delays. You must keep your unit on schedule."

"*Nam chim,* Comrade General," Colonel Yi answered. He recognized his commander's voice. There was no reply that would make the general happy. Only the use of explosives could remove the obstacles from the rock drop. All Colonel Yi could do was wait for the engineers to do their duty.

Yi scanned the scene around him. Time was running short. The southern fascists were now on the run, but the rain and their stubborn defense had cost the attackers valuable time which must be made up. Intelligence reports indicated that the enemy was outnumbered seven to one and running south. It was merely a matter of pushing a few die-hards out of the way.

"What do you want me to do with the prisoners?" Colonel Yi asked.

"They will only slow you down," General Park answered from the top of his command car. "Kill them. Kill all the warmongering imperialist fascists you catch. Don't let anything slow you down or force you to deviate from the plan."

Colonel Yi saluted as the general ducked inside his APC to listen to the latest reports. The colonel's deputy commander, full of communist faith in the glory of the task at hand, looked eagerly at Yi.

The lieutenant colonel barked some orders. The prisoners slowly stood up. The guards charged their weapons and leveled their submachine guns at the group of forlorn men. Several of the South Koreans, understanding what was about to happen, screamed and put out their arms in protest. The lieutenant colonel gave the order to fire. The guards didn't hesitate. The submachine guns rattled, cutting down the defenseless men in rapid succession. In seconds it was over.

The lieutenant colonel shouted new orders and the guards raised their weapons. Precise to the end, the lieutenant colonel moved forward, kicked each corpse, and fired his pistol into the brain of any victim who showed the slightest signs of life.

The explosion of another rock echoed in the valley.

Colonel Yi walked forward to the rock drop. As he walked he

gazed at the broken bodies of the South Korean soldiers lying in the mud next to the road. He had no pity—only contempt— for soldiers who surrendered. They were the pampered soldiers of a rich country. They had eaten three meals a day and listened to rock and roll music while his countrymen died of disease and starvation.

A tired, sweat-stained engineer captain ran up to the colonel. "Comrade Commander, we will be executing the last demolition in a few minutes."

"Quickly, Captain. I must get moving."

"*Nam chim,*" the captain yelled and saluted.

The colonel moved around the rock drop and climbed the steep wall of dirt and rock to the left of the opening. He walked over the top and to the other side, wishing to survey the battle that had been there. Two M1985 light tanks and a T55 tank from the 45th Mechanized Division lay in ruins on the south side of the obstacle. A few surface-laid antitank mines sat in open view to the left of the destroyed hulls. A bunker to the left of the rock drop had been the source of many of the casualties the 45th had taken. Colonel Yi looked above the bunker and spied a tiny South Korean flag hanging limp in the thick air, its white background mixing perfectly with the fog. Only the red and blue yin and yang center gave any indication of the flag's presence. He wondered how many more of his roads had been blocked by men as tough as the ones who had defended here.

Colonel Yi turned back to his tank, walking slowly to enjoy the last puffs from his dying cigarette. The soldiers of his armored brigade were busy with the business of mechanized war; inspecting metal track connectors, adding oil to hungry engines, and checking weapons. Yi could sense that his men were eager to fight as they waited for the word to move.

The colonel climbed up the front of his T62 and leaned on the turret. The rain had stopped, but the sky was still filled with low black clouds. Yi listened to the radio loudspeaker and mentally traced the routes of other units as they crossed their designated reporting lines. For a few moments he relaxed, reached into his pocket, and took out a brown aluminum foil packet. He opened the combat ration and munched the boiled rice as the engineers completed their work.

The final explosion to clear the rock drop detonated in a shower of dust and falling debris. The engineers shouted in victory. The choke point was cleared. Yi barked orders over the command radio frequency to continue the march. The 1st Brigade, 820th Armored Corps, began to move again.

5:40 P.M., 2 October, defensive position in the eastern Chorwon Valley, ten kilometers south of the DMZ, South Korea. "Dragon Six, this is Saber One-Six. Over," the commander of Alpha Troop, 4-7 Cavalry, sounded on the radio.

"This is Dragon Six, Saber One-Six. Over."

"My 1st Platoon is ready to pass through your lines now," the voice answered.

"Roger, Saber One-Six. Send them through. We'll hold our fire. Confirm how many are passing. Over."

"Three tanks and two Bradleys. They lost a tank and two Bradleys in a fight three kilometers north of you. They report that the lead elements of a North Korean tank brigade are headed south on 43. Over."

"Any ROKs north of us?" the lieutenant colonel queried.

"Not on Highway 43. There are plenty of ROKs heading south on Highway 47, east of your position," the cavalry captain reported. "I estimate that the enemy will be on you in an hour or so. Break . . ."

Rodriguez scanned his map. Highways 43 and 47 joined at a Y intersection a few kilometers south of his position. Rodriguez's task force was west of Highway 47, on the top left side of the Y. The main strength of the Alpha Troop, 4-7 Cavalry, was in the east, on the top right.

"I'm delaying a North Korean armored brigade along Highway 43," the cavalry commander added. "I've got my hands full. There's no fucking artillery, and I can't get any air. The ROKs have jammed the roads. You have to hold them on Highway 43, or they'll block my line of retreat and we'll be surrounded. Can you hold? Over."

"We'll hold, Saber One-Six," Rodriguez answered. "We won't let them get behind you. I'll send your three tanks and two Bradleys south to the junction of 43 and 47 as soon as they pass through my lines."

"Roger, Dragon Six. Thanks."

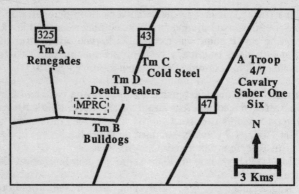

Dragon Force Positions and A/4-7 Cavalry

"Good luck, Saber One-Six," Rodriguez replied, and he said a silent prayer for the captain and his men. "This is Dragon Six. Out."

Rodriguez stood in the turret of his M1A2 and looked down to check the IVIS screen for messages from C Company. Cold Steel was his most northern company team on Highway 43. Seeing no messages from Cold Steel, he checked the digital connections to the mortar platoon.

In spite of his familiarity with the M1A2 tank, Rodriguez still marveled at the tank's command and control system. The radio interface unit managed the digital information gateway of the tank. The AN/VRC-92A SINCGARS secure, frequency-hopping radios could not be intercepted or easily jammed. At the push of a button, an IVIS-equipped tank could laze to a target, transmit its exact location, and rapidly send a digital call for artillery fire to the artillery or the battalion mortar platoon. This new system took only a fraction of the time it would have taken to get fires the old, voice radio way. The digital system saved seconds. In battle, the side that could decide and act faster than the other usually won.

Night came in stages. First the cloud sky changed slowly from dark gray to black as the unseen sun departed. Then the drizzle and fog that had saturated everyone during the day grew suddenly colder. The American task force commander gazed with sad reminiscence at the slowly darkening sky.

"We're all set, boss," Command Sergeant Major Dougan said as he walked over to the side of *Firebreather,* the battalion commander's M1A2 tank.

"We still don't have digital linkage with the mortars," Rodriguez complained to his gunner.

"You sure it's not your system?" the sergeant major asked.

"I've checked it three times."

"Let Obrisky handle it; that's why I put him on your tank," Dougan scolded.

"Sir, let me up there," Obrisky said. "I'll have it working in a few minutes. Why don't you step outside and have a cigar or something."

"Okay, supertanker," Rodriguez chided. "If you weren't so damn good, I'd fire your ass. This baby's all yours."

The colonel muscled out of the tank commander's hatch and climbed down to the front of the tank to join his sergeant major. Obrisky took his place in the turret and started a diagnostic check.

Rodriguez reached into his Nomex breast pocket and took out a cigar. He had only five left. He felt the need to conserve them, but he needed a break. One of his simple joys was sharing a cigar with his sergeant major. He handed one to Dougan.

"I figure we'll be up against a tank brigade and lots of infantry early in the morning," Rodriguez announced.

"Have you received any orders from brigade?" Dougan asked, taking the cigar.

"No. The only other U.S. unit I've talked to is a troop from 4-7 Cav."

"I just came from Team Alpha's positions at the river," Dougan replied, changing the subject. "Captain Sharpe has set the Renegades in a strong position. They've occupied some empty concrete bunkers that overlook the stream and the bridge, some large enough to protect tanks and Bradleys. His infantry is well dug in with overhead cover. They could hold off an army from those positions."

"Good; they may have to," Rodriguez said, nodding as he thought about his young infantry commander, Capt. Joe Sharpe. If anyone could stop the enemy's attack along Highway 325, it was Joe Sharpe and his Renegades—one M1A2 tank platoon and two Bradley infantry platoons.

"Yeah, let's hope they don't have to," Dougan replied, biting off the cellophane wrapper of his cigar.

"It looks like the main enemy attack will come down Highway 43," Rodriguez replied, unwrapping his own cigar. "If Sharpe can hold the North Koreans from coming south on 325, I'll trap the bastards along Highway 43. Did the extra ammo arrive?"

"Roger that. I moved up the last HEMMT of ammunition to them. We're lucky we had so much 7.62mm and .50-caliber machine-gun ammo here for tank gunnery; otherwise we'd be hurting. Captain Sharpe stockpiled the machine-gun ammo in bunkers near each platoon. For insurance, the Volcano is positioned just like you ordered—to lay a minefield to backstop him if anything breaks through. The Volcano team says it will take an hour to lay a minefield a thousand meters long by sixty meters deep."

Rodriguez nodded and lit his cigar. He shared the match with Dougan. The sergeant major puffed away until his stogie was burning cherry hot.

"Cold Steel is set to defend in depth along Highway 43," Dougan continued. "I've also checked their positions. Mackenzie has his 3d Platoon forward and ready to execute three MOPM minefields, as you ordered. As soon as they see the first three companies pass their location, they'll execute the minefields. Behind them is Team Dealer, tucked away in good overwatch positions."

Rodriguez thought about Sergeant Hardee and the 3d Platoon at the tip of the trap that he was about to set. His plan was bold—maybe risky—but he had studied the North Korean tactics. He knew that he had to break the enemy's formations into bite-sized pieces. The MOPMs—boxes of antitank mines that scattered and armed at the push of a button, scattering twenty-one mines, each in a semicircle around the container—would serve that purpose. Three MOPMs, sixty-three mines, would not hold the North Koreans for long, but they should break up their formations for just long enough. After Mackenzie destroyed the first echelon of the enemy's attack, he could reposition his forward platoon and Rodriguez would start the process all over again farther to the south. Timing, as always, would be important to pull off this maneuver.

"I want to divide the first North Korean battalion from the follow-on battalions," Rodriguez replied. "They'll be stacked up bumper to bumper in column as they hit us. If I can trap the first battalion, the second and third will be easier to kill. After the second battalion is smashed, I'll counterattack with B Company to finish them off."

The two men stared at the map as a dozen different options raced through Rodriguez's mind.

"Zeke, what haven't I thought of?" Rodriguez asked, sharing doubts that he could share only with his command sergeant major. "Are we ready?"

"Boss, we're as ready as we'll ever be," Dougan answered. Then he looked at his commander in a quiet moment of truth. "No bullshit now. I've been a soldier all my life. Tell me the truth. Do you think we can stop an entire armored brigade by ourselves? Do you think you can pull this off?"

Rodriguez set his jaw tight and nodded. "This first enemy brigade is mine. It's the six or so other tank brigades, followed by infantry and artillery, that'll be pushing up behind the spearhead that have me worried."

7:50 P.M., 2 October, eastern Chorwon Valley, eight kilometers south of the DMZ, South Korea. The officer pinched the dying cigarette from his lips and flicked it into the mud. The butt died slowly, turning from glowing red to ashen gray. The officer leaned against his armored personnel carrier and turned up his collar to the damp air.

North Korean People's Army captain Yin Ch'un-chu stood in the vehicle commander's station of his Chinese-designed, North Korean–built VTT323 armored personnel carrier. The 14.5mm antiaircraft machine gun in front of him pointed straight up into the dark sky. For a moment, Yim tried to forget that he was in a war. If he had a choice, he might have been a poet, but there was no need for poets in North Korea. He thought about his wife and the hard life he had as a soldier in the Inmun Gun. He thought about the lost souls of the dead that surrounded him on this battlefield. He yearned for a chance to sleep.

So far, Yim had merely road-marched his unit to their start line as other units in the great colossus that was the Inmun Gun moved to the attack. The battle had been fought by others, and the grim testimony of the struggle had littered his route of advance. Now he waited for his orders.

In ten minutes it would be time to cross the first reporting line. Yim shivered as he checked the firing mechanism of his machine gun, then loaded the red- and orange-tipped 14.5mm bullets into the machine gun's feed tray. He snapped the tray shut and pulled back the bolt, slamming a round into the chamber. He was ready. He looked at his watch and counted the minutes.

Yim's VTT323 APC had a crew of four soldiers—a driver, an assistant driver, a radio operator, and a commander. One of his crewmen, Corporal Kim, the radio operator, offered a cup of hot barley tea that he had brewed on a small fire by the side of the APC. Kim's job, maintaining communications for the reconnaissance effort along the line of attack, was one of the most important in the brigade.

"Thanks, comrade," Yim said politely to the young corporal who handed him the tea. The soldier nodded, then returned to his duty of monitoring the company radio.

My soldiers, Yim thought with a smile, are like my family. I

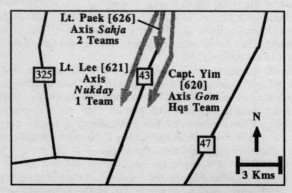

Captain Yim's Reconnaissance Plan

am proud of them and their quiet confidence, their dedication. They had already transcended that point where hard soldiering was considered an inconvenience. They were used to living off the land in their armored vehicles. The unit had become their natural environment; a world of orders, loyalty, and dedication, where they were at their best. Yim's men seemed intensely proud of this fact. He was sure they saw themselves as the most fit and able combat soldiers in the Inmun Gun.

Yim's brigade reconnaissance company consisted of ten VTT323 APCs. He was reinforced with four T55 tanks—one with a mine roller and three with mine plows—and one eight-wheeled BTR-60 chemical reconnaissance vehicle. Yim had divided this force into three recon teams and a headquarters team. Each recon team consisted of three APCs and a T55 mine plow tank. His headquarters team consisted of his VTT323, a mine roller tank, and the BTR.

Yim's plan was simple. His teams would advance in an inverted V. From west to east he deployed teams under Lieutenant Lee—one to reconnoiter the western side of Highway 43, along Axis Nukday (wolf); two teams under his deputy commander, Lieutenant Paek, to trail the other two by moving straight down Highway 43 along Axis Sahja (lion); and his own headquarters team to move down Axis Gom (bear) east of 43. Yim chose to be on the eastern side, along Gom, because the high ground east of Highway 43 would help him maintain radio communications with his elements and the brigade headquarters. Yim knew that in the restricted terrain of Korea, reconnaissance was ineffective if the information could not be transmitted rapidly to higher headquarters.

Yim's mission was to determine the exact location of the enemy's main defenses along Highway 43. Once this location was found, the artillery would fire, flanking infiltrations would begin, and the armor fist would ram forward.

Yim's VTT323—number 620—sat silent. Yim felt as if he were a racehorse waiting to jump out of the starting gate. Yim knew that Lieutenant Paek—his deputy commander, in VTT number 626—was also eager to move.

An authoritative, crisp voice boomed over the brigade command frequency and informed Yim's radio operator that the enemy was rapidly falling back to the south. Yim had been trained for years to be bold. Now it was time to put that training to the test. Delays were out of the question; he must press on with all speed.

"Six-Two-Six and Six-Two-One, this is Six-Two-Zero. Over," Yim called to Lieutenant Paek.

"Six-Two-Zero, this is Six-Two-Six," Paek answered.

"Six-Two-One here," Lee replied.

"Move now. All units execute Report Line One at this time and report on contact. Over," Yim said. Each group was to cross their start points along their designated axis, maintain the formation, and immediately initiate radio contact with the enemy.

"Affirmative, Six-Two-Six. Out," Paek answered. *"Nam chim."*

"Nam chim. Six-Two-One acknowledges," Lee replied.

Yim smiled. His men were ready, the enemy was on the run, and the smell of victory was in the air. Soon all the sacrifices of his people would be justified, he thought. He searched ahead and tried to scan the horizon with his night vision goggles, but the fog was thick and limited his view.

"Driver, start the engine," Yim ordered into his throat microphone. "Move out to your left front."

With a loud roar the armored vehicle's diesel engine came to life. The APC quickly jerked forward and turned south onto a concrete road that paralleled Highway 43. Yim sat in the thinly cushioned commander's seat, peering out of his hatch, straining his eyes to see what lay ahead. The cool, moist air refreshed him.

The armored personnel carrier moved slowly as the thick fog reduced visibility to less than a hundred meters. Yim's stomach tightened as the fog made navigation by terrain features all but impossible. At least, he hoped, the fog would hide him from the enemy. With any luck, the South Koreans would mistake him for one of their own and let him pass by in the misty night.

He turned around in his hatch to observe the rest of his headquarters team and make sure they were also moving. The BTR and the T55 tank trailed directly behind, as they had in a dozen practice maneuvers.

The tracks squeaked in the foggy, thick night air as Kim's VTT churned along. Yim followed the road, navigating at short range, knowing that most roads in the Chorwon Valley ran north to south.

He turned to the front and stared through his night vision goggles, a recent and welcome addition to the reconnaissance team's list of equipment. He adjusted the monocular eyepiece as he stood in the open hatch. The goggles were made in Japan and had been reverse engineered from American models. He laughed quietly at the irony that his equipment had been designed by his enemy and sold to his country by his enemy's ally.

"Corporal Kim," Yim said over the intercom system, "did you hear any reports from the long-range recon teams about the enemy on the brigade radio frequency?"

"No, Comrade Captain, not a single report. Would you like me to try to reach them now?"

"No. Just stay tuned to their frequency in case they call us," Yim said. Why hadn't the 820th Corps chief of reconnaissance coordinated the efforts of the long-range recon teams to contact him? The teams were the NKPA's forward eyes. They were deep inside South Korean territory, having been dropped off by AN-2 Colt aircraft and Hughes 500D helicopters the night before the attack. Hundreds of four-man special forces teams had spent days behind South Korean lines, waiting for the right moment to attack. Other teams were to avoid contact and occupy observation posts to aid the advancing North Korean columns. From their high vantage points, these teams were expected to provide the corps with critical intelligence information, vital to the plan of attack.

Yim wondered why he had received so little intelligence information from these teams. Had the enemy killed or captured the long-range recon teams? Was the thick fog hiding the enemy, or had the South Koreans withdrawn? All Yim knew was that the radio was hot with messages from brigade headquarters, urging him to press on quickly and make contact with the enemy's next line of resistance.

KARRUMMP! The rumble of artillery sounded to the far south and west.

"Driver, move off this road at the next turnoff," Yim ordered. "We must get to higher ground along Axis Gom and try to reach the special forces teams by radio."

The VTT moved slowly off the road and onto a dirt trail that traveled southeast across rising ground. Yim peered through his night vision goggles but had a difficult time seeing anything. Empty farmhouses lined the road, and a few abandoned cars were overturned in ditches along the side. Terraced rice paddies and ginseng fields were patchworked between the houses. The driver continued on, able to see only twelve meters in front of his vehicle, even with the aid of his infrared night-driving periscope.

Yim cursed. The laws of physics hadn't changed, and infrared night vision sights, which were good for driving on clear, dark nights, couldn't see through fog and rain.

Yim bounced against the hard circular hatch of the VTT as the vehicle dipped into a shell crater in the road. Moving across rough terrain in a VTT323 is not a pleasant experience; the vehicle is cramped and meant for fighting rather than comfort. The poorly designed suspension system reflected every jolt. The metal sides of the vehicle dug at Yim's ribs with every bump, telegraphing endless pains into his aching body.

The trail narrowed and became more difficult as it zigzagged up the eastern side of the Chorwon Valley. The trails shown on Yim's excellent Japanese-made satellite maps appeared trafficable, but the reality was something else. The problem of the narrow roads was exacerbated by the challenge of navigating in the dark and the thick fog. Yim couldn't use a compass in his armored vehicle—a compass doesn't work around so much metal—and he couldn't take the time to dismount every few minutes to check his orientation.

As Yim's vehicle ascended a hill, Corporal Kim tried several times to reach the special forces teams, but with no success. At least, Yim thought, this difficult route and the thick fog provide security from enemy observation. Yim looked behind and saw the BTR and T55 trailing.

Yim's APC stopped abruptly.

"Comrade Captain, which way?" the driver asked.

The trail came to a fork. Yim checked his map and saw that the trail to the right appeared to offer the only route that paralleled Highway 43.

"Stand by," Yim ordered as he waited for the BTR and tank to catch up. He studied his map and hoped that he had guessed his location correctly. In the thick fog, without any real reference, he was becoming more confused. Maybe he should have stayed on Highway 43. "Turn right," he said finally.

The VTT clanked down the dark trail, moving less than five miles an hour. The narrow road soon entered a complex of farmhouses and huts of various sizes. The houses came right up to the road. Two more damaged cars painted a scene of a mad evacuation that must have occurred the day before. Yim thought that his APC ran over a body in the road, but it was too hard to tell in the fog. After a few tense minutes, Yim saw fewer buildings and then none. The column moved onto a muddy trail that led down a steep hill.

Yim's APC moved slowly. A wrong turn would drop them off into a ditch or could lead to a time-consuming dead end. Yim's column moved dutifully behind, as if tied by a tether.

"Six-Two-Zero, this is Six-Two-One. Report Line Two, time now. No enemy contact," the VTT323 group on Axis Nukday reported.

"Affirmative, Six-Two-One. This is Six-Two-Zero. Continue mission," Yim answered, pleased that his plan was working. "The enemy must have run away."

"Six-Two-Zero, this is Red Six," Colonel Yi's powerful voice resonated over the radio speakers. The brigade commander's tone demanded an immediate answer.

"Red Six, this is Six-Two-Zero. Over," Yim replied, nervous that the brigade commander was listening to his internal communications.

"I have monitored your transmissions. Long-range recon team communications are ineffective. The identification of the enemy's defenses is up to you. Have you seen anything that would designate their main line of resistance?"

"Negative, Red Six," Yim replied. "We are still looking . . . heading south."

"Move rapidly," Colonel Yi ordered. "Corps headquarters reports that the fascists are withdrawing on all fronts. I don't want to give them a chance to set up a strong defense."

"Affirmative, Red Six," Yim replied. He struggled with his map, trying to determine his location. In the thick fog it was nearly impossible, but he knew that the commander would require frequent updates on his unit's location. Frustrated, he guessed at it. "I am continuing the mission. I am one thousand meters short of Report Line Two. All clear. No sign of the enemy. He has abandoned this sector. Over."

"Continue to move south. Find the enemy. This is Red Six. Out."

Yim took a deep breath. Every time he talked with Colonel Yi he felt uneasy, as if he were a truant pupil being upbraided by a mean schoolmaster. It wasn't that Colonel Yi was his commander and the center of all authority. It was more than that. It was as if the man thought of Yim as little more than a tool with little worth to be expended to accomplish the mission. Yim was a captain, a member of a proud unit. His reconnaissance company was his family, and he resented the colonel's tone. But, of course, he always obeyed.

Yim shook off his thoughts and focused on his movement. A few moments later, the team on Axis Nukday reported that they were a thousand meters north of Report Line Two. There was no sign of the enemy anywhere along Axis Nukday, just more smashed civilian cars and a couple of overturned military trucks. Indications of the enemy's complete withdrawal seemed overwhelming.

Yim's VTT323 moved forward, farther to the south. The terrain was not cooperating. The ground was a series of rough fingers that jutted east-west off the main mountain ridge. To traverse this ground Yim had to roll up and down one finger of the mountain after another, or find an east-west trail to get around an impassable finger. Yim felt as though he were on a ship at sea. The constant rocking back and forth across a sea of ridgelines was making him nauseated.

"Six-Two-Six, this is Six-Two-Zero. Situation report. Over."

Yim waited in silence. He tried again, keying his throat microphone for a few extra seconds to lengthen his signal. Still no response. He looked behind him as his APC moved steadily forward. The BTR and the T55 tank trailed close behind, like a parade of geese walking to a pond.

"Six-Two-Zero, this is Six-Two-Nine," the BTR commander following his APC answered. "We read you loud and clear, Comrade Captain."

"Acknowledged, Six-Two-Nine. Six-Two-Zero. Out."

These damned mountains, Yim cursed. Even on this higher

ground, the black hills are blocking my communications. Why aren't the radio retrans units, who were supposed to deploy on high ground to the rear of the main effort, supporting me?

Minutes passed, but they seemed like hours as Yim squinted through his night vision goggles, continuously adjusting the focus. The driver picked his way along the treacherous ground. In the dark and fog, Yim feared that he was becoming hopelessly lost. Axis Gom was too difficult, no matter what the planners had thought when they issued him the reconnaissance plan. The idea of moving to the highway flashed in his mind; it seemed the only way.

7

BATTLE IN THE FOG

For his own sake, and of those around him, a man must be prepared for the awful, shrieking moment of truth when he realizes he is all alone on a hill a thousand miles from home, and that he may be killed in the next second.
—T. R. FEHRENBACH

12:10 A.M., 3 October, alternate command bunker, 2d Infantry Division headquarters, seven kilometers northeast of Seoul, South Korea. Lieutenant Colonel Steve Wallace needed to see on the other side of the hill, but he was blind and he knew it. Without sensors from satellites and spy aircraft, his intelligence system relied largely on reports from the forward units. Most of these reports were confused and incomplete. The picture that was emerging, however, was not impossible to guess. He didn't need anyone to tell him what was happening to the friendly forces; he could see the graphics on the map. Confusion and disorder had a new spelling, the lieutenant colonel thought. It was spelled D-E-F-E-A-T.

Wallace picked up a note and read the latest report from Major Beady, the assistant G3. Colonel Hassay, the chief of staff, had been evacuated yesterday afternoon by wheeled ambulance along with forty-three other wounded. The convoy was guarded by a single squad of MPs. On their way south the convoy was ambushed by a North Korean sniper company that had infiltrated behind the lines. No one survived the attack.

Wallace crumpled up the report, closed his tired eyes, and shook his head.

The air inside the command post was stale. It smelled of burned coffee, mildew, and unwashed bodies. Officers and sergeants scurried around, dropping off reports and answering phones and radios. The building hummed with computer printers and electronic noises. Somebody in the back of the room cursed that his radio was inoperative.

"Okay, what do you have for me?" Maj. Gen. George Schmidt said as he walked into the briefing room and took a seat at a long wooden table.

Major Jim Cooper, the assistant division intelligence officer, stood at a large map board of Korea that hung on the wall. Cooper placed a red enemy marker south of the ROK's second line of defense in the Chorwon Valley.

Schmidt, commanding general of the 2d Infantry Division, took a seat opposite Cooper. Lieutenant Colonel Wallace sat at the general's left. Wallace could sense that the other two men were as tired as he was. Their faces showed the strain of having to make important decisions on too little sleep.

"Have you seen the report on the casualty convoy?" Wallace asked.

"I've seen it," Schmidt glowered. "Now let's see what we can do to strike back at these bastards."

Wallace nodded and gave Cooper the signal to start the briefing.

"The ROK/U.S. counterfire effort has not been as successful as we had hoped, General," said Major Cooper like a doctor relating the latest condition of a dying patient. "The enemy destroyed a lot of our artillery in the surprise attack. In addition, his special forces hit most of our prestocked ammunition dumps hard. We're running out of artillery ammunition."

"Okay, I know the counterfire fight has failed, so tell me about the ROKs," Schmidt said, looking at the map. "Do we know they've broken? CFC hasn't reported any penetrations of the second line of defense in the Chorwon Valley."

"Sir, the ROKs are withdrawing in the Chorwon," Wallace announced. He winced in pain as his shoulder throbbed. His left arm rested in a green sling that was tied in a square knot behind his neck. "They've lost the equivalent of three divisions. They're withdrawing what they can from the Chorwon to defend south of Uijonbu."

Schmidt shook his head in disbelief. "Three entire divisions destroyed?"

"Sir, many of them have probably gone to ground in squad- and platoon-sized units. They may still be fighting, but they aren't holding back the enemy's advance," Wallace said.

Major Cooper moved to the side of the map and handed the general an empty coffee cup. While the general held the cup steady, Cooper poured some of the lukewarm brew from his metal thermos. "It didn't help much that the enemy's attack coincided with the transition of their brigades on the DMZ."

"Damn," the general cursed, his face a canvas of disbelief. "The ROKs picked a lousy time to rotate units."

"There's no doubt that this had something to do with the timing of the attack," Wallace replied. "This one was well planned."

"And, sir, the NKPA doesn't have to clear out all the ROKs in each defensive line," Cooper interjected. "As long as they fix the defenders to their bunkers and keep the roads open, the NKPA has a clear axis of attack to Seoul."

"Have we found out what's wrong with our electronic systems?" the general asked, looking at Wallace. "Why isn't our global positioning satellite system working?"

"This report explains the whole deal," Wallace replied, handing the general a manila folder. "It appears that the North Koreans aren't as technologically unaware as we thought. They purchased the means to desynchronize our GPS system. They used a special Japanese commercial satellite communications system to scramble it. It's kind of like having a computer virus in your personal computer scramble all your data. The satellites then shared the virus, and the entire system went out of action."

"You mean they used our own satellites against us?"

"That's about it, General," said Cooper. "Remember in May 1998 when one satellite went down and turned off all the pagers in the United States? Well, the North Koreans have somehow done the same thing. We rely on the GPS system to navigate, plot artillery, and synchronize our frequency-hopping FM radios. Scrambling the system was a brilliant way to temporarily desynchronize our command and control. When they scrambled the system, it affected the U.S. military worldwide."

"When will we have this fixed?"

"No way of knowing, sir," Cooper answered. "Our side is working now to debug the scramble."

"Damn. What's the latest on our casualties?" the general asked, staring at the map as if he could stop the enemy with his glance.

"Heavy casualties, sir," Cooper said grimly. "We pulled back most of the division out of range of their artillery. G1 reports that our division has lost four hundred and fifty-three confirmed killed in action. We've got about five hundred wounded."

Schmidt shook his head and paused for a long moment. Wallace could see the impact of the loss of life, as if the general was seeing the face of each lost soldier parade in front of his mind's eye.

"I want to hit them back, Steve," the general said slowly, with emphasis on the word *hit*, "but the ROKs need three days at least before they can launch any kind of counterattack. I need to slow them down. I need to buy twenty-four hours."

One day. Wallace stared at the operations map. The war had started only two days ago. Since then the Combined Forces Command, the ROK/U.S. headquarters responsible for leading the defense of South Korea, had become a shambles. The enemy's surprise attack was well planned and executed. The senior leadership of the ROK/U.S. alliance was the main target of the enemy's suicide attacks. Seven senior generals and dozens of the essential members of the Combined Forces Command staff had been killed or wounded.

It was all happening so fast. Wallace realized that these attacks had almost sealed the fate of South Korea. Most of the critical headquarters were now deploying to alternate facilities in the southern portion of South Korea. In short, the Combined Forces Command was in no shape to provide command, control, advice, or analysis. The 2d Infantry Division, hard hit itself, was now under the command of a ROK corps that was struggling to get organized and recover from the surprise attack. The division was, for the time being, on its own.

To add to the pandemonium, Seoul was in a panic and the South Korean government was in utter disorder. Dozens of Nodong rockets had hit the city, blasting huge sections of the urban area to rubble. Much of the city was on fire. For thousands of people in South Korea it was a difficult time, but for thousands of others it was their last time. Refugees jammed the roadways to the south in a mad, undisciplined dash to get away from the bombs and missiles.

Wallace knew that the ROK Army was also in a frenzy. Antimilitary sentiment before the North Korean attack had placed the country's military at a severe disadvantage. Rehearsals and mobilization practice exercises that should have been conducted were canceled to reduce political opposition. Some reserve units had failed to arrive on time; no one wanted to call it desertion. Confusion and lack of command and control had hopelessly delayed the mobilization of the republic's reserve infantry and artillery divisions—key factors in the defense of the capital. The time required to mobilize enough force to push the enemy back, by Wallace's best guess, was four to six days. By that time the North Koreans would be having breakfast in Suwon.

Wallace rubbed his eyes and stared at the map. The Chorwon Valley defenses were a mess. The enemy had penetrated the ROKs first and second lines of defense. The enemy was committing his armored forces, a major indication that the communists sensed that the crack in the dam was about to give way. The major danger was now along Highway 43.

Higher headquarters, again, wouldn't believe Wallace's assessment. The belief that the North Koreans had committed their exploitation forces was not accepted by experts in Japan or at CINCPAC, but most of these experts were safe in Japan or Hawaii, giving their advice over the telephone. Their ideas were based on a long war scenario, where North Korea mobilized all its forces. Wallace knew that this had not occurred. He saw the North Koreans aiming for a quick, lightning type of victory. Why else would they have risked a surprise attack without calling up all their reserves? They must believe that they could win in a week to ten days. With the enemy's success so far, Wallace anguished, nobody could dispute that claim.

At least the north hasn't used chemical weapons, Wallace observed. If they had, the casualties would have been catastrophic. Such an enemy attack, using a chemical nerve agent, would have demanded a lethal counterresponse from the United States. Because the United States no longer stored chemical weapons, there was only one other means, and Wallace didn't want to think about that option. His sense of humanity didn't wish that on anyone, even the North Koreans.

"We need to hit the North Koreans hard, stun them, and slow their advance," Schmidt said as he stared at the operations map. "I talked to the CINC a few minutes ago on the TACSAT. The ROK casualties have been heavy. Civilian casualties are even higher. He's concerned that the ROKs might start negotiations with the north and stop fighting. If this happens, the North Koreans win, pure and simple."

"Well, sir, since the beginning of the North Korean Army, the basic tactics have changed very little. A penetration force composed mostly of infantry and supported with massed artillery causes heavy attrition of the enemy's defenses and cracks the line. Then a mobile tank and mechanized force rush forward through the gap to secure a decisive political objective—in this case, Seoul."

"They don't have the force, or the time, to take Seoul," the general replied.

"Yes, sir. Their plan must be to cut off Seoul from the rest of the country and hold the city hostage," Cooper offered. "Twelve million people, all in range of North Korean artillery, would make quite a bargaining chip."

Schmidt bit his lip and paused for a moment. "How do we slow the bastard down?"

Wallace shrugged. "Most of the division is still moving south, regrouping after the beating we took in our base camps. We lost a dozen attack helicopters on their airfields, and we won't have any significant airpower for another two days. Right now, General, we don't have a damn thing to put in their way."

"Find me something," the general said, obviously annoyed. "Scrape together some units that can fight and get them north. We need to buy some time or we're going to lose this war."

The briefing room grew silent as the general studied the map. He pulled a bag of tobacco from his pocket and filled his empty pipe. "Do we have communications with the 1st Brigade?"

"Communications are a nightmare," Wallace confessed. "We don't have mobile subscriber equipment working right now, and our FM communications are out of range. All of the radio retransmission sites have been knocked out by enemy special forces. I've ordered a Blackhawk retrans bird to get comms. We lost one yesterday, but I've got another one standing by on twenty-minute alert."

"Steve, find a way to contact Task Force 2-72 and tell Rodriguez to buy us a day," the general said with determination. "I don't care what you do, but make sure he understands his mission. He's not to allow the enemy to penetrate Highway 43 south of the tank range. Is that clear?"

Wallace nodded.

"He's to fight until I tell him to move," Schmidt continued. "He must buy me twenty-four hours. Withdrawal is not an option."

"If I have to," Wallace promised, nodding, "I'll fly up there myself and deliver the message."

1:00 A.M., 3 October, along Highway 43, five kilometers north of the DMZ in North Korea. The rain fell in a persistent drizzle. Major Chun cursed as he shuddered in the dark mist. His nylon raincoat was slick with water. Tired and hungry, he pulled the hood of his raincoat over his Russian-style steel helmet.

"If the weather continues like this," he said to himself, trying to rationalize some benefit from his discomfort, "it will at least deny the enemy the use of their airpower."

A long line of ammunition trucks and fuel tankers snaked slowly down the center of a narrow, mud-splattered road that led south. The two-lane concrete route was bordered on both sides by rice paddies. Each vehicle moved forward at the mercy of the vehicle in front of it. The convoy stopped abruptly.

Major Chun Yong-ho, the commander of the 136th North Korean People's Army 152mm self-propelled howitzer battalion, shined his flashlight down on his map and calculated the distance and time it would take him to establish his guns in a position in South Korean territory. Whoever was in charge of organizing the march tables for the support of the attack should be shot, he cursed again. Only an idiot would hold up the artillery from making its timing of the march. Gaining time was the all-important factor for achieving the objective of the march. Success comes to the side that knows how to make decisions and deliver strikes the most rapidly. To win time is to win the battle, and he could sense the time slipping away.

Chun's open-topped half-ton utility jeep was at the head of his column. Behind him, eighteen 152mm howitzers squeaked slowly forward, their tracks laying one pad at a time. Chun waited, watching the wipers move slowly back and forth on the windshield of his jeep as the cool, wet night passed.

Chun thought about his wife and two boys. They had a hard life in North Korea. The last year was a dismal time of shortages. Even a major of artillery was rationed barely enough food to survive. During the spring famine period—the *chun-gungki,* as it is called in Korean—there were many sad days when his young boys cried because their bellies were empty. Widespread starvation had brought a modicum of international aid, but the breakdown of the means of distribution and a deteriorating road and train network caused most of this food to rot in warehouses. Well-fed commissars expounded the virtues of eating only one meal a day while Chun's children slowly wasted away.

The Americans were to blame, Chun was told. They were the ultimate enemy that was referred to throughout North Korea by the term *wonsu,* meaning "someone who has killed your father." They had caused the starvation that was gripping the North Korean people by the throat. The Americans hoped to break the people's will and turn North Korea into a slave sweatshop to run their capitalist factories. The only alternative to ignoble defeat and surrender was a war of liberation.

Chun watched the windshield wipers sway back and forth. He slowly nodded off to sleep for a few minutes, then instinctively jolted back to consciousness. Shocked at his own indiscipline, he shook his head and sat straight up in his seat. How long had it been since he last slept? He tried to remember. On 1 October he had spent the entire night in preparation; on 2 October he had fired his batteries all morning and moved all night. Now it was the morning of 3 October—three days without more than a few hours to catnap. There was so much to do, he didn't have time for sleep now. They would all rest soon, in the beds of their enemy's houses, when the Inmun Gun tore down the flags of the southern fascists and their imperialist warmongering American allies.

Chun looked at the luminous hands of his wristwatch—0210. His column of artillery hadn't moved an inch for more than ten minutes. The tiny white slit lights on the back of each truck looked like the eyes of huge animals. They seemed to defy the major to move them. Frustrated with the delay, Chun jumped out of his jeep and dashed toward the left side of the Zil-151 cargo truck blocking his way.

"Idiot, get this damned truck out of the way," Major Chun screamed.

The big five-ton truck didn't move. The windshield wipers flicked back and forth madly, making an annoying racket. The driver looked down on the major from inside the cab with the window rolled up. A confused look of disbelief and impotence registered on his face.

The major jerked open the door to the cab. "My column has priority movement on this road. You will pull your vehicle off to the side of the road immediately or I will have you arrested."

The two young North Korean privates in the cab of the truck looked paralyzed with fear. "But comrade officer—sir—our platoon commander . . . ," the driver stammered.

"I am a major in the artillery," Chun said, the fire in his words striking the privates like projectiles shot from cannons. "I have eighteen 152mm self-propelled howitzers behind you. There are six battalions of artillery behind me. Your truck is stopping the movement of the corps' artillery group. Move off the road now or my howitzers will push you off."

The private shrugged. "Yes, sir."

Carefully the truck moved against the left rim of the glistening, water-splashed road. Chun walked forward to the next truck, and the next, ordering each one to move aside. He stomped through the puddles of water as if he were a man possessed by some powerful demon. Finally he came to an intersection manned by three North Korean security guards. All were wearing white armbands that designated them as military police. Trucks were moving slowly down the intersecting road, effectively halting the column that blocked Chun's way.

"Who is in charge here?" Chun shouted, his voice full of energy from the altercation with the drivers of the ammunition trucks.

"I am," a voice in the dark replied. "Who are you?"

"I am Major Chun, the commander of the 136th Howitzer Battalion," Chun shouted loudly enough to be heard over the noise of the passing truck column. "My howitzers are the lead elements of the 820th Corps Artillery Group."

"Show me your orders, Comrade Major," the voice said with a tone that displayed a policeman's predilection for issuing rather than receiving instructions.

"You will immediately stop this truck column and pass my artillery forward," Chun demanded, visibly incensed, as he handed the guard written orders.

The dark figure turned on his red-filtered flashlight. He quickly scanned the paper, then saluted.

"Yes, Comrade Major, at once," the voice responded quickly with a dramatically different and more respectful tone of voice. "We have been waiting for your artillery. Everything is going slower than planned."

"Then stop wasting time and do as you are told," the major howled.

The military police sergeant saluted again and abruptly barked orders to the soldiers conducting traffic control of the intersection. The military police immediately stopped the lead vehicle of the next serial, had a short, sharp-worded conversation with the vehicle commander, and stopped the column moving on the intersecting road.

"Your convoy has priority," the sergeant shouted. "You may proceed."

Chun turned back, facing the front of his column. For a few seconds he waved madly with a red-filtered flashlight to signal his vehicles forward. His jeep arrived; he hopped in and slammed the thin metal side door shut. Slowly the howitzers cleared the trucks on the left side of the road and proceeded down the road to the south.

Major Chun saw the faint flash of explosions in the distance. There was a battle going on up ahead, and he was determined to get his guns in position. The artillery, behind schedule and out of range of the front, was at least moving again, he consoled himself. He looked at the overcast sky, devoid of stars from the cloud cover, and hoped that his howitzers could make the required twelve kilometers before morning.

3:00 A.M., 3 October, defensive position in the eastern Chorwon Valley, ten kilometers south of the DMZ in South Korea. They say that the waiting is the worst part of war. Short of battle, which Pvt. Jamie Emerson hadn't experienced yet, they were right. Right now, he wished he was anywhere but here.

Dark clouds hung low over the valley, blocking out the stars. The rain-filled night had been ominous with the noise of artillery shells. Now, in the early hours of morning, only an occasional shell lit the pitch-black valley. A busy highway that was normally frequented by civilian cars, buses, or numerous ten-ton dump trucks—affectionately called terminators by American soldiers serving in Korea—was empty. The civilians had long since left the area.

Emerson hadn't slept—really slept—for three days. The thick, moist air chilled the young tanker manning the 7.62mm machine gun on top of the tank. He shivered in his open hatch, as much from the cold as from his thoughts. He feared that the gentle hum of the tank's external power generator would give away their position. He worried about being surprised. He feared that a North Korean would lunge out in the dark and kill him and his crew.

Emerson coughed quietly, covering his mouth with his gloved hand. Nomex fire-retardant clothing covered almost his entire body. His one-piece tanker's suit and gloves—and the balaclava that covered his face and revealed only his mouth, nose, and eyes, like the wool pullover caps worn by northern folks in winter—were carefully designed by the American tank crew equipment experts to prevent flash burns in the event of a tank fire. Because the 120mm main gun ammunition of the M1A2 tank was encased in combustible cartridges, with a powder combination that ignited instantly if a spark touched it off, protective clothing was worn by every tanker. The Nomex clothing, Emerson was told, was heat resistant up to 700 degrees Fahrenheit. He hoped he wouldn't have the opportunity to verify this.

Emerson checked the ammunition belt that fed into his M240 machine gun, exactly as he had been taught by Sergeant Hardee. His hands trembled as he felt the cold, sharp points of the armor-piercing incendiary bullets. He was scared, no doubt about it. He never thought it would be like this.

He had, of course, envisioned battle. On television and in the movies he had seen the terror of battle, the blazing fire of machine guns, and the loud roar of cannon. He had read about battles and imagined his role and reactions in heroic proportions. In his youthful imagination, he was always in the central role of the conflict. He would be an invincible warrior, like John Wayne, Sylvester Stallone, or Steven Seagal, winning the day single-handedly against terrible odds.

Ever since he was a small boy, Emerson had wanted to enlist in the military. He burned to be a part of the pride, the pageantry, and the importance that he saw in military service. The youngest in a family with three sisters, he viewed warfare as his manly right, a task that made him distinctly different from his siblings. It all seemed so silly now.

His father, a construction worker, had died shortly after Jamie's birth in a building accident. His mother, a strong-willed Kentucky woman with a great sense of the real nature of things, had worked hard to raise Jamie and his three older sisters. She discouraged Jamie from considering the military as anything but a waste of time. Her family had no tradition in the military. Her convictions against joining the service were strong. Throughout his high school years, she had tried to channel his energies toward college. She wanted him to earn a degree toward a profession and enter the business world.

But college was not in the cards, at least not yet, Emerson promised himself. Partly out of rebellion, partly to leave Kentucky, and partly to find himself, he volunteered for the

U.S. Army two months after graduating from high school. The recruiters gave him two choices: infantry or armor. It didn't take long for him to make up his mind. He knew he didn't want to walk anywhere he could ride. He chose the tank corps.

He had only one problem after he enlisted: He had to tell his mother. To his surprise she took the news well. She was upset, to be sure, and wailed about his missed opportunities, but something in her voice told Jamie that she was proud of his determination. Reluctantly she blessed his actions. On the day he was ordered to report to Fort Knox, she drove him all the way in their 1986 Ford station wagon.

Emerson's thoughts were interrupted by the sharp crash of artillery several kilometers to the north and resonating in the valley. Emerson looked into the fog with trepidation. The enemy was coming closer each minute; Emerson could feel it. Would he measure up? Would he meet the test of battle? He had performed well so far. He felt that he was a valued member of a team—his crew—led by the indomitable Sergeant Hardee.

Sergeant First Class Nathaniel Hardee was Emerson's great source of strength. In a few short days Hardee had become like the father Emerson never knew. The sergeant looked and played the part of the professional soldier. A combat veteran, Hardee was God on earth to Emerson. The tough sergeant knew what he was doing. Emerson felt that he would make it as long as Hardee was there.

Emerson was surprised when Hardee had defended him to his company first sergeant for the round that was fired out of impact at the MPRC the other day. When Emerson found out that a television crew had videotaped the incident, he was even more surprised that he wasn't punished. Loading the wrong round had been his fault. Emerson confessed to Hardee that he had gotten confused in all the excitement. Instead of being punished, Hardee chewed him out and took the blame for the entire incident. He told the first sergeant and company commander that he was responsible for his crew. The company commander agreed.

After seeing such a display of loyalty, Emerson admired Hardee even more. He didn't even mind that Hardee made him load training rounds all evening, one hundred times, under the sergeant's watchful eye. Then just a few hours later, the enemy artillery slammed into the tents at the tank range.

That night seemed like a world away. Right now, Emerson thought to himself, I'd give anything to be back home, safe and dry in Kentucky.

Emerson's mind buzzed with a swirl of ideas and emotions. He was worried, anxious, excited, tired, and scared all at the same time. He suddenly realized that he really didn't know himself very well.

A lightning bolt of panic shot through his mind as several shells fell high on a hill to the northeast, their crimson billows illuminating the far-off ridge. My God, he thought, they're coming. The war is coming.

His hand glanced over the wet metal feed tray of his machine gun. All he could think was that he was an unknown quantity, untried and untested. He wondered how everyone else could remain so calm. He wondered if his crew suspected him of being afraid, if they questioned his ability to stand up to the test.

"See anything, 'cruit?" Hardee asked over the intercom as if he were reading Emerson's mind.

"No, Sergeant," Emerson replied a little too loudly as he forced the words out of his throat. Somehow, when Hardee called him a 'cruit—slang for new recruit—it seemed more like a badge of honor than a term of ridicule. "Just a couple of shells landing on the hill to the north."

"Yeah, nothing to worry about," Hardee remarked calmly over the tank's intercom set. Emerson marveled at how cool the tank commander sounded. He was in control. Nothing could shake Sergeant Hardee. "Those shells fell near the northern edge of our engagement area."

Hardee, standing in the tank commander's station with the hatch locked open, looked over at his loader. "Do you understand how we designate direct fires in the Dragon Force?"

"Kind of," Emerson replied, whispering into the microphone attached to his CVC—his tank crewman's helmet.

"Our engagement areas, or EAs, are the large, open areas we expect to kill the enemy in," Hardee explained like a teacher in school. "They're designated on our maps from one line of visibility to another. We name them after states. This one is Maine. It goes north from the ridge where those shells fell to a line a couple of hundred meters behind us. When we see the enemy coming, I'll identify their location by the cardinal directions— north, south, east, west—or center, depending on the enemy's location in the EA. Got it?"

"I think so," Emerson said, glad to get his mind off the thought of his conduct under fire. "The shells that just landed fell in EA Maine, northeast.

"Right," Hardee replied, with emphasis on the word to show his satisfaction with his pupil. "Now add to that the elevation. Alpha terrain is the valley, bravo terrain is the ascending slope, and charlie terrain is the near top to the actual top."

"EA Maine, northeast, charlie," Emerson remarked.

"You got it, kid," the veteran sergeant answered, a kind laugh in his voice. "Keep that up and you may make private first class."

Emerson smiled. Maybe everything would be all right.

A great, strange silence overcame him. He hated the silence. He wanted, he needed, to talk, to be reassured, but there was nothing to say.

A multiple volley of artillery reverberated in the hills. The explosions echoed in the valley like a wave hitting a rocky cliff. Suddenly four more shells detonated in plain view, on the crest of the far northeast ridge.

My God, thought Emerson as he watched the shells slam against the northeast side of EA Maine, they're coming.

3:40 A.M., 3 October, eastern Chorwon Valley, eight kilometers south of the DMZ in South Korea. Danger flickered and blinked in the air like the twinkle of a burning candle. The reconnaissance commander bravely moved forward. What else could he do? He had his orders.

A critical bridge along Highway 43 had been destroyed. Yim had searched in vain for a bypass. After several hours he found a single trail that his VTTs and tanks could travel, and he was back on his main direction of attack. He radioed the location of the destroyed bridge to his commander, Colonel Yi. The commander would have to fix the bridge on Highway 43 before the brigade could continue the attack.

A wave of artillery explosions banged off in the hills far to Yim's left. They were North Korean shells, Yim was sure of that, and they were falling in a wide, scattered pattern of fire. Shells had smashed all over during the night, some falling closer than he wanted, with no effect other than to strain his already taut nerves. The pompous gunners of the proud North Korean artillery were trying to win the war by shooting blindfolded, thought Yim. The damn forward observers can't see their targets in the fog, so the artillery fires by map to prove they are actively supporting the plan.

"Damn this blasted fog and our gloriously stupid artillery," the North Korean captain cursed. The fog was slowing him down to a crawl, and he feared that his own artillery fire might fall on him any minute.

A single artillery shell detonated nearby. The ground shook, but Yim could see only a brief splash of light up ahead in the fog. "See that, Kim?" said Yim to his radio operator. "If the enemy doesn't shoot us, our own artillery probably will."

"Comrade Captain," Kim announced, "the brigade commander is asking for an update. He reports that the engineers will take several hours to fix the bridge. He wants us to continue our reconnaissance."

"Maybe we should ask him to stop shooting at us first," Yim said, shaking his head. Headquarters seemed convinced that the fascists were on the run. He hoped that they were right, because every increase in speed caused greater risk of falling into an enemy ambush. Obedient to the letter of his instructions, Yim ordered his men to move faster, but he knew that it was an order without substance. Drivers who could not see their hand in front of their face knew it was suicide to rush down roads and mountain trails, even if an enemy wasn't waiting in ambush. To compensate, the captain did what he had learned to do in training—report to his superiors what they wanted to hear.

The fog thinned out as the night wore on, and Yim's company moved farther south. Around 3:50 A.M. the visibility improved; Yim could see almost three hundred meters. No one had heard from the special forces teams along the route of advance, so Yim moved forward like a blind man in a dark room.

He needed information on the enemy's defenses. He needed a prisoner, or an enemy map.

"We should be at Report Line Two soon," Capt. Yim Ch'un-chu announced with a lack of confidence that was obvious to his radio operator. He was still six hundred meters from the attack axis. "Tell him we are back on the attack axis, continuing the mission."

Yim's eyes strained to see through the fog. The advance guard battalion was far behind him. He could talk to them only intermittently. The FM radios required line-of-sight contact, which was problematic at best in this rough terrain. Yim's commander, however, expected him to reach his reconnaissance objectives and overcome all obstacles. Colonel Yi was not a man to be denied.

This added pressure and Yim's tight, vehicle helmet made his head ache. Increasingly, things were getting on his nerves. First, he was out front, all alone. The destroyed bridge cut him off from any support he might have received from the advance guard battalion. To make matters worse, he had received no assistance from the dozens of special forces teams that were expected to help guide him forward. Second, he wasn't sure if he was making the right decisions. He worried that he might have made a mistake by bypassing the destroyed bridge and getting too far ahead of the advance guard. Was he moving too fast down the wide, four-lane highway without first checking the flanks? The brigade commander solved his dilemma by ordering him to keep going and move faster.

"All reports indicate that the enemy is in full retreat," Yim said, more as a hope than as a statement of fact. In his country, he had lived all his life in a society that believed that if it was officially reported as being so, it was. Still, he worried. "Corporal, keep your eyes open for the enemy. The fascists may have left units behind to ambush us."

The VTT323 moved south along Highway 43 as a wind from the south thinned the fog, allowing Yim to see almost four hundred meters with his night vision goggles. He sensed danger. Thinking quickly he ordered the driver to exit the highway and take a secondary road that paralleled Highway 43. Carefully, at about five miles per hour, the VTT moved south in the fog; the rest of Yim's element trailed right behind.

"Driver, stop," Yim ordered into his throat mike. He focused the night vision goggles on a hill three hundred meters to his left front. In the thinning fog Yim saw the silhouette of an armored personnel carrier. "It looks like a South Korean K200 APC."

"What do you want to do, Comrade Captain?" Corporal Kim asked.

"Maybe we've reached the forward edge of the enemy's counter-reconnaissance screen," said Yim. "Driver, engine off."

The armored personnel carrier became quiet. The trail vehicles halted behind their leader and quickly shut off their engines.

"Comrade Captain, I see no security around the vehicle. He is an easy target," Private Hwang, the assistant driver, said with glee.

"Yes, and too valuable to bypass," Yim said, hesitating to think what he should do. "Corporal Kim, come up and man the machine gun. Hwang, you grab the RPG rocket launcher. We will pay a visit to our enemy. I need information."

"Nam chim," Hwang replied, eager to go hunting for the first kill of the night.

"They look like they're sleeping to me," Yim said as he clicked off the safety on his AK-47 assault rifle. "Kim, cover us with the machine gun. Hwang, I need information. I want to take anyone inside alive."

Hwang nodded. Yim and Hwang gathered their gear and quietly dismounted from their APC. They huddled together by the side of the VTT for a few minutes as Yim worked out their angle of approach.

"Hwang, it looks like he's facing to the south. We'll slowly walk up this hill to our right and get within fifty meters. He may think we're South Korean. If I run into trouble, shoot him with the RPG," Yim ordered.

"Yes, Comrade Captain," Hwang whispered.

The two men walked slowly in a crouch as they worked their way over the rocky ground toward the South Korean APC. The night grew suddenly quiet. Yim heard his heart beating faster and faster as they got closer.

Hwang grinned a white toothy smile. Yim pulled his AK-47 bayonet out of its scabbard and attached it to his assault rifle.

The South Korean K200 was directly in front of them, engine off. Yim heard voices whispering in Korean. If only he could pull open the door, he might capture them all.

Yim inched forward, his AK-47 thrust forward, listening to the heavy noise of his own breathing. Hwang knelt to his left rear with the RPG on his shoulder.

Yim moved to the door. With a loud creak, the heavy metal back door of the K200 opened. A red light flashed on Yim's face, and he fired automatically at the open door. The green tracers from his AK-47 tore into the dark figure that stooped in the doorway of the armored vehicle. Other tracer rounds flashed against the armored back of the APC. With a muffled cry, the South Korean soldier fell out of the vehicle onto the ground.

Another soldier inside the APC fired at Yim.

Yim dived backward, away from the enemy's bullets, firing a full burst from his AK-47 as he fell.

Instinctively, Hwang fired the RPG. In a bright flash, the missile shot right into the side of the K200. The high-explosive warhead detonated inside, searing everything in its path. A tremendous shower of sparks and burning aluminum shot up through the hatches.

Yim rolled away and lay in a ditch as the force of the blast swept over him. In the next moment the K200's fuel and ammunition ignited. The exploding APC illuminated the surrounding area with bright orange flames. Yim hugged the cold, wet mud, waiting for the explosions to subside. Finally they ended and Yim stood up.

Black smoke poured out of the burning APC. Nothing was left of the crew. Hwang had aimed his shot well.

The body of the man Yim had shot had been thrown near the ditch that Yim had been lying in. Yim quickly searched the dead man's pockets, but he came up empty. No map, no information. He went through the man's wallet. In the light of the burning APC, he saw the pictures of the soldier's family and friends.

The bloody body in front of Captain Yim revealed a young man, not more than nineteen. A sense of painful remorse engulfed Yim as he contemplated the death of fellow Koreans by his own hand. He had never considered the enemy as men. Now he saw them as human beings, much like himself and his own soldiers. Yim looked at the bloody face and wondered about the man who was alive only seconds before.

The remorse didn't last long. Years of training kicked in to overpower his guilt. He remembered that the South Korean fascists were the cause of his people's suffering. He released his pity for the dead enemy soldiers and concentrated on the mission. Suddenly he was focused again. If he wanted to live, if he ever wanted to go home, he had to win. Winning became his driving force. Winning at all costs.

"Hwang, let's go," Yim shouted. The two men picked up their weapons and ran back to the VTT323. The glow of the burning South Korean armored vehicle flickered in the dark night.

"Good job, Comrade Captain," Corporal Kim replied as the two climbed back into the cramped VTT323. "Was there any sign of other vehicles?"

"No, he was all alone," Yim answered.

"First kill of the morning. We will be heroes for this action," Hwang said proudly, hoping to receive an award for gallantry in battle.

"Right," Yim said soberly, putting on his crewman's helmet and connecting the cord of his throat mike to talk on the intercom. "We needed a prisoner, but it couldn't be helped. We must move forward. We've wasted valuable time."

The sound of artillery fire echoed in the hills far to the west.

5:10 A.M., 3 October, defensive position, eastern Chorwon Valley, South Korea. Sergeant Hardee rested uncomfortably in the commander's seat of his M1A2 tank. His tank commander's hatch was partially closed, in the open protection position. The half-open hatch allowed him to see out and yet covered him from rain and—its more important design factor—artillery shrapnel. Dressed in his Nomex uniform, Hardee had his neck and most of his face covered in a balaclava, and gloves covered his hands. His CVC helmet padded him as he leaned his forehead against the wall of the tank.

We're ready, he thought as he looked at the dark figure of his loader, Private Emerson, sitting to his left. Below him, at his knees, sat his gunner, Corporal Oh. Oh was alert, looking through his excellent thermal sights, peering into the gloom of the early-morning fog and drizzle.

Sergeant Hardee coughed. His throat ached from the damp air. In another life, in another time, Sgt. Nathaniel Hardee might have been a blacksmith. He was a big man with a big head. His thick arms seemed perfect for gripping a forge hammer. He struggled to be comfortable in the cramped confines of the tank commander's station of his M1A2.

"Sarge, how many of our guys got killed yesterday?" Hernandez asked solemnly over the intercom.

"I don't know, kid," the sergeant answered seriously. "Don't think about it."

The tank's intercom was silent for a few minutes. Hardee could hear the steady hum of the external unit that powered the M1A2's fire control system while the engine was off. Thank God for our auxiliary power generators, he thought. Fuel was now more important than ammunition.

"Sarge, aren't we kind of far away from the rest of the company?" Private Emerson said, filling up the silence.

"Look, I've explained this to you guys before," the veteran sergeant snapped. He was tired and irritable, but he quickly took a deep breath. If the kids are nervous, he thought, it doesn't help to bite their heads off. "Look, Emerson, in this terrain we'll fight in the valleys. That means we have to defend in depth to gain security so we can shoot and scoot. Each company sends out a section forward of the main defense. This gives us a chance to detect the enemy early and pick off his reconnaissance."

"What about those mine things?" Hernandez asked.

Hardee looked at the demolition clackers hanging on the side of his tank commander's station. "When the right moment comes, I'll press these clackers and set off three MOPMs. The mines will block the narrow point in the valley, and we'll have North Koreans for breakfast."

"Oh," Hernandez answered. "Kind of like shutting the door behind them, huh?"

"That's the idea. Now, you need to get some sleep. Three up and one down, those are the orders."

"Sarge, I can't sleep," Hernandez complained over his intercom.

"Then keep your eyes peeled forward. We may be seeing something soon. The platoon leader says they're on the way."

Sergeant Hardee peered out into the foggy gray morning through the thermal sight of his CITV. The engagement area, an open stretch of valley traversed by a paved four-lane highway, was as empty as a graveyard. On the first day the road had been jammed with desperate civilians. On the second day, as the civilians thinned out, ROK Army vehicles started fleeing south. Hardee saw almost a hundred vehicles carrying wounded and dazed soldiers on top of tanks and artillery guns. Many were crammed into overcrowded trucks. Most of the ROKs were pretty shot up. From the sound of the shelling he had heard to the north, Hardee could imagine just how rough it must have been.

Soon, Hardee knew, the North Koreans would arrive. The thing he feared most was the enemy's dismounted infantry. In this weather, a determined infiltrator could pop up on top of the tank before you knew it. He rubbed his tired eyes. When, he thought, was the last time he had a good night's sleep?

"Emerson, pop your hatch and keep a keen eye out for any movement," Hardee said to his loader. "If you see anybody walking out there, sound off immediately. Just remember, C33 is off to our left."

"Wilco, Sarge," Emerson responded. His anxious voice cracked as he made his reply.

The air was heavy with moisture as the drizzle continued. The seconds passed by slowly.

"Sergeant, I see a vehicle moving toward us," Corporal Oh said over the tank intercom system. "It looks like an enemy APC."

Hardee locked on with his CITV. The tank turret slewed in the direction of the threat.

"Crew, action front," Sergeant Hardee shouted. The tank commander of C34 looked with tired eyes through the green-tinted thermal sight of his M1A2. "Good eyes, Oh."

"Loader up, HEAT loaded," the excited voice of Private Emerson shouted. "And I mean HEAT."

"Sarge, you want me to crank up the engine?" Private Hernandez asked over the tank intercom.

"Negative," Hardee said, listening to the mild purr of his tank's external power unit. "Not yet. We have to save our fuel."

The tank commander quickly grabbed the override control and tracked the movement of the enemy vehicle, maintaining the crosshairs of his reticle on the center of mass of the enemy vehicle. He pushed the thumb button on his firing handle to engage the laser. The green digital range display at the bottom of his thermal sight read 2300.

Sergeant Hardee looked at his map. "Emerson, check the plugger grid again."

Emerson read the LCD screen of the global positioning satellite receiver that the tank crew had bolted to the wall of the tank close to the radios in the loader's station. "The plugger's still going crazy."

"Check it again," Hardee bellowed.

"Yeah, Sarge," Emerson replied. "It says 'NO SATELLITES.'"

"Great, I guess we'll have to do this the old-fashioned way," Sergeant Hardee said as he pointed to the grid location of his tank on his plastic-covered 1:50,000 map. He extrapolated the enemy location from his map. "Blue One, this is Blue Four. Spot report. Over."

"Blue Four, this is One. Send it," the voice of the young leader of the 3d Platoon answered back.

"Observing one APC—looks like a VTT—moving south, engagement area Maine, northeast, alpha, at grid CT488151." Hardee's unemotional voice announced over the platoon radio net that the enemy vehicle was in the northeast corner of the company's engagement area in alpha (valley) terrain.

"This is Blue Three. We see 'em too," the voice of the tank commander of C33, Hardee's wingman, reported. "He's coming right down the fucking road."

"It's probably a recon patrol," Hardee added. "We can take them out before they know what hit them. Request permission to engage."

"Stand by, Blue Four," the nervous voice of the platoon leader responded. "We're still at direct fire cold, waiting for more ROKs to move south through us. IVIS POS/NAV isn't working. Keep tracking him. I'll get right back to you."

"Sergeant, I see two more vehicles," Oh said, switching his

thermal sight from wide field of view to high magnification. "They are much closer. Nine hundred meters. Both APCs."

Hardee looked through the viewer of his CITV and verified the report. Two VTT323 North Korean APCs were moving down the left side of the highway. The VTT was a lightly armored APC built off the old Chinese design. Its puny 14.5mm machine gun wouldn't even scratch the depleted uranium armor of an M1A2. It wouldn't stand a chance against M1A2 tanks.

"That's got to be a brigade reconnaissance patrol," Hardee announced over the intercom.

"Blue Four, this is Blue One. We just got word from the TOC," the lieutenant's voice called.

Hardee understood what had happened. The task force command center had verified that no friendlies were in engagement area Maine and radioed that information to Hardee's platoon leader. Simultaneously, because the POS/NAV system was on the blink, Hardee manually indexed his grid location into the IVIS and sent a digital report to his commander.

"Go to direct-fire hot. Engage and destroy any vehicles in EA Maine," the voice of his lieutenant ordered.

"Wilco, Blue One. Break. Blue Three, sabot, you take the far tank; I'll take the two near APCs. At my command. Over."

"Roger, Blue Four. We're ready."

Corporal Oh moved the turret slightly, tracking the uneven movement of the enemy vehicle.

"Driver, halt," Captain Yim abruptly ordered. "I can't see a thing in this damn fog. The enemy could be waiting in ambush for us and we wouldn't know it. Kim, we need some artillery to flush out the enemy along the route of advance. Call for two rounds of artillery one kilometer south of Report Line Two."

"Affirmative, Comrade Captain," Corporal Kim replied as he took the radio hand mike to request artillery fire. "That may take quite a while. Most of the artillery is not yet set in range."

"Request mortar fire," Yim ordered as he scanned the fog with nervous eyes. Kim made the radio call. Seconds passed into minutes. Yim felt like a sitting duck, unable to do anything until the illumination was fired. Finally Corporal Kim received word from brigade that the shot would be fired soon.

"Six-Two-Two, this is Six-Two-One," the VTT commander on Axis Gom shouted over the radio frequency. "Six-Two-Four has been hit. I am trying to . . ."

The radio went dead in midsentence.

"Six-Two-One, this is Six-Two-Zero," Yim replied anxiously. "Report. What's your situation?"

The radio remained silent. Yim took off his helmet and heard the boom of a tank cannon to the southwest. The area to his right front, about fifteen hundred meters ahead, was lit with the glow from a burning vehicle.

"Hell, the enemy isn't running away," Yim shouted into the intercom. "Kim, where is that artillery? I've got to get some support."

"Comrade Captain, we should get it soon."

"Damn the fucking artillery," Yim said impatiently. The sound of explosions echoed in the valley. "We can't wait. I must see what's happening up ahead. Driver, move straight ahead."

"Gunner, HEAT, two APCs, left PC," Hardee ordered.

"Identified," Oh answered coolly.

As Corporal Oh lazed to the target, Sergeant Hardee sent a digital contact report over his IVIS system to the rest of the platoon and the company at the push of a button. This report traveled automatically to the task force commander, Lieutenant Colonel Rodriguez. Every M1A2 tank in the task force could now read its IVIS screen to acquire the exact location of the enemy.

"Up," cried Emerson as he pushed the mechanical safety lever to the fire position.

"Fire," Hardee shouted over the radio.

As the first HEAT round exited the muzzle of the tank's gun, the inside of the turret echoed the fury of the shot. The gun breech recoiled and ejected the base cap of the combustible projectile. This aft cap bounced on the floor of the turret.

"Target, right PC," Hardee yelled over the intercom, his right eye glued to his thermal sight.

Immediately Emerson twisted to his right, activated the

ammo door knee switch, and opened the armored blast doors that protected the crew from the ammunition storage compartment. He hefted the sixty-pound HEAT round out of its retaining canister and released the knee switch to the ammo doors. The blast doors snapped shut. He twisted to his left to insert the round into the breech of the M256 cannon. Standing clear of the breech, Emerson pushed the safety handle to fire and yelled, "UP."

BOOM! The 120mm tank cannon roared. The gun leaped back in its carriage with fifteen tons of force, ejecting the aft cap onto the turret floor. Emerson pushed the knee switch and opened the ammunition blast doors with drilled precision. Quickly the young loader fed another HEAT round into the open mouth of the gun.

Direct hit. Hardee grinned as he looked through his CITV and saw that both enemy APCS were flaming wrecks. In this fog the M1A2s had the decisive advantage. The enemy never knew what hit them.

"Identified tank," Oh screamed.

Hardee saw the outline of a T55 trying to move off the road. There was no need for a subsequent command. The enemy tank burst into a blaze of orange flame. Another tank from Hardee's platoon had taken the shot before Oh could fire. The high-explosive antitank round tore through the thinly armored North Korean tank and blew it into fragments of burning metal.

Hardee watched in grim fascination through the thermal sight of his CITV as the tank burned like a blowtorch. After several seconds the hull exploded, showering the roadway with sparks and fire as the onboard fuel and ammunition detonated.

"Poor bastards," Hardee said as he watched the tank's soul flicker in the fog, "but they started this fucking war."

"Identified PC!" Oh screamed.

The VTT jerked forward, throwing Yim against the side of the turret. The driver moved the vehicle quickly to the new position. The lead vehicles were on fire, blasted away by an unseen enemy.

Yim looked back. The T55 tank, usually twenty to fifty meters behind, was within arm's reach. Yim thought that the T55 commander must have closed the distance for fear of losing sight of the lead vehicle in the rugged, broken terrain.

A burst of white light exploded directly over Yim. "Tell them to cease fire," Yim screamed. "They're dropping it right on us. Driver, move out. Get out from under this light."

The VTT driver roared the engine and raced off to the east as fast as the vehicle would go. The second round of illumination landed directly over the T55 as it drove frantically to catch up.

A huge explosion erupted to the rear of Yim's APC. Yim looked back and saw a ball of flames. The exploding T55 belched fire and thick, dark smoke. Then, abruptly, the turret ripped off the hull and sailed into the air as the onboard ammunition detonated. The crew was vaporized in a second.

"Damn, they're shooting us like cattle at a slaughter pen," Yim screamed. He looked to his left, over the open hatch that protected him from small-arms fire like a shield. Peering through the fog, he suddenly saw the dark outline of a big enemy tank directly to his left flank. "Shit. Driver, turn right. Get us out of here."

The world suddenly exploded in a shower of flame, light, and sparks. A 120mm high-explosive antitank round cut through the poorly armored VTT like a hot knife through butter. Everything was over in a millisecond. Yim didn't even have time to feel the pain of dying.

"Cease fire," Hardee commanded. "Scan for additional targets."

"Good shooting, Blue Four." The voice of the C33 commander filled Hardee's earphones.

"Knock it off, Blue Three; this ain't no basketball game," Hardee said seriously. "Blue Three, continue to scan. They may have friends following them."

"Wilco, Blue Four," C33's commander answered in a voice still full of victory.

"Blue One, this is Blue Four. Destroyed three APCs and one tank, vicinity EA Maine, northeast, alpha terrain. Continuing to observe."

"Roger, Blue Four," the platoon leader replied. "It looks like we took out most of an enemy recon company. You can bet there's more where they came from. We expect a major push soon."

"My POS/NAV's still not working," C33's commander said to his platoon sergeant. "I may have a system malfunction."

"Negative, Three-Three. Everyone has the same problem. Something's wrong with the satellites. Index grids manually and adjust from there."

"Wilco, Blue Four."

Hardee took off his Nomex tanker's gloves and sat back in the tank commander's seat. He destroyed that last VTT at less than three hundred meters—too close for comfort. Patches of dense fog and the rough terrain of Korea were sometimes a match even for the thermal sights of the M1A2. He took off his helmet and balaclava and rubbed his tired face with his dirty hands. Maybe in a couple of hours this blasted fog will burn off, he thought.

"Oh, Hernandez, Emerson," Hardee announced over the intercom. "Well done."

8

DEFEND

Men who did not obey were shot. . . . Given ammunition, the North Korean soldier could fight on three rice balls a day.

—T. R. FEHRENBACH

8:35 A.M., 3 October, Chorwon Valley, South Korea. Colonel Yi Sung-Chul, the commander of the 1st Brigade of the 820th Corps, was troubled. A strange uneasiness had floated in with the thick morning fog. He hated waiting. In the past two days, one agonizing delay after another had taken its toll on his force. His men were tired. More than thirty vehicles had fallen by the side of the road due to mechanical problems. Fighting against clogged roads, myriad enemy obstacles, blown bridges, and stupid mistakes, his tank brigade had finally moved forward to its attack positions.

Worst of all, he was behind schedule.

Colonel Yi looked at his map portraying the suspected dispositions of the enemy. The South Koreans had been fighting harder than expected. They had destroyed most of the bridges that led south and contested each piece of ground inch by inch. In addition, mistakes disrupted the plan; the artillery was late, convoys lost their way in the dark, and communications had been haphazard. The fighting that captured the penetration points in the enemy's first and second lines of defense had consumed the best NKPA infantry battalions. These blunders and difficulties caused frustrating delays that Yi could not afford.

He felt like a thoroughbred racehorse being held back by a herd of cattle. The North Korean People's Army had always adopted a policy of fashioning some elite brigades to provide the smashing combat power at the tip of the spear. This was the role of the brigades of the 820th Corps. Marshal Kim Seung-Hee had explained this in his lectures. Yi believed in the Daring Thrust concept with all his heart and was assigned the honor of leading the exploitation for the main attack to Uijonbu. The eyes of the nation were upon him, and he was eager to get into the fight.

He stood by the side of his command tank, looking at a wrecked South Korean sedan several meters to his left. A strong force, probably a large truck, had pushed the car into the wall. There were no bodies in the auto, but the shattered, blood-stained windshield told the horror of the accident.

The wreck of a civilian automobile really did not bother him. Casualties among the civilian population were the nature of war. What nagged him more than anything was the car. Everywhere his tank columns had moved, the roads were littered with the wrecks of expensive, well-built cars. There were too many cars, as if the South Koreans were conducting a ceremony the day of the attack. He had never seen so many civilian automobiles, or so much wealth.

In the "North Korean Workers' Paradise," cars were reserved for a privileged few. Government officials and senior ranking military officers were the only ones who could afford to have cars. Buses were the main means of transport by vehicle. In North Korea you could walk for kilometers on empty asphalt roads and seldom see a passenger car.

For Yi, South Korea, with its cars, luxurious homes, restaurants, and gas stations, was like another world. Never having traveled outside North Korea, he found it incredible that the capitalists had accumulated such wealth.

A specially rigged VTT323 armored personnel carrier, with four antennas sticking out of its thin armored roof, was parked next to the brigade commander's T62 tank. A lieutenant colonel, the brigade deputy commander, stood in the open hatch of the VTT323 listening intently on his radio earphones.

Colonel Yi paused, trying to visualize the battle. He saw, in his mind's eye, the attack of his splendid tank brigade. In the next few hours the brigade would uncoil from its attack positions and leap like a snake assaulting a frightened, cornered mouse. The artillery covering plan was to start twenty minutes before H hour. The brigade would have six artillery battalions in direct support from the corps artillery group. A walking wall of fire would precede the attack along the direction of advance. Fourteen hundred artillery shells would pulverize the attack corridor, destroying enemy antitank positions and killing their infantry. Heavy smoke screens would blanket the entire direction of attack, hiding the advancing tanks and APCs from the surviving enemy guns. If the South Koreans were not crushed by the weight of the artillery, his brigade would kill them all with tank cannon, missile, and machine-gun fire.

Yi's first echelon consisted of the advance guard battalion. They would lead the way with twenty-one T62s, seven VTT323s, nine 107mm multiple rocket launchers mounted on VTT APC chassis, and twelve 122mm self-propelled howitzers. The advance guard was designed to be a combined-arms organization that could gain contact with the enemy and either overrun the defenders or fix them for destruction by the main body of Yi's armor brigade.

The main body of the brigade formed the second echelon. It would follow five kilometers behind, closer than the normal ten to fifteen kilometers they had practiced in training but necessary against a retreating enemy. The main body of the brigade consisted of two tank battalions and one mechanized rifle battalion. The light tank battalion of M1985 tanks formed the brigade reserve and followed the second echelon. Yi would maneuver the light tank battalion as needed.

A third echelon, consisting of two truck-mounted infantry battalions, would be used in the case of stubborn resistance. These battalions would dismount their infantry farther back to attack any position that blocked the lead elements. Yi doubted that the infantry would have to leave their trucks.

Yi had tasked each echelon to accomplish a specific mission. The advance guard makes contact, breaches enemy obstacles, and paves the way for the next battalion. Depending on the ground and the success of the artillery fire, the lead VTT323 company will dismount about two hundred meters behind the leading tanks, when the assault force is about four hundred meters from the enemy.

If the lead elements are involved in a major fight, the follow-on battalions will dismount their infantry companies from their VTT323 APCs. As the infantry attacks along the ridges, moving behind the enemy's frontline defense, the tanks and APCs of the lead element form a firing line and plaster the enemy with fire. As the infantry maneuvers and the tanks and APCs blast the enemy with tank cannon and machine guns, the self-propelled artillery deploys and pulverizes the enemy defenses. After a firestorm of artillery, the infantry and tanks then assault and break the enemy's defense. Once the advance guard penetrates the enemy's defenses, the remaining two battalions race through the gap and continue south.

Yi was ready. His brigade was ready. He waited.

9:40 A.M., 3 October, Chorwon Valley, South Korea. The drizzle had stopped. The air smelled fresh and clear with a keen scent of pine. Up on the ridgeline, the young South Korean officer felt as if the war were passing him by. He hiked unmolested along a slender mountain trail. The trees swayed with the wind, sending a shower of mist onto the trail below. The idyllic surroundings made it seem as if the events of the past two days were some horrible, mist-filled dream.

But he knew they were real. The sound of distant artillery, rumbling like a violent thunderstorm, confirmed the reality.

Second Lieutenant Sung-Joo trudged south, hoping to reach the ROK Army's second line of resistance. The sound of firing to the south was not encouraging. He considered the options. Can I make it back to friendly lines? Will the enemy already be there? Should I hold up here and wait for the eventual counter-attack? Should I stop and rest in the day and travel only at night? A million questions swirled through his mind. His heart beat faster as he climbed up a steep slope.

Sung-Joo's guilt burned in his stomach. He was tired and hungry but alive, and his soldiers were dead or captured. Walking along the ridgeline, he seemed to have escaped the horror that was happening in the valleys. It was as if he were a spectator of the battle, not a combatant. It didn't seem fair.

The trees are beginning to change colors, he thought as he marched. He remembered the picnics with his family during their frequent visits to their ancestral grave sites. His grandfather, grandmother, and great-grandfather were buried in the traditional Korean way, in a rounded mound on the side of a high hill. Every month, but especially on holidays, Sung-Joo would walk with his father, mother, brother, and two sisters to pay homage to his dead relatives. His mother packed the best-tasting dishes to enjoy once the climb to the burial mound was complete. After honoring his ancestors by bowing three times at each grave, his father would tell a short story about the life of each person buried in the mound. In this way, his father said, no loved one is ever really forgotten.

Suddenly Sung-Joo felt ashamed. How could he think of his family when every soldier in his platoon had been killed? Their mangled and shattered bodies were probably still lying in the trenches where they had fallen. His men might never be given a proper burial; the North Koreans might just dump them in the nearest ditch. They were good men, with families and loved ones, and did not deserve to be butchered by the communists. They were dead and he was alive. They had fought and he was running from the enemy. He felt ashamed.

He stopped and sat down on the side of the trail, resting his heavy pack on the ground. He carried the equipment he had salvaged from the dead Americans—an M16 rifle with twenty rounds, the backpack radio, a canteen of water, an empty 9mm pistol, and a pair of binoculars. He reached for the canteen, unscrewed the plastic cap, and took a swig of water. Explosions echoed in the hills. They sounded only a few kilometers away, he thought. He checked his M16 rifle, slung it on the pack, and headed down the trail.

Crouching low, he crawled off the trail and through the pine trees to a position that overlooked the valley. He raised his binoculars to his eyes to scan the scene below. The fog hugged the valley like a thin cotton blanket, diffusing with each passing moment. Pillars of black smoke about a thousand meters away billowed up to the low-hanging clouds. Another battle had been fought in the valley along the road that led south. The large open area directly below him had been an ROK Army artillery position, apparently caught in the night by North Korean infantry.

Sung-Joo was appalled at what he saw. The valley was filled with the wreckage of burned trucks and smoldering ROK artillery vehicles. Black smoke rose from several of the ammunition carriers. The mangled artillery trucks and support vehicles were grouped together like blackened clumps of junk. Trucks that had once been full of infantry and jeeps had been blown apart. Vehicles were capsized. Bodies of South Korean soldiers lay everywhere.

The second line of resistance had fallen to the enemy. The line, which his superiors had boasted would never be penetrated by the North Koreans, had been punctured in less than two days. North Korean armored vehicles, trucks, and command cars were quickly moving south along the two-lane concrete road.

Sung-Joo lay prone against a small pile of rocks, observing the carnage. Those men have been slaughtered just like my men, he thought.

North Korean tanks and armored personnel carriers jammed the road. The sound of the explosions of artillery shells, falling far to the south, filled the early morning.

Sung-Joo shook his head. The ROK defenses had dissolved. "We are losing the war," he said out loud. "It is all over."

10:00 A.M., 3 October, along Highway 47, ten kilometers south of the DMZ, South Korea. North Korean military police, wearing orange reflective vests and green helmets with big red stars painted on the front and sides, pointed the column into its planned position. Seventeen big North Korean 2S3 152mm self-propelled howitzers of the 136th NKPA Field Artillery Battalion led the way. The howitzers followed the directions of the military police exactly, moving quickly off the muddy road into an open field. Additional artillery units, some consisting of truck-towed howitzers and others composed of self-propelled guns, moved rapidly to other fields and open areas to the left and right of the corps artillery group's firing position.

Major Chun's jeep splashed through a mud puddle and moved to the center of the area he was expected to occupy. The mud had slowed them, he thought, and so had the stubborn

South Korean defenders who had persisted in holding on in spite of the fury of his cannons. His men had fired countless missions in the last fifty-five hours. They were tired and hungry, but they were performing like the well-oiled machine he had trained them to be.

"Stop here," Chun shouted to his driver. "Radio the battery commanders to meet me here in five minutes."

Chun dismounted his jeep, walked to the front, and placed his battle map on the jeep's hood. The corps chief of rocket and artillery troops had selected an ideal site for the corps artillery group, he thought, surveying the scene. High mountains flanked the east and west sides of the position. Highway 47 ran northeast to southwest, following the east Chorwon Valley. The highway continued all the way to Uijonbu and then to Seoul. Seoul was only eighty kilometers away, a couple of hours' hard drive if unopposed.

Engines roared and gears grated as the mud-covered vehicles pivoted and turned on the wet ground. A single five-ton truck loaded with soldiers bounced abruptly to a stop at the far southern end of the large, unsown rice paddy field. Pairs of soldiers jumped out of the truck, each carrying a red-and-white-striped barber pole. The survey teams quickly ran to prerehearsed distances, checked the alignment of their stakes, and pounded them into the ground with hammers. Each howitzer then moved to a designated position behind each pole. The 2S3s raced into position as if they were competing for a prize as part of an annual training test.

The battalions of the corps artillery group deployed in rapid succession. A long line of trucks, filled with fresh stocks of ammunition, moved off the road and parked in wet rice paddies to the far right of Chun's guns. The ammunition trucks also deployed to set up an artillery resupply point that would feed the insatiable appetite of the guns. Platoons of soldiers dismounted their trucks and started to dig shallow shelters to protect the ammunition.

Another group of artillerymen worked to set up the battalion headquarters in an abandoned house at the eastern end of the field. Antennas were positioned and erected off the line of movement. The battalion and its support elements executed the well-rehearsed drill as if they were dancers in a prearranged choreographed spectacle.

"Move faster. We are behind time," Major Chun yelled as a captain ran up and handed him a sketch of his guns' firing positions. The captain stood at attention. Chun was not pleased. The battery commander had already lost one gun to poor maintenance. The precious 152mm self-propelled howitzer had been left behind early this morning just south of the DMZ. Chun could not afford additional losses. He needed every tube. He knew that Marshal Kim Seung-Hee had designated his guns for a special mission that had strategic implications. Every 2S3 howitzer was a precious asset.

The major reviewed the sketch quickly, then glared at the captain. He drew his right hand across the left side of his face, then suddenly struck the captain with the back of his hand. The captain's head moved slightly, absorbing the blow, but he maintained a rigid stance, his hands stiff by his side.

"This is sloppy work," Chun yelled. "Your inefficiency has already cost me one gun. I will not lose another. Redo this immediately. Move gun number four ten meters to the left and gun number six fifteen meters forward. I will not tolerate your continued incompetence."

"It will be done, Comrade Commander," the captain shouted in reply, standing stiffly at attention.

Chun nodded, signaling that the battery commander was dismissed. The officer, red faced and humiliated, saluted and ran back to his battery.

Chun watched him as he charged back to his guns. The officer kicked a private who was standing idle and holding a red-and-white-striped artillery stake. The captain then yelled and screamed. His men moved furiously, shouting orders to their subordinates, changing the lay of their howitzers to please their enraged commander.

Chun smirked. The skillful commander treated his men with calculated brutality, he thought. This is how you mold a peasant army into a fierce fighting force. Men were, by nature, lazy cowards. The discipline that each soldier learned in the Inmun Gun would make the difference between victory and defeat. Discipline was the force that conquered in war. Chun was sure that the lack of brutal, ruthless discipline was what was causing the South Koreans to lose.

It's the discipline, he thought, that drives the men on. In the NKPA discipline was everything. The army's values and discipline were absolutely brutal. Physical abuse and corporal punishment of lower enlisted soldiers was commonplace, particularly if the punishment would provide the greater number of soldiers a vivid lesson of how to behave. Chun cautioned his junior leaders against being lenient, for he felt that hate directed at an officer could easily be redirected toward the enemy. The end result of this kind of training was the creation of a breed of vicious fighters. Individuals whose dignity and manhood had been so cruelly violated would hardly refrain from doing the same to their enemies.

One battalion of artillery after another moved off the road and set up in tight, triangular firing formations. Dozens of soldiers with SA-17 surface-to-air missiles ran across the fields to take up positions on the outskirts of the corps artillery group's firing position. Trucks towing ZSU-57-2 antiaircraft guns moved onto the high ground surrounding the open area to reinforce the missile air defenses. Rooftops of buildings were set up as air defense fortresses, each with an SA-17 gunner and tripod-mounted 14.5mm air defense machine guns. A battery of ZSU-23-4s and a dozen S-300s took up positions on the outside edges of the perimeter.

One by one Chun's battery commanders assembled at his jeep for their orders. The major took their reports, made corrections and several caustic rebukes, and handed back the corrected forms to his subordinates.

"The battalion will be ready to fire in fifteen minutes," he said. "We will be the first battalion ready. Is that clear?"

"Nam chim." The battery commanders, standing at attention in front of him, shouted their concurrence in unison.

The radios squeaked the transmission of detailed firing instructions to the artillery fire direction centers as Chun visualized the chain of events that he had set in motion. Every action of the guns was synchronized by time. The batteries would fire their prescribed ammunition allotments at each designated location before moving on to the next planned target. Battalions would fire in mass at one location at a time, as prescribed in the order. Mass was what was required to obliterate the enemy in front of the advancing forces.

Chun made some quick calculations of the amount of fire requested and the time to complete ammunition reloading. He knew from his instruction at the artillery academy that prone infantry unprotected in the open would likely suffer 100 percent casualties if subjected to artillery and mortar fire of the intensity prescribed by NKPA doctrine. Bunkers would take more fire to destroy but would eventually crumble to his howitzers. Tanks would take even more fire.

The orders called for artillery fire on a broken enemy, one that was disorganized and running away, so Chun calculated the amount of fire for unprotected troops. The NKPA high-density rate of artillery fire would place forty high-explosive rounds on a single hundred-meter-square box. These fire boxes were used to maneuver the strike of the artillery fire. The massed fire of hundreds of guns would be walked from box to box to annihilate the defenders.

The first fire box was planned two kilometers south of Report Line Two, where the most recent enemy defenses had been identified. The rest of Chun's fires would fall farther to the south in a walking sheet of exploding death along the main axis of attack.

"When will you be ready to fire?" Chun taunted his assembled captains as he looked up from his calculations.

"Ten minutes more, Comrade Commander," answered a tall, thin captain wearing the red shoulder boards of an NKPA artillery officer. The other two captains standing by his side nodded.

Chun quickly jotted down the firing instructions on a notepad, then handed a sheet of firing coordinates to each officer.

"Let's burn them into ashes," he said keenly, a fiery glint in his eye. "Show them how they must fear the Inmun Gun's artillery."

The officers saluted and ran back to their batteries. Around them, other batteries were conducting their own firing occupation drills. Across the valley, through the thinning fog, Chun could see four battalions of multiple rocket launchers lining up, preparing to fire. In this four- by six-kilometer chunk of South

Korea was the largest concentration of artillery that Chun had ever seen.

Smiling at the precision of his soldiers, Maj. Chun Yong-ho, the commander of the 136th North Korean People's Army 152mm self-propelled howitzer battalion, grabbed his radio transmitter. "The guns are ready," he reported to corps headquarters.

10:10 A.M., 3 October, Team B (Bulldogs) assembly area, just south of the MPRC. The vehicle commander stood up in the hatch and manned the .50-caliber machine gun. Alice Hamilton, sitting inside the dark armored personnel carrier, could see only the soldier's legs. She zipped up the flak jacket she was wearing and glanced at Paul. The cameraman was nestled in a heap in a corner of the APC, his eyes closed.

"I can't stand it anymore, Paul," she said. Her shoulder-length blond hair fell over her left shoulder as she reached for the door handle of the APC. "I've got to go outside."

Paul opened his eyes and shook his head. "It's too dangerous."

"Nothing's happening right now," Alice said. "Besides, I have to go outside."

Paul waved his hand, exhausted from the terror of the past day.

Alice turned the long metal handle and pushed the door open. It clanged against the back of the vehicle. The vehicle commander bent down inside the APC and announced, "Ma'am, it's my orders to keep an eye on you. You aren't supposed to leave my APC."

Alice looked across the muddy, barren field and saw a vehicle pull up to a tank just within view. She saw Lieutenant Colonel Rodriguez exit the vehicle and walk over to the tank. A man stood in front of the tank and saluted Rodriguez. Another man climbed down from the turret of the tank to join the group.

"I must talk to your commander, Sergeant," Alice said to the soldier inside the armored personnel carrier. "Colonel Rodriguez is right over there. I'll be back in a few minutes."

Before the sergeant could argue with her, she climbed out of the APC and slammed the door shut. Her once white tennis shoes, now smudged with dirt and mud, hit the rain-soaked ground. Struggling in the mud, she trudged over to Rodriguez.

"Al, any questions about what I want you to do?" Rodriguez asked Capt. Al Grey as they huddled over the map on the front slope of Grey's tank.

The captain pulled his trim black mustache as he considered the graphics on the map. "Sir, it'll take me fifteen minutes once you give me the word to be in position to counterattack north up Highway 43. It'll take me about eighteen minutes to counterattack up 325. Are you sure you want to counterattack an enemy brigade?"

"Yep, and you're just the man to lead the charge," Rodriguez said with a sly smile.

"Any artillery support?" asked Lieutenant Lopez, the third man in the group and Captain Grey's artillery support officer. "I sure would like to get into this fight."

"Not yet, Lopez," Rodriguez answered with a grin, "but we're working on it."

Captain Grey suddenly noticed Ms. Hamilton and motioned with a jerk of his head for Rodriguez to turn around.

"Colonel Rodriguez, I want to know when you're going to get me out of here," Alice demanded. "And I want my cell phone back."

"Why Ms. Hamilton, I thought you wanted to report the news," Rodriguez replied sarcastically.

Suddenly two men rushed out of the fog as if they had just sprung out of the earth. Both wore U.S. Army battle dress uniforms, but one carried an M16 and the other carried a pack and had a stick grenade in his hand.

The machine gun on top of Captain Grey's tank fired at the two intruders. Spires of mud kicked up as the .50-caliber bullets struck the barren field. The man with the M16 fired at the turret, hitting the American manning the machine gun.

Rodriguez jerked Alice to the ground and pulled his .45 pistol from his side holster. Grey and Lopez ducked for cover. The intruder fired his M16 again and Lopez spun to the ground.

Alice screamed as Rodriguez fired his .45 at the two men. He fired twice, hitting the man with the M16 in the forehead, splattering his face all over the field. The second man, only thirty meters away, charged forward and ducked as Rodriguez fired three more times and caught the charging man in the shoulder, chest, and head. The man tumbled backward and fell on the grenade.

Rodriguez jumped on Alice to shield her from the blast, and Grey rolled Lopez to the side of the tank as the grenade exploded.

Pieces of steel, mud, and bits of human flesh fell over the field. Rodriguez opened his eyes and saw that he was staring into the face of the terrified and confused lady with green eyes and blond hair.

Rodriguez pulled himself up as soldiers rushed from other areas to lend assistance. The colonel picked up Alice in his arms and sat her on the ground next to the side of Grey's tank.

"Al, you okay?" Rodriguez yelled, still looking at the speechless expression on Alice's face.

"Yes, sir. Lopez looks bad. Shot in the chest," Grey said as he scrambled up the tank to check on the soldier who had manned the .50-caliber machine gun.

"Are you okay, Ms. Hamilton?" Rodriguez asked as he quickly scanned the reporter for signs of injury.

"I don't know . . . I mean, I'm not sure," she stammered.

"Medics!" Captain Grey shouted. "I've got wounded men here."

A sergeant ran up to Rodriguez and saluted. Rodriguez just nodded. "What?"

"I've checked the bodies, sir. They're both North Koreans, as best I can tell, wearing our uniforms. The pack that one guy was carrying was full of explosives. We're lucky the son of a bitch didn't go off."

Rodriguez nodded again.

Alice, now soaked in mud from the ordeal, managed a trace of a smile. "Okay, Colonel, it's a deal. You can keep the phone if you just get me out of here."

11:00 A.M., 3 October, along Highway 43, ten kilometers south of the DMZ, South Korea. Yi glanced at his watch, wishing that mere willpower could fix the bridge. He knew that his attack would be the decisive blow that win the war, but first he had to cross the bridge. Nothing had stopped the attack of the

Inmun Gun so far. He was sure that nothing could, if the engineers would only repair that bridge.

Yi had faith in superior numbers, particularly in the tanks, artillery, and infantry of his tank brigade. Over the radio he heard that the enemy was pulling back. There had been no time to get infantry forward. The Inmun Gun was pushing south with determination, breaking through the weak spots in the defenders' lines, infiltrating behind his strong points, and putting pressure on the enemy all across the front.

Losses in the NKPA were heavy, but in several key areas the ROKs had broken and run. Yi considered this proof of their loose discipline and soft living that he had been told about.

The attack was delayed while the destroyed bridge on Highway 43 was being repaired. The delay would at least allow the artillery to catch up. The plan was still working. As soon as the bridges were ready and Yi's artillery was set, he would wipe the South Koreans off the face of the earth. Then his tanks would drive through the gap and race to Uijonbu. There was no doubt in Yi's mind that the victory of communism was near. He relished the thought of being the first to raise the red-starred North Korean flag over the government assembly building of his enemy's capital.

One report, however, particularly bothered him. The brigade reconnaissance company had reported tanks blocking the 1st Brigade's approach. The report was received around 0500, only four hours ago. Unfortunately the brigade lost contact with the reconnaissance company commander before the exact composition of the enemy could be confirmed. No further transmissions had been received. Yi assumed that they were still driving south, out of communication range because of the high hills that narrowed the line of sight of FM radio communications.

Yi would have to relieve the reconnaissance company commander, Captain Yim, as soon as he could. It was inexcusable not to maintain contact. Reporting was too important to be ignored, no matter what the difficulties of terrain. Yi hated the thought of going into battle without knowing where the enemy was in front of his battalions.

Yi glanced at his wristwatch again. The time didn't matter; the attack from the march would not wait. Even if there were a few diehard defenders, they couldn't stop his brigade. Besides, the 820th Corps commander had reported that the way was clear. Speed was critical. Yi didn't have time to send out an independent reconnaissance patrol to reconfirm the information or make contact with the brigade reconnaissance company. As soon as the artillery preparation had done its job, he would move his tanks and APCs forward. Once the battle was over, he would deal with his recalcitrant company commander.

"Any word on the bridge yet?" Colonel Yi screamed from the top of the turret of his T62 tank. Yi's deputy commander shouted, "Comrade Commander, the engineers are working as fast as they can. They estimate one more hour before the bridge is ready for tanks."

"Is the artillery set yet?" Colonel Yi asked scornfully, knowing that the artillery was carefully controlled and synchronized to fire according to a meticulously established time schedule.

"The roads are jammed, Comrade Commander," the deputy commander reported with a shrug. "The artillery is still moving into position."

Colonel Yi shook his head. Special forces teams had been designated to take the bridge intact. Apparently they had failed. The plan was being trampled by a countless number of minor mistakes. He understood inefficiency—in North Korea he had lived with it all his life—but he had hoped that the call to action would somehow improve things. Tasks were dragged out in innumerable ways, and poorly trained staffs aggravated the problem. Orders were long, detailed, and filled with wordy expressions and political jargon that did little to inspire the readers and offered less clarification of the task and purpose of missions. Lack of attention to detail of the ground and the enemy's obstacles was a particular problem. A well-known military proverb came to his mind: "The plan was smooth on paper, only the general staff forgot about the ravines."

"Don't worry, sir," Yi's deputy commander promised. "The bridge will be completed soon. In a few hours we will crush the fascist bastards, and you will have the honor of leading the brigade into Seoul."

Yi nodded. After so many years of preparation and training, after years of privation and sacrifice, he was finally going to destroy the despised enemies of his country. He would break whatever hasty line of resistance was left and speed south.

Yi tapped his map board against the hard steel of his tank turret. They were now twelve hours behind schedule.

11:30 A.M., 3 October, Task Force 2-72 tactical operations center at the MPRC, Chorwon Valley, South Korea. Lieutenant Colonel Rodriguez scanned the sky, hoping for the possibility of air support. The fog was thinning, but the haze and low cloud ceiling argued against effective ground-to-air coordination.

Rodriguez ducked into an open rear compartment of an M577 armored command post vehicle. "Any news from brigade?"

"Nothing, sir," a sergeant answered, taking off his headset. "I've been trying for hours."

Rodriguez nodded. He stood alongside the M577, wearing his Nomex coveralls and Kevlar helmet. His high tanker's boots were splattered with red mud. His ancient .45-caliber pistol and an M42 chemical protective mask hung from his belt. The five M577 armored command post carriers were in a circle facing toward the center, their ramps down. The task force headquarters was carefully sited in an abandoned quarry. Its steep northern rock sides offered effective protection from enemy artillery.

Radio antennas were placed on the high ground and linked to the armored vehicles by thick, rubber-coated cables. Soldiers armed with M16 rifles and squad automatic rifles stood guard in hastily dug fighting positions. Two M1A2 tanks—Rodriguez's *Firebreather* and Major Bradford's *Defiant*—were situated near three M113 armored personnel carriers. This small force made up the Task Force Command Group. The vehicles were lined up and ready to move forward to the battle area.

"Keep trying to get brigade," Rodriguez said as he stepped out onto the ramp of the armored vehicle.

Major Lucas stood in the center of the circle of M577s. The tall Texan wore his camouflage, charcoal-lined chemical suit, a Kevlar helmet, and the traditional infantry-style load-bearing equipment with ammunition pouches, suspenders, and canteen. He held a computer-generated maintenance report form in his hand.

"Sir, we lost Lieutenant Lopez in Bravo Company. Total casualty report for the task force is now twelve dead and fourteen wounded."

Rodriguez closed his tired eyes and nodded. "Combat power?"

"We have thirty-nine tanks and fourteen Bradleys operational," Lucas said, checking his report. "Three of the tanks are down for electrical problems, two for mechanical parts. We're low on fuel."

The battalion SINCGARS radios whined in the background, adding to the noise of the generators.

"I'm taking spare parts off damaged tanks to get a few more working. I should have one up for Bravo and one more for Delta. Both tanks are in the combat trains right now."

Spare parts had always been a problem with the M1A2. But now that the friction of war had severed the automated, just-in-time logistics system, the repair parts problem was a nightmare. The XO was doing a superhuman job of keeping the task force running. Rodriguez could see the strain in the bleary, sleepless eyes of his executive officer.

Rodriguez blinked, wishing for sleep himself but forcing his mind to check off the long list of things he had yet to do.

Wham! A single artillery shell slammed into the empty rice paddy four hundred meters south of the command post.

Everybody was visibly shaken. Rodriguez gauged their fear and spoke up.

"Relax, gentlemen. The North Korean guns aren't accurate enough to hit us in this quarry."

"We should move to TOC," the XO replied, his nerves visibly reaching the breaking point. "You seem to think you'll live forever, but you're as mortal as the next man."

Rodriguez didn't reply.

"Sir, we've got brigade on the radio," an excited sergeant yelled from the ramp of one of the M577s. "It's Iron Five, the brigade XO."

Rodriguez leaped toward the sergeant to grab the radio hand mike. Lucas stood next to his commander in the crowded command post vehicle, listening to the squawking speakers. The two NCOs who were in the vehicle work area wriggled to the other end.

"Dragon Six, this is Iron Five," the voice of the brigade executive officer announced.

Rodriguez took a deep breath and keyed the mike. "Iron Five, this is Dragon Six. Damn, am I glad to hear from you."

"Dragon Six, this is Iron Five. If you hear me, break squelch twice."

"Damn, they aren't picking up our transmission," Rodriguez cursed, pressing the hand mike twice as directed. He looked at the sergeant in charge of the TOC. The sergeant was covered with mud, and his left hand was bandaged. "Is the big antenna up?"

"Yes, sir," the NCO answered. "I checked the connection myself ten minutes ago."

"Check it again," Rodriguez barked.

"Dragon Six, if you can hear me, orders follow." The voice on the radio faded in and out. "Move south to—"

Rodriguez and Lucas moved closer to the speaker, but the transmission ended in midsentence. The two officers waited pensively. Nothing followed in spite of Rodriguez's attempts to initiate a response.

"Sergeant, keep trying until you get 'em back on the radio," Rodriguez ordered as he handed the sergeant the hand mike. He stepped outside the armored vehicle, took off his helmet, and rubbed his close-cropped hair with his right hand.

"You heard the orders," Lucas said, appearing at Rodriguez's side. "We were ordered to pull out."

Rodriguez shook his head. "What about the cav? Have they pulled south to the junction of 43 and 47 yet?"

"No, they need a few more hours. I just received the report a few minutes ago."

"Then we're staying."

Lucas looked at his commander. "We can't fight without artillery and air support. You know we've got only one load of service ammunition for the tanks. Do you expect us to fight with training ammunition?"

"Yes," Rodriguez answered firmly. "It's too late to withdraw now. I can't obey an order I know is wrong. We're here. This is the critical point. There's nobody else. We'll make do with what we have."

"What about our wounded? What about our casualties?"

Rodriguez shook his head. "We're all staying. I can't spare a force to protect a convoy of wounded. There'll be more dead than wounded if we try to evacuate them without a proper escort. The North Koreans have small teams all over the place."

Ten artillery shells landed eight hundred meters away, smashing against the hills to the west.

"How can you risk the entire task force?" Lucas pressed. "How can you disobey orders?"

"Dave, when they made us officers, they expected us to be smart enough to know when to disobey orders."

"Are you sure we can do this?" Lucas questioned. "Are you sure?"

Rodriguez looked into the grim eyes of his friend and put his hand on his shoulder. The touch seemed to work wonders, as if Rodriguez was suddenly transferring energy to his worried executive officer.

A wide grin stretched across the commander's tired face. "With Dave Lucas as my second in command, nothing is impossible."

"Okay, okay," responded Lucas. "I never could say no to you."

"That's the style," Rodriguez said, nodding, then he turned toward the sergeant who was trying to contact the brigade headquarters on the radio. "Any luck getting brigade?"

The sergeant shook his head.

"Sir, we have to get forward now," Maj. Tony Bradford yelled from the top of *Defiant,* interrupting the discussion between Rodriguez and Lucas. "Scouts just reported that they have vehicles moving into EA Maine."

"Dave, I'm counting on you," Rodriguez replied in a quiet, steely voice. "It's my call. I'll take the heat for it."

"Hell, sir, we're in this together. You know I'll do my part." Lucas raised his right arm in a brisk salute. "Just come back in one piece. We don't have this in writing, and I don't want to be the only one at the court-martial."

Rodriguez grinned, returned the salute, and ran toward his tank. *Firebreather* roared as the driver cranked the big 1,500-horsepower gas turbine engine. Bradford's tank, named *Defiant,* and three additional M113 armored personnel carriers made up Rodriguez's command group. He had designed the group to help him fight the battle. One APC acted as a tactical command post and radio relay station, the latter an essential element for fighting in restricted, mountainous terrain. Another APC was the enlisted tactical air control party (ETAC), commanded by an air force sergeant who controlled requests for immediate close air support with his special high-frequency radios. The third APC was the engineer commander's vehicle.

Rodriguez managed a forced grin as he looked up at his fire support officer, Captain Fletcher, and the steady Captain Drake. "Radios set? Are you ready?"

"I've only got mortars on the net, sir," Captain Fletcher said nervously. "I can't raise any artillery units on voice or digital."

"How about the air force? Any CAS?" Rodriguez questioned, asking about the possibility of close air support.

"Sorry, sir. I've talked with the guys in the ETAC. They've been sending radio requests for close air support all day. No one's answering right now, but I told them to keep trying. We just might get lucky."

"Let's hope so," Rodriguez said with a nod, then he climbed up the left side of his M1A2 tank. He crawled over the top of the turret, slid into the commander's station, and waved his arm forward.

12:20 P.M., 3 October, Chorwon Valley, South Korea. Colonel Yi observed the damaged bridge with his binoculars. North Korean engineers climbed over the broken structure like ants trying to fix a disturbed anthill. A dozen huge trucks inched forward, and heavy steel beams were unloaded and manhandled to the damaged bridge. The engineers bolted the metal sections together as if connecting a giant Erector set, but the work was difficult and time-consuming.

Nothing was going as planned, Yi fumed. His trail battalion of M1985 light tanks had found a way around the destroyed bridge and moved down a parallel route along a steep mountain ridge. A few kilometers south the lead tank was destroyed at a bend in the trail by an antitank mine. The minefield was quickly cleared, but the damaged tank blocked the route and halted the entire column. It would take hours of towing and maneuvering to push aside the mangled wreck and continue the march.

The fog thinned as the day wore on. The weather was breaking, Yi sensed, looking up at the heavens. This afternoon or to-morrow the sky will clear. Clear skies would aid the defender. These delays may cost us, he brooded.

"The damned engineers," Yi cursed scornfully, raising his bushy, dark eyebrows at his deputy commander. "How much longer must we wait?"

"The engineers report that the bridge will be ready in fifteen minutes," the man replied. "The corps chief of rocket and ar-tillery troops says that the entire corps artillery group will be ready to fire in twenty minutes."

"At last. Any news from our brigade reconnaissance com-pany?"

"None, Comrade Commander, but communication is diffi-cult in this restricted terrain. We should hear from them soon."

"What is the news from the other axis of attack?" Colonel Yi asked.

"Comrade Commander, the news is excellent," the deputy commander said with a grin. "Official radio broadcasts have signaled the success of our attack. The enemy is withdrawing everywhere. The fascist air forces have been destroyed on the ground."

"What about the Americans?" Yi asked.

"The Americans were hit hard in their garrisons. They have taken tremendous casualties. The latest report is that they are all running away, toward Pusan."

Colonel Yi smiled a big, toothy smile. He had learned over the years to suspect the official broadcasts, but he wanted to be-lieve this news. Dreams of victory filled his mind. It appeared that the Daring Thrust plan was working. All they had to do was strike, and the enemy's house of cards would collapse of its own weight. The great war to liberate Korea would be over in a week, as predicted.

Vehicles lined up, filling the cramped attack positions, ready to push across the bridge. Colonel Yi was glad that the enemy air forces had been destroyed. His brigade would be a tempting target. If the enemy used their aircraft on his brigade, which was bunched up while waiting for the word to attack, it could be disastrous.

The deputy commander waved his arms wildly. "The bridge

is ready. The artillery is in position, ready to fire. You can commence the attack."

Yi grunted and keyed his radio transmitter. "All Red elements, this is Red Six. Attack and drive the enemy south. Grind them into dust."

Seconds later, with a tremendous roar, seventy howitzers from five artillery battalions hurled explosive shells along the direction of attack, clearing the way for the tanks. Five batteries of multiple rocket launchers shot their screaming missiles into the sky. The screech of soaring projectiles and the distant rumble of explosions signaled the start of the attack.

The squeaking noise of the moving tanks was barely audible over the terrible rumble of the artillery. To Colonel Yi, the big, dull bangs in the distance sounded like a giant blacksmith pounding on a huge anvil. The clouds hung low in the sky, but visibility was six to seven hundred meters.

Yi stood in the turret of his T62, observing the movement of the advance guard battalion. Everything can still go as planned, he thought as he looked at his watch again, even if we are hours behind schedule. As the last tank of the advance guard headed south, he waved his arm and ordered the rest of the main body forward. The first battalion revved its engines and moved south in perfect column formation. The thin fog mixed with the black exhaust of the T62 tanks and VTT323 armored personnel carriers.

The colonel's T62 tank jerked forward, quickly traversed the hard, rocky riverbed that led to the north-south highway, and slipped into the order of march behind the lead tank company of the main body. The main body contained Yi's headquarters section, two tank battalions, a motorized rifle battalion, an antitank company, an artillery battalion, and an antiaircraft platoon of ZSU-57-2 self-propelled guns.

"Red Six, this is Red One-Six," the commander of the 1st Tank Battalion, the advance guard of the brigade, reported to Colonel Yi. "We have reached the line of departure. No enemy contact. Over."

"Affirmative, Red One-Six," Yi replied quickly, trying to minimize excessive chatter over the brigade's command frequency. "The 2d Tank Battalion will move in five minutes."

The enemy seemed to be acting exactly as predicted. The

brigade was working like a well-oiled machine, Yi thought. Nothing could stop such power. The iron monsters continued south, cheered on by the moan of rockets and artillery shells flying overhead.

"So far our echelonment is working fine," Yi said to his tank gunner over the vehicle intercom system as he watched the advance guard battalion, five hundred meters in front of him, driving hard to the south. "Radio to corps that we are still in march formation. The advance guard should contact the enemy in about twelve minutes."

The fog began to clear. Visibility was now almost eight hundred meters.

We will smash them, Yi thought. We will smash them into dust.

12:35 P.M., 3 October, Chorwon Valley, South Korea. With a crash like the roar of a giant freight train, North Korean artillery shells fell all around Hardee's position. Hardee buttoned up and watched the flashes through his vision blocks. Because of a combination of skillful tank positioning and luck, the rounds missed, as though the tank was blessed by angels. The keyhole position that Hardee's tank occupied protected it from the angry, exploding shells.

KARRUMMP! The noise was overpowering. A continuous rain of shells fell in a tumultuous, rolling barrage. The fire crept toward them, covered them in fury, then passed like a crushing wave. After the firestorm, Hardee opened the ballistic shield on his CITV and surveyed the battlefield.

"Corporal Oh," Hardee said calmly, "I expect that the North Koreans will be coming soon. Remember, we want to let the lead tanks pass. We'll open up on my command. When I think the lead battalion has passed, I'll detonate the MOPM mines. Our job is to separate the lead battalion from the second battalion."

"Then we fire?" Oh asked.

"Roger that."

"Affirmative," Oh said over the intercom. "I understand."

Oh didn't have long to wait.

A few minutes later the first tanks streamed past Hardee's position. The enemy attacked in a long column of vehicles, moving at twelve kilometers per hour through the fog, with hatches buttoned down tight. Hardee peered through his CITV. The M1A2's thermal sight saw the targets as black hot spots moving across a white background. From this angle of fire, they would be shooting at the enemy's flanks and grill doors.

Hardee knew that the enemy couldn't see his tank. Hell, he thought, with their hatches locked down tight they could barely see the road. He watched as the second company of the lead battalion passed.

"Blue Four, this is Blue One. They're getting awful close," Hardee's platoon leader called over the radio. "When are we going to open fire?"

"Steady. Wait for the word from Steel Six," Hardee clicked back a reply.

The third company of the advance guard rolled by. Through the thermal image in his CITV, Hardee could see the distinct outline of a North Korean VTT nine hundred meters away. Hardee glanced down to his left. Emerson stood in the loader's station, prepared to load on command. He looked anxious but ready.

"Steel, this is Steel Six. Fire at will," Captain Mackenzie shouted over the company command net.

"Blue Four, this is Blue One. Observing six tanks, Maine, north, alpha," the lieutenant's voice answered. "Direct-fire hot. We'll get the tanks, you take the Vetts. Over."

"Roger, Blue-One," Hardee answered coolly.

"Identified, PC," Oh screamed, his palms sweaty and his trigger finger eager to send a HEAT round into an enemy vehicle. The enemy was moving south in perfect column formation. The T62s and VTT323s were about twenty-five meters apart, maintaining their formation as if they were on parade.

"Fire," the voice of his lieutenant ordered over the radio.

"FIRE," Hardee yelled over his tank intercom.

A VTT, the target in Hardee's cannon sights, disintegrated from the impact of the 120mm high-explosive antitank round. The four well-trained M1A2 tank crews of the 3d Platoon fired almost simultaneously even though they were dispersed in the terrain and out of sight of one another. Four enemy APCs went up in flames, their wreckage thrown about in fantastic contortions of broken metal and burning rubber. Other enemy vehicles quickly bypassed the burning wrecks. The enemy column picked up speed. Several sections broke off the main road and formed platoon columns.

The enemy was looking to their front, Hardee thought as he hit the slave button on his override and placed Corporal Oh on the center of mass of another enemy APC. Hardee grinned. The enemy still didn't know where he was. In the fog and smoke, they were dying to a force they could not see.

The lead enemy battalion melted in front of C Company's guns so fast that the engagement area seemed to spawn two dozen bonfires in the first few seconds. More T62s and an APC were destroyed in the smoke. Two T62 tanks halted to return fire at their unseen foe. Confused as to where the firing was coming from, the enemy tanks formed a firing line facing south.

"Gunner, two tanks," Hardee shouted, swinging the gun over in the direction of the enemy tanks. "Left tank."

"Identified," Oh replied.

"Fire." The shot from Hardee's gun tube hit the first enemy tank squarely on the left side of its turret. The T62 shuddered from the strike and jerked quickly to a stop from the force of the explosion. Through his thermal sight Hardee could see a plume of black smoke belching from the turret of the dead North Korean tank. "Right tank, fire sabot."

Emerson loaded a depleted uranium sabot round. "UP."

"On the way," Oh screamed.

This round knocked the second North Korean tank on its side. It smoldered for a brief second, then exploded in a shower of sparks and orange flame. The enemy kept coming. Two more T62 tanks appeared in Hardee's tank sights.

"Identified two tanks," Oh shouted as he moved the crosshairs onto the lead enemy tank.

"Fire and adjust," Hardee ordered.

Oh's next round hit one of the T62s on the front slope, just below the turret at the point where its armor is thickest. The depleted uranium sabot round punched through. A flash of flame and spall—molten metal that had once been the inside of the tank—shot out the T62's engine compartment. The dead tank stopped immediately, shuddered, smoldered, then exploded as the onboard ammunition cooked off. The turret flew into the air like a giant Frisbee.

In quick succession the tanks were turned into burning tombs for their unsuspecting tank crews. Another T62 incinerated in almost the same instant, proof that the rest of Cold Steel had the enemy in their sights. Tanks and VTTs were smashed into junk as soon as they came into range. The valley was now littered with thirty or more burning enemy vehicles.

"Execute the minefield," Captain Mackenzie's calm voice sounded over the radio.

Sergeant Hardee pressed the clackers one at a time. Five hundred meters to his front, at the narrowest point in the valley, the well-camouflaged mine boxes exploded. Around each box a circle of deadly antitank mines spread out like a fan.

The lead tanks of the second battalion hit the mines and exploded. The second battalion ground to a halt as the tanks maneuvered around the mines and returned fire to the south. The VTTs stacked up behind the tanks were rained on by 120mm mortar rounds that ripped through the APCs' thin top armor.

Hardee watched as the confused enemy attack slowed to a crawl. He ran out of targets; the only thing moving was now north of the MOPM minefields. Slowly the enemy tanks drove to the flanks of the engagement area, trying to avoid the mines and the fire of their tormentors.

Hardee waited without a target. He scanned the battlefield with his CITV. The thermal sight registered dozens of fires in the engagement area. Machine-gun tracers from the tanks and Bradleys of teams C and D cut down the enemy infantry as they tried to flee the wrath of the guns.

1:00 P.M., 3 October, Chorwon Valley, South Korea. "Red Six, this is Red One-Six," the battalion commander of the advance guard battalion reported. "Contact, enemy tanks in Fire Box Five."

Colonel Yi was furious. The enemy was farther forward than expected. Why had the reconnaissance failed? His advance guard was being decimated. "Red One-Six, are you sure? Check the location again."

There was a short pause. Yi could visualize the harried commander of his first battalion moving quickly south, trying to verify the coordinates of the enemy sighting.

"Confirmed, Comrade Commander. The enemy is everywhere."

"How many enemy tanks?" Yi demanded.

"Unknown," was the quick reply, then silence.

With a curt order to his driver, Yi pushed his tank forward toward the developing battle. The VTT with the multiple antennas followed. The squeak of the tank's tracks and the roar of its diesel engine resonated in Yi's bones as he held on to the tank commander's hatch. The hatch opened forward and protected the front of his body as he peered over the top, giving instructions to his driver on where to go. He halted his tank and his deputy commander's APC on top of a rise that overlooked the smoke-filled valley. He raised his Japanese-made binoculars and searched for indications of the success of the advance guard fighting to the south. Through the smoke and fog he could see the flash of fire.

"Red Six, this is Red One-Six. We are being hit by superior forces. Request artillery support—Fire Box Five—for my attack," the advance guard battalion commander screamed. "We need support."

Yi looked at his map. This was not foreseen. Corps headquarters had declared the enemy in retreat. His own reconnaissance had declared the area clear. Besides, it should have been destroyed by the artillery preparation. He did not have fires planned to repeat on Fire Box Five. The artillery was firing preplanned targets farther to the south. Yi could see the advance guard battalion, now only a kilometer to his front, firing with all weapons to the south.

"Continue the attack," Yi replied, acknowledging the advance guard battalion commander's report. "Continue to execute the plan. Artillery fires are being shot as scheduled. Keep moving south. There can be only a few disorganized remnants at Fire Box Five."

The advance guard battalion commander did not reply.

"Red One-Six, this is Red Six," Colonel Yi repeated, trying to make contact with his subordinate commander. "Red One-Six, this is Red Six."

Yi watched as the main body of the brigade, seventy vehicles strong, began a right turn onto the main highway leading south.

The crash of artillery grew closer. He observed bright flashes of red and orange explosions from the main formation of the advance guard battalion. He steadied his binoculars and tried to observe the enemy firing line, but it was too far away to be seen in the fog.

"Red Six, this is Red Two-Six," the 2d Battalion Commander reported rapidly over the radio. "The advance guard battalion is in heavy contact. We've found the Americans. I say again, we've found the Americans."

Colonel Yi grimaced—another surprise. He glanced at his deputy commander, who had heard the same report and was standing in the back of the VTT. So the Americans are not running to Pusan, he mused, studying his battle map.

"Fire artillery on Fire Box Five," Yi yelled to his deputy commander. "I need artillery and infantry support. The enemy is prepared. Order the truck mobile infantry to dismount here and attack both flanks."

"Sir, it will take ten minutes to deploy the guns," the deputy commander protested. "The truck mobile infantry is behind our last battalion. They will take a long time to move forward."

"Just do it," Yi shouted, irritated by the response of his deputy, which reflected an attitude of procedure over requirement. We have created a generation of bureaucrats and robots, Yi thought. "Report our situation to the corps commander and request the corps artillery support I need."

The deputy commander nodded and dropped inside the VTT. Yi looked at his battle map again. There was no turning back now; he was committed. This was not how he had expected it to be. In the military academy and in tactical lectures, he had learned to expect that the armor would be sent in after the enemy had been knocked off balance. The artillery and the infantry were supposed to make the gap; his forces were to exploit the gap. Now it appeared that he was facing a defense that had already trapped half of his brigade.

He could see the billowing black smoke from the charred remains of dozens of T62s. The enemy tank cannon fire was unbelievably accurate. Yi still could not see his attackers. The trail tank company deployed on line in assault formation as best it could and returned fire.

"Red Two-Six, this is Red Six!" the slender colonel screamed over the command radio frequency. "You must break through the enemy's defenses. Answer me."

There was no response.

The plan was falling apart. Yi couldn't believe what was happening. He had to think quickly. He had a sinking feeling in the pit of his stomach. It was now or never.

There was only one thing to do—press on. Yi ordered his artillery battery to fire smoke on the enemy positions. Within ten minutes his artillery was sending rounds downrange. The smoke mixed with the fog would screen the attack.

"All commands, this is Red Six," Colonel Yi shouted over his radio transmitter. "Turn on vehicle smoke generators. Increase speed. All units attack. Continue mission. Everyone advances."

Reducing the visibility was his only chance. If they could get close enough to overwhelm the defenders, Yi felt that his superior numbers would win.

"Driver, move out," Yi ordered, angered by the inability to strike back at his enemies. His tank passed a column of stationary vehicles as he struggled to get to the front. The sound of heavy tank cannons was like a thunderous firing squad—a nightmare.

"Red Six, this is Red Two-Five," the 2d Battalion's deputy commander screamed over the radio. "The commander is dead. We have lost most of our tanks. The enemy has a minefield to our front and we have not been able to breach it."

"Don't stop," Yi answered, incensed at the thought of losing his finest battalion in a matter of minutes. "Keep moving forward. Continue the mission with whatever you have left. Find a way through the minefield."

There was no response.

"Did you monitor my orders?" Yi demanded. "Answer, now."

"Red Six, the deputy commander is also dead," a youthful, agitated voice announced.

"Who am I speaking to?" Colonel Yi demanded.

"This is Lieutenant Paik, platoon leader, 1st Platoon, 2d Company, Comrade Commander."

"Listen carefully. Keep moving south," Yi shouted over his

radio. There was no more he could do. He ordered the rest of his brigade, including the reserve, into the fight.

1:05 P.M., 3 October, Chorwon Valley, South Korea. An enemy tank filled Hardee's sights. This tank was close—too close. Hardee didn't have time for a fire command.

"SHIT!" he screamed, firing the gun himself from the tank commander's override.

His tank rocked backward from the recoil of the 120mm cannon. Hardee's aim was good, but he could hardly have missed at this range. The shell exploded a few feet in front of C34, hitting its mark in one terrible blinding flash of metal against metal. The T62 tank, sixty meters away, crashed to a halt, its turret ripped off in a terrific explosion.

Hardee heard the battle chatter on the platoon radio net. The rest of the platoon fired madly, furiously. The battlefield was now covered with smoke. Tanks and VTT323s were racing south as fast as they could travel over the rough terrain along the fringes of the minefields. A company of APCs moved rapidly through a rice paddy on the south side of the minefield, in plain view of Hardee's sights.

"On the way," Oh screamed as another round fired from his deadly gun.

The shot struck the VTT directly center of mass. The HEAT round punched through the vehicle's armor and blew the VTT apart.

"Target," Hardee announced, absorbed by the moment. The enemy was everywhere. There was no time for pity, no time for remorse. He was fighting for the survival of his crew. If he was ever to get out of this position in one piece, he had to kill them all. "Left VETT, fire."

"On the way." Oh aimed at the left VTT that was now trying to break for cover. At this range he could not miss. The gun fired and recoiled back in its carriage. The small metal stub of the expended shell clanged to the floor.

Hardee saw the second VTT take the high-explosive shell. The HEAT round detonated against the left side of the thin-skinned APC. The energy from the explosion spun the crumpled hull ninety degrees. Fragments of metal and the torn and twisted pieces of an eight-man infantry squad that was seated inside were strewn all over the ground. The charred remains of the APC began to burn.

"Gunner," Hardee yelled as he sat in his tank commander's weapons station, his right hand gripping the tank commander's override control tightly and his right eye pressed against the tank commander's sight. "Where did the third one go? Find him."

The third VTT fired its 14.5mm machine gun at C34. The gun raked the front of the M1A2 in vain, making a futile pinging sound against the tank's superior armor. Oh fired another M830 120mm high-explosive tank round. The third VTT was obliterated, its small turret ripped off and thrown to the ground by the tremendous power of the 120mm HEAT round.

"Got the mother," Oh screamed with delight.

Four T62s came out of the smoke and immediately engaged Sergeant Hardee's tank at point-blank range. Oh fired again at a tank less than three hundred meters away and smashed a HEAT round into the turret ring. The T62 lurched backward as if snapped in two, its turret moving several feet to the rear of the hull. Black smoke billowed from the loader's and tank commander's hatches. Firing rapidly, Oh disabled another T62 as the tank swerved into view. There was a splash of sparks as the tank jerked quickly to a stop from the force of the explosion. This T62 spun to the left in a violent half circle, blocking the path of the other tanks. The hatches opened and the North Korean crew quickly abandoned their smoldering vehicle.

The North Koreans kept coming. More vehicles advanced along the eastern edge of the valley, moving by Hardee at close range. One at a time the enemy vehicles blundered into his engagement area.

Hardee's crew fired as the enemy came into view. They stopped counting how many they had killed. The actions of the crew were automatic. Emerson reloaded rounds into the massive breech of the 120mm cannon. Oh, now in control of the gun, aimed with a vengeance and killed every enemy he shot at.

As Hardee was engaging the tanks, enemy APCs moved forward behind the burning T62 and disgorged their infantry. Hardee scanned to his right and saw North Korean infantry running toward him on the high ground to his right flank and rear.

"Enemy infantry," Emerson shouted, alerting the crew. Looking to his left and right, he saw men running everywhere.

"Gunner. Coax. Troops," Hardee screamed and immediately jumped up in his hatch and manned his .50-caliber machine gun. "Fire and adjust."

Hardee plastered the ridge with bullets. Oh's 7.62mm machine gun also blazed away at the North Koreans.

"Hernandez, let's get out of here," Hardee ordered over the intercom. "Move forward, fast."

Oh continued shooting his M240. Enemy infantry squads roamed all over the place, trying to avoid the fire from the tank's machine guns. Moving the turret from the gunner's position, Oh jerked it back and forth, firing at targets.

A North Korean suddenly stood up within fifteen feet of the tank in an attempt to launch an RPG rocket at C34. The tank shot out of its position and pulverized the enemy gunner against the side of the rocky hill. Other North Koreans fired RPGs at the rampaging tank.

Two brilliant explosions detonated against C34's left side, forcing the tank to stop. Hardee poked his head above the turret and saw the tank's left track roll off the support rollers. Hernandez, not knowing that the left track was broken, revved the engine. The right track churned in the mud and jerked the tank to the right, forcing C34 into the side of the hill.

1:15 P.M., 3 October, Chorwon Valley, South Korea. Yi bit his lip. The two lead battalions were gone. If that was the cost of victory, he would pay it. So be it.

"Where is the light tank battalion?" Yi screamed.

"Red Six, this is Red Four-Six," the light tank battalion commander answered. "I have found a way around the enemy's defenses. I am moving southwest toward the junction of Highway 325 and 37. I will be there in fifteen minutes. Over."

"Excellent," Yi answered. "Continue the attack and flank the enemy from west to east. Over."

"Nam chim," the officer shouted.

Yi trained his binoculars toward the south. The battle area was filled with the smoke from generators, blazing vehicles, and burning smoke pots. "Continue the attack, 3d Battalion. All units, continue the attack." Machine-gun tracers arched high over the area, ricocheting off rocks and hitting the tops of small hills. The crash of artillery and the roar and dust from tank cannon obscured the movement of the individual vehicles as they continued in their deadly shuffle of attacker against defender. The lead North Korean tanks and VTTs were all firing to their front. Most had stopped, opened their back doors, and dismounted their infantry.

The T62s and VTTs of the fresh 3d Battalion raced toward wreckage of the lead battalions. The fresh wave of T62 tanks fired with their 115mm cannons in controlled volley fire on the American positions. AT-5 antitank missile gunners in VTTs also sought targets and let their missiles fly.

Now we have them, Yi said to himself with a grim smile. I will fix them here with the 3d Battalion while the light tanks flank them from the east. We can still crush them.

The 3d Battalion increased its fire as the infantry dismounted and rushed forward. Through gaps in the smoke and fog, Colonel Yi could see his infantry climbing out of their APCs. With explosives, grappling hooks, and bare hands, they threw themselves at the enemy minefield in a desperate attempt to clear the way for the tanks. The soldiers then marked the entrance and exit of the minefield with bright orange panels and engineer tape. One after another North Korean soldiers fell to the devastating fire of the unseen enemy. Finally, after much sacrifice, one wide lane was cut through the American minefield.

Colonel Yi's armor raced to the breach.

9

BREAKOUT

Troops were getting killed, in pain and fury and dust and filth. What has happened to the widely heralded push-button warfare where skilled, immaculate technicians who had never suffered the misery and ignominy of basic training blew each other to kingdom come like gentlemen?
—T. R. FEHRENBACH

1:35 P.M., 3 October, Chorwon Valley, South Korea. Rodriguez thanked his luck as the enemy's artillery fire fell harmlessly in the valley behind his task force. The dense fog and the destruction of the enemy's reconnaissance forces had given the Americans a temporary advantage. Rodriguez wondered how long he could maintain this edge.

The radios barked madly, adding their discordant screech to the thud of explosions and the loud crack of 120mm cannon. Rodriguez's IVIS screen flashed one digital message after another. He scanned them quickly, looked at the location of his forces on the screen, then switched to his CITV thermal site and surveyed the valley to the north.

Blazing and shattered North Korean armored vehicles littered the battlefield. The enemy's courage and determination had not been enough to escape the trap that he had carefully constructed. In the first few minutes of the fight, the combined firepower of Team Steel and Team Dealer devastated the enemy's advance guard formation. Then the second North Korean battalion hit the command-detonated MOPM minefields and was chopped up in the confusion. The enemy's main force charged into the melee, rushing into the smoke and debris without a sense of the trap that Rodriguez was about to spring.

"Lovely, just lovely," he said to himself. He panned the width and depth of engagement area Maine through his CITV. He rechecked his digital display to determine his losses. The digital report depicted none. This report did not tell him about losses to Bradleys or M113 vehicles—only the M1A2s had the IVIS terminals that sent automatic digital reports—but this was good news.

Rodriguez nodded as if he were approving his next move. He depressed the button on the battalion radio hand mike. "Renegade Six, this is Dragon Six. Send me a SITREP. Over."

"This is Renegade Six. Engaging enemy tanks and Vetts in engagement area New York, center, alpha. We're amber now and killing them as fast as they come up. They keep coming, but we can hold them. I've lost two Bradleys. Six KIA, four WIA. Request mortar fire on Michigan center and New York north."

"Hold 'em, Renegade," Rodriguez answered sternly, wincing at the casualties that Sharpe reported. Amber meant that Sharpe's team was at 75 to 89 percent strength. "You have priority for mortar fires right now."

"Roger, Dragon Six. We'll hold. We've got them stacked up on Route 325. They can't bypass us."

Rodriguez noted the location of his tanks on the IVIS screen. Now is the time to commit the reserve, he thought. "Bulldog Six, move to ABF Two-Two, now."

"Wilco, Dragon Six," answered Capt. Al Grey, the Bravo Company commander, in response to Rodriguez's request that he move to attack-by-fire-position Two-Two. "My lead platoon will be there in a few minutes. I'll set the entire team on a firing line at ABF Two-Two. We'll be close together, but we'll stop them. I'm sending you my graphics now. Over."

"Get 'em, Bulldog," Rodriguez answered as he simultaneously scanned his IVIS screen and saw Grey's attack plan superimposed on a 1:50,000 map. Rodriguez felt a surge of confidence in his men and their machines. He realized that the central problem in combat was motivating men to fight; the training and discipline were paying off.

Rodriguez scanned engagement areas Maine and New

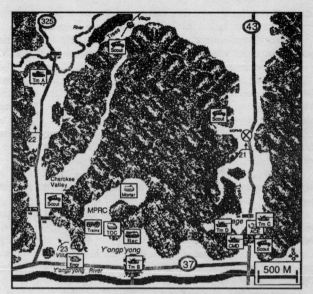

Dragon Force Defense Plan

Hampshire through his thermal sight. His tank commander's hatch was open. The noise of battle rose to a fever pitch, so loud that he heard the explosions through his CVC helmet inside *Firebreather*'s turret. Team Steel and Team Dealer were firing so rapidly that Rodriguez couldn't make out the individual shots. The explosions seemed to center on the area west of the road, right where the enemy was attempting to breach the mine-field.

"Bulldog Six," Rodriguez added, doing his best to remain calm on the command frequency, "once you gain fire superiority at ABF Two-Two, I want you to drive through them all the way to ABF Two-Four. Take out everything in your wake."

"Wilco, Dragon Six," Grey shouted over the radio.

"Bulldog Six, this is Steel Six," Capt. Ken Mackenzie interjected. "We've destroyed at least two battalions of tanks and a dozen Vetts, but they're still coming. They can't see us in the fog and smoke. They're headed right for ABF Two-Two."

"Roger, Steel," Bulldog replied, cross-talking on the battalion commander's net with his fellow company commander. "We'll be there in four minutes. Hang on."

Rodriguez considered his options as the crash of battle intensified. The sound of hypervelocity armor-piercing rounds tearing through metal turrets punctuated his thoughts. Was he making the right decisions?

Rodriguez glanced at Captain Drake in the APC positioned a few meters from *Firebreather.* "Anything from brigade or division?"

"Negative, sir," Drake shouted back, shaking his head. "I'm eavesdropping on the Renegade net. They're in quite a fight right now."

"Renegade will stop them. They don't make them any better," Rodriguez yelled back confidently, taking off his CVC helmet to hear the reply better. "But let's hedge our bets. Keep trying to get us some air support. If we get it, I'll use it to finish the enemy in the east. Once that's done, we can shift one of the other companies to support Renegade."

Drake nodded, climbed out the back door of his APC, and ran over to the ETAC. A few minutes later a young sergeant wearing U.S. Air Force stripes on his BDUs looked up at Rodriguez from *Firebreather*'s side.

"Sergeant, if there's anything flying, I sure could use it now," the task force commander shouted, his voice cracking from the strain. "We have them now; we need to finish them. I just committed my reserve. The only reserve I have left are these two tanks and three M113s. It sure would be nice to get the air force into this fight."

The airman nodded, beaming a smile that went from ear to ear. "I've got a flight of A-10s inbound in fifteen minutes, sir."

"I don't know how you did it, but, by God, if you get me that flight of A-10s I'll take back everything bad I ever said about zoomies." Rodriguez grinned and wiped the sweat and dirt from his face with his right hand. "Just get me those damn planes."

The airman nodded and raced back to his armored personnel carrier.

Rodriguez put his CVC helmet back on. The nerve-racking ordeal of commanding a combined-arms task force in battle was quickly draining his energy. His confidence was bolstered by the knowledge that the task force would finally get some air support. We're not alone and forgotten, he thought. He reached down inside *Firebreather*'s turret, removed the canteen from the side wall rack, and took a quick gulp of water.

The boom of tank cannon resonated in the valley and increased to a crescendo.

"Dragon Six, the Bulldogs are set at ABF Two-Two, attacking by fire. We're cutting them down before they even see us."

"Take them down, Bulldog," Rodriguez said fiercely into the radio transmitter of his CVC helmet. "Everybody fights; nobody quits. Attack, and don't let a single one of the bastards get away."

1:45 P.M., 3 October, Chorwon Valley, South Korea. The battle was grinding on like a huge machine pounding out products until there were no more parts left to stamp. The machine would grind to its inevitable conclusion. A few more minutes, Colonel Yi imagined, and he would have them. He had never lost at anything in his life. He swore that his proud brigade would not lose now. He dreamed of victory.

"Enemy aircraft," the panicked cry resounded over the brigade's radio frequency. "Air defense alert. Enemy aircraft."

A pair of American A-10 attack aircraft flew in low out of the thick, dark clouds, avoiding the S-300 air defense missile system by masking their movements with the steep ridgelines. Flying only a few meters above the remnants of the advance guard battalion, the A-10s made a determined run at their targets. The lead aircraft, like a winged avenger, discharged a Maverick missile as it flew directly over Colonel Yi's tank. The colonel, incensed by the enemy attack aircraft, rapidly turned his 12.7mm antiaircraft machine gun in the direction of the retreating aircraft and let off a long burst of fire.

Other T62s and VTT323s engaged the enemy aircraft with 12.7mm and 14.5mm machine guns. The bullets chased the American planes like maddened hornets defending their hive. Massed machine-gun fire, however, could not stop the attackers. A cluster bomb fell on top of the column of T62 tanks behind Yi, reducing ten vehicles to smoking wrecks.

"Damn them, damn them," Yi cursed as he searched the battlefield for his air defense artillery. "Where in hell is the air defense?"

The A-10s flew into the clouds again. A swarm of air defense missiles shot into the heavens toward the aircrafts' direction of flight. Undaunted, the A-10s returned and made a second pass. They fired their 30mm cannon at the stalled North Korean column and dropped more cluster bombs. A dozen vehicles staggered to a stop as the bomblets fell on their thin-skinned roofs. Metal struck metal with a hollow boom. A fleeting glow of orange-red molten metal was followed by a thick *KARRUMP* as the warhead detonated ammunition or fuel inside. The armored personnel carriers exploded in fiery balls. Yi watched in terror as his infantry squads struggled to escape from the burning vehicles and the rain of death from above.

A pair of ZSU antiaircraft guns finally got into the action. Two ZSU-57-2s riddled the sky with 57mm cannon fire, but the A-10s flew away undamaged. In their wake they left three burning VTT323s and seven shattered tanks.

The stricken vehicles burned fiercely and the attack slowed down. More tanks and APCs rushed to the sides of the road and tried to disperse or seek cover. As the attack slowed down, more vehicles were hammered by tank cannon fire from attackers hidden in the fog. The distinctive crack of enemy tank fire filled the air as Yi's armor jammed tightly together in the valley. Ten armored vehicles that had been in the lead were now nothing more than hunks of twisted metal projecting jaggedly from clouds of swirling flame. Follow-on vehicles, with nowhere to turn, were blocked by the exploding wrecks and jerked to a halt. Others peeled off right and left, attempting to find routes through the burning hulks.

Damn them, Colonel Yi cursed again to himself. Everything is going wrong.

North Korean artillery shells screamed overhead, blasting away at an enemy that Yi could not see. Missiles and tracer bullets filled the air, but the enemy fire never slackened. A new wave of T62 tanks surged forward, spraying cannon and machine-gun fire to the south.

Battles revolve on courage, Yi thought. These devils we're fighting will see how real soldiers fight. Yi pushed his radio transmitter forward. "Press the attack. All battalions attack south. No one stops."

The fire from my tanks and missiles is ineffective, Yi thought. The artillery fire is not moving them. A chill raced down his spine. He would not break through the enemy's defenses. His brigade was dying.

"We must break through," Yi shouted, slamming his fist against the top of his tank. "We must break through."

The enemy aircraft returned for a second attack and were greeted by a wall of antiaircraft fire. In spite of it, the A-10s strafed the column with 30mm cannon fire. Two tanks of the lead element were engulfed in a flurry of explosions. In seconds the aircraft raced east, dipping low over the ridges to avoid the antiaircraft fire. Hundreds of green machine-gun tracers chased the low-flying aircraft. Antiaircraft missiles, shoulder-launched versions of an improved SA-14, streaked through the air at the retreating A-10s. The trail aircraft exploded in a brilliant red-yellow fireball as the lead A-10 made a large arc to the north to return for its final attack.

2:00 P.M., 3 October, Chorwon Valley, South Korea. "There's fucking infantry all over the place!" Hardee screamed as he grabbed the tank commander's override control and slewed the turret to the right rear. The turret jolted to an abrupt stop as it hit the rock and dirt wall of the mountain.

"Damnit," Hardee cursed as he struggled with his hatch to stick his head and shoulders outside the turret. "Emerson, man your loader's machine gun, now."

With a mighty heave, the tank commander opened his hatch to the full open position. A sudden bright flash and a wave of hot air forced Sergeant Hardee back inside the turret.

"Sarge, I think we were hit," Emerson yelled.

Emerson looked through his left vision block. An RPG round had struck the tank's left sponson box. Emerson opened the hatch, then abruptly fell back into the turret.

He couldn't move. He felt dazed, and his arms and legs didn't want to work. His mouth was dry and his heart was racing. Suddenly he felt as if he were going to die. He just stood there, next to the radios, his 7.62mm machine gun sitting in its mount above the turret, silent. He couldn't find the strength to push his body up to stand on the loader's seat and man his machine gun.

"Emerson, what's wrong? Are you hurt?" Hardee shouted into the intercom, his big hands charging the machine-gun bolt to the rear. Within seconds his .50-caliber was rattling loud, long bursts of fire. "Get that gun firing."

Rifle and grenade fire resonated outside Emerson's open hatch. Trembling like a trapped animal ready for a snake to strike, Emerson didn't move.

"Emerson," Hardee yelled again.

"I'll man the gun," Oh shouted as he pushed past Hardee's feet and climbed past Emerson to man the loader's machine gun.

Perspiration streamed down Emerson's face. His balaclava and Nomex uniform were soaked with sweat. He cringed in horror, unable to make himself move as he watched his crew fight for their lives.

Emerson could see Hardee only from the waist down as the tank commander madly fired his .50-caliber machine gun. Hardee stood with his head outside the turret to see his attackers on the ridge to his right and rear. The noise was tremendous. Fifty-caliber hot brass casings fell inside the turret as Hardee swung back and forth wildly in his tank commander's weapon station.

Emerson's eyes burned from the exhaust of machine-gun rounds and smoke. He rubbed his eyes and discovered that he was crying. He realized with shame that he was trembling uncontrollably. He couldn't believe what was happening.

"Hardee, there's an RPG team, direct front," Private Hernandez yelled over the tank intercom.

The steady hammer of the .50-caliber stopped. Sergeant Hardee ducked down into the turret and reached for another box of ammunition. He looked scornfully at Emerson. "We need your help, now," he shouted.

"Sarge, RPG, direct front," Hernandez screamed again over the tank's intercom.

Hardee stood up in the turret just as the high-explosive warhead hit the top of the tank commander's hatch. The force of the blast cut Hardee in two, leaving his bisected torso hanging off the side of the turret bustle rack.

Emerson screamed as blood gushed into the turret. He vomited uncontrollably. The turret started to smoke as pieces of burning cloth and debris fell through the tank commander's position. Hardee's smoldering half torso lay crumpled in the tank commander's stand, the cut portion facing Emerson. He had to get away from the horror of the thing that sat gushing blood just a few feet from him.

Oh, standing above Emerson, continued to fire the loader's machine gun. Swiveling quickly to engage a new target, his knee forced Emerson against the radios. Choking from smoke and vomit, Emerson took off his CVC helmet and threw it on the turret floor. In a panic he tore his soaking-wet balaclava off his face.

Bullets ricocheted off the top of the tank. Oh suddenly stopped firing and fell inside the turret, bleeding from the face and neck. Emerson jumped aside. He glanced at Oh and saw the bloody face of his friend. Oh's eyes seemed to beg for help, but his mouth was shot away and his attempts to talk only brought up bright-red blood. Emerson laid him down on the turret floor. A sickly, gurgling sound emanated from Oh's throat, then a final death rattle.

Emerson stood paralyzed. Oh was dead at his feet, and Hardee's bloody, dismembered body lay in front of him. The turret was awash in blood. Emerson's heart was racing and his mind was in chaos. He felt impotent and ashamed. In sheer panic he realized that someone had jumped onto the back deck of his tank. Like an animal making his last stand against a predator, he found his senses abruptly sharpened. He feverishly reached for the loader's hatch release, pulled hard, and closed the hatch.

A screeching sound, the roar of an attack aircraft, resonated in the turret. A huge rumble of hundreds of explosions overwhelmed his senses as the cluster bomb exploded above the tank. He felt as if he were being crushed. Falling to the bottom of the turret, he pushed Oh's blood-soaked body away with his feet. The tank shook from the thunder of hundreds of small explosions. The fire scarred the tank, striking the outside with shards of flying steel. Emerson could hear the dull whack of high-explosive bomblets detonating against the sides of the tank. This is the end, he thought. He closed his eyes, waiting to be eaten by the horrible red monster of war.

The tank slowly filled with smoke. Choking for air but unwilling to open the hatch for fear of the enemy, Emerson waited until he could no longer breathe. Finally he forced himself up, pushed open the hatch, and gasped a huge gulp of fresh air. Slowly he slithered onto the top of the turret and climbed off the tank.

Surveying the scene, he realized that there wasn't anyone on top of C34 anymore. A VTT and a North Korean tank burned just a few meters in front of his tank. Pieces of dead North Korean infantrymen were strewn everywhere. Clumps of mangled bodies lay on the ground as if they were seeking company in the mournful sorrow of death. It looked like a scene from Dante's *Inferno*. No one in the open had survived the cluster bomb. No one could have survived.

Emerson ducked instinctively as a round cooked off in the glowing North Korean tank. The explosion hurled a piece of jagged metal the size of a car door fifty feet into the air. The noise of the battle was growing. It seemed to get nearer and nearer as it echoed in the valley. The smoke, the smell of burning diesel fuel, and the scenes of the dead dominated Emerson's senses. C34 lay smoldering in a graveyard of dead and dying men. He saw Hernandez lying in a bloody heap near the front of the tank, the driver's hatch wide open. Smoke wafted over the battlefield, rolling in like a low-flying cloud.

Emerson's chest tightened; it was difficult to think, hard to breathe. Gripped by real and imagined terrors, he thought only of escape. Ashamed and defeated, and without a helmet or provisions, he ran to the east, up to the high ground, away from the battle.

2:05 P.M., 3 October, Chorwon Valley, South Korea. "Red Six, the breach in the enemy's minefield is blocked with wrecked tanks," the commander of the 3d Tank Battalion reported. The noise of firing and the rattle of machine guns sounded in the background of the radio transmission.

"Red Three-Six, you must establish a new breach," the

brigade commander screamed over the command radio frequency.

"Yes, Red Six," the 3d Battalion commander answered frantically.

The 3d Battalion charged through the smoke. The rest of the main body, still north of the obstacle, massed its tanks and APCs for the final push. Colonel Yi, his tank intermeshed with the lead company of the 3d Battalion, moved south toward the sound of the guns. The vehicles in the tightly packed column were twenty meters apart. The firing was so substantial that he could feel it in his stomach.

"Red Six, this is Red Two-Six. We will make a new breach fifty meters to the west of the main highway. We're marking it with panels now."

"Excellent. Keep moving forward. Get through the new breach and charge them with everything you have left," Yi answered. He realized that he had taken heavy casualties, but if he could push through and take out the defenders, his sacrifice would have meaning. He depressed his throat mike button to key the radio. "Push on to seize the brigade objective. One last rush will force us through."

"Red Six, this is Red Three-Six. The breach is established fifty meters west of the highway," the voice of the lead battalion commander of the main body announced over the command frequency.

"All elements, move through the marked lane west of the highway," Yi ordered. "Keep moving. Our objective must be reached at all costs."

Yi's tank rushed steadily through the smoke down the axis of attack. Yi strained to see what was happening. The sound of explosions increased. He broke through a cloud of smoke and saw the advancing line of tanks. Yi could not see the enemy.

The smoke grew thick again, and Yi could suddenly see little. Oily black smoke covered the battlefield. Thick clouds of burning diesel fuel emanated from dozens of flaming VTT323 APCs and T62 tanks. Enemy tank fire forced the 3d Battalion to form a firing line a thousand meters from the initial objective.

White smoke blanketed the valley. Blotches of thick black burning diesel indicated the death of dozens of North Korean armored vehicles. Unable to see anything but the smoke of the vehicles in front of them, the tanks and APCs floundered in the chaos, queuing up at the entrance of the breach like people lining up to see a movie. As the new lane became choked with burning tanks, VTTs and T62 tanks charged to the right and left rather than stand still. The tanks and APCs moved forward, unable to avoid the deadly antitank mines as they tried to bull through the minefield. A few exploded. Others charged and got through the mines only to be ripped apart by a buzz saw of 120mm fire on the southern side.

"Damn them," Yi cursed. He realized that the Americans with their thermal sights could see right through the smoke. "We are being slaughtered."

He sensed a bitter copper taste in his mouth. Could this be the taste of defeat? he wondered. The sound of explosions resonated across the valley.

"Red Six, this is Red Three-Six," the commander of Yi's last remaining battalion reported. "Enemy defense has not been penetrated. The attack from the march has . . ."

The radio transmission ended in midsentence.

Yi's T62 rolled on through the smoke and carnage. To his right flank, toward the west, he saw a line of burning T62 tanks. Their turrets, lying upside down on top of their hulls, was grim testimony to the accuracy and power of the enemy's weapons. The line of blazing wrecks discharged thick clouds of oily black smoke.

Yi shuddered, unnerved by the ferocity of the devastation. His hatred for the enemy intensified. How can this be happening? he thought. What kind of devils am I fighting? My plan is falling apart. My brigade, a force of ninety-one T62 tanks, forty-six M1985 light tanks, and thirty-one VTT323s, is being obliterated.

A line of VTTs formed to force its way across the minefield. The lead VTT in the queue, only two hundred meters to Yi's left, exploded as it triggered an antitank mine. The high-explosive charge detonated through the belly of the thin-skinned APC, igniting the onboard fuel and ammunition. The rest of the column stopped. The second VTT was hammered by a sabot round and exploded in an orange fireball. Thick black smoke billowed to the sky as vehicles burned.

The vehicles crossed the intervisibility line, a crest that the tanks could not see over, and were met by the crash of accurate 120mm tank gunfire. One T62 after another burst into flames as turrets were ripped from hulls. Through his vision blocks, Yi could see pillars of smoke rising high into the air. It was a slaughter. They are killing us all, he thought. He considered turning around but knew that such an idea was impossible. Honor would not allow it. Besides, the column of vehicles pressing behind him would just push him forward. Even if he did get back, he would only be shot for cowardice.

"No, the way is forward," he muttered defiantly.

But the North Korean infantry had taken enough. Because their tanks and APCs carry their ammunition exposed in the turret, the risk of explosion is great. Shocked soldiers opened the hatches and doors of their halted APCs and staggered away from the devastating tank fire.

Vehicles from several formations were intermingled in the smoke. Yi's tank was third in line. All at once, the lead tank burst into flame. The turret exploded and separated from the hull. To avoid a collision, Yi's tank moved quickly to the right, past the burning, stalled wreck. The second tank moved to the left and passed the burning tank. With a shower of sparks, a 120mm tank round slammed into the side of the second tank, flipping it over.

Yi was now leading the attack. He saw the breach markers. Burning tanks and APCs littered the path to the markers. "Gunner, disregard the fire. Face front. Driver, go through the breach. Stay within the markings."

Yi's T62 moved through the breach lane, then jerked to an abrupt halt. A burning tank blocked the entrance. The report had been false or incorrect. The minefield had never been completely cleared.

"Driver," Yi screamed over his intercom, "hard right. Don't get close to that burning tank."

It was already too late. An armor-piercing round hit Colonel Yi's T62 in the left side before the driver could execute the command. The tank spun violently to the left and flipped upside down. Yi crashed against the top of his turret. Battered but alive, he struggled to exit his tank. The driver screamed as smoke billowed from the driver's compartment. Yi clawed at the hatch to find an avenue of escape. The turret quickly filled with smoke. Trapped inside a steel coffin, Yi screamed in panic.

Mercifully, the T62's ammunition ignited. Engulfed in a flash of flame and burning, twisted metal, Yi and his crew disintegrated in the blast.

2:25 P.M., 3 October, Chorwon Valley, South Korea. "Dragon Six, this is Dragon Five," Major Lucas reported. "Flash spot report. Over."

"Send it," Rodriguez answered. The voice of his executive officer carried a tone of worry and shock that Rodriguez had never heard before. Something was wrong.

"Scouts report that the enemy is advancing in battalion strength down Cherokee Valley, heading southwest. Two scout Hummers are down. The North Koreans are flanking us. I ordered the Volcano to start laying mines ASAP."

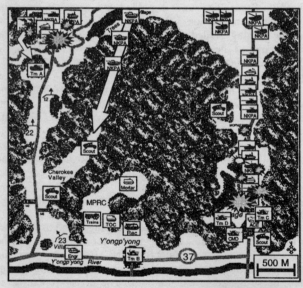

Battle at Highway 43 and Highway 325

"Acknowledged," Rodriguez answered. A hundred thoughts bombarded his mind at once. The enemy had split his defense by coming down a trail he hadn't expected.

"The engineers are laying minefield M3 now," Lucas added.

Time was pressing on. Lucas had done the right thing by ordering the engineers to execute a Volcano minefield at location M3. Now, Rodriguez had to react to this new move quickly, before the enemy broke out of Cherokee Valley. He'd already committed the Bulldogs, his reserve company. Captain Grey's ten tanks were fighting against the remnants of the brigade on Highway 43. The only force that Lucas had left was the two tanks and three APCs of his command group.

"Dragon Six, this is Renegade Six. I monitored. I'm committed here. If I try to move back, they'll have clear shots at my grill doors as I withdraw."

"Roger, Renegade Six. Stay where you are and continue mission. I'm moving to ABF Two-One to block the enemy's attack now. Dragon Five, organize a new reserve, at least a platoon, from Steel or Dealer and send them to help me."

"Wilco, Dragon Six," Lucas answered. "I've got scouts with eyes on Cherokee Valley. I'll switch priority of mortar fire to them to slow down the enemy."

Rodriguez didn't have time to answer. He waved his right arm in a circle above his head. Major Bradford, standing in the turret of *Defiant,* only fifty meters to the right of *Firebreather,* nodded. "Follow me, Dragon Three. We're all there is."

"Moving now," Bradford replied as his tank backed out of its fighting position.

The command group moved swiftly to the west. The tanks kicked up spires of muddy water as they raced ahead of the slower M113s.

"Scouts report that the lead enemy tanks are M1985s," Lucas said. For some reason Rodriguez couldn't hear the scouts, probably due to the rough terrain. Lucas was doing a great job of managing the fight while Rodriguez moved toward the action.

Firebreather arrived at ABF Two-Three just as the lead elements of the North Korean battalion turned the southern corner of Cherokee Valley.

The engineers were still laying mines. The lightly armored

M548 chassis that carried the Volcano mine dispenser was sitting in the open, directly in front of the advancing enemy.

"Volcano crew, get out of there," Rodriguez screamed in vain over the task force radio frequency.

The Volcano exploded in a shower of sparks and flame. Two soldiers who had been outside the vehicle ran away from the enemy, but they were too late. The fast-moving North Korean tanks gunned them down.

"Damnit," Rodriguez cursed. "Gunner, sabot. Four tanks. Fire and adjust."

Rodriguez stood in the open hatch of his tank commander's station, firing his .50-caliber machine gun at the advancing enemy tanks, trying to draw their fire away from the engineers.

"Turn right," Rodriguez shouted to his driver over the intercom. "Hold your right track." The big tank lurched forward, moved off the trail, then pivoted to face toward the enemy.

Firebreather and *Defiant* swung into the attack. Their tank cannon boomed. The enemy returned fire at their attackers with a ragged volley of twelve tanks.

Three 76mm cannon shells hit the ground to *Firebreather*'s right. Another round exploded in front of them, erupting in a billow of white smoke. *Firebreather* charged through the smoke. Dozens of enemy vehicles now spilled into the valley and raced to the cover of a tall rice paddy embankment.

"Jones, move forward to the right, through the rice paddies," Rodriguez yelled. "Let's get them. Move to the right . . . move right. . . . MOVE."

Enemy tanks were advancing in a staggered column, firing at the M1A2s as they went. Tank shells landed all around *Firebreather* as it surged forward. *Defiant* lunged ahead to Rodriguez's left, firing as it moved. The two M1A2s killed a tank every seven seconds, but the enemy kept coming, racing into the low ground. The valley filled with smoke as the North Koreans closed the range.

Rodriguez's tank raced off the narrow dirt trail to their front. Obrisky fired the tank's main gun on the move. Two more enemy tanks exploded from his fire. Moving the turret from the gunner's position, Obrisky jerked it from one target to the next, picking off targets in rapid succession.

Obrisky fired another sabot round at an advancing M1985 as

Rodriguez swung his .50-caliber in the direction of a second enemy tank. A steady, continuous burst of heavy machine-gun bullets sparked against the flank of the enemy tank.

North Korean tanks swarmed toward them across the muddy rice paddies and trails in the open valley. The lead North Korean tanks were now only a hundred meters away.

Jones turned *Firebreather* violently to the left in a last attempt to avoid an unseen paddy dike. Missing the dike by inches, Jones crashed the tank into a deep ditch in the muddy rice paddy. The tank pitched forward forcefully, throwing the crew against the turret walls. At the same time, Obrisky, who was tracking a light tank only fifty meters to the right front, fired.

The M1985 blew apart, its turret flying wildly into the air. More enemy tanks bypassed the wreck and moved past *Firebreather*, strafing the tank with 7.62mm bullets.

"Back up," Rodriguez cried as he ducked down and a flurry of lead struck the periscopes in his tank commander's station.

Reacting quickly, Jones slammed the tank into reverse. The tank jumped backward just as two enemy tanks were passing them. The powerful engine of the M1A2 threw the tank straight into them, smashing it against one North Korean tank before Rodriguez could avoid the collision. Rodriguez, out of machine-gun ammunition, swung the turret around and fired the main gun.

The 120mm projectile screamed through the air. It burst the North Korean light tank apart at the seams, showering the rice paddy with pieces of metal.

The loader shouted "UP," having loaded another sabot round into the cannon.

"They keep coming," Bradford screamed over the radio.

Rodriguez heard Bradford but didn't have time to answer. He looked through his vision blocks toward *Defiant*. Suddenly there was a blinding flash. The air ripped apart with a shattering explosion as Bradford's tank took a direct hit from a 76mm cannon. The top of the turret burned brightly for a few seconds as the .50-caliber ammunition cooked off in a fiery, terrible stream of sparks.

"On the way," Obrisky shouted, barely making out the clumps of enemy rushing toward his sight. The 120mm projectile tore into another lightly armored North Korean tank. Obrisky fired two more rounds, blunting the enemy's drive. The enemy tanks moved forward in groups of three or four, firing 76mm cannons, frantically trying to close the distance to destroy the Americans.

Clouds of smoke hung low over the battle position.

"Keep firing. Get the bastards," Rodriguez yelled to his gunner.

A 76mm round had struck *Firebreather* on the left side of the turret. The hard armor of the M1A2 took the blow as nothing more than a slap across the cheek in a fistfight.

Machine-gun bullets ricocheted off the hard armor of the American tank. The sleeping bags and personal gear in *Firebreather*'s bustle rack burned, billowing smoke from the top of the turret.

BOOM! Obrisky fired another round, torching another North Korean tank.

Bullets ricocheted off the top of Rodriguez's tank. He slammed the hatch shut and looked through his right vision block just in time to see two enemy soldiers running toward the tank and carrying a large satchel. His .50 was out of ammunition. Thinking quickly, Rodriguez drew his .45 from his shoulder holster, pulled back the slide, and chambered a round. He took a deep breath and pushed open the hatch.

In one quick move he stood up in the turret, aimed, and fired a magazine of .45 slugs at the two North Koreans. Quickly he ducked down and slammed the hatch closed.

His heart racing, he looked through his vision blocks. The two enemy soldiers lay dead fifteen feet from *Firebreather*'s right flank.

Rodriguez felt the ground shake as the enemy satchel charge exploded. Rocks and debris banged against the tank. He reached for a new magazine for his pistol and quickly reloaded.

The enemy was now more cautious. Three M1985s took up hasty positions behind a rice paddy dike and fired at *Firebreather.* Obrisky returned fire, destroying another North Korean vehicle.

"We're with you now," the jubilant voice of Capt. Ken Mackenzie sounded over Rodriguez's earphones.

Rodriguez sighed with relief. He looked to his rear with his

CITV and saw five M1A2 tanks racing north, their guns blasting away as they moved. The few remaining enemy tanks abandoned their hasty positions and tried to flee to the north. Team Steel's tanks ran them down.

In seconds the battle was over.

Rodriguez scanned forward with his CITV. Burning enemy tanks were scattered all over the valley. None of the North Korean tanks had survived. Then he noticed that *Defiant* was seeping black smoke from the top of its turret.

"Dragon Three, this is Dragon Six. Report."

There was no response.

"I'm headed outside," Rodriguez announced over *Firebreather*'s intercom. "Obrisky, get up here and man the turret."

Rodriguez muscled out of his hatch, his .45-caliber pistol cocked and ready to fire. The battlefield was ominously quiet except for the rumble of C Company's tanks as they moved north and fired machine guns at withdrawing enemy soldiers. Carefully Rodriguez climbed down off the tank.

As he touched the ground, a dazed enemy soldier suddenly staggered in front of *Firebreather*. Surprised, the North Korean hesitated for a second, then fired his weapon. Rodriguez ducked as AK-47 bullets ripped wildly against the tank's metal sides.

Rodriguez dropped to one knee and fired his .45 three times. The North Korean took all three slugs. The rounds shattered the man's chest and flung him off his feet. He landed on his back in a puddle of stagnant water. Rodriguez kept his pistol trained on the dead man, then looked back at the tank.

Obrisky peeked his head out of the TC's station.

"Obrisky, stay with *Firebreather* and man the machine guns," Rodriguez ordered with fire in his voice. "I'm going to check on the S3."

Rodriguez arrived at Bradford's tank and climbed onto the back deck. Sergeant Lanham, the major's gunner, was outside leaning against the side of the turret, ashen faced. The loader stood on the ground near *Defiant*'s left side with an M16 cradled in his arms.

"The major's dead," Lanham said, sobbing. "I told him to button up. He had the hatch in open protected."

Rodriguez didn't reply. Major Tony Bradford was a tough

warrior and his good friend. Tony had always supported him with an eager, can-do attitude that made every mission a challenge rather than a task. Rodriguez had never known a better man.

"The bastards hit the TC's station. The blast took off the top of his head. He's still in the turret. There's blood everywhere," Lanham continued, tears streaking down his face. "I told him to button up. I told him . . ."

Rodriguez put his hand on Lanham's shoulder. The touch was worth more than words. The two men stood together for a few minutes.

"I'll send Obrisky over with some medics to give you a hand with Major Bradford. We'll be moving out soon and I need every tank in the fight."

Rodriguez looked inside the turret at the body of his friend. Bradford was unrecognizable with half his head shot away. Rodriguez turned away and stumbled back to *Firebreather*. Before he reached his tank he knelt down and heaved for a few moments until there was nothing left to spit up. Slowly he wiped his chin and slumped down on the ground against *Firebreather*'s track.

He had never felt so exhausted, so totally drained from the exertion and the emotion of the fight. He was sick of making life-and-death decisions, but he knew he couldn't quit. Grieving for the loss of his friend, he gazed at the smoking battlefield. Forty burning enemy tanks dotted the valley—an entire enemy battalion destroyed. He could smell nitrocellulose, the distinct odor of the combustible 120mm tank rounds, mingled with the acrid scent of flaming rubber and burned flesh. Three hundred meters away a burning enemy tank exploded, shaking the ground and shooting metal fragments into the air.

I really hate this madness, he thought.

10

WITHDRAWAL

But acquiescence society may not have, if it wants an army worth a damn. By the very nature of its mission, the military must maintain a hard and illiberal view of life and the real world. Society's purpose is to live; the military's is to stand ready, if need be, to die.

— T. R. FEHRENBACH

3:00 A.M., 4 October, Task Force 2-72 command group, Chorwon Valley, South Korea. An occasional explosion and the incensed, distant rattle of a machine gun punctuated the thick night air, reminding Rodriguez that there were few safe places on a battlefield.

He sat down on the ramp of the armored personnel carrier with his back against the aluminum rear wall. He was exhausted. There was still plenty of work to do, but he knew that things were getting better. He now had a firm link by FM radio with brigade, which meant that the brigade TOC and radio retrans teams were up and working.

He scanned the dark sky to the south. His armored personnel carrier, nestled into a U-shaped draw that protected it from enemy fire and observation, served as the task force's tactical command post—TAC for short. A large antenna, stuck into the ground and tethered by guidelines, stood on the hill to the north. A thick black cable ran from the antenna down to the radio receiver inside the TAC. Rodriguez hoped that the U-shaped hill would also protect the helicopter landing zone.

"I just passed the latest report to division, sir," said Major

Lucas, interrupting the commander's thoughts. He handed Rodriguez a canteen cup filled with hot instant coffee. "The choppers will be here soon."

"Dave, thanks for all you did today," Rodriguez answered, quietly taking the cup. "This is just what I need."

"Sir, I've put all the dead in body bags and loaded them in a truck," the executive officer replied. "There's only room on the choppers for the wounded. I wish . . ."

"I know," Rodriguez answered, filling in the blank in Lucas's sentence. "We are our choices. Tony chose to be a soldier. There was nothing I could do. There were too many enemy tanks. I couldn't save him."

"Sir, I just want you to know that you made the right decision to stay and fight. Tony was damn proud to be a part of this battalion. I'll miss him a lot." Lucas paused. "Well, I'd better get the landing zone operation set up."

Lucas walked away.

Thankfully the rain had stopped. As the air grew colder the fog cleared. Rodriguez stared at the sky and prayed that his wounded would be evacuated in time. A few were in critical condition, and minutes might make the difference between life and death.

He thought about his choices and the decisions he would have to make in the hours ahead. The Dragon Force was trading space for time, making the North Koreans pay an expensive price for the real estate. Five hours ago a regiment of NKPA infantry climbed along the western and eastern mountain ridges to infiltrate behind Rodriguez's positions. He pulled the force back a few kilometers, and his crews watched through thermal sights as the enemy crested and spilled onto the forward slopes of the hills. Rodriguez ordered everyone to hold their fire until the majority of the enemy was almost to the valley floor. Then the task force plastered the slopes with fire from machine guns, 25mm Bradley chain guns, tank cannons, and mortars. Wave after wave of North Koreans fell as they tried desperately to assault the tanks and Bradley fighting vehicles. More infantry poured over the hills, and the slaughter continued. When the enemy infantry finally got close enough to engage the armor with RPGs, the company teams withdrew, took up new positions farther south, and engaged the infantry again at long range.

A South Korean artillery battery then sealed the enemy's fate. Captain Fletcher earned his pay as an artilleryman by coordinating the fires of an ROK multiple rocket launcher battery. With the aid of a KATUSA soldier who translated the call for fire, he placed several deadly volleys of 130mm rockets on the advancing enemy infantry. The North Koreans were caught on the slopes of the hills and pulverized by fire. Each MRL rocket exploded over the target area in a glowing shower of antipersonnel bomblets. The fire devastated the enemy infantry, smashing their attack and lighting up the tree-covered mountains on the east wall of the valley in flames.

At 2:00 A.M. the attacks stopped and Rodriguez's forward elements reported no contact to the north. Rodriguez wasn't sure how many North Koreans his force had killed. He had no doubt that it was a substantial number, but he wasn't interested in keeping score. He was worried about his men.

The task force had taken casualties. In the last day's fighting, the Dragon Force had lost four tanks, three Bradleys, six M113s, and the Volcano; the total was now twenty-nine dead and thirty-four wounded. Most of the casualties came from crews of thin-skinned trucks and lightly armored APCs. Rodriguez remembered the faces of his dead men. Because he didn't have a clear picture of how the rest of the war was going, he could only wonder if his fight in this desolate valley was making a difference or was just a useless sacrifice.

The maintenance situation was getting critical. Rodriguez's M1A2s needed spare parts. Many were fighting in degraded mode, with critical systems damaged in the past days' hard fighting. The major digital components of an M1A2 tank—the pieces that made it an M1A2—could not be replaced except by cross-leveling from damaged tanks.

Rodriguez looked inside the crowded APC. Captain Drake, exhausted from four days of constant fear and tension, sat crumpled in a corner, asleep with the radio hand mike still pressed to his ear. Sergeant Jeddy, a big, burly, no-nonsense noncommissioned officer, stood alert and on guard in the vehicle commander's hatch. The sergeant, who had PVS-7 goggles strapped to his face, manned the APC's deadly .50-caliber machine gun.

"Sir, there are four choppers approaching," Maj. Dave Lucas reported efficiently as he walked up to the back door of the old man's APC. The short, wiry officer was full of energy in spite of the four days of arduous fighting. Rodriguez felt lucky to have such a superb executive officer, even if he was hardheaded sometimes. "I'll give them the signal to land and get the wounded loaded."

Lucas ran off to turn on the blue-filtered flashlights that designated the landing zone. Rodriguez struggled with his pistol belt, slung his M3 submachine gun around his neck, and carefully stepped out of the APC.

"I'll watch the radios, sir," Sergeant Jeddy said in his deep Alabama accent.

A group of soldiers lay on stretchers while two medics walked down the line caring for them. The wounded were waiting for the helicopters, hoping to leave the inferno of the battlefield. Few of the wounded men made a sound; each seemed absorbed in his own personal struggle. Next to the wounded were two other people to be evacuated, the TV news reporter and her cameraman.

Rodriguez walked over to the wounded and knelt down next to a few of the men on the stretchers, offering words of encouragement. At the end of the line he came to Alice Hamilton and Paul Schaefer; both were sitting on the cold Korean dirt waiting for the helicopters. Alice was wrapped in a muddy Gore-tex parka; Paul wore an olive drab flak jacket over his tan jacket.

"Colonel, I never thanked you for saving my life," Alice said as she stood up. "I guess you must think we're some kind of jerks. I've changed my mind. We'd like to stay."

"No, Ms. Hamilton," Rodriguez answered.

"Alice, please."

"Okay, Alice," Rodriguez replied. "We're still not out of the fire yet. Besides, you can't report the news if you can't get your messages out. You'll be better off in Seoul. You can tell them what we did here. My men would appreciate that."

She pressed next to him and quickly kissed him on the cheek. "Good luck."

The swirl of helicopter blades filled the air. Rice straw from the empty field blew around them. Rodriguez turned and lowered his head to avoid the debris from the backwash of the rotors.

Four UH-60 helicopters, each carrying sling loads, flew low over the field. They hovered a dozen feet above the ground as the external cargo loads gently touched down. Soldiers ran forward to unhook the slings and detach them from the choppers. Using night vision goggles to see, the men unfastened the sling-loaded supplies—three blivets of diesel fuel and one pallet of machine-gun ammunition. Carefully the four helicopters moved to the left and touched down in a line in the open rice paddy.

A dark figure jumped out of the nearest Blackhawk and headed toward the TAC. Lucas and a squad of medics started to load the helicopters with wounded. The helicopters whined as their blades swirled, ready to take off on short notice.

Alice turned to Rodriguez, her hair blowing in the wind of the helicopter blades. "Maybe when this is all over . . ."

Rodriguez nodded. "I have to go."

He quickly turned and walked toward the TAC as the blades of the helicopter continued swirling. Rodriguez immediately recognized his fellow warrior and friend, Lt. Col. Steve Wallace, standing next to the TAC. With a tired but proud gesture, Rodriguez raised his hand to his helmet. Wallace returned the salute and grabbed Rodriguez by the arm. "Mike, you've done a great job here."

"Steve, you took a helluva risk flying out here," Rodriguez said in disbelief. "Thanks."

"Mike, you don't know how glad I am to see you," Wallace replied as they moved inside the armored personnel carrier. "I can't stay long. You've bought us some valuable time. Now you've got to get your guys south. We need you for the counterattack."

Rodriguez shut the door and turned on the lights. Both men sat down on the narrow bench that faced a map board fixed to the wall of the APC. "Show me where the old man wants me."

"Pull back before daylight," Wallace said. "The ROKs are establishing a delay line seven kilometers south of here. Get your guys through their lines and head for the brigade assembly area. Colonel Jakes has the rest of the brigade moving now.

They'll be in their assembly area by 1000. You need to get there before noon."

Rodriguez nodded. "I only have about six hours of fuel left. My fuelers have sucked dry every gas station and abandoned vehicle we could find. I've even used some fuel from a few dead North Korean tanks."

Wallace paused. "How's that working?"

Rodriguez shook his head. "Some of my M1A2s are running like old jalopies. But don't worry, we'll make it. What's the plan for the counterattack?"

"We're going to hit them hard," Wallace said with fire in his voice. He pulled a small light from his pocket and shined the red beam on the map. "We've got some CAS and attack helicopters just in from the States, but we need you back in good shape. We'll need every tank you've got."

Rodriguez nodded as he watched the G2's light travel down the map.

"You'll mass through ROK lines here, just north of Uijonbu," Wallace explained. "The ROKs have dug in to hold Uijonbu. You'll refuel there and join us in the assembly area to the south. We plan to counterattack on 7 October."

Rodriguez took a long look at the attack graphics. The arrows on the map were more than symbols now; they indicated the cost in blood that the Dragon Force would pay to reach the designated objectives. He felt tired.

"Mike, I've got to go. The choppers can't stay here any longer. General Schmidt needs you in this fight."

"We'll be there. . . . Steve, I need you to do me a favor."

"You name it."

"The reporters are still here. They'll be leaving with you and the wounded. Make sure Ms. Hamilton and her cameraman get out of here safely."

A flare went off high in the sky several kilometers to the northwest.

"I'll take care of her for you," Wallace said, nodding. He dug into his BDU pants pocket and handed Rodriguez a pack of cigars. A wide grin lit his face. "Thought you might need these."

"Thanks," Rodriguez said with a smile as he took the cigars and stuffed them in his pocket.

The G2 ran back to the helicopter. Rodriguez watched as the

last of the wounded were placed aboard the waiting choppers. The figures stooped low as they ran to the sides of the UH-60s and quickly loaded the aircraft. The four birds revved their engines and took off one at a time, banked sharply to the left, then raced south.

Rodriguez pulled a cigar from his Nomex cargo pocket. It was his one luxury, in the shivering cool night, and it helped to keep him awake. He ducked inside the APC and carefully lit the cigar.

8:00 A.M., 4 October, 1st Army Group headquarters near Kaesong, North Korea. If there was one thing that Major General Kang hated, it was cigarette smoke. He was a nonsmoker, a rare breed in the NKPA. In a nation that allowed few legal pleasures, smoking was the simplest vice of the North Korean elite. Kang had suffered through years of stuffy, smoke-filled rooms and smoke-clouded briefings.

Almost all North Korean Army officers smoked—mostly strong, unfiltered Russian and Chinese brands. Of them all, probably no one smoked as much as Kim Seung-Hee. Kang could not remember if he had ever seen the Heroic Leader without a cigarette. If the general did not die in battle or from his painful headaches, he would surely expire from lung cancer. Kang laughed, visualizing that statues of Kim Seung-Hee would have to include a cigarette dangling from the man's dour mouth.

The chief of staff of 1st Army Group strained his tired eyes to stare at the large, multicolored battle map. The bright lights that lit the 1:20,000 scale situation map of Korea were beginning to annoy him. He would have to make a note to have them changed.

Behind the glass map wall the operations staff toiled, updating the map with the latest information, adjusting the location of units. The reports were promising. The number of enemy units that were surrounded, destroyed, or retreating was growing.

How tidy war is from here, Kang thought, observing the southern advance. How different it must be on the muddy slopes and ridges of the Chorwon Valley.

An aide entered the room carrying a cup of tea. The general

closed his eyes. The strong aroma of the tea reminded him of happier days. Unlike most of the officers in the Inmun Gun, Kang had been honored to travel abroad. Years ago, during the early 1980s when he was only a colonel, he had attended the Voroshilov Soviet Military Academy of the Soviet General Staff. In Moscow, he and his family lived like the privileged class. There was plenty of food, a fine house. When he was not deeply involved in developing plans for the attack of army groups against a mythical Western enemy at the academy at Khol'zunova Pereluk, Dom 14, in Moscow, he was able to spend peaceful weekends with his wife and two children.

The Voroshilov Academy's primary purpose was to prepare cadres for working in large military formations—army and army groups. His most important instructor, Col. V. V. Larionov, had praised Kang Sung-Yul on his official efficiency reports as the brightest student in classes on the history of war and military art. For a Russian, Larionov had been a good teacher. Now that the Soviets have surrendered to the capitalists, Kang pondered, I bet he's out of work and forgotten.

Since those halcyon days, Kang's impression of the great communist brotherhood had soured, though not officially or publicly. He saw the contradictions and saw through the lies. He understood the inefficiencies and the injustices.

He knew that it was the nature of things to report successes and minimize failures. The high command knew that things were in a bad state down below, but they didn't want to know precisely how bad. They lived a fantasy life. If they bothered to discover the truth, they would have to account for the very situation that they themselves had created.

Kang understood that North Korea's future was bleak. Because it could no longer use its entire army to attack—it couldn't feed, fuel, and prepare so many men—it had devised Daring Thrust. Using only the best-trained and best-prepared units of the army, North Korea created an option for a lightning strike. The timing of the attack, the use of special forces teams, and the disabling of the enemy's satellites were strokes of a master strategist. All of this, however, offered only a temporary advantage if the tanks couldn't isolate Seoul.

Now came the depressing, gut-wrenching indications of an offensive losing steam. Many of the ROK positions that had been bypassed, expected to surrender after they discovered they were cut off, resisted fiercely. Night attacks by NKPA infantry were driven off, with substantial losses. The 820th Corps had taken a beating at the hands of an American task force. Repeated delays afflicted almost every unit across the entire front. In response, Kang's frustrated staff officers rushed reinforcements and supplies to the 820th Corps.

Kang sifted through a pile of reports from the Chorwon front. Every report cited one glorious victory after another. No reports mentioned the 1st Brigade of the 820th Corps. Kang knew. The brigade was gone and the 820th Corps had been badly mauled. The corps had rushed into the fight before the enemy was pushed off balance. The American battalion that opposed them had ground them to a halt. The 820th commander, unwilling to admit defeat, had thrown his supporting infantry brigades into a prolonged fight that caused only heavier casualties. Now the infantry brigades of the 820th Corps were scattered over the ridges of the Chorwon Valley, with many dead and wounded.

Kang could read between the lines. He felt as if he had uncovered a great secret. He knew in his heart that they had underestimated their enemy. He sensed that if they didn't win in the next few days, they would lose the war. He knew that defeat would mean the end of North Korea.

The latest reports showed that the ROKs were digging in at Uijonbu. A tough battle for the city loomed. Success depended on who would crack first, the ROKs or the Inmun Gun.

Kang's most immediate problem was to determine if he should tell his Heroic Leader, Marshal Kim Seung-Hee, of this development. Kang shifted his stance and stared at the operations map as he sipped his tea. The hot beverage invigorated him.

Kang nodded his head as he saw the location of the red and blue markers. We have the capability for one more thrust and one thrust only, he thought. A resolute attack now might knock the enemy off balance and force him to sue for peace on our terms. Kang's intuition told him that the enemy's determination was wavering. Kim Seung-Hee's great gamble might work, but only if the 820th could push through.

Kim believed that the capture and destruction of a major

population center would force the South Korean government to waver and submit. Kim wanted Uijonbu taken and destroyed. Excuses would not be tolerated. The marshal risked everything on this one throw of the dice. He wanted only to hear that the Inmun Gun was advancing.

Kang could tell that Marshal Kim's headaches seemed to be increasing. Kim Seung-Hee had become increasingly irritable each day. Kang feared he might not be seeing the situation realistically. How would he tell Kim that the plan should change, that the attack on the city should be abandoned, that the forces at hand were inadequate for the task?

The door opened. Six armed guards moved rapidly inside the briefing room and secured the massive eight-foot steel blast doors. Major General Kang stared at the mammoth North Korean flag that decorated the back wall of the bunker as he awaited the arrival of his master.

Colonel So, Marshal Kim's aide, entered first. He strutted in, his chin raised, his arms swinging, and his legs moving stiffly at a deliberate pace. This is a pretentious, pompous ass if there ever was one, Kang thought.

Kang stood in front of the map, patiently anticipating his call to recite. Kim Seung-Hee, with gray hair and a large, glistening forehead, a black patch over his left eye, followed a few moments behind and took his customary seat opposite the situation map.

General Kang saluted. Kim Seung-Hee nodded, then reached inside the pocket of his tunic for his gold cigarette case. Obligingly, Colonel So provided a light for the general. Rings of noxious cigarette smoke soon floated throughout the room.

"Comrade General, there has been a pause in the battle," Kang said, using the euphemism for trouble. He pointed to the map. "We are making a steady advance in the strike sector and are having varied progress at other areas along the front. The decisive point is here, at Uijonbu. A determined defense in the Chorwon Valley by an American force has delayed our penetration."

"The Americans," Marshal Kim growled. "Why is it always the Americans? I thought we destroyed most of them while they were in garrison."

"Apparently we were not as successful as our reports led us to believe."

"Will we seize Uijonbu as scheduled?" Kim demanded.

Kang paused. This was a difficult moment. All his prior training focused on this day. He knew that he should convince the marshal that Uijonbu was no longer important. The plan must be modified. The 820th should bypass Uijonbu. Then the combined weight of the 820th and 815th Corps could continue the offensive. What was important, Kang was convinced, was to keep up the tempo of the attack. He realized that the 815th Corps was still a day and a half away. Time was fleeting. Victory would be decided in a matter of days, if not hours.

Kang looked at Marshal Kim as the leader of North Korea blew cigarette smoke into the air. Can I change his mind? wondered Kang.

"I am waiting for your answer, General," Kim Seung-Hee prodded, glancing at the cigarette between his right index finger and his thumb as if there were words of great wisdom written on its white wrapper.

It is by small mistakes that we are undone, Kang thought. Countless small disruptions that eventually tear down the plan. Would the marshal view his desire to change the plan as prudence or cowardice?

Kang answered as he knew he would. A lifetime of living in a totalitarian state had conditioned him to obey and not ask questions. "Sir, we will regain the time. The 820th will break through and attack Uijonbu tomorrow night. The artillery is in position, and final ammunition allocations will arrive at the army artillery group on the morning of 6 October to complete the destruction of Uijonbu. The 815th will arrive on the night of the sixth and attack at dawn on the seventh. We will be at the gates of Seoul by 8 October and force the surrender of the fascists."

Kim Seung-Hee nodded, rubbing his black eye patch with his left hand. "Order all commanders to make their maximum effort. I want no one left idle. We will take Uijonbu and crush it like an egg. I want the reactionaries in Seoul to see what will happen if they do not surrender."

A door opened. All eyes in the room turned to the new arrival. A colonel from General Kang's signal staff carried a message in a folder. The red and yellow on the folder signaled correspondence for Kim Seung-Hee only.

Colonel So took the folder, making a sideways glance at General Kang, and quickly handed it to Kim. The colonel's gesture communicated suspicion, as if the message was not to be opened in Kang's presence. This only spiked Kang's interest.

Kim Seung-Hee snubbed out his cigarette in the ashtray on the table. He took the folder, opened it, and quickly read the note, looking up at So several times. Then he sat back in his big, overstuffed chair, the message dangling from his left hand. His face turned tight as he stared at the operations map. Abruptly he jumped up and walked toward the door.

He turned around and addressed his chief of staff. "General Kang, you will remain here and control operations. I want Uijonbu to suffer. I want our southern brothers to see what happens to a city that resists. My strategy depends on this; it acts on the mind of our opponent. The death of Uijonbu will be an example for the southern fascists to see. Use whatever additional force is necessary. Force the enemy to capitulate."

General Kang nodded, placing his heels together and bowing slightly.

"I will move forward," Kim continued, "to control the final steps of the battle."

Kim exited the briefing room, followed by Colonel So and the general's bodyguards.

Kang looked perplexed as he stood in the room filled with the pungent odor of tobacco. *I wonder what was in the message?* thought Kang.

3:00 P.M., 4 October, ridge of the Chorwon Valley, South Korea. Sung-Joo woke with a start as he heard the crack of AK-47 rifle fire echo close to his shallow foxhole.

He had walked for kilometers without rest, always moving toward the sound of the gunfire. Unable to go any farther, he had found a place to hide and catch some sleep. His goal to join a South Korean defensive position seemed less realistic by the hour. Everywhere he had traveled, he had witnessed only the devastation and defeat of his once proud army.

The angry rifle cracked again. Sung-Joo cocked his ear as he heard the sharp, high-pitched snap of a 9mm pistol bark back at the rifles.

He peered up over the rock that hid him from the trail below. He was in a perfect position to observe the firing. A hundred meters below him, a man wearing an olive-green uniform but no helmet was running down the muddy trail. He was fleeing from two helmeted North Korean infantrymen.

Sung-Joo could easily see that the man was an American. The North Koreans moved forward by bounds, one soldier running while the other fired a few rounds at the man in green. The American, finding himself pinned down by the enemy's fire, popped back at them with his pistol. The enemy rifles barked back. It would be only a matter of minutes and they would have their victim.

Sung-Joo saw the American crawl behind a large, jagged rock outcropping. The American then spun around on his belly and leveled his pistol in the direction of the enemy. He blasted off two more shots, then his pistol quit.

The American was now obviously out of ammunition. The North Koreans waited a few moments, then moved out into the open and walked forward arrogantly. One soldier fired his AK-47 from the hip at the cornered quarry. The North Koreans laughed. The American cowered behind the rock.

Sung-Joo raised his M16 rifle to his shoulder and released the safety with his right thumb. Time hung in the air, still and frozen. He felt his heart beating fast. He carefully placed the farthest North Korean in his sight picture. He exhaled slowly and gently squeezed the trigger.

His M16 made a cracking sound. The enemy soldier crumpled to the ground. The second North Korean screamed and ran forward, firing a full blast from his assault rifle at the American. Sung-Joo quickly shifted his M16 to the second man and fired. The enemy soldier fell to his knees, dropping his rifle. The wounded North Korean looked up, a mask of surprise and confusion on his face. Sung-Joo fired again and the man collapsed, falling backward into the mud.

"Don't shoot," the American yelled. "Don't shoot. U.S. Army."

Sung-Joo stood up and walked down the muddy slope. Dirt and rocks tumbled down the hill that had given him such an advantage over the North Koreans. He reached the trail and walked over to the American, looked at him for a few seconds, then moved forward to check the North Koreans.

Sung-Joo kicked the nearest man with the tip of his boot. The dead soldier lay on his back. Two large red holes adorned his chest. A pool of blood gathered in the mud beneath him, soaking into the soil. Sung-Joo stared at the North Korean as if he were a creature from Mars. His victim couldn't have been more than twenty years old. Somehow, however, Sung-Joo didn't feel that he was looking at a man—just an enemy.

His anger burned. He thought about the scenes of destruction he had viewed on his trek south and how the North Koreans were killing his countrymen like sheep at a slaughter. He thought about his lost comrades. His platoon had been his family. They were comrades in arms. Each one had been his special responsibility. Now they were gone. He spit on the body.

He walked over and checked the other dead soldier. He rolled the corpse over with a swift kick to make sure the soldier was dead.

The American walked up to him. "Thanks," he said, extending his hand. "Do you speak English?"

Sung-Joo slung his rifle and took the American's hand. "I am Second Lieutenant Ri Sung-Joo, of the Republic of Korea Army. You are a tank soldier?"

"Yes," Emerson replied, lowering his head. "I'm Private Jamie Emerson, U.S. Army. My tank crew is dead. I survived. Everyone else is dead."

The lieutenant eyed the private carefully, seeing his bloody Nomex uniform. "Are you injured?"

"No," Emerson replied.

"Do you know if we have stopped the communists?" Sung-Joo asked.

"No. It's not going well for us."

Sung-Joo picked up the AK-47 rifles and as much ammunition as the two North Koreans had left. He handed one of the rifles to Emerson. Together they searched the dead North Koreans for ammunition, food, and water, taking everything that would help them survive.

"We must go," Sung-Joo said, his voice noticeably cool and controlled. Suddenly, Sung-Joo knew how he could do something that might make a difference. He looked over his shoulder at the summit of a hill to the southeast.

"Where can we go?" Emerson asked. "There are North Koreans all over the place."

"The enemy will come looking for these two. We will hide them in the bushes and then we must leave," Sung-Joo replied. He pointed to the top of the mountain range high beyond the hill behind him. "We will hike up there."

6:00 P.M., 4 October, New Chosun Hotel, Seoul, South Korea.
"I wonder how the soldiers of the Dragon Force are doing," Alice thought out loud. "I wonder if they'll make it?"

"What?" Paul asked as he busily connected his video equipment. "Did you say something?"

"Nothing." Alice Hamilton managed a nervous smile at Paul, her faithful friend. She shook her head as if to argue with herself that the events of the past four days were really only a horrible dream and that soon she would wake and everything would be as it was. Unfortunately she knew better.

A shudder of revulsion ran through her mind. The previous days had seemed like a lifetime, a frightening, personal experience. She had escaped alive but not untouched. She was suddenly no longer a tourist to the events unfolding around her. Now, like all the people in Seoul, she was also a target.

In the past she had remained aloof from her stories, enjoying a special detachment from the issues she had reported on, no matter how sincere she appeared on the TV screen. It wasn't that she hadn't seen death before, or that she didn't care. She had seen plenty in Liberia, Sudan, and Bosnia, and she did care. Somehow she felt that this time was different. She had stepped over the line. She was not just reporting the news; she was part of the story. She felt a strong connection with the men on the battlefield. She had lost her objectivity, and she knew that this was a serious problem for a reporter.

Seoul seemed like a city under siege during the Middle Ages—dark, ominous, and desperate. Thick, dark clouds of smoke hung high over the city, blocking the sun's early-morning rays. Several tall skyscrapers, black and charred from explosions, marred the once modern and picturesque skyline. Oily black spires of smoke from dozens of fires—the work of

North Korean artillery and rockets—rose high into the atmosphere.

Alice looked at the city skyline from the top floor of her forty-story hotel. It stood on the bank of the Han River on Seoul's south side, an undamaged building in a scarred, forsaken city. The bridges over the river were jammed with military traffic heading south. Traffic clogged the southern routes, and only military traffic moved north on the roads. Rumors spread that the ROK Army was about to destroy the bridges over the Han River, to deny the North Koreans a means to cross to the south.

The ROK military police did all they could to keep the roads open, but their efforts were futile. Northern movement was forbidden to civilian cars on all roads without special passes. The ROK Army checkpoints scrutinized the papers of everyone entering or leaving the city. The army was taking no chances, because car bombs had devastated critical installations in the city during the first few days of the war.

Kimpo airfield, the main terminal that served the 12 million inhabitants of Seoul, had been closed since the first night of the war. The wreckage of civilian and military aircraft attested to the ferocity of the North Korean missile, air, and commando attacks on this vital airport. Kimpo was not alone; North Korean attacks had left most airfields in South Korea a shambles. No one was leaving or entering Seoul by air.

Alice felt lucky to have made it back to Seoul and, for that matter, just to be alive. Once she landed in the 2d Infantry Division's hospital area with the wounded from Task Force 2-72, she was transported to a reporters' pool set up by the ROK government at the New Chosun Hotel. Other reporters in the pool updated her on the events of the past few days. They told her of the fanatical North Korean suicide attacks against ROK and U.S. installations throughout South Korea and against American airfields and seaports in Japan on the first day of the war. Alice watched video replays of chaotic scenes of ROK border forces retreating south. She saw pictures of thirty American prisoners executed by North Koreans at Panmunjom. These pictures were particularly repugnant; the Americans had their arms tied behind their backs with barbed wire and were lying dead in a pile by the side of a muddy road.

As she saw the video of the American dead, Alice thought about Rodriguez and the young men she had lived with in the first, horrible days of the war. Shivering as she watched the video, she found herself saying a silent prayer for the men who had kept her safe.

Alice moved to a large window and gazed at the chaos in the city below. A huge Z made of thick tape decorated the window—the hotel's pitiful attempt to reduce fragments should the glass shatter. Alice studied her reflection in the glass. She still wore the bloody, mud-splattered Gore-tex parka given to her by the young medic on the first, confused day of the war. Her blond hair was dirty and disheveled. Her green eyes, usually bright and dancing, were red from worry and lack of sleep.

She looked at Paul, who was just as tired and dirty. His beard seemed to have grayed. Good old, dependable Paul, she thought. He clung to his camcorder as if he were born with it. She mused how he had become almost like a big brother, someone to trust in a dangerous world where life and death changed in the flash of an eye. How long had they worked together without her really acknowledging him? She realized how little she really knew about him, how much she had remained a stranger in their daily work. Now, in this hell, she knew that he was also her only friend.

"Paul, those soldiers we were with. If they don't stop the North Koreans, the enemy will take Seoul. Thousands of people will die. Whatever happened to all this push-button warfare we were told about?" Alice asked, not really expecting an answer.

"Those soldiers we were with—they're the push-buttons," Paul responded seriously.

Alice thought about this answer for a moment, then nodded, understanding his insight in a way she had not considered before.

"Let's make this report and get out of here," Paul offered. "I'm not excited about being in the highest building at ground zero."

She nodded again, then cleared her throat and signaled for Paul to start the camera. "This is Alice Hamilton reporting live from the center of war-ravaged Seoul, Korea. As you can see behind me, the city has taken a terrible beating in the past few days. The same has occurred at the battlefront. I was visiting a U.S. Army unit when the war began. The footage you will see after this live broadcast was taken during the first few days of the war. American soldiers, fighting alongside the South Koreans, have fallen back all along the front. Most significantly, the allied air forces have yet to arrive in force on the battlefield, because most of the aircraft are being used to target the North Korean artillery and missile batteries that are inflicting such terrible damage on the city of Seoul."

The sound of air-raid sirens wailed harshly in the background. Alice looked quickly over her shoulder to the skyline and caught her reflection in the window. A look of sheer terror splashed across her green eyes. She looked back to the camera. "Oh, my God, we're under missile attack and will have to get back to you later. This is Alice Hamilton in Seoul, reporting."

"Everyone to the basement," a man shouted as he helped the cameraman pick up his equipment.

Alice took one more look out the window. She heard a loud noise and saw a streak of light shoot into the sky. Frozen in apprehension, she watched the detonation of a Patriot air defense missile striking an incoming Nodong rocket several hundred meters above the city. Sparks showered from the sky as pieces of the missile fell onto the buildings and streets below.

Wham! The building shook from the concussion of the missile.

"Alice, let's go, *now*," Paul yelled as he took the camera off his shoulder.

She turned as Paul grabbed her hand. Together they raced down the corridor to a stairwell. He pushed open the door and the pair ran down one flight of stairs. Dozens of other people were racing to the basement in the same stairwell. The sound of explosions and the wail of sirens increased with each successive flight. Finally, gasping for breath, Alice and Paul reached the basement.

A large group of people, mostly news reporters, were already in the shelter. Most sat on the concrete floor and some stood against the wall. Many had already donned gas masks. Hamilton recoiled in horror as the thought of a gas attack filled her brain. What would she do? She didn't have a mask.

Paul smiled and looked at her as if to say, don't worry.

"What makes you so confident?"

"They haven't used gas yet," he said gently. "They might, but I think they know what would happen to them if they did. Besides, as long as they're winning, they don't really need it."

Alice leaned back against the basement wall. The sirens continued their maddening squeal. Several people sitting next to her were sobbing. She covered her ears and wished it would all just go away. She never thought that anything could be so terrifying.

An immense explosion resonated outside, shaking the ground and the foundation of the building. Dust fell from the ceiling. A woman screamed and other people sobbed. A man near Alice mumbled a prayer and crossed himself. Another terrible Nodong warhead detonated thirteen hundred pounds of high explosive somewhere in Seoul.

"They say the city will be taken by the North Koreans in two days," Paul whispered. "We don't want to be here then. Maybe we should head south."

8:00 P.M., 4 October, five kilometers southeast of Uijonbu, South Korea. The captain looked up at the heavens. The rain had stopped, which was a relief, but the night was still black as pitch without a trace of the moon. Heavy clouds hung oppressively low in the sky. Mackenzie felt uneasy but happy to be moving away from the enemy.

His tanks were met by soldiers on the ground who carefully guided the lumbering, seventy-ton beasts forward in the dark. Waving small, green, chemical light sticks, like ground crews at an airport, the guides led the tanks into predesignated refueling positions next to large fuel trucks. Twelve HEMMTs—huge, eight-wheeled, 2,500-gallon fuel trucks—lined the road. The trucks were spaced about sixty meters apart.

The high-pitched whine of the turbines filled the humid night air. In the darkness, with the aid of thermal viewers and night vision goggles, soldiers lined up next to the HEMMTs and refueled their armored vehicles. The chem lights identified the trucks and the soldiers on the ground. Soldiers from the battalion support platoon—the men who did the hard work of fueling and rearming the task force—guided the tanks into predesignated locations on both sides of the road. The HEMMTs refueled two vehicles at a time from hoses extending from their back ends. Tank loaders jumped from hatches and stood on the flat back decks of their M1A2s as the men on the ground handed them metal-tipped fuel nozzles. Within seconds JP8 was flowing into the thirty M1A2 tanks.

Captain Ken Mackenzie pushed out of his tank commander's station. He opened the fuel cap on the back right rear of the M1A2, and his loader inserted the nozzle held out to him by a soldier on the ground. Each tank could take 500 gallons, but each tank received only a six-minute shot of fuel. At a flow rate of 25 gallons per minute, the six-minute shot would provide each M1A2 with almost 150 gallons. At the M1A2's consumption rate, that was enough fuel for only three hours of operation.

A HMMWV suddenly pulled up next to Mackenzie's tank. It was the old man, Dragon Six. Mackenzie looked down from his tank's back deck and touched his hand to his CVC helmet.

"I'm glad to be getting this fuel, sir," Mackenzie shouted with a loud grin as his loader held down the HEMMT fuel nozzle in the M1A2's rear fuel tank. "We were running on fumes."

"Right. Just make sure you thank Command Sergeant Major Dougan," Rodriguez shouted back. "He's the one who got the ROKs to refuel our HEMMTs. Without him, we'd end up fighting from right here."

"Well, you know the old saying, sir," Mackenzie said, cocking his head to the left. "If you run out of fuel, become a pill-box. If you run out of ammo, become a bunker. If you run out of time, become a hero."

"Okay, hero," the Dragon Force commander said with a smile, nodding his head. "Just keep 'em rolling. The XO just contacted me on the radio. Our assembly area is only ten kilometers from here. We'll be set by oh-two-hundred. Get your men some rest, but don't forget security. They say it's hell back here in the rear."

Mackenzie smiled. "You're killing me, sir. Don't worry, we'll all get there. Just give me a three- to six-second advantage over the bastards and we'll send them all to hell."

"Orders at oh-six-hundred tomorrow," Rodriguez said. "I'll see you there, at the TOC."

"Sir, sorry to hear about Major Bradford. He was one of the best."

Rodriguez nodded, then walked over to his HMMWV and drove away.

The old man's taking it hard, Mackenzie thought, and there's nothing I can do about it. He's done everything right so far. He's kept us alive and fighting. It might be luck, but I don't think it's luck alone. It's how the team operates, as if there isn't anything we can't do if we do it together.

Rodriguez's leadership is an important factor, Mackenzie thought; it nurtures us. He never prescribes in long and detailed written orders how to carry out a mission. Detailed orders might reduce the risk of failure in the case of a bad company commander, but Mackenzie knew that it would also tie the hands of a good commander. If a commander was preoccupied with controlling his company commanders, he could hobble them. Exploiting the situation at a decisive moment was what commanders at all levels got paid to do.

Mackenzie thrived in this type of environment. He found pleasure in taking risks. It suited his hell-bent-for-leather image. He liked running with the ball and not looking over his shoulder every minute to see if the boss approved of which way he was running. He had learned in his six short years in the army that the more complex a situation was, and the fewer the forces involved, the more often a higher commander was tempted to meddle in the business of his subordinates. He had also learned, at places such as the National Training Center— the army's premier war-game training ground in the California desert—that oversupervision didn't work.

Of course, there was such a thing as being too bold, as the old man had warned him on more than one occasion. That was one of the reasons Mackenzie liked Rodriguez. He took the time to teach and coach his company commanders. He trained his commanders to make rapid decisions, which was emphasized during training. He said that decisive action was the first prerequisite for success in war, and that plans were a basis for change. He expected everybody, from the highest commander to the youngest soldiers, to make decisions based upon the mission and their understanding of the commander's intent.

"Sir, we're ready to roll," Mackenzie's loader said, handing the fuel nozzle back to the soldier on the ground.

Mackenzie and his loader crawled back inside the turret.

With the signal of a chem light from a support platoon soldier on the ground, Mackenzie's tank drove down the dark road to the south.

11:30 P.M., 4 October, 1st Army Group headquarters, near Kaesong, North Korea. Marshal Kim Seung-Hee crumpled the secret message into a ball and threw it on the floor. Colonel So, Marshal Kim's aide, picked up the paper and put it in his pocket.

"Admiral Bae," Kim seethed. "Get Comrade Bae on the secure telephone, immediately."

"Comrade Marshal, I have the signals officer working on that now. Admiral Bae cannot be reached. We have not heard from him in the past eight hours. Our communications with Pyongyang have been disrupted by the Yankees."

"Bae would get a message through in spite of everything if he wanted to," Kim seethed. "I never trusted him."

Kim stared at the latest report from the Chorwon Valley. The enemy was in retreat, and the way to Seoul seemed open. The general moved to the edge of his chair, his body leaning forward, his head slightly tilted and supported by his left hand, as if he were sitting on a hill somewhere, watching the battle unfold. His right eye blinked slightly. "We are almost there. Victory is in our grasp."

"Yes, Comrade Marshal," Colonel So announced. "The plan is almost complete."

"Traitors can always disrupt the best plans," Kim replied with a sneer. "Maybe if you had been more careful in assigning agents to watch Bae, we wouldn't be in this situation."

Colonel So stood stiffly, his hands behind his back, facing his master without flinching. "No, Comrade General. No. Bae is guided by self-interest. He was a reliable asset throughout the planning and execution of the coup. Maybe he was influenced by the southern fascists from the beginning."

"I do not believe that," Kim answered deliberately. "Bae is a coward. He bends with the wind. He had something turn him."

Kim thought of words he had read once. "It is like insects," he said to his aide. "If they gather on an ox, they do not fly more than a few paces, but if they stick to a swift horse, they can chase the wind and pursue the sun simply because of the superiority of what they cleave to."

Kim ran his hands through his graying hair. "I have come a long way to this exact moment in time. I have planned the attack carefully, anticipating every contingency. Now I am faced with two dilemmas.

"The first is the delay of the offensive. Speed is everything and the attack has been seriously delayed. The attack must break through to Uijonbu. The destruction of Uijonbu is a critical part of the psychological pressure that is needed to achieve the plan. Now, because of one feeble American force, the breakthrough has been delayed two days."

Colonel So listened obediently.

"Today will make the decisive difference. When the 820th takes Uijonbu, enemy morale will crack. When the 815th Corps attacks on 7 October, the enemy will be destroyed. But with every delay, enemy power grows. Forces moving to the front and supply columns are being damaged by air interdiction. The 815th has to be protected on its long march to Uijonbu. I must use my power to create a situation that will cause the Americans to withdraw their airpower."

Kim opened his gold cigarette case, picked out a cigarette, and quickly lit it. He used cigarettes like tranquilizers, taking one to his lips during the intervals between moments of tension. He puffed for a few seconds, considering his options. He thought about that day in the snow when he had taken the cigarette case from the American sergeant.

"The second matter is more surprising and possibly more damaging," continued Kim. "Somehow a countercoup is brewing in Pyongyang. My spies report a growing threat of assassination."

"Marshal Kim, I swear that no man will get close enough to harm you. Our security is airtight. You are safe here."

"Nevertheless, the plot exists. No suspects have been identified, but the information and the source seem reliable enough. Some unknown traitor is organizing against me. What am I overlooking? Who has the power to oppose me?"

"To defend against the possibility of trouble, I have written the order to assign the People's Militia to support security operations," Colonel So explained. "The militia will take over control of critical sections of the capital on your order. I will instruct them to arrest Admiral Bae."

"Yes. Find our dear admiral and bring him to me. I want this insect alive. I must know what he knows before I smash him like the insignificant bug that he is."

"It will be done, Comrade Marshal," So answered.

"We will move forward with our troops. It will be more difficult to plot against us this way."

Colonel So nodded.

Kim looked over to the table in the center of the room. The special satellite communications box, which gave him personal control over the detonation of the nuclear device in the Romeo-class submarines, was on and ready. The arming switch stood in the standby position. With a flick of that switch, Kim would detonate the twenty-kiloton nuclear bomb and devastate the South Korean Army island fortress of Paengnyongdo in the Yellow Sea.

The North Wind, he thought. His gaze turned to the *paduk* game board. What do they say in *paduk*? "As the edges go, so goes the board."

He took the final puff from his dying cigarette, then extinguished it in the already full ashtray. Lately his headaches had bothered him more than ever. His temples throbbed. He rubbed his left eye and quickly took a pill from his pocket and placed it under his tongue before continuing.

"The explosion of a bomb will turn the small hunk of rock into a glistening piece of glass. The explosion will display our power. Coupled with the capture and destruction of Uijonbu, I will surprise my enemies when they are at their most vulnerable. The uncertainty of additional devices, with a clear example that we will use them, will end the war and force the vacillating Americans and cowardly South Koreans to negotiate on my terms."

"Marshal Kim, what if the Americans decide to attack us with nuclear bombs?"

"They are hostage to their own fears. Besides, the island is garrisoned by a mere regiment of ROK soldiers, not U.S. soldiers. The Americans cannot risk the devastation of Seoul or Tokyo. Unless they are sure of how many bombs we have and how they were launched, they cannot act without great risk.

That is the beauty of the submarine. It will not be detected. The Americans will not know how the explosion occurred. This uncertainty will work for me. With the risk of nuclear attacks on their forces, the Americans will be prudent and withdraw their fleets and move their air forces south to protect them. The ROK government—reeling from the fact that we have nuclear weapons and that their army is on the verge of defeat, and realizing the loss and devastation of Uijonbu—will go into shock. They will be forced to consider negotiations or face the destruction of Seoul."

"It is a daring thrust right at the hearts and minds of the enemy," Colonel So praised his master.

Kim nodded. "Ruthlessness always succeeds. I will attack the enemy through his fears of mass destruction. With such power, why should I be concerned about a weak, ineffectual traitor such as Admiral Bae?"

Kim smiled as he rubbed his eye patch with his right hand.

"Here is the latest report on the location of the submarine," So offered. "It is in position now, Comrade Marshal."

The general lit up a cigarette and puffed vigorously for a few seconds. "It is time for the North Wind," Kim said. "It is time to show the enemy the power we possess."

Colonel So bowed his head and marched over to the transmitter. Without any display of emotion, he tapped in the Morse code signal for North Wind. The device responded, displaying the command to enter the numerical sequence. Deliberately, he punched in the multinumber arming command and pushed the detonation switch forward.

11

PASSING LINES

It was in the misty valleys and on the cruel mountains and hills that the fighting took place, and it was in these narrow valleys and barren hills that the story of Korea was told. —T. R. FEHRENBACH

4:30 A.M., 5 October, 820th Mechanized Corps headquarters, North Korean People's Army, Uijonbu, South Korea. The city of Uijonbu was dominated by the sound, smell, and look of a place crushed by war. The skeletons of crumbled ruins spotted a skyline that had once boasted modern thirty-story apartments and high-rise office buildings. Collapsed walls exposed blackened rooms. Tall buildings were torn open, exposing their souls to the outside world. Broken power poles, snapped like bent matchsticks, held sagging power lines. Smoldering rubble lay in mounds. In this hell the battle continued.

The light of the fires outlined the destruction of the urban area. From the east, the city gleamed with patches of fire. Major General Park Chi-won trained his binoculars on the urban battlefield, hoping to see the defenders give up the contest. He had brought total war to Uijonbu, a kind of war that had been witnessed before at places such as Verdun, Stalingrad, and Hue. Park knew that he was winning this battle. He also knew that his units were being used up at an alarming rate.

The question was, who would be used up first?

The sounds of explosions echoed in the valley. Bullets ricocheted furiously over the buildings even as flying cinders floated to the heavens. An explosion ignited a spire of fire that shot up high into the sky. Some streets in the southeastern portion of that battlefield burned like furnaces, as if they were the flaming corridors of hell. In that hell, Park knew, men were hunting one another with tanks, machine guns, rifles, grenades, and in some cases their bare hands.

He stood in the open hatch of his armored command vehicle. The officers manning his command radios sat two to a side. The engines of the BTR-60 armored personnel carriers hummed as the officers inside sat glued to their radiotelephone headsets. Dutiful officers quickly jotted down reports from the forward units and posted the information on map boards attached to the inside walls of the BTR.

"Sir, the 417th Infantry Division has arrived at the attack point," an officer shouted to Park.

"Send them in immediately to support the 415th," Park commanded, pointing to the fire that was the city of Uijonbu. "No further delays. Drive out the fascists. They will break soon and the city will be ours."

Park knew that time was critical. Each delay worked against the plan. The enemy air forces were growing stronger. American aircraft had attacked his columns earlier in the day, killing truckloads of infantrymen before the S-300 air defense missiles drove the planes away. The enemy jammed his radios, causing him to change frequencies repeatedly, and FM communications with army group headquarters were intermittent. Park was sending more orders by messenger now than by radio. His only effective link with Marshal Kim Seung-Hee was the special Japanese satellite radio in his corps headquarters.

A volley of artillery rained down abruptly on the city in a tremendous torrent. The ground shook as the bright bursts of high explosive smashed into the southern portion of Uijonbu.

Park kneaded his bandaged left palm with his right hand. He feared that the wound was infected in spite of the ointment he had spread on the lacerations. He could disregard the pain, but he knew that he could not put off medical attention much longer if he wanted to keep the hand.

"Sir, the enemy is falling back to the southwestern portion of the city," the officer reported. "We control the highway. The 415th Infantry Division is continuing the attack."

Park smiled as he thought about the battle he was winning. He reached for the binoculars that hung around his neck and brought them to his eyes. He couldn't see the units locked in combat, but he pictured the exhausted ROK defenders running from the fierce attacks of his tanks, infantry, and flamethrower teams.

Nothing will stop us now, Park thought. Today my forces will be in command of the city and the vital road junction that leads to Seoul. The enemy will see the destruction of the city, the loss of its defenders, and the seizure of the crossroads to Seoul. The Inmun Gun is now linked by Highways 3, 43, and 47. These avenues of attack run from North Korea to the south and point at the capital of Seoul like a bloody dagger.

The enemy must be at his wit's end, Park thought. Their technology is superior, but their will is weak. We have negated their high technology through preparation, surprise, ruse, bluff, and, most of all, discipline. We are willing to die to achieve victory. Now our enemies will pay for their arrogance. Now they will truly learn to fear us.

"What is the strength of the 415th Division?" asked Park.

The officer searched his reports and looked up on the red-lit battle board along the wall of the BTR-60. "Comrade General, they report thirty percent strength. They have just seized the local government headquarters."

Park nodded, calculating the numbers. Thirty percent strength. The division had started the attack with almost 13,000 men. Now it was down to 3,900.

"Order the commander of the 415th to continue the attack. Tell him to pursue the enemy until he drives them out of the city."

"It will be done, Comrade General."

"Who is the commander of the 415th now?" Park asked, knowing that the casualties had hit the leadership hard.

"The officer issuing the report was Lieutenant Colonel Yu Chung-Nin, Comrade General."

Park nodded. Casualties were indeed high. Lieutenant colonels were now commanding divisions. That meant that sergeants were probably in charge of companies.

A series of explosions erupted from the city, sending another shower of debris and glittering sparks skyward.

"What is the strength of the 416th and 417th Divisions?" Park asked, raising the binoculars to his eyes to see the extent of the large fireball that reached to the sky from the center of the city.

"The 416th is defending," the officer answered in a cold, mechanical tone as if he were reading from a prepared script. "We have lost contact with their commander, but the battle rages in their zone of attack. They will reach their objective by daylight or die to a man."

This is why we will win, Park thought in silent satisfaction. We are not afraid to die and pay the cost. The Americans and the South Koreans expect to fight wars without casualties. In the Inmun Gun things are different. Each soldier of the Inmun Gun is part of a great machine. Each does his job, unthinking, obedient, not letting the events around him stop him from accomplishing his duty. If one part of the whole is chopped off, the rest will step forward to take his place.

"The 417th is still attacking," the officer continued. "Their last report, received ten minutes ago, put them at fifty-five percent strength. We have the 420th in reserve; it should arrive at dawn."

General Park understood the cost of the attack. He also knew that there were no more reserves. The 815th Corps was the last uncommitted unit in the North Korean force. The Daring Thrust attack plan had achieved surprise at the expense of mass. The plan could work only under special conditions—conditions that the weak South Koreans had been only too eager to supply—the partial disarmament of their army and the mass rotation of their units along the DMZ. It was a plan that had to succeed in ten days, or the war would turn into a longer battle of attrition that the north could not win.

"Commit all reserves. The lead divisions have done their duty. Now we need fresh forces to continue, to finish the job. Press the attack. There is no turning back."

Tracers flew wildly through the sky over Uijonbu. Somewhere in the city a tank gun boomed, and boomed again. Flames leaped from the southwestern portion of the city as artillery smashed into the defender's enclaves. The rocky hills to the west glowed red, reflecting the light of the fires.

A jeep with only slit white driving lights jolted down the road toward Park's command group. A North Korean guard standing outside the commander's BTR stopped the vehicle and challenged the occupants. The guard, obviously satisfied with the response to his challenge, sent the vehicle forward. The jeep raced up to General Park's BTR and stopped. A young major, Park's chief of operations, exited the jeep and climbed the metal footholds on the side of the general's armored car.

"Comrade General," the officer reported, handing Park a specially sealed folder, "I have an urgent message for you from Marshal Kim Seung-Hee."

Park opened the folder eagerly and unfolded the message. With the aid of a red-filtered flashlight, he read the contents of the report.

"We will win the war," Park bragged to the young major. He held the message in his right hand as if it were an omen from the gods. He dropped inside the BTR and motioned for the staff officers to take off their headsets. Each sat patiently, looking at their commander. "This message is from Comrade Kim Seung-Hee. We have detonated a nuclear bomb against the fascists at Paengnyongdo Island. Marshal Kim says he has more nuclear bombs and that we must not fear the Americans. He expects the enemy to withdraw their airpower for at least two days."

Park's subordinate officers listened with eager ears. Covered with the dirt and grime of five days of constant battle, the officers watched him attentively. Their dream of victory, Park could see, was fueled now with a new hope.

His officers cheered. "We are ready to march on," yelled a young captain at the far end of the BTR.

"His orders to us are clear," Park bellowed dramatically. "The enemy has not stopped fighting. We must capture Uijonbu. Death to the enemy."

"Nam chim. Mansai," the officers shouted.

A long, rolling thunderclap of artillery explosions echoed against the western hills. The scorched ruins of Uijonbu burned brightly in the night.

6:40 A.M., 5 October, 2d Infantry Division headquarters, ten kilometers south of Seoul, South Korea. Wallace traced the movement of the enemy on his situation map. North Korean 152mm howitzers were now in range of the outskirts of Seoul.

"We're losing," Wallace said aloud to himself. "The North Koreans are playing us like a fiddle, and now the fiddler has nukes."

Wallace sat down in a hard metal chair, exhausted and dispirited. His deputy sat to his left, drinking a cup of warm coffee. The two men were in a fifteen- by twenty-foot room that had once been the main office of a large furniture factory. The walls were covered with 1:50,000 scale maps. From his desk, Wallace could look out the large, plate glass window into the open bay area that was serving as the operations center for the division.

"Why waste a nuke on an island when they could have used it on us?" Cooper asked. He paused and scratched his head. "I don't get it."

Wallace shook his head and pushed the top secret report toward Cooper. He looked outside the room, through the large glass window, as the division staff worked feverishly to complete the hard science of moving a modern combat division into offensive operations.

"Will we still attack now that the enemy has nuclear weapons?" Cooper questioned.

"Other people way above us will have to figure out a response to the enemy's nuclear strike," said Wallace. He leaned back in the chair. "We'd better get on with our planning. If General Schmidt finds out we don't have a plan, he'll nuke us."

"I'd rather low-crawl naked across crushed glass than get on Schmidt's bad side," Cooper joked.

Wallace smiled a faint smile, but his mind was focused on the problem at hand. He closed his eyes and tried to visualize the plan that they were about to finish, wondering if he had forgotten anything. The plan put the might of the entire division into a narrow, powerful attack. While the enemy fought off ROK attacks to recapture Uijonbu, the Americans would seize the initiative by bypassing the city and striking at the enemy's artillery groups. The 2d Infantry Division, refitting in assembly areas southeast of Seoul, would break through the North Korean lines and run amok in the enemy's rear. If that could be accomplished, the North Koreans would be in one hell of a mess.

Cooper interrupted his superior's trance with a whisper. "The old man's here."

Wallace looked up to see General Schmidt heading toward the office door. As he entered the office, Wallace and Cooper stood up.

"Relax, gentlemen," Schmidt snapped, looking more worried than Wallace had ever seen him. He was splattered with mud from head to foot and was red eyed from fatigue, which gave his face a hard, eaglelike appearance. He had been forward with his lead brigades, keeping in touch with the headquarters by helicopter and radio and returning once or twice a day for briefings. "What's the latest on the North Korean nuclear situation?"

"Sir, one small-yield nuclear explosion obliterated Paengnyongdo Island. Casualties among the regimental-sized ROK garrison are unknown but presumed catastrophic. The delivery means is unknown," Wallace answered. "They could have used anything—missile, plane, or ship—although no missile launches were detected. Right now, all U.S. forces are on nuclear alert."

"Who else in the division knows about this?" Schmidt asked, pointing his right hand at the window to the operations staff working outside.

"Nobody but you, Major Cooper, and me."

"Is there anything we could do to protect our force if they launch another nuke at us?" Schmidt asked, putting his pipe in his mouth.

Wallace took off his glasses, pinched the bridge of his nose, and closed his eyes. "No, sir."

"Any reports of chemicals or nukes anywhere else? Anywhere in South Korea?" the general asked.

"No, sir. Nothing's been reported," Wallace replied.

Schmidt plopped down in a metal folding chair with the back side forward. "I don't have to tell you that the ROKs are screaming for us to turn North Korea into a nuclear-tipped cruise missile test site. They're pissed—frothing mad. If they had nukes, they'd be dropping them on Pyongyang right now."

"Any chance we'll use nukes?" Wallace asked, almost afraid of the answer.

Schmidt shook his head. "So, what can we learn from the enemy's nuclear attack?"

"I believe that this was a warning," Wallace answered firmly. "It was a demonstration of potential."

"A demonstration?" Schmidt said with tired eyes. "The poor ROK garrison on Paengnyongdo would probably disagree with that; that is if there is anyone left alive."

"Sir, suppose you have a limited number of nukes. If you use them, they're gone and you get nuked in return. Their value is in having them, not using them. If you're North Korea and you've never used a nuke before, you have to demonstrate that you can. What better demonstration than to kill South Koreans in a place that doesn't automatically trigger a nuclear response from us?"

"But why not use them against us, to punch a hole through our lines or to hit Seoul itself?"

"That option makes sense only if they're resigned to suicide," Wallace argued. "Our enemy is smart but apparently not suicidal, at least not yet. He's fighting to win, not just to die. He's gambling everything he has. He wants us to believe he's more capable than he really is. He picked a target that would show his potential without forcing us to respond with nuclear missiles of our own. That's why he hit the island. That's also why he hasn't used chemicals."

"So you think he's bluffing," Schmidt said, using his pipe as a pointer. "He's trying to get the ROKs to negotiate by stepping up the pressure."

"That's my read, sir, and he seems to be desperately trying to end it soon."

"You may be right. The ROKs are acting like passengers moving around deck chairs on the *Titanic*. They want to counterattack, but the thought of having the North Koreans drop a nuke on their attacking forces has them paralyzed.

"We may lose the war in the next few hours," Schmidt continued. "We must launch a counterattack that will drive his artillery back from Seoul."

Wallace nodded. A short sergeant carrying an M16 rifle

slung over his shoulder, muzzle down, entered the room and handed Wallace a computer printout.

"The latest top secret orders from the Combined Forces Command," Wallace announced, handing the message to General Schmidt.

"Great," Schmidt said. "I just love surprises."

9:00 A.M., 5 October, mountain overlooking the town of Pochon, Chorwon Valley, South Korea. It doesn't matter what kind of background you come from—rich or poor, American or Korean, Pvt. Jamie Emerson thought. Cold and wet is cold and wet.

The sun was somewhere behind the overcast, but Emerson couldn't tell where. The temperature was about fifty degrees Fahrenheit, but it felt colder. A spattering, frigid rain had started at sunrise and continued all morning. The drizzle made the rocky slope of the mountain shine like polished stone. Unequipped for cold weather, Emerson and Sung-Joo shivered in the rain.

The shriek of cannon and the whoosh of rockets seemed almost continuous in the wet, drizzling morning air. The noise reverberated between the hills of the fog-filled valley, creating an eerie roar, as if giant monsters clamored in some colossal struggle.

"Stay low as we get close to the edge," Sung-Joo whispered, pushing his helmet up on his head to get a better view of the mist-covered valley below. "The enemy may have patrols out looking for us."

"Hell, a mountain goat couldn't follow the path we took to get here. I just wonder how we'll ever get down."

Sung-Joo didn't answer.

Emerson crouched low as he crawled to the edge of the precipice. The view from their perch was breathtaking. It was as if he were looking into a misty white sea speckled with islands. The hills that ringed the valley stood out from the low-hanging fog like the backs of long, sinuous dragons. After staring at the view, he understood why the ancient Koreans and Chinese were so fascinated with dragons.

The last few days seemed so overwhelming that Emerson felt numb. The death of his crew gnawed at his heart. He kept thinking of the machine gun, Sergeant Hardee's lacerated torso, and Corporal Oh's face. He tried a hundred times to explain it to himself. He told himself that it wasn't his fault, but in his heart he knew better. If he had manned the machine gun and driven off the attackers rather than cringing in fear in the turret of the tank, maybe they would all be alive right now.

His head drooped down as he lay on the cold ground that seemed to suck the life from his bones. He shivered again and looked up to the turbulent, cloudy sky. He wished he was far away, safe back in Kentucky.

"There," Sung-Joo said sternly, pointing at the fog. "I have been watching their fire. That is the center of the artillery group."

Emerson looked below. Flashes of fire brightened the fog as enemy cannon, firing twelve to eighteen at a time, discharged their shells. The lieutenant handed the American a pair of binoculars.

"I can't see anything."

"Once the fog clears, we should be able to see the entire valley from here."

The two men lay flat, watching the bright orange-red bursts in the fog, as a battery of multiple rocket launchers loosed a shower of rockets into the air.

"But what good will that do us?" Emerson asked.

"From the sound of the artillery fire, and the flashes I have counted, the North Koreans must have most of their artillery right here, near Pochon."

"We can't just sit up here and watch the war go by," Emerson said, a sharp determination adding steel to his words. "I want to even the score."

"Even the score?" Sung-Joo questioned, looking puzzled.

"My tank crew was killed. They were good men. They were my friends."

"I too have lost good friends," Sung-Joo answered, his accented English sounding formal but comprehensible. Sung-Joo looked seriously at Emerson. "We both, then, have a score to settle. That is why we are here."

Sung-Joo handed Emerson the backpack radio that he had been carrying since the first day of the war.

"You will help me put this to use," Sung-Joo explained. "If

we can contact a friendly unit, we may be able to direct artillery fire or attack aircraft on the enemy's guns."

Emerson looked at the pack and pulled out the radio. "We'll never range them from here," he said, shaking his head.

"This mountain is very high," Sung-Joo replied. "You must try."

"Look, sir, I'm a tanker, not a radio expert."

"We will try. It is our duty. It is our chance to even the score."

12:10 P.M., 5 October, 1st Brigade Tactical Operations Center, fifteen kilometers southeast of Uijonbu, South Korea. "That completes the orders," Colonel Jakes announced. "We can't execute until we get the go-ahead from division. Any questions?"

There was a pause as the commanders looked at one another. After four long hours in the operations order briefing, Rodriguez was eager to leave and get back to his task force.

"Okay, gentlemen. Good luck. I'll call you when we get the exact time to launch the attack," Colonel Jakes ordered. "Rodriguez, join me outside. I need to talk to you."

Colonel Jakes, wearing his helmet, web harness, 9mm pistol, protective mask, and BDUs, walked outside the TOC extension and found a corner of muddy rice paddy that was unoccupied. Rodriguez, wearing his Kevlar helmet, tanker's Nomex, web belt with .45 pistol, and protective mask, and with his M3 submachine gun slung over his shoulder, followed silently behind. Rodriguez carried his Plexiglas map case in his left hand.

Jakes turned around and put his hand on Rodriguez's shoulder. "I'm counting on you to lead this effort. Your task force has already done more than its fair share, but I know you can do it."

"Sir, my men understand," Rodriguez answered. "If we're not careful, we could still lose this war."

"You're right," Jakes said. "We've all seen the cold equation of war played out in the past few days. We've applied the science we know and were taught, but the rest is art, guts, determination, and luck. Your battalion has paid the reckoning of this tough calculus in blood, as the other battalions have. Now I've got to ask you to lead the effort one more time. Is there anything you need?"

Rodriguez felt unexpectedly exhausted, drained. "No, sir,

we're pretty well set with fuel and ammo. A couple of hours' rest and maintenance would be nice."

"Mike, time is the one thing I can't give you," Jakes replied. He handed Rodriguez a cigar. "Good luck."

Rodriguez took the cigar, beamed a quick smile, and snapped his brigade commander a salute. Jakes returned the salute and walked back into his headquarters. Rodriguez stood quietly alone for a few moments, then walked over to his HMMWV. He opened the door and sat in the right-hand seat without saying a word. He was bone-weary tired in spite of the three and a half hours of rest he had had last night.

With a snap he buckled his seat belt, shut the door, and placed the map on his lap. His driver, Specialist Finley, turned on the ignition and roared the engine for a few seconds. Rodriguez nodded, and Finley pulled out of the brigade headquarters site. The HMMWV moved through a series of concertina-ringed checkpoints and guards, then bounced across the narrow road toward the Dragon Force assembly area.

Rodriguez considered what he had learned about the North Korean method of war; it was inexorable and politically rigid and required nothing more than mindless obedience from those who execute it. Would the American counterattack succeed? He thought about his casualties. He thought of Tony Bradford.

Rodriguez looked up at the cloudy sky. The weather had turned rainy and foggy. The brave sun was fighting a fierce battle against the gloom, and losing. The early-morning fog that had blanketed their assembly area wasn't evaporating at all.

The bad weather wouldn't help the counterattack, he thought. Yesterday had been a fairly good day, and he had seen dozens of aircraft. There would be few planes flying today to interdict the enemy's columns. He stared down at the map in his lap. Another tough mission, he thought. I pray to God that the weather clears and we can get some air support.

Finley maneuvered the HMMWV down a muddy, narrow road and arrived at the task force tactical operations center. He pulled up next to a cluster of M577 armored command post vehicles and parked. Each of the big, square, tracked M577 APCs had its back ramp down. Inside the vehicles, officers and sergeants listened to the crackle of radios and posted operations maps.

Command Sergeant Major Zeke Dougan, wearing Nomex and carrying an AK-47 strapped over his back, opened the colonel's door. In a quick move, he reached in with his powerful right hand, grabbed the colonel's hand, and pulled him out of the HMMWV. Together they conferred at the back of the HMMWV as the company commanders gathered near the hood.

"All right, boss, we're ready," the sergeant major said with a big, toothy grin. "The task force is refueled, rearmed, and as fixed as we're gonna get her. Your combat power is thirty-eight M1A2s and eleven Bradleys. I acquired some parts from direct support maintenance, enough for the maintenance tech to fix three other tanks."

"Sergeant Major, you're a miracle worker," Rodriguez replied with a wide smile to match his command sergeant major's grin. "How did you ever get three more tanks up?"

"Besides raiding direct support maintenance, I helped the maintenance officer to cross-level Charlie Two-One," the veteran NCO said. He unscrewed the lid of his thermos, poured a warm drink, and handed his boss the cup. "We got enough parts off Charlie Two-One to get three tanks up. I had to take apart most of the turret, but Two-One can still run and can fire machine guns. I'll move it with the combat trains. It might come in handy."

"Good thinking," Rodriguez said with fatigue in his voice.

"How do you feel? You okay?" Dougan asked, seeing the look on his commander's face.

"Jakes is counting on us to lead the main effort," Rodriguez said. "This attack may determine the war. We can't let him down."

"We won't," Dougan said with a smile. "Don't worry, boss; only the good die young."

"Then I guess I'll live forever."

"That's right." Dougan continued grinning as the two of them walked to the front of the HMMWV to join the company commanders.

The men were already assembled. Rodriguez's officers gathered around him. Captain George Maxwell commanded Team Dealer, the advance guard; Capt. Ken Mackenzie, Team Steel, the breach company; Capt. Joe Sharpe, Team Renegade, the mechanized infantry heavy company; Capt. Al Grey, Team

Bulldog, the task force reserve. Captain Kurt Richardson, the task force engineer officer, and Capt. Pat Meyer, the headquarters company commander, stood at Rodriguez's side.

Rodriguez paused for a few minutes to look at his commanders. They were like any other group of company team officers in the U.S. Army, dressed in stained Nomex uniforms, muddy leather boots, and Kevlar helmets. They carried their pistols and chemical protective masks at their sides. They were typical, but there was an air about them. They were veterans now and they projected the aura—a sensation, like a cold breeze or a bright light, that precedes the onset of absolute certainty—that nothing could stop them. Rodriguez wondered, knowing how strong his tanks were and how fragile flesh was, how long this would last.

Rodriguez eyed his sergeant major as if he were seeing him for the first time. Dougan wore his tanker Nomex uniform, infantry-type harness, pistol, long bowie knife at his side, several pocket knives and two grenades taped to his harness. He looked like a picture from the cover of *Soldier of Fortune* magazine.

"Sergeant Major, you carry more weapons than any man I know," Rodriguez announced. He touched the barrel of the AK-47 slung around Dougan's shoulder. "Where'd you steal this?"

"Sergeant majors never steal, sir, they acquire," Dougan beamed with pride. "It seems that some communist son of a bitch was playing sniper and tried to take a potshot at one of the mechanics in the combat trains. I happened to be near a fifty-caliber. Let's just say he was a lousy shot and I'm not."

Rodriguez smiled. "Are you sure you won't reenlist? The thought of you as a civilian scares the hell out of me."

"Yeah, Sergeant Major," Captain Mackenzie joked. "You look like some kind of a medieval warlord. We can't have you frightening the civilians, can we?"

"Shit, sir, I'm here for the duration. Then it's off to retirement land," Dougan responded, shuffling his stance. "Besides, my wife, Kaye, may just kill me if I don't get this fucking war over with pronto and get back to her. She was going to meet me in Hawaii in a few weeks, and she has all the goddamned credit cards."

The officers chuckled. Rodriguez slapped Dougan playfully

on the back. He knew of Kaye's formidable charms from the never-ending series of colorful tales told by Dougan.

Captain Grey, who sported a scraggly, wild mustache that always exceeded the regulation standard, had a Band-Aid taped to his chin. Rodriguez stared at the bandage with a smile and stroked the stubble on his own chin. "That's a closer shave than the one I had this morning. Which reminds me, you guys are beginning to look like refugees."

The officers laughed again. Captain Joe Sharpe, the commander of the mech-heavy team, the Renegades, touched Grey's face and ripped off the bandage. "Al, I've got a bayonet you can use if you really want a shave."

"Ouch." Grey put his hand up to his neck in mock shock. "Hell, I just didn't want to get another counseling statement from the old man for my mustache. If I'd known that no one else was going to follow the regulations, I would have started growing a beard."

There seemed to be a desperate need to share small things. Rodriguez was happy that, in spite of the deadly combat they had witnessed, they could still share a joke. The horrors of the past few days had aged them all. The humor helped ease the tension, and he encouraged it. They needed the strength they drew from one another. Now he had to ask them to go back into the fight and face the elephant again. What had he read once? "A mysterious fraternity born out of smoke and danger and death." Whatever it was, this group had it.

"Okay, let's get serious," Rodriguez said as he placed his 1:50,000 scale map on the hood of his vehicle. "The brigade will tell us in a couple of hours if the attack is on or not. In the meantime, we prepare as if it is. We're leading the brigade night attack. Our plan is simple. The ROKs call this a sweeping attack. We'll punch through enemy lines on the eastern side of Uijonbu, bypass everything we can, and race up Highway 3. We'll keep going and smash through anything that blocks our path. Nobody stops; nobody quits. Everybody fights. Keep attacking until we're through to their artillery. When we find the army artillery group, we'll destroy them before they can move. The NKPA artillery is the grand prize."

"A hell of a prize," said Capt. Joe Sharpe, the commander of

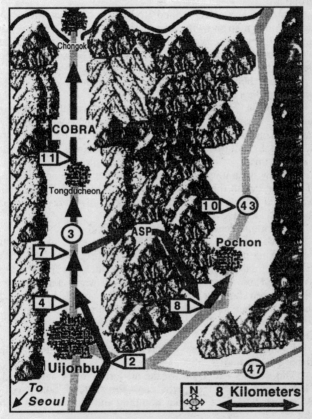

Dragon Force Attack Plan

A Company, the Renegades. "They'll be defending those guns like a mother bear guarding her cubs."

Two of the company commanders shook their heads. Sharpe whistled in surprise. "Sir, do we know where this artillery group is?"

"North of Uijonbu," replied Rodriguez. "The enemy positions on this map show the latest intel reports. Don't worry. An army artillery group is a hard thing to hide. We'll find it. Once we take out the guns, we'll head back for our lines or go on the defense and link up with the rest of the brigade."

"Behind their lines again," Sharpe complained. "Been there, done that, didn't like it."

"Lucky us," Maxwell added, a look of disbelief flashing across his weary face. "Sir, my men are dog tired. We've barely had a chance to pull maintenance on our tanks, let alone rest. The plan doesn't give us a lot of preparation time. Whose great idea was this?"

"I know it's a tough mission, George, but make no mistake. If we don't push the North Koreans back soon, we'll lose this war," said Rodriguez. "I don't want those guys who died near the MPRC to have died for nothing."

The commanders eyed Rodriguez pensively.

"We've got some advantages," Rodriguez explained. "We'll be attacking in the dark, and heavy fog is expected. The GPS system is finally up, so that will help. Besides, the enemy's got to be tired too. They've been fighting all week, and their artillery's been shooting almost nonstop. The brigade S2 reported that the weather will break tomorrow morning. As the main effort, we should get all the CAS and attack helicopter support in the division."

"I've heard that story before," Mackenzie chided. "The check's in the mail."

"This sounds like a job for the air force," Grey announced. "If it's such a big target, why can't the air force take it out? What ever happened to radar bombing and all their high-tech shit?"

"The air force is moving south," the fire support officer, Captain Fletcher, interjected, kicking a rock with his boot. "I heard they got orders to reposition farther to the south."

"That's great timing," Captain Mackenzie retorted.

"Who told you that?" Rodriguez asked, raising his hand to silence the cynicism. He was annoyed that no one had mentioned this fact during Colonel Jakes's operations briefing.

"Sir, the brigade fire support officer told me that as you were driving up," Fletcher answered.

"Typical air force," Captain Grey announced. "Remember, the air force ain't just a job, it's an occupation."

The officers chuckled.

"It doesn't matter," Rodriguez said, disregarding the disparaging remark concerning the army's sister service. "I don't have to tell you guys we won't get a second chance."

"Looks pretty rough, sir," Grey offered, looking at the map graphics. "The enemy's had a day or more to prepare his defenses. There will be plenty of enemy infantry dug in and waiting to greet us."

"Well, rough or not, Al, we've got to break through. We'll attack along Cobra. Asp is the branch plan. We'll have to attack all night and all day. After that we'll either fight our way back or they'll link up with us."

"Asp doesn't look like much of a direction of attack," Command Sergeant Major Dougan said with a whistle.

"If we can get up Asp, we can flank them and hit them on Highway 43 from the west," Mackenzie explained, pointing to the map and a connecting road that ran west to east.

"Right," Rodriguez answered. "I've been up that trail several times. It's tank capable and, I'm betting, not heavily guarded."

"We can do it," Mackenzie replied confidently. "We've been up worse trails."

"That's for sure. That's for damned sure," Maxwell said with a grin. "Maybe if we get some artillery support, we can catch them napping."

"That's what I'm counting on," Rodriguez said. "And we should have plenty of artillery, at least at the start."

"What about our flanks?" Captain Sharpe asked.

"Forget the flanks, Joe," Rodriguez answered, his eyes narrowing as he emphasized the words. "All of you must keep the column moving. Break through, find his artillery, and kill it."

The company commanders nodded.

"If we get the word to attack, we'll move out at twenty-three hundred and cross the line of departure at twenty-four hundred.

Remember, possessing the terrain doesn't matter. What matters is shattering the enemy. The terrain will fall into our hands by itself. If we can get at their artillery, destroy it or make it move, we'll save a lot of lives."

Rodriguez looked up to the black clouds that filled the sky. If only the weather would break, he prayed.

"That's all. As soon as I get the word that the attack is on, I'll call you. In the meantime I expect you to get ready as if we already have the word to go. No hesitation. Brief your men."

"Dragon Force," the officers shouted as they saluted.

Rodriguez smiled as they dispersed. Their tone was proud. There was a challenge in it. Rodriguez liked that. He needed it right now.

4:00 P.M., 5 October, Uijonbu, South Korea. The sound of heavy artillery fire echoed in the Korean hills. The city of Uijonbu burned continuously, as if it were a huge furnace composed of hundreds of separate conflagrations. The flames mingled with the thick fog. Machine-gun fire still sounded from the close-quarter melee. Apparently the South Koreans weren't surrendering.

Major General Park Chi-won, the commander of the 820th Armored Corps of the North Korean People's Army, sat in a black high-backed swivel chair. His new headquarters, a large, thick-roofed building, was ideal. It had plenty of room and offered protection from everything but a direct hit.

The building had once been a Hyundai car dealership. A poster showing a pretty Korean girl in a short skirt caressing the side of a new Hyundai car was pinned to the wall. In Korean the poster read, "Isn't it time you fell in love with a Hyundai?"

Park shook his head. The poster seemed to be mocking him. In North Korea he had a Mercedes, the official property of the People's Republic. In his country, individual citizens didn't own personal automobiles.

"Comrade General, here is our situation," a young major announced, tearing the general away from his thoughts. The major pointed to the area south of Uijonbu on the multicolored map. Six subordinate commanders, all young majors and lieutenant colonels, sat with him in the room, waiting to receive their orders.

Park looked at the young faces. The cost of the attack on the NKPA's senior leadership had been stiff. The war was at a critical point, he thought. The North Korean plan, to attack with only twenty-five divisions, required speed and an unrelenting advance. The initiative was still in the hands of the Inmun Gun. The attack on Uijonbu, however, was eating up Park's forces and slowing the drive.

The southern fascists were defending bitterly, more fiercely than Park had expected. North Korean losses were staggering. The attacking units had stalled and taken many casualties in front of their third line of defense north of Seoul. Park wondered why Marshal Kim Seung-Hee didn't order him to bypass the city. He felt uneasy.

"The enemy is completely spent," the major announced, pointing to the map. "He is still fighting in Uijonbu, but his defenses are collapsing. The enemy is withdrawing everywhere else across the front. His major forces are now southeast of Seoul. He has six weak divisions defending the capital."

"Excellent."

"We still have two infantry divisions and the elements of half a dozen brigades fighting in the city of Uijonbu," the major continued, putting down his copy of the corps operations order that had been issued the day before. "We expect to wipe out the small pockets of fascist resistance by sunrise."

"The purpose of the battle for Uijonbu is to defeat the enemy's will and set the conditions for the next phase," Park commented. "The 815th Corps will arrive just before dark. They are moving from their UGFs in the motherland now. When they arrive, I want them to move immediately into assembly areas outside Uijonbu. I want them rearmed and refueled. They will continue the attack at oh-eight-hundred tomorrow."

"Sir, as you know, we have continued to work to refine the plan," commented the chief of staff. "There is a strong possibility that the Americans will replace the southern fascists as our main adversaries in the next phase of the battle."

"What is their strength?"

"Comrade Commander," a major said, pulling out a chart that depicted the American order of battle, "the enemy is estimated to be a depleted brigade of three battalions: one armor, one Bradley-equipped mechanized infantry battalion, and one ROK mechanized infantry battalion."

"Defeating them wins the war," General Park said, a look of revenge in his eyes. He remembered his first battle against the Americans in the fog. He had lost an entire brigade in a matter of minutes. The success of his defense depended on stopping the Americans. "How will the Americans deploy?"

"I believe, Comrade General, that they will defend against the 815th from positions near Seoul. The Americans seem obsessed with their flanks. Every time we get around them, they withdraw. In any event, American forces haven't yet left their assembly areas. We will attack before they can get into positions to defend."

Park nodded, tossing aside a copy of the thick operations order he had received from 1st Army Group headquarters. None of the details of the order made any sense now. The timetables for fires and movement were completely desynchronized. "Show me the new plan of attack, Major."

Thick red arrows on the map depicted the line of attack for each corps. The major stiffened and handed a copy of a thirty-page operations order to the general. "All commanders have already received the timetable for the attack on 7 October."

"What is our strength?"

"Comrade General, our strength in infantry is still strong but we can muster only forty-four tanks, sixty-two VTT323s, and nineteen AT-5s in the entire corps."

Bitter close combat had reduced Park's forces to a mere shadow of their prewar strength. Fortunately, decades of preparation still inspired his men with the will to fight. Other armies would have stopped the attack by now, Park mused. These men would fight; he could see it in their eyes. They had not lost their faith.

"We have reorganized tank and mechanized infantry units to defend," the major reported. "Our total artillery strength is good—seven artillery battalions and five multiple rocket launcher battalions. The 1st Army Artillery Group is located south of Pochon."

"I want these forces to defend tonight and shield the 815th. The enemy has not attacked us yet in this war," General Park announced, pacing back and forth in front of the terrain model. "But I want to be ready just in case."

"We have infantry and tanks guarding every approach," Major Lee reported, indicating the map with a long wooden pointer. "The brigade artillery group is in range, just north of Uijonbu, prestocked with plenty of ammunition."

General Park smiled. "The moment of decision has arrived. Our enemies are trembling before us. Tomorrow morning we will launch the 815th Corps to attack and win the victory we deserve."

5:00 P.M., 5 October, mountain overlooking Pochon, Chorwon Valley, South Korea. "I've checked everything out six times and I can't hear anyone," Emerson said, comparing the time on his watch to the time on the digital radio's readout. "It's got to be the timing."

Lieutenant Sung-Joo scanned the valley, ignoring the American's comments. The fog was still thick but the rain had stopped. From the flashes in the fog and the noise, Sung-Joo had identified the location of seven artillery battalions and five multiple rocket launchers. The enemy's howitzers and mobile rocket launchers were hidden in a blanket of fog. The howitzers were firing at regular intervals.

"Try again," the lieutenant said. "We must reach somebody and tell them what we have here."

Emerson checked the large, collapsible antenna. He turned on the radio and made a functions check. "Maybe it's not the radio. Maybe we're just out of range. Maybe everyone is so far south we can't pick them up."

"They will return," Sung-Joo answered. "Save the battery. We'll try again in a couple of hours. If we don't reach anyone by tomorrow morning, we'll have to move south."

Suddenly Emerson perked up. He heard Korean voices.

"Hey, I hear—"

"Shhh," said Sung-Joo, putting his index finger to his lips. He quickly brought his M16 rifle to his side and looked back toward the trail, the way they had come up. They were in a good position to observe but a bad one to fight. Although the precipice was a perfect lookout point, it was also a dead end.

There was no place to run. The only way out was back the way they had come.

The voices grew louder. A man laughed. Sung-Joo motioned for Emerson to get closer to the rock wall, hoping that the intruders would not see them. He crawled back, trying to line up next to the stone surface of the cliff, and carried the radio with him.

Emerson heard the sound of footsteps as the safety on Sung-Joo's rifle clicked off. The lieutenant aimed at the trail. Emerson was tense with expectation. Stay calm, he said to himself.

A North Korean with a rifle slung over his shoulder sauntered ten feet in front of him. The soldier saw Sung-Joo and froze. Sung-Joo fired.

The M16 cracked and the man fell down. A second North Korean, walking behind the man who had fallen, fired several shots, then quickly turned to run back down the trail. Sung-Joo jumped up and fired three rounds. The well-aimed shots tore into the man's back, and he fell to the ground.

The ROK lieutenant moved forward and checked the two North Koreans. Both were dead. He stripped them of their weapons, water, and ammunition. One of the dead men carried a stick grenade. Sung-Joo stuffed it in his web belt. Emerson helped him gather every useful item—helmets, ponchos, even boot laces. Then they heaved the North Koreans over the cliff.

The two men walked quietly back to the precipice with the equipment they had taken from the North Koreans. The American sat against the rock wall, his newly acquired AK-47 at the ready. They each had four magazines of twenty 7.62mm bullets, a bottle of water, a poncho, and a bag of rice.

"Not much to fight a war with," Emerson announced. "Do you think they'll send any more patrols?"

"They will return when they do not hear from this patrol. Probably at sunrise."

"Then we've got to get the hell out of here. Where can we go?" asked Emerson.

"There is no place to go. The top of the mountain is almost straight up. They're sure to be waiting for us at the bottom. We're better off right here for now."

"If they come back in the morning, we won't stand a chance," said Emerson.

"I am tired of running," Sung-Joo answered. He put down his M16, which was now out of ammunition, and grabbed the AK-47, inserted a magazine, and pulled back the bolt. "Our mission is here. We are staying. Try the radio again in two hours."

5:10 P.M., 5 October, 2d Infantry Division temporary headquarters, ten kilometers south of Seoul, South Korea. "General, sir, wake up," Major Cooper said, nudging the commanding general carefully. "We have him, sir. By God, General, we have him."

"What . . . huh?" General Schmidt replied. "Cooper? Have who? What the hell are you talking about?"

The general sat up on his aluminum-framed, canvas-covered cot. He rubbed his eyes and raised his left arm to scan the watch on his wrist. He had been resting for a few hours.

"Hell, I feel like I just closed my eyes."

"Sorry, General, but the ROKs have the North Korean code and their high command frequency. Here's the latest message that the leader of North Korea sent to his troops opposite us a few hours ago," Cooper said, handing the general a piece of paper. "We knew you'd want to see it right away."

Schmidt read the message out loud. "Commanders of the Strike Zone: The war is almost over. We have destroyed the enemy garrison on Paengnyongdo Island with a nuclear device to show our nuclear potential. We have more nuclear weapons, but we will use them only if the Americans try to attack us with nuclear missiles. Everything now depends on the battle you fight. In a few more days we will complete our victory. I have committed the 815th Reserve Corps in your sector. The lead elements of the 815th Corps will attack and complete the encirclement of Seoul. The corps artillery groups are positioned to fire chemical weapons at the city if they refuse to negotiate. Signed: Marshal Kim Seung-Hee."

"Sir, we have confirmed the report," Cooper said, pointing to the map. "The 815th Corps is on the road, moving now to exploit the NKPA's success at Uijonbu. This is their last mobile reserve."

"How do you know that?" Schmidt asked.

"We received detailed reports from the South Koreans," said Major Cooper, pointing to the map. "The 815th Corps is moving from their UGFs now. They've smoked large portions of the route to camouflage their move, but the ROKs have been able to track them. They'll arrive in pieces tonight, one battalion at a time, and close before dawn."

"If that's true," Schmidt said thoughtfully, "the next twenty-four hours will decide the war."

He looked at the map, then began to pace. Head down, hands clasped behind his back, he walked slowly in front of the map. He reached for a report on the table and turned it over.

Cooper didn't speak. He knew better than to interrupt the general when he was trying to make a decision. Silent, he bit his tongue and watched the old man go through his decision-making ritual.

Schmidt abruptly stopped pacing and looked at the map for a few more seconds. He reached for his pipe, fiddled with the side pocket of his BDU trousers, and brought out a bag of tobacco. He opened the bag, pinched a wad of brown tobacco, and stuffed it in his empty pipe, then placed the pipe between his teeth.

A telephone rang on the table next to the situation map. Major Cooper picked up the phone. "Sir," he said, turning to Schmidt, "CINC's on the secure line for you."

The general moved in front of the map and took the phone from Cooper. "Schmidt here, sir. Uh-huh. Yes. We can do that. We've got a plan already in the works. Yes, sir. We're ready to execute. Roger, sir. Out."

10:30 P.M., 5 October, flying south of Kaesong, North Korea. Four MI-17 HIP helicopters flew in tight formation through the dark, wet Korean sky. The lead helicopter banked to the west, making its final approach to the landing site.

Kim Seung-Hee considered his next move. Few of his staff realized what a razor-edged gamble he was taking. Few of them understood the intricacies of his strategy. Few, he mused, were masters of *paduk*. No one understood the critical importance of the endgame.

Kim hated flying in general and helicopters in particular. He frowned as he put the radio intercom on his head. He hated that he couldn't smoke in the cramped aircraft. He hated being confined to the dark, noisy, compressed compartment of the HIP.

The marshal looked out into the blackness of the rainy night. His personal staff, Colonel So, and four lieutenant colonels were flying with him. Three other ships flying in formation around him carried other staff officers and his bodyguards. The last helicopter carried the precious nuclear artillery shell.

The HIP's big 1,900-horsepower engine surged as the blades swirled in the wet night. The helicopter moved quickly across the blacked-out countryside, crossing the old border and heading south to Pochon.

There were four reasons why Kim had decided to fly to Pochon. First, it was critical that he take personal command of the operational exploitation forces. No one else knew the entire picture. He had to be close to the fighting to decide the endgame, the final victory. Everything depended on this. Second, he had only one nuclear weapon left and he didn't trust anyone with the arming key. If needed, the weapon would be launched from a 2S3 howitzer and would vaporize a large section of Seoul. Third, if he miscalculated, he would not be safe from a nuclear attack on his command bunker in Kaesong or Pyongyang. He didn't believe that the Americans would use nuclear weapons on North Korea, especially because they couldn't know if he had any more to throw at the south. But it was prudent to be out of Kaesong. The Americans, even if they went insane and devastated Kaesong or Pyongyang, wouldn't dream of exploding a nuclear bomb inside South Korea. Last, a North Korean traitor trying to assassinate him would have a tough time finding him in "liberated" South Korea, where he was surrounded by soldiers of his loyal shock divisions.

Kim's nuclear bluff was working. The enemy air forces had not flown in significant numbers since the explosion at Paengnyongdo Island. The plan was still achievable. One more attack and we've won, he thought.

The destruction of Paengnyongdo Island and the seizure of Uijonbu were all propaganda statements designed to terrify the paper tigers of South Korea and the United States. The mobile columns of the Daring Thrust plan were part of an indivisible whole that was designed to place maximum pressure on the enemy at precisely the exact psychological moment. Kim Seung-Hee expected that the emotional, degenerate South Koreans, assailed militarily, politically, and psychologically, would fold. He expected the debate between the ROK and U.S. allies over nuclear release to divide them and cause confusion and paralysis. He knew that Washington would not drop nuclear weapons on another Asian country for the sake of a small island. He also knew that the ROKs, seeing the vacillation of their nuclear protector, would feel abandoned and alone. In the end, the ROKs would collapse to a lack of will.

Kim Seung-Hee wondered—hoped—that it might not be necessary. Would the enemy capitulate before the 815th attacked? He knew that his ultimatum had been received by the South Korean government, the United States, and the United Nations. In his radio message he demanded the immediate cessation of hostilities and the withdrawal of all U.S. forces from Korea. He imagined the chaos that must be rampant in the weak-willed southern government that dared to call itself a democracy.

In the next few days, Kim Seung-Hee expected the ROKs to declare a unilateral cease-fire. He expected them to demand the withdrawal of all U.S. forces. He had watched a CNN broadcast of the events in Seoul today, a great gift of what the capitalists called the information age, and was pleased with his handiwork. The world was watching on live television the North Korean juggernaut swallow its southern neighbor. It was almost as if CNN was working for him to pressure the South Koreans to negotiate a truce.

Kim did, however, expect to win. A new order would rise in Korea, and Kim Seung-Hee would be its leader.

He scanned the latest reports that his efficient General Kang had prepared for him prior to his leaving Kaesong. Casualty figures in the advancing 820th Corps were high. Many senior officers had been killed in the fighting—grim testimony to the leadership and loyalty of the Inmun Gun's officer corps. The rest of the fronts had ground down to a bloody attrition match. This, however, was irrelevant; the psychological trap had been set, and the stage was ready for the advance on Seoul. The fresh 815th Corps was exiting its underground staging areas and moving south. The fog and a blanket of white smoke from hundreds of smoke generators concealed their night advance along the highways that led south.

The last report in his stack of papers concerned the activation of the People's Militia to defend Pyongyang. Enemy air attacks on the capital had caused extensive damage in the first few days of the war. Kim chuckled. Luckily, the People's Militia would not see any ground action. They were busy scurrying away from the enemy's bombers. So much the better, Kim thought. *Every bomber they waste against North Korea gains time for my divisions to drive south.* The People's Militia was serving an important role—that of a diversion. *Let them keep the enemy's planes busy.* It didn't matter how many buildings and dams the Americans destroyed. They would all be rebuilt with South Korean money after the war.

In Pochon, Kim's forward headquarters was set up in a large stone building in the city university. The plans for the final strike against the enemy were being laid out on the big map boards that depicted the terrain around Seoul. By now, the enemy government had had time to discuss the devastation of Paengnyongdo Island and Uijonbu. The fascists could see the continued southward drive of Kim's mobile corps. Seoul, reeling under the bombardment of Nodong missiles and huge KOKSAN 170mm cannons, was now in range of all of his artillery. The southern reactionaries were, indeed, in a rapidly closing vise.

"Colonel So," Major Rhee, Marshal Kim Seung-Hee's personal pilot, announced over the helicopter intercom. "We will be landing in Pochon in one hour."

"Excellent," Colonel So replied curtly over the intercom.

"Colonel So," Marshal Kim ordered, interrupting, "contact Major Chun as soon as we are on the ground and make sure he has three howitzers set aside for our special mission, as planned."

"It will be done, Comrade Marshal."

The Old Wolf lowered his head, raised his hand to his left eye, and gently rubbed the black eye patch. His headaches were stronger than ever. They seemed to grow with the stress of each day. He opened the pillbox in his pocket and choked down three small white pills.

I must be strong for the coming battle, he thought. *I must not be sick.*

11:30 P.M., 5 October, five kilometers south of Uijonbu, South Korea. The tanks moved in a tight column down the road like great armored dragons roaring in the night. The thick fog transmitted the whine of turbine engines as the tanks left their final refueling stop prior to moving into enemy territory.

The sounds of battle emanated from the north in the firestorm that had consumed Uijonbu. If the fog wasn't so thick—visibility was less than five hundred meters—Rodriguez was sure he would see Uijonbu from here. In the fog the only things he could see were the tanks in front of him and the faint red glow of light on the northern horizon.

The thirty-eight M1A2 tanks, eleven Bradley fighting vehicles, one Grizzly breaching vehicle, four MICLICs, two Wolverine assault bridges, and twenty-two M113s that made up the Dragon Force clanked down the road. Rodriguez knew that he had ten hours of fuel, which he could extend if he stopped, set a defense, and ran on auxiliary generators. Fuel was always his greatest concern. The North Korean People's Army ran a close second.

Firebreather rolled north along the two-lane concrete road. The TAC, like a dog on a leash, followed close behind him. In this battle, Rodriguez knew, he would have to move, shoot fast, and keep in communication with brigade and all his companies. In the restricted terrain of Korea, where the hills constantly interrupted the line of sight required for FM radio communications, this was a big challenge. The TAC's four radios and a long, OE254 crank-up antenna were almost as important to command and control as the IVIS system on *Firebreather*.

"Dragon Six, this is Dealer Six. We're at the passage lane now. Everything's on track," Captain Maxwell reported. "No sign of the enemy."

"Roger, Dealer. Continue mission," Rodriguez answered, then switched to *Firebreather*'s intercom. "Obrisky, keep scanning to our right. *Defiant* is looking to the left. I'll cover the blind spots with my CITV."

"No problem, sir. This fog ain't nothing for our thermals. Of course, this damn road's so narrow that the first time we see the enemy he'll be knocking on *Firebreather*'s sides. We'll be so close when I open fire that I might as well just stick the gun tube down their throats and tell them to say ahh."

"You just fight the tank while I fight the task force."

"Yes, sir," Obrisky said with a laugh. "I just thought I'd mention how close the targets will be coming up. You better keep your hatch closed. I don't want to have to train a new tank commander. Remember what I always say—"

"I remember. 'I tank, therefore I am.'"

"You got it, sir."

Rodriguez smiled. His gunner, SSgt. Steve Obrisky, exuded great faith—arrogance would be closer to the mark—in his skill as a tanker and in the capabilities of his M1A2 tank. Obrisky treated *Firebreather* as his tank. To Obrisky, *Firebreather* was human—a female, to be exact. Obrisky often said that you had to treat a tank like a "babe," with tender care and affection. Obrisky wasn't politically correct, but he was the best tanker Rodriguez knew and worth his weight in gold in a tank fight.

Rodriguez checked his IVIS screen and read the latest digital report. The advance guard was moving on schedule. In fifteen minutes, the artillery preparation would begin. Five battalions of 155mm artillery and two MRLS batteries would fire nonstop to pulverize the area in front of the attacking force. So far, so good, he thought.

12
COUNTERATTACK

But ground battle is a series of platoon actions. No longer can the field commander stand on the hill, like Lee or Grant, and oversee his formations. Orders in combat—the orders that kill men or get them killed—are not given by generals, or even by majors. They are given by lieutenants and sergeants, and sometimes by PFCs.

—T. R. FEHRENBACH

1:00 A.M., 6 October, NKPA defensive position along Highway 3 east of Uijonbu, South Korea. The newly appointed North Korean captain looked south. Yu Sum-Chul hoped he wouldn't see anything moving north.

The long race to Seoul had been hard on his unit, he thought. At first the heady, intoxicating drive through the South Korean defenses had seemed like a fantastic dream. The Inmun Gun had swept all before them. Yu felt like a zealot on a holy mission to free a sister from the hands of infidels. Then the fighting had grown harder with every kilometer they moved south. The enemy's final stand at Uijonbu was ferocious and bitter. The fighting for the city had shattered three NKPA divisions.

It will be worth the sacrifice, he mused, to achieve victory. Seoul lies within our reach. The long-awaited liberation of our nation is surely at hand.

The thin, twenty-two-year-old captain stood in the open hatch of his BMP. He wore a dirty, slightly torn combat uniform. A belt with a gray metal buckle with a red star gathered his tunic at the waist. The holster attached to his belt carried the standard North Korean 9mm pistol. The four stars on his shoulders signified his new rank as captain but did not reveal his new responsibility as the commander of a battalion.

It wasn't a real battalion, Yu argued with himself. Not like the proud BMP battalion that had marched as a part of the May Day celebrations in Pyongyang only six months ago. No, not a real battalion. This battalion was a ragtag battle group of pieces of units from all over his wounded division.

The fighting for Uijonbu had decimated so many North Korean units that the 820th Corps commander had organized the survivors into hasty battle groups. Yu had taken command of such a force—men from several units, men he did not know.

He glanced at the red epaulettes on his shoulder. There had been no time to sew on proper shoulder boards, so he had attached them to his battle jacket with safety pins. The rank insignia had once belonged to his revered company commander, Captain Chan. The death of Chan and most of the battalion officers in the fighting at Uijonbu catapulted Yu, the senior first lieutenant in the battalion, to battalion command. His battle group consisted of a BMP company reinforced by a tank platoon and a half-strength battalion of infantry. The brigade commander moved Yu's battle group to a quiet sector of the fighting, on the eastern rim of the Uijonbu pocket, to rest and reorganize. His new deputy commander was a senior NCO, the sturdy Sergeant Ee, from the platoon he had commanded only a week ago. The rest of his force, except a scattering of sergeants, was made up of two-year draftees unknown to him.

The hills echoed with the staccato hammering of the guns of tanks and assault teams in the city. Distant explosions punctuated the night as if the dying city were screaming in agony. Yu glanced over his right shoulder and saw Uijonbu glowing like the embers of a huge campfire. The fog was thick and reinforced by the smoke of the burning city. He scanned the darkness with his night vision goggles. Scattered artillery flares fell to the southwest, providing just enough illumination for him to make out the undeniable silhouette of a North Korean T62 tank, waiting in ambush for an enemy foolish enough to enter his engagement area.

The tough fighting in Uijonbu, however, was not Yu's only worry. There were rumors about hundreds of enemy aircraft burning the supply columns to the ground like dry matches.

There were rumors about enemy counterattacks. His latest crisis was the lack of food, fuel, and ammunition for his battalion. The support system had broken down. Fuel was scarce. His men had kept the advance going by scavenging supplies from the enemy. They had an adequate load of small-arms ammunition but not enough antitank rounds for AT-4 antitank launchers and RPGs.

Yu took solace in the fact that his battalion was in strong defensive positions. Nothing was supposed to happen tonight. The big, final attack would kick off tomorrow after daylight.

In spite of heavy losses, Yu was confident. His BMPs were sturdy vehicles, and he was proud of their capabilities. In the 1980s the NKPA had acquired BMP infantry fighting vehicles from Russia. The BMP had much more firepower than the typical North Korean APC, the VTT323. The VTT had a 14.5mm machine gun, whereas the BMP carried a powerful 73mm cannon. The BMP could fire AT-3 Sagger and AT-4 Spandrel antitank missiles. This made Yu's infantry fighting vehicles the most powerful in the NKPA inventory and more than a match for the South Koreans' APC, the lightly armored K200.

Yu listened earnestly as he heard the distant sound of a machine gun. He had much more to do before he could rest—check positions, talk to nervous crews, send a written report of his defensive plan to the brigade commander—but fatigue was overcoming him. He looked down at his watch and saw that it was just past two in the morning. It was going to be a long night. Hours of planning, preparation, and tense combat without much rest were taking their toll. He rubbed his weary eyes and wondered what the morning would bring.

Yu's orders compelled him to occupy a two-kilometer stretch of narrow secondary roads in a suburb that bordered the six-lane highway on the eastern side of Uijonbu. His unit was the second line of defense. Another mechanized battalion battle group defended forward of his positions to the south.

Yu really didn't have much to defend, he thought, gazing at his battle area. Artillery fire had flattened and burned most of the buildings. A narrow, winding road slithered through his sector. The main avenue of approach, the wide four-lane Highway 3, was off to the west. He was, he brooded, defending the forgotten far flank of a charcoal-pungent charnel house.

Yu's brigade commander had laid out the plan for his defense in detail. With characteristic efficiency, Yu followed his detailed orders with great precision—something that his mortally wounded company commander would have been proud of. He organized his six BMPs and three tanks into three platoons of two BMPs and one tank each. He deployed the platoons two up and one back in well-prepared defensive positions, placing his tanks and antitank weapons in keyhole shot positions. A keyhole shot allowed his weapons to fire at the flanks and rear of his enemy while remaining masked to the front.

True to the discipline of the Inmun Gun, Yu had forced his exhausted soldiers to prepare defensive positions. In the past ten hours, his men had dug hasty trenches, prepared tank and BMP fighting positions, and laid a few mines on the road. They linked his BMP and the critical fighting positions with communications wire, because the FM radio was almost useless due to enemy jamming and interference. The old, reliable field telephone offered him the surest means of communication.

About a hundred infantrymen in trenches reinforced his T defense. Their positions targeted the roads and offered excellent flank shots at anyone moving north. His infantry had nine AT-3 Sagger missile launchers, twenty RPG launchers, six 12.7mm machine guns, and seventeen 7.62mm machine guns.

Yu smiled to himself. He was proud of his work. He knew that his precise deployments would earn praise from his commander. In the North Korean Army, commanders were rigidly controlled. Adherence to orders was absolute. Yu did not have the authority to move a single vehicle, or soldier, anywhere other than where the plan directed them to be. If the enemy came, Yu would be exactly where he had been ordered to be. In the morning the 815th Corps would pass through his lines and relieve him of this sector.

"Any reports from brigade?" the captain asked his radio operator.

"No reports, Comrade Captain," Yu's assistant answered. "All frequencies are still jammed."

Yu rubbed his dirty, sweat-stained face. There will be no action tonight, he thought. Even his brigade commander had told him that. It would be best to catch a few hours' sleep. He sat back in the commander's seat of his BMP, the field telephone pressed against his ear, and nodded off.

1:40 A.M., 6 October, mountain overlooking Pochon, Chorwon Valley, South Korea. Jamie Emerson worried whether the North Koreans would return. He looked at his partner and saw Sung-Joo as alert as an owl surveying his territory for the movement of prey. The Korean lieutenant's AK-47 assault rifle was at the ready as he stared down the dark trail.

Emerson coughed. When was the last time I had a decent rest? he thought. Tense from living a twenty-four-hour nightmare, he found sleep—real sleep—impossible. Instead he would nod off for a few seconds, then awake in fear, imagining the enemy all around him. We'll never get out of here if I don't get this radio working, he thought.

"If I can match a frequency, maybe we can get some help."

"Match a frequency?" Sung-Joo whispered.

"This radio jumps frequencies every other second. If I can match this radio's frequency with other radios, we can talk. If not, it's just high-tech junk."

"Try," Sung-Joo replied. "Start with the frequencies you remember from your unit."

Jamie turned on the SINCGARS radio. He checked the battery reading, saw that it was still good, and corrected the timing to match his G-Shock watch. He tuned the frequency knobs to the only unit station he knew, the 2-72 Armor hop set.

"The enemy artillery has been silent for almost two hours now," Lieutenant Sung-Joo whispered. "They are either rearming or repositioning. You must hurry with that radio."

"I almost have this licked," Emerson said as he extended the radio's long antenna. "We're high enough on this mountain to get a clear line of sight to friendly lines, if there are any friendly lines left. If anyone is transmitting within range, I should pick them up."

Emerson coughed again. The weather was getting colder. The fog thinned and rolled slowly to lower ground. He shivered as the cold, wet air wrapped around him like an unwelcome blanket.

The wild scream of a multiple rocket launcher battalion blasting off a volley of deadly rockets suddenly filled the valley below. The missiles shot into the heavens and headed south. They illuminated the valley, clearly showing the locations of several artillery batteries in the thinning fog. Both men jumped nervously from surprise.

Emerson moved the antenna around, trying to pick up a station. He pressed the handset receiver to his ear and flipped through the hop sets he remembered from his battalion. After several minutes of static, he exclaimed, "I can hear someone."

Lieutenant Sung-Joo's eyes narrowed in anticipation. He scooted closer to Emerson, who turned up the volume. A voice in English issued instructions to some unseen unit, replacing the rushing, static noise in the receiver.

"Damn. It sounds like my tank battalion," Emerson exclaimed as he pressed the push-to-talk button. "Any station, this is Private Jamie Emerson, C Company, 2-72 Armor, U.S. Army. Can you hear me?"

With a loud, whooshing sound the missiles arced through the dark sky, their glowing white tails illuminating the night. Another volley of death was on its way south.

2:00 A.M., 6 October, along Highway 3, southeast of Uijonbu, South Korea. Rodriguez nervously tapped the map board on his lap with a blue alcohol pen as his tank rumbled ahead in the fog. His instincts told him to go forward. Every fiber of his body urged him to go forward to see the battle with his own eyes. He knew that was the wrong answer. In restricted terrain, such as the narrow valleys of Korea, being forward meant being consumed by the fight. He had to command the task force; he didn't get paid to be a tank commander. He had to use his IVIS display and his map and trust in his team commanders. He knew he needed to be where he could best make decisions, and that location right now was following Sergeant Lanham's tank, *Defiant,* and Team Dealer, the advance guard team. From this location in the advancing column, Rodriguez had communications with his critical subunits and good line of sight to receive information for his IVIS.

His tank column had 119 armored vehicles. He couldn't control his force; he had to guide it, to command it. Behind him traveled his TAC, the 120mm mortar platoon, Team Steel, Team Renegade, and Team Bulldog—two-thirds of his force. If he

Dragon Force Attacks Along Axis ASP

had to change direction or execute a branch plan, he could leave Team Dealer in contact and send Team Steel forward along a different line of attack.

The crash of friendly artillery fire muffled the steady noise of American tanks moving forward in attack column formation. For the moment, Rodriguez felt out of control. A mix of emotions running the gamut from pride to anxiety consumed him as his armored columns passed through ROK lines. On the one hand he felt that his armored vehicles were irresistible, a force with unrelenting power. On the other hand he knew how risky this attack was, and how desperate the situation. He worried that the enemy might block his attack on the narrow roads. It took only one well-designed ambush to stop his armored column from moving forward. In his experience, something like a magic curse usually attaches itself to hastily planned night attacks. Let's hope, he thought, that the curse is on the enemy.

It all depended on the factor of surprise, timing, and training. He mentally checked off the critical elements of the attack. The fog was acting as a natural smoke screen. He carefully chose the direction of attack. Lieutenant Red Whitman, the task force scout platoon leader, had spent the previous six hours finding the least defended secondary road to aim the penetration. The route that Red had picked moved around the eastern edge of Uijonbu, where suburbs of prefabricated buildings had once housed thirty thousand people. The enemy's artillery had leveled the entire area. Uijonbu wasn't much of a city anymore. What scorched and gutted houses remained were mere facades. The flattening of these buildings created fields of fire in some places as long as twelve hundred meters.

A quote had been going through Rodriguez's mind: "For all your days prepare, and meet them ever alike; when you are the anvil, bear—when the hammer, strike." The Dragon Force had been the anvil before. Now he was going to strike, and strike hard.

The secondary road picked for the direction of attack reconnected to the four-lane Highway 3 at checkpoint 4. The task force would then continue the attack north, up Highway 3, until it reached checkpoint 7. There it would continue to attack north or turn east and hunt down the enemy's artillery groups.

There was nothing for Rodriguez to do right now but ride behind *Defiant* and Team Dealer and wait for first contact.

He monitored his radio and plotted the forward movement of the task force, checking the location of his tanks on the IVIS and scanning to the flanks with his CITV. In spite of the advanced technology of the M1A2, he was unable to see much of the battlefield. Visibility was about six hundred meters because of the fog, but the latest weather report promised improving conditions. The thermals were picking up targets as far away as eighteen hundred meters. The thermal tank sights and the driver's thermal viewer, valuable additions to this version of the M1A2, gave the American task force a decided advantage in fighting and maneuvering in fog and smoke.

"Dragon Six, this is Dealer Six. I've got enemy in trenches at alpha-charlie one-zero-six. Digital SITREP sent. I don't think they see us yet."

"Roger, Dealer Six. They'll get an education soon," Rodriguez acknowledged into his CVC helmet microphone as *Firebreather* rolled on. He glanced down at his IVIS screen and read a list of four ten-digit grid locations that designated the enemy trench line. "Dragon FSO, the series alpha-charlie one-zero-six. Over."

"Wilco, Dragon Six," Captain Fletcher, the fire support officer, responded. "I monitored and processed the report. Rounds on the way."

Rodriguez couldn't see the artillery that was ten kilometers to his southeast, but he knew that the howitzers of the 1-15 Field Artillery Battalion were rapidly pumping shells at his target. The IVIS-TAC-FIRE interface—composed of the digital computers in the lead M1A2s, the fire support officer, and the artillery fire direction center—was transmitting the hard mathematics of war, the artillery end of Colonel Jakes's "cold equation." The digital messages transmitted the enemy's exact location to the guns. The fire control computers determined the charges and howitzer settings in rapid time.

In a few seconds Rodriguez observed a tremendous burst of orange flame buffeting the stretch of highway in front of and to the western flank of his advance guard company team. The ground shook as if an immense cudgel was hammering the earth. Smoke shells and 155mm high explosive burst in a cascade of loud eruptions. Others exploded just above the ground, billowing in bright bursts of flames. The white-hot fragments fell on the North Korean trench line, sending the fortunate running for cover and pounding the bodies of the unfortunate into the mud like a hammer hitting nails into soft wood.

The shellfire abruptly shifted north, leaving the tanks and the surprised North Koreans facing one another in the fog at close range. In this lopsided confrontation, the charging tanks had all the advantages. Even with his tanker's helmet on, and the whine of *Firebreather*'s engine roaring as he drove along the road, Rodriguez could hear the distinct loud blast of tank cannon firing in the valley. The high-pitched whine of his M1A2's turbine engine was quiet by contrast.

The crash of enemy mortar rounds fell six hundred meters to the southwest of the column. The enemy was reacting clumsily, like a punchy prizefighter swinging after the bell, Rodriguez thought. They're shooting their mortars blind, trying to hit us on the move. Trying to hit a moving armor force in this fog is like trying to win the million-dollar jackpot at a Las Vegas casino with a single quarter.

Team Dealer plunged through the fog and hit the North Korean main line of resistance while the North Koreans were placing a minefield on the route of attack. The lead tank platoon cut through the startled North Koreans like an ax chopping through a cardboard box. The lead tank, its mine plow already lowered, pushed aside the antitank mines that lay on the surface of the road. Before the communists could recover, the heavy armored beasts of Team Dealer scoured both sides of the road with withering machine-gun fire. The machine guns quickly cut down the enemy soldiers who stood and fought.

Team Dealer had knocked on the door of the enemy's defense and, in a few minutes of intense combat, kicked in the opening. Speed, surprise, and bold planning caused the breakthrough—Team Dealer provided the means.

"Dragon Six, this is Dealer Six," Capt. George Maxwell shouted to his commander, his excited voice loud over the task force command frequency. "Contact, Texas, center, alpha. Minimal return fire—only a few RPG rounds. We've broken through. It was no sweat. We've broken through."

The narrow secondary road chosen to break into the enemy's

lines was working like a charm. Rodriguez thanked his luck as the column drove forward. Every tank in the column fired machine guns to the flanks. Stunned enemy soldiers struggled in the fog to run away from the steel monsters.

"Roger, Dealer Six," Rodriguez said calmly as his tank lumbered behind *Defiant*. "Good job. Continue to shift the artillery to your front and flanks. Don't stop, don't stop. Keep moving."

Maxwell's men had verified their namesake, the Death Dealers, in the previous fighting in the Chorwon Valley. They were proving their reputation again. Rodriguez felt that nothing would stop Maxwell's ten tanks and three Bradleys tonight. He knew that the turrets of his tanks were impenetrable to the enemy's RPG rounds and their best tank cannons. He knew that his depleted uranium armor could resist 1,300mm of explosive force. A 115mm high-explosive round from a T62 provided only 450mm of penetration; a puny RPG provided a mere 325mm. As long as the tanks kept moving and maintained the momentum of their attack, they would be safe. Like panthers hunting in the dark, the tanks lunged forward for the kill.

2:20 A.M., 6 October, defensive positions along Highway 3, just east of Uijonbu, South Korea. Someone was fighting to the south. The sounds of explosions up ahead had Yu on edge. He struggled in his turret and tried to focus his Japanese-made night vision goggles to see through the thick fog.

"Damn this weather," he cursed. He turned to his radio operator and assistant gunner. "Can you get anyone on the brigade radio frequency?"

"No, Comrade Captain," the young soldier replied nervously. "The radio is working, but all frequencies are filled with noise."

The sound of fighting echoed to the south. The noise grew closer with each passing minute.

"Commander," Sergeant Ee shouted over the field telephone to his motorized rifle company commander, "I see a vehicle moving near Target Reference Point One. It appears to be a tank coming right toward us."

"Damn," Yu said over his intercom. "Can you tell if it is a friendly or an enemy tank?"

"It is impossible to tell, Comrade Captain," the sergeant reported. "I will need to shoot flares. The fog is too thick to see much, even with night vision goggles."

"Do so immediately," the captain ordered briskly.

Tense seconds ticked by as the captain's apprehension grew. Explosions reverberated in the thick fog.

"Comrade Captain, a vehicle is moving within range," the sergeant announced. "He is moving very fast."

"All elements, get ready to fight," Yu screamed over the company wire net. "Enemy tanks at Target Reference Point One."

"Commander," Sergeant Ee reported again, "I can now identify four tanks. They are two hundred meters north of Target Reference Point One."

A flash from a 73mm cannon erupted forward of Yu's ambush position.

"Engage with all weapons," Yu replied quickly, realizing that his forward elements were already in a fight. "Red Two-Four, volley fire at the enemy as soon as they move past the bend in the road at Target Reference Point One."

"Commander," Sergeant Ee shouted over the company wire net. The bang of machine guns dominated the background of the telephone transmission. "They are breaching the mines on the road with some kind of plow. Our guns are not stopping them."

"Stay in your positions and fight," Yu yelled back into his telephone transmitter. "Acknowledge, Red One-Four."

There was no reply from Ee.

A wave of cascading explosions, fire, and white-hot steel fragments engulfed the company positions. Artillery fire supporting the Yankee attack crashed into the NKPA positions all along the valley. Hundreds of small bomblets landed along the left and right sides of the highway, hitting armored vehicles from the top like sledgehammers striking empty tin cans. Yu struggled with the thinly armored hatch of the BMP and quickly closed it. Flying shrapnel tore through the air, pelting the side of the turret of his BMP.

"Where is our vaunted artillery now?" the captain cursed as the enemy's artillery played havoc with his defenses. The ground shook with the explosions, weakening Yu's resolve. The noise was so loud that he couldn't even hear his telephone.

Shards of metal scraped against the side of his BMP, making a terrifying sound.

Yu scanned the bend in the defile through his periscope sights. A few mortar illumination rounds floated slowly toward earth. The enemy, moving forward somewhere to his left front, was nowhere in sight.

"Red Six," Sergeant Ee screamed, "two enemy tanks have formed a firing line east of Target Reference Point Three. They are firing at us. I have lost two BMPs. I am now down to one tank and one BMP. I am not getting any support from the infantry."

North Korean mortar flares continued to fall forward of Sergeant Ee's battle position. Captain Yu watched the intermittent bursts of light change the dark landscape into an eerie, whitewashed scene. A machine gun opened up on the advancing tanks. A few rifles fired erratically from the trench line, but most of the North Koreans were silent, ducking the fire that cut them down whenever they lifted their heads over their positions to peer into the thick fog. Yu cursed. The constant fighting had worn his men down. A state of inertia gripped the defenders. The ad hoc infantry groups were not fighting. Thrown together with men they did not know, tired, low on ammunition, and woefully underarmed against the heavy enemy tanks, the defenders clung to the bottom of their trenches.

The loud banging of machine guns and the tremendous boom of tank cannon echoed from the south. Yu knew from the flash of the fire in the fog that the enemy was only seconds away.

2:35 A.M., 6 October, along Highway 3, east of Uijonbu, South Korea. Scanning through his CITV, Rodriguez realized that his task force was in the middle of a large enemy force, probably an NKPA mechanized infantry brigade defensive position. The huge tactical advantage of surprise had worked to his benefit. The dazed North Korean infantrymen staggered up from their trenches like zombies and ran into the swath of the advancing American fire. The North Koreans were unable to run or hide from the tanks.

The Dragon Force rolled on at high speed, firing on the move. The destructive M1A2s surged forward, protecting the boxy M2 Bradleys that followed closely behind. The Bradleys fired their 25mm cannons through thermal sights, knocking down any resistance. The North Koreans, barely able to see the attackers until they were face-to-face with snarling, seventy-ton death machines, melted away.

The tanks blasted both sides of the roads, knocking down anyone who rose above ground level.

Firebreather was only twenty-five meters behind *Defiant.* Obrisky, in control of *Firebreather*'s turret from his gunner's station, fired the 7.62mm machine gun, mounted coaxially with the main gun, at North Korean infantrymen who were running away to the east.

Two North Korean VTT323 APCs and a BTR emerged from a side road and were destroyed by Dealer's tanks before the enemy could react. By the time *Firebreather* reached the point of the short skirmish, the burning hulls of the three shattered armored personnel carriers lined the road. Rodriguez saw the BTR-60 blazing in front of *Defiant.* Momentarily unable to use his CITV in the heat and glare of the fires, he glanced at the burning vehicle through his tank commander's hatch. The remains of the crew were clearly visible, slumped in their positions.

The enemy BTR partially blocked the intersection of the road. *Defiant* unceremoniously smashed into the wreck's side, pushed it onto its flank, and moved around it. The smoldering BTR burst into flames as its fuel spilled in all directions.

The battle picked up in intensity. An enemy machine gun suddenly opened up. Machine-gun bullets ricocheted off the sides of Rodriguez's tank. *Defiant* quickly charged the enemy and butted into a concrete telephone pole, snapping it in half. The M1A2, unshaken, rumbled forward, firing its machine guns and silencing the enemy fire.

Rodriguez watched as a North Korean soldier stood straight up, obviously in shock, and walked diagonally across the field of fire as if nothing was happening. *Defiant*'s machine guns knocked him down in a split second.

Firebreather rolled on, advancing into the scene of devastation left in Dealer's wake. Houses burned on both sides of the road. A few determined defenders pelted the trail section of Team Dealer with small arms and RPGs. The source of the fire was the ruins of a roofless brick house. Rodriguez saw Team

Dealer's trail tanks and Bradleys execute a perfect massed fire engagement against the enemy of the building. Three tank rounds and hundreds of machine-gun tracers tore into the building. In seconds the walls collapsed and the enemy fire ceased.

"Conserve your ammo, Dealer Six. It's going to be a long battle," Rodriguez warned over the radio.

"Roger, Dragon Six," Maxwell responded triumphantly. "We're entering engagement area Oklahoma now. Contact, PCs, Oklahoma, center, alpha. Out."

Firing to both sides, the tanks rushed on through the fog into a sea of rubble and panicked North Koreans. Blackened vehicles and burning wrecks blocking the road were shoved aside by the surging seventy-ton armored beasts.

Rodriguez could see a dozen bright hot spots displayed on his CITV. He knew that these were the result of Dealer's tanks lighting up enemy vehicles and buildings. A line of dozens of smaller, colder spots represented the bodies of dead or dying North Korean soldiers. Rodriguez couldn't see any moving hot spots.

The battle grew more confused as firing and explosions occurred all around. The dull thud of secondary explosions rattled in the fog. Orange fireballs lit up the night. In the thick fog the explosions resonated like the banging of a great, deep-sounding bell. Machine-gun tracers whistled and sparked in all directions. Whenever the road was blocked, a tank pushed or smashed the obstruction out of the way.

"Look for the CIP panels; pick your targets carefully," Rodriguez rasped on the command frequency, concerned that the tanks might not accurately identify friend from foe in the fog. Each tank carried large thermal panels called CIPs—combat identification panels—which gave off a distinctive thermal signature in the M1A2's excellent sights. "Watch out for friendlies to your southwest as we enter EA Oklahoma, and turn right on Highway 3."

"I don't see any friendlies, only enemy," Captain Maxwell replied over the battalion command frequency with a cockiness in his voice that communicated confidence. "Let's get 'em now while they're on the run."

Rodriguez radioed his satisfaction. "You're doing a great job, Dealer Six. Keep moving."

In the middle of the report, Rodriguez saw three North Koreans dart onto the road. One man with an RPG on his shoulder was preparing to fire at *Defiant*'s grill doors. The men were right in front of *Firebreather.*

"Troops!" Obrisky screamed over the intercom as he quickly laid the gun to the front. The gunner's 7.62mm machine gun cut them down. They crumpled to the side of the road as if swept away by an invisible hand.

"Ski, tank to our right," *Firebreather*'s driver shouted over the intercom. "It just drove up to the road. Right front."

Rodriguez heard the loader cry, "Up."

The battalion commander rapidly slewed the CITV to the right, like a gunfighter in a western movie getting a bead on the bad guy. In less than three seconds he identified the target from his thermal sight, pushed the turret slave button, announced "on the way," and fired. The tank gun recoiled, expending the ejected base stub of the 120mm HEAT round.

"Target!" screamed the gunner. "You blew the fucker's turret right off."

Firebreather raced past the flaming T62 tank. The American tanks fired on the move. Enemy machine-gun fire, RPGs, and tank fire flew through the air hot and heavy, but most of it seemed to be fired blindly into the fog, detonating harmlessly

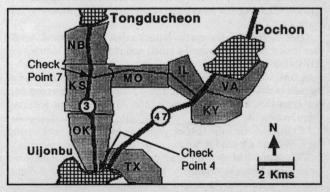

Dragon Force Attack with Engagement Areas

into the ruins on both sides of the direction of attack. Enemy tanks that fired immediately gave away their positions and received the massed vengeance of Team Dealer's guns.

2:45 A.M., 6 October, defensive positions along Highway 3, just east of Uijonbu, South Korea. "Fire flares now," Yu screamed over the FM radio. "Target Reference Point One."

The NKPA captain trained his binoculars on the bend in the defile. Sergeant Ee's platoon was being slaughtered. Yu had to do something to stop the enemy onslaught.

Unexpectedly an American tank burst through the fog. The armored monster moved forward rapidly, firing machine guns to the left and right. To Yu in his lightly armored BMP, the American tank seemed unstoppable. An artillery flare fell directly in front, so he could see the tank clearly now. He took the firing controls of his BMP and armed the firing switch for the Sagger antitank missile.

"Prepare for AT-3 missile launch," Yu shouted to his crew over the BMP's intercom system. He pushed the launch control. "Missile launching."

Sparks and flames exploded from the top of the BMP's 73mm cannon. The missile arched high into the sky, trailing smoke and flame from its tail. Just as it was on line with the target, the artillery flare fell to the ground, blanketing the enemy vehicle in darkness. Without illumination, Yu was unable to direct the flight of his missile, and it crashed harmlessly to the earth.

"Get another missile on the launch rail," Yu screamed. A soldier inside the BMP opened a hatch and struggled to load a new AT-3 missile.

A BMP on the left side of the strongpoint fired its cannon at the advancing American tank. The 73mm rounds bounced off, not even slowing down the tank. The American tank returned fire, devastating the North Korean BMP.

"Complete, sir," the soldier yelled as he jumped back inside the BMP and closed his hatch.

Two more BMPs fired madly at the advancing American tank. Their fire also seemed to have no effect. A North Korean tank, off to Yu's left flank, took advantage of the distraction and fired a high-explosive round at the advancing enemy. The round struck the angry monster on the lower right side, cutting its track. The M1A2 suddenly peeled off to the right and stopped. The turret quickly slewed to the T62. Within seconds a 120mm round had turned the T62 into a flaming hulk. The tank continued to lacerate the North Koran trench line with machine-gun fire. Artillery flares burst overhead, lighting up the night.

"Shit, nothing will kill these demons," Yu cursed over his intercom. "Let's get out of here. Driver, move to the alternate position."

"Yes, Comrade Captain," the driver answered as he slammed the BMP into reverse. Yu's BMP quickly darted into its new position. He scanned to his left and right. All he could see was smoke and dust.

"Comrade Captain," Yu's driver shouted, alerting the crew, "enemy tank."

A tank lumbered into his sight picture. From the stadia lines on his missile choke-sight range finder, Yu determined that the M1A2 was only six hundred meters away. He pushed the fire button and peered through his optical sight. The missile exploded from its launching rail, trailing a plume of thick white exhaust smoke. It raced high into the sky, then flew on-line with the enemy tank. He pushed the joystick, guiding the missile and diving it into the enemy tank. The Sagger hit the American tank squarely in the turret, showering the enemy with sparks and flame.

Yu's crew cheered, but then the cheer turned to panic. Wreathed in smoke, the enemy tank surged forward. Wide eyed, Yu saw that the American tank had not been damaged. The big steel monster just kept coming. The Sagger had made no difference.

"Enemy tank, three hundred meters," Yu yelled. "Main gun, firing."

The captain grabbed the 73mm cannon firing trigger and blasted away at the charging American tank. The BMP shook from the recoil of the cannon's loud bark.

The puny 73mm round bounced off the thick armor of the tank. The American continued his rush. More tanks appeared behind the first. They seemed to be everywhere, machine-gunning the infantry and crushing all opposition before them.

Yu's vehicles, chained to their fighting positions by his orders, were smoking and burning in their holes.

"Damnit," Yu screamed with frustration. "Driver, back up. Get us out of here." The driver slammed the BMP's transmission into reverse. The engine sputtered for one terrifying second, then the vehicle rapidly jerked backward.

Yu opened his hatch and quickly directed his BMP toward an alternate command position. He could see a burning BMP two hundred meters to his right as his BMP churned to the rear. Another BMP farther to the left was billowing flames in its firing position.

"Driver, faster," Yu ordered at the top of his lungs.

It was too late. Before the driver could get more speed out of the Russian-designed APC, the tank fired at point-blank range. The round ripped into the BMP. The vehicle ignited in a sheet of flame that shot right up through the open hatch.

An enormous wave of heat and pressure lifted the captain into the air and threw him out of the BMP. He smashed to the ground and blacked out momentarily. Regaining his senses, he struggled to move his legs but couldn't; they were mangled, bleeding stumps. Clawing the ground with his hands, he painfully dragged himself away from the burning furnace of his BMP.

The poor crew, he thought.

A soldier grabbed him by the collar and pulled him over the rough, rocky ground. He scraped along, then was slammed into the protection of a shallow depression. A tremendous blast from a tank's cannon sounded a few feet away. He looked up to see an M1A2 coming right for him.

"Help me," the captain ordered the infantryman, the words barely leaving his dry, scorched throat.

The infantryman rose to pick him up but was immediately cut down by machine-gun fire. The tank rolled closer, quickly clearing the ground in front of his position. The turret of the evil beast moved left and right, belching machine-gun fire.

The tank doesn't even know I'm here, thought Yu. To it, I am irrelevant, just something in the way.

The last thing that newly promoted Capt. Yu of the Inmun Gun experienced was the weight of the seventy-ton American tank crushing the life from his charred, wrecked body.

3:10 A.M., 6 October, alternate command bunker, 2d Infantry Division headquarters, three kilometers north of Seoul, South Korea. "Sir, you asked us to find their weakness," Wallace announced, "a center of gravity that we could target."

"Right, but make it fast, Steve," General Schmidt answered. "I've got my Blackhawk waiting to take me forward to the 1st Brigade TOC."

"Wilco, sir," Wallace replied. "I believe the center of gravity of this North Korean attack is their commander."

"Okay, keep talking," the general replied. He took his pipe from his left cargo pocket and pulled out a bag of tobacco. He grabbed a big wad of tobacco and stuffed it in the pipe.

"General, we just received some top secret reports concerning Marshal Kim Seung-Hee. Here's the folder we have on him."

Schmidt put the pipe in his mouth, reached for the folder, and thumbed through ten pages of faxed information. After a few minutes he looked up, took the pipe out of his mouth, and eyed Wallace carefully.

"Apparently Kim Seung-Hee is some kind of brilliant, ruthless renegade," said Wallace. "He's their best strategist and possibly quite mad. They say he suffers from some kind of brain tumor. As long as he's firmly in command, the war will continue. In fact, the report hints that certain parties are waiting to see how well he does. If, on the other hand, he was to be killed, the ROKs believe that another leader would immediately come to power—a leader with whom they have been doing business for quite some time."

Schmidt reviewed the ten-page file, reading each line as rapidly as he could.

"Shit, this guy is the Prince of Fucking Darkness. He'd sell out his mother to seize power. How do we suddenly have so much on this guy?"

"The ROKs apparently have a high-ranking man in Pyongyang," Wallace answered with a half smile. "They won't tell us the whole story, but the stuff is good—verified by our highest levels."

"That's pretty good intelligence information." General Schmidt tossed the folder onto the table in front of him and shook his head. "Too good, if you ask me."

Wallace took off his glasses, pinched the bridge of his nose, and closed his eyes. "We've studied this Kim Seung-Hee character. If he wins, he'll be a national hero. If he dies, we might change the fate of the war. The bottom line is that someone in North Korea is so nervous about him that they've sold him out."

"So you're saying if Kim Seung-Hee is killed, the leadership in Pyongyang will end the war?"

"The ROKs told me thirty minutes ago that they think it would," Wallace said.

"Very interesting," Schmidt replied. He took a deep draw from his pipe and blew out a small cloud of smoke.

"It would be like severing the head from a body," Major Cooper interjected, "and we may be the closest ones to his location."

"Do we know where he is?" asked Schmidt, his left eyebrow raised in a gesture of skepticism. The general took his ever-present pipe out of his mouth and used it as a pointer.

"The ROKs just intercepted his personal command helicopter frequency," Major Cooper said, beaming. "He flies in a formation of four special MI-17 HIP helicopters. If we can find out where he's headed we just might be able to get him."

"What do you have in mind?" the general questioned, sitting down in his chair and leaning back. He fumbled in his pocket and lit his pipe.

"Sir," Wallace said seriously, "the ROKs think he's headed for Pochon."

"OK," the general nodded. "That's where we'll go."

3:30 A.M., 6 October, 820th Corps headquarters, northwest corner of Uijonbu, South Korea. The rumble of explosions shook the foundation of the big building. From the sound, fighting was occurring to the northeast of Uijonbu.

"I need information immediately," Major General Park shouted into the telephone transmitter. "All commands will report the situation to headquarters immediately."

He slammed down the transmitter and looked up at his operations map, illustrated with red arrows depicting tomorrow's attack plan. Red circles showed the corps' immediate objectives. Dashed red circles, located farther to the south, designated the subsequent and final objectives. The map clearly indicated the future isolation of Seoul.

Park listened to the rising clash of battle to the northeast, then plopped down in the comfortable chair, tilting his head to the white ceiling. A grim frown was frozen on his face. He had had so many battalions destroyed under his command in the past week that he understood the predicament unfolding. His dream of victory was fading.

"Comrade General, the Americans have attacked in strength about an hour ago," his thin, young major reported. "I cannot contact the 815th Corps."

A greater calamity could not have been arranged, Park thought, rubbing his tired eyes. He had to determine what was happening and gain control of the situation.

Time. It was all a matter of time. Previous attacks by the South Koreans had been methodical. The southern fascists had been stubborn in the defense but reluctant to counterattack. This pattern had blinded Park to the possibilities. He had not expected the enemy to attack, and he had not expected the Americans to lead the effort so soon.

The general looked at his watch. The 815th was still closing on their preattack positions. One tank brigade and several mechanized infantry battalions were refueling. Could they be ordered to attack south in time? Could they beat back the Americans?

On paper he realized that Kim Seung-Hee would not understand how a battalion or two of American tanks could penetrate his defenses. The Heroic Leader would see this counterattack by the Americans as an act of desperation. Kim would expect Park to block the Americans, surround them with infantry, and kill them with artillery. Such set-piece actions took time and planning.

General Park, however, had developed a realistic appreciation of his adversary. He knew the power of the American tanks and the speed with which they were able to mass their awesome firepower. He had learned about the agility of the American army in the past few days. Their combat units had fought well. They had defended fiercely in the Chorwon Valley, using the terrain and their powerful tank systems to great advantage. If they attacked boldly and recklessly and smashed through his tired, spent forces before he could organize the defense, they would disrupt the 815th Corps attack.

This, he knew, must not happen. A sour sense filled his tired mind. The sense was not so much of defeat as fumbled victory. The fate of North Korea, the dreams of victory—not to mention his own future—depended on stopping the Americans. Kim Seung-Hee would not forgive the commander who failed to accomplish the design of the Daring Thrust.

Park rubbed his face with his good right hand, then looked at the map, trying to guess the enemy's objective. The Americans must be trying to gain time for the ROKs to improve their defense of Seoul. Considering the halting motion of the ROK counterattacks in the battle of the Uijonbu Pocket, Park hoped that the enemy drive would be shallow, that they would not try to go too far north.

"Rush every reserve to block off the Americans," Park grunted to his chief of operations. The general stood up and glared at the map, arms crossed on his chest, fists clenched, and jaw tight. "Send in every available rifleman. Strip the headquarters and support units. Get every man an RPG. I want the Americans stopped before they break through and interrupt the attack of the 815th. Is that clear?"

The major stared at General Park with unblinking eyes, his body taut and erect. "*Nam chim,* Comrade General," the young major shouted, proving his obedience. Without changing his stance, he paused, then continued. "Comrade General, it will take time to reorganize the forces to move against the counterattack. Our communications are jammed. We will have difficulty reaching the subunit commanders. Every unit is acting according to the plan."

The plan, Park thought. We are slaves to our plans. We do not have the ability to react. How often we plan perfectly and find that execution is impossible. Only the liar, Park mused, comes out of a great campaign and says that everything happened as it was planned. Quite frequently nothing happens exactly as it was planned.

The crash of artillery shook the ground. Dust settled from the stucco ceiling onto the richly varnished wooden table in front of the map. The sounds of multiple explosions resonated outside.

"I don't care what the problems are," Park screamed, his voice rising in volume and rage with each word. His left hand throbbed in pain, making it increasingly difficult to concentrate. "Redirect the artillery to smash the Americans. Move antitank forces to block their advance. All units will obey, or I will find those in command who hesitate, charge them with cowardice, and have them shot."

"Nam chim," the major answered like a trained dog.

"Get my BTR ready. We are going to the fight."

3:50 A.M., 6 October, Highway 3, three kilometers southeast of Uijonbu, South Korea. "Roger, Iron Six," Rodriguez replied confidently to his brigade commander over the brigade FM circuit. "I acknowledge that the enemy artillery group is south of Pochon. I will turn east off Highway 3 at checkpoint seven and execute direction of attack Asp."

"Warrior Six says you are the main effort," Colonel Jakes replied. "You'll get all the support we have. We're jamming his command and artillery frequencies. If you can knock out the enemy's S-300s or make them move north, we can get some ROK aircraft and our attack helicopters in the air. Iron Six. Out."

Flares popped overhead, suspended by small parachutes, and slowly drifted earthward. Continual explosions shook the earth and illuminated the early-morning sky with columns of flame. A BRDM armored car and two BMPs burned furiously. Their onboard ammunition exploded and illuminated the heavens with shooting sparks and tracers.

Team Dealer sliced through the crust of the North Korean defense. The rest of the Dragon Force followed, spraying death and destruction at everything that moved, ran away, or stopped to fight. The masonry and stone debris that littered the road was ground to dust by the tracks of the heavy tanks. Some shattered walls, still standing upright by some miracle of balance, fell to the ground as the rumbling tanks passed by.

"We've just reached the intersection of Highway 3, checkpoint four," Rodriguez said to Sergeant Obrisky. "We'll head north for another seven hundred meters, then turn east at checkpoint seven." We've caught the bastards with their pants down, he thought in silent satisfaction. For once in this damn war, we have the initiative.

The blast of a tank cannon firing rapidly up ahead resonated in the valley. Rodriguez, standing in the open turret, struggled to see.

"Dragon Six, contact, Kansas, north, alpha!" an excited Captain Maxwell screamed. "They're lined up on both sides of the highway. Tanks, PCs, and trucks are everywhere."

"Roger, Dealer Six. Keep moving," Rodriguez ordered, worried that he may have run into more than he could handle.

"Dragon Six, we've caught them refueling," Maxwell shouted. "By God, they're parked on the sides of the road refueling. A whole goddamned brigade. Shit, maybe more. Fire series alpha-charlie one-one-four."

The digital artillery requests were transmitted in seconds. The tank column picked up speed as it moved along the four-lane highway. Secondary explosions erupted in huge fireballs in the fog, sending shock waves that Rodriguez could feel against his face. He jumped back down to his IVIS, scanned the screen, and punched a button to fire a series of artillery strikes that would fall along the front and flanks of his direction of attack. He intended to create a wall of fire that would fall a thousand meters forward of his fast-moving tanks.

Dealer's M1A2s fired on the move in rapid, alternating patterns on both sides of the wide road, one tank shooting right, the next left, and so on. Every round struck a tank, an APC, or a fuel truck. Surprised North Korean soldiers suddenly found themselves in between the burning vehicles and the charging tanks. The men on the ground panicked and were crushed by tank treads or cut down by machine-gun fire. Team Dealer lit up the road with a line of raging fires.

Defiant fired machine-gun bullets to the left of Highway 3 while Obrisky fired his 7.62mm machine gun on *Firebreather* to the right of the road. *Firebreather* plunged through the pall of black smoke masking the road. As Rodriguez passed by, he witnessed a series of gutted, burning T62 tanks, many without their turrets, blazing like blowtorches. The tanks lay end to end, as on a parade field, because the enemy had parked them to the side of the road to conduct a maintenance halt and refueling operation.

Bullets bounced off the side of Rodriguez's tank as an enemy machine gunner tried to even the score. Rodriguez ducked inside the turret and closed the hatch as Obrisky turned the turret on this foe. *Firebreather*'s machine guns blazed as Obrisky raked the right side of the road, silencing the fire. *Firebreather* rolled on. Rodriguez checked his IVIS screen. So far, only one American tank had been put out of action.

The M1A2s were about thirty meters apart, moving as one connected armored snake, the tanks blasting everything in sight. The Bradleys raked the sides of the road with explosive shells. The direction of attack turned into a road of flame.

Rodriguez, his hatch now in the open protected position, peeked out of the slit between the hatch and the top of the turret. The twisted and charred wreckage left in the wake of the Dragon Force's attack was grim—pure, bloody chaos. Bodies lay all about. A tremendous fireball raced skyward as an enemy fuel truck exploded. Sparks, flame, and debris showered down like rain. Burning liquid splashed onto a dozen enemy soldiers. The men ran in flaming agony as the searching machine guns of an advancing M1A2 cut them down.

"Dragon Six, we've destroyed twenty or so tanks and more PCs than I can count. Continuing to attack. Over," Maxwell shouted over the radio, his voice exuberant. "We've taken no casualties. I say again, no casualties."

"Press on, Dealer," Rodriguez answered. "We've got to keep going to checkpoint seven. Don't stop for anything."

Explosions ripped through the air as the ammunition on board the enemy tanks exploded. The force of the detonations threw enemy soldiers onto the road. The M1A2s picked up speed and rolled on, firing as they raced forward, not stopping for anything or anyone. The shocked enemy ran away, leaving their burning tanks behind. Soon there was nothing left to oppose the tanks.

"Steel, this is Dragon Six. SITREP."

"We're right behind you, Dragon Six," Mackenzie shouted over the roar. "We're firing at what's left with machine guns. I count about two battalions' worth of tanks destroyed, maybe more. They're running from us like quail from a bird dog."

"Dragon Six, this is Dealer Six. Some of my lead tanks are running short of main gun ammo in their ready racks. Over."

"Roger. Kill the tanks and leave the Vetts and trucks for the Bradleys. Keep moving to checkpoint seven, then set up a firing line facing north. I'll pass Team Steel behind you to take Axis Asp. Guidons, guidons. Renegade, Bulldog, respond."

"Renegade. Roger."

"Bulldog. Roger. These guys are C students. We're smashing through them like they're not even here."

"We're taking direction of attack Asp. Dealer will form a firing line north of checkpoint seven. Team Steel will lead down Asp. Keep dressed up tight and don't stop. Dragon Six. Out."

With a loud roar another wave of artillery shells fell to the north, adding to the carnage. The volley of 155mm shells crashed into the road in front of Team Dealer, blasting a path clear for the Dragon Force.

No battle plan survives contact with the enemy, Rodriguez thought with a grim grin, but this was fantastic. The North Koreans were fighting back, and it didn't matter. The Dragon Force could not be stopped.

"Dragon Six, this is Dragon Five," Rodriguez's radio barked.

"Send it, Dragon Five," Rodriguez answered.

"I've picked up a station on our old battalion hop set," Lucas reported. "It's one of our men. He says he's observing the enemy's artillery group at Pochon."

"If he checks out, get him to pinpoint targets for artillery and send me the digital info over IVIS," Rodriguez asked. "Who is it?"

"A Private First Class Jamie Emerson," Major Lucas replied over the battalion command frequency. "He was the loader on C34."

6:00 A.M., 6 October, 1st Army Group headquarters bunker, Kaesong, North Korea. Since the surprise decision by Kim Seung-Hee to execute the Paengnyongdo Option and the destruction of Uijonbu, General Kang had been troubled. He feared the American response to the North Korean use of nuclear weapons. He understood that once weapons of mass destruction were used in the war, the possibility of rapid escalation, to a force level that far outclassed North Korea's limited means, would overwhelm them. He feared that he would lose control.

The general kept his fears to himself. He was a soldier, obeying the orders of his appointed commander. His duty was clear. He was not the person who would make decisions. He was merely the man behind the power, the efficient chief of staff.

The operations staff worked like bees in a hive, updating the large operations map. The information was intermittent. Only a few reports were getting through by AM radio. The satellite communications system, purchased at such great expense from their Japanese friends, was suddenly ineffective. Most of Kang's information came by telephone lines that had been tediously established by hundreds of hardworking communications teams.

The Americans, no doubt, had turned off their ability to communicate with their high-technology jamming systems. They were magicians, Kang thought, with a few surprises still up their sleeve. It was apparent to him that the war had taken a sudden, dramatic turn.

Hard fighting was occurring all over the battle area. Many of the bypassed fascist positions still resisted fiercely. Rather than surrender to their northern brothers, they fought back like tigers. In several places these forces had sallied forward to interdict North Korean supply lines. Night attacks by NKPA infantry to take out these stubborn islands of resistance had been driven off, with substantial losses. Kang's staff was frustrated by the unwillingness of the enemy to surrender. As more S-300 air defense systems were destroyed, enemy air attacks increased. Supplies of ammunition and fuel were running seriously short. Difficulties in communications and resupply afflicted every unit across the entire front. Rumors concerning an invasion by an ROK-U.S. amphibious group in the Yellow Sea, off the west coast of North Korea, threatening Kaesong, seemed to be gaining more validity.

More pressing, however, were the confused reports of a counterattack near Uijonbu. This situation created a significant new turn in events.

Kang sipped a cup of ginseng tea and looked at the operations map. The latest reports of the enemy counterattack were fragmented and confused. He really didn't have a clue what was happening, but his experience told him that the plan was failing. The depressing, gut-wrenching indication of an offensive losing steam was in the air. Kang knew that this counterattack would have to be defeated to renew any hope of victory.

His aide entered, carrying a pot of copper-colored tea. The major bowed slightly and, with a gesture, offered to refill the general's cup. Kang held out his cup obligingly, balancing it carefully while the major filled it to the brim.

The door opened abruptly. A captain in full battle gear, the commander of the bunker security force, strutted in and saluted.

"Nam chim," the captain screamed. He stood at rigid attention and saluted as if he were standing at a dress review.

Kang looked at the captain as he raised his left eyebrow and tilted his head. "What is so important, Captain, that you must interrupt me in the operations room?"

"Sir, there is a General Jong from the People's Militia here to see you. He says it is urgent. He will not wait."

Kang looked puzzled. The People's Militia, he thought. What could they possibly be here for? Kang looked at his aide. The major shrugged his shoulders in a gesture that expressed his bewilderment over the significance of the visitor.

"All right then," Kang said, drinking the tea quickly and handing the empty cup to his major. "Send him in."

Kang folded his arms over his chest and stood in front of the huge operations map. He had dealt with the People's Militia before and was not overly impressed with these political soldiers who played at war. They probably wanted to use his precious truck transport battalions for some inane task.

A pudgy, short, serious-looking major general entered. The officer, whom Kang hadn't met before, was alone. He walked in quickly, looking around at the guards and Kang's aide. The officer was in his forties. He wore the uniform and black armband of the People's Militia.

"Comrade Major General Kang Sung-Yul, chief of staff of 1st Army Group," the officer said stiffly, as if he were talking to a person with a highly contagious disease. "I am General Jong

Chang Ryol. We must speak privately. It is a matter of the gravest concern."

Kang politely smiled. He looked placidly at the shorter man and arched his eyebrows without a furrow in his forehead. "I have no secrets from my aide."

"I insist on secrecy," Jong persisted, waving his arms dramatically as if to clear the room with his gesture. "The survival of our people depends on it."

Kang nodded at his aide and uncrossed his arms, indicating that he had favorably changed his mind. The aide quietly withdrew, taking the guards with him.

"Now, what can I do for you, Comrade General?" Kang replied, his curiosity piqued.

The People's Militia general handed Kang a sealed envelope.

He opened it and unfolded the letter. He read slowly, holding the paper with both hands in front of his face. His eyes opened wide as he understood the meaning of the words. The look on his face registered both surprise and resignation.

7:20 A.M., 6 October, Highway 3, four kilometers north of Uijonbu, South Korea. Captain Ken Mackenzie's M1A2s pressed on, passing Team Delta. As soon as he was leading the task force, he dashed harder. His philosophy was that if you go through boldly enough, the enemy doesn't want to stop you. Maybe you're the spearhead of a tank division. The enemy doesn't know; they just want to let you through and then get out of there themselves. But if you hesitate, that's something else; they'll destroy you. It's hard to stop a thunderbolt forged from M1A2 tanks, and that's what Mackenzie planned to give them.

A smoldering S-300 battery, four chassis that had burned to the ground, stood in an open field to his left flank. A dozen bodies lay among the wreckage, a tribute to the security detachment's futile defense of their missile launcher.

Mackenzie grinned as he looked through his CITV and scanned to the east. The Dragon Force had turned east at checkpoint 7 and taken the direction of attack Asp. The narrow secondary road led through the mountains to Highway 43. Team Dealer was off to his left, firing at an enemy infantry position to the north.

The sun's rays broke over the jagged mountains. The fog had dissipated. Visibility was now in excess of a kilometer. Mackenzie smiled: It was a great day for a tank attack.

The valley in front of Mackenzie narrowed like a funnel, the end of which was a two-lane secondary road. It was the key to the door that would unlock the enemy's defenses and allow the Dragon Force to attack into the enemy's artillery group. A rock drop guarded the road as a sally port in the wall of an ancient fortress. Rock walls, designed to stop tanks from coming from the opposite direction, effectively blocked the west-to-east movement of the task force. Mackenzie's job was to remove the heavy concrete blocks in the opening of the funnel and punch through to the other side.

He surveyed the ground that covered the western exit of the rock drop. There was no bypass. He would have to secure the rock drop with fire, obscure it with smoke, and send in his engineers to blow the rocks blocking the route to dust. Dangerous business, but something his Team Steel had often trained for in peacetime.

Looking straight ahead, he could see the rock drop that blocked the task force. A line of trenches filled with enemy infantry was situated on a low ridge to the north of the rock drop. He could see heads popping up and down inside the trench line, trying to get a look at his tanks. This flank would pose a problem to his engineers and would have to be eliminated. At least six enemy tanks and a dozen VTT323 armored personnel carriers were positioned on the southern side of the rock drop, waiting for Mackenzie's attack.

Brave souls, he thought, realizing that these North Koreans were in front of their own obstacle with no route of retreat. Mackenzie looked to his loader, who was up in his hatch manning his 7.62mm machine gun. Mackenzie pointed to the enemy. "In a few minutes we'll get to see how good the North Koreans are at tank gunnery."

For the moment the task force had air support, and Mackenzie wanted every advantage to help him break through. He quickly orchestrated a terrible concert of death to overwhelm the dazed North Koreans.

Flying low, three ROK F-16 aircraft burst across the horizon. The aircraft suddenly split; one dived toward the hill to the east and dropped a fish-shaped silver canister directly on the rock drop. The object fell for a few quiet seconds, then exploded in orange fire along an area a hundred meters wide and five hundred meters long. Napalm.

The hills on the east side of the valley burned, and dark, oily smoke rose into the sky. The second and third F-16s dropped half a dozen silver canisters of napalm on top of the North Korean infantry. A huge fireball engulfed the enemy trench line with the hellish liquid flame. The fire attacks incinerated the defenders in their trenches. Those who weren't burned to death were cooked or suffocated inside their bunkers by the enveloping wave of liquid fire.

Captain Mackenzie, riding behind the lead tank platoon in his command tank, watched the ROK aircraft fly off to the south. Steel's tanks rolled east down the secondary road without hesitating, firing as they moved forward. Two T62 tanks that were dug in on the eastern side of the rock drop fired desperately at the advancing M1 tanks. Sagger missiles from the trench line and the fire from four enemy tanks on the southern side of the road blasted away at the Americans in platoon volleys.

"Steel One-One, form a firing line eight hundred meters short of the rock drop," ordered Mackenzie. "Plaster the area with fire. I want every vehicle on the south side of the rock drop burning in five minutes. Out."

"Roger, Steel Six. Executing now," the obedient platoon leader replied. Almost immediately the four tanks of the 1st Platoon executed a battle drill to change from column formation to a modified firing line. Two trailing tanks moved to the side of the road and fired HEAT from stationary positions. The two lead tanks charged forward in an echelon left arrangement, racing down the two-lane road, firing sabot as they moved.

Enemy tank turrets ripped into the air as they were struck by the powerful silver bullets of the M1A2s. The lead M1A2 was hit twice by enemy tank rounds but kept on rolling, unscathed. With their rounds bouncing off, some of the North Korean tanks stopped fighting, and their crews tried to run away. The machine guns from the M1A2s cut them down.

"This is Steel Six. Steel Two-One, support by fire 1st Platoon. Steel Three-One, fire STAFF at the far side of the rock drop."

The platoon leaders acknowledged their commander on the FM radio. Mackenzie read the digital readouts of his IVIS, checking the location of his tanks. In less than two minutes the company team deployed in the cramped area between the road and the rice paddy. The fierce 120mm cannon of Cold Steel's M1A2s hammered away in a cruel, rippling wave of fire.

Black clouds of smoke billowed into the air from the burning napalm and the turretless T62s. Tracers and high-explosive antitank rounds punctuated the skyline to the west as Team Dealer fired at a separate enemy. American artillery fell on top of the rock drop and the trench line, adding to the enemy's dismay. The one-sided battle seemed almost unnecessary, but Mackenzie knew that the enemy had to be cleared from the southern entrance to the rock drop before he could let his thin-skinned engineer APCs move forward.

"Dragon Six, this is Steel Six," Captain Mackenzie reported over the FM radio. "Combat power, twelve and one. I've destroyed at least six tanks and twelve PCs. I have no casualties. Preparing to breach the rock drop. I'm firing HEAT at the rocks to bust them up for the engineers and STAFF on the far side to kill what's behind the wall. Request artillery smoke on target alpha-charlie one-six-three. Over."

"Roger, Steel Six. Dealer's blocking an enemy counterattack coming north to south on Highway 3. Get through the rock drop as fast as possible."

"As soon as I get good smoke, it'll take me about fifteen minutes to blow a hole through for us."

"Roger, Steel Six. You've got the ball. Keep me informed. Dragon Six. Out."

Mackenzie drove his tank, nicknamed *Conan,* to the left of a 1st Platoon tank that had just stopped to take up a hasty fighting position. Burning enemy tanks and armored personnel carriers littered the landscape.

The Bradley to Mackenzie's left rear launched a TOW missile at a BMP that had managed to get on a hill overlooking the rock drop. The BMP was a thousand meters away to Mackenzie's left front. The missile arched through the air, a red-hot exhaust designating the flight of the warhead to the target. Within seconds it had crashed into the lightly armored BMP, exploding the vehicle like a strong wind smashing a house of cards.

Mackenzie smiled. He always believed that a commander's job in battle is to keep confusion organized in his own command and disorganized in the enemy's. So far, he was doing just that. He was confident that in a few minutes he would be through the constriction and into the rear of the enemy's defenses.

Smoke billowed from the rock drop as the task force's 120mm mortar rounds struck the area near the obstacle and blanketed the target in billowing white phosphorus smoke. Mackenzie shifted the artillery to fall behind the obstacle, then moved the fire farther east.

The 1st Platoon tanks fired main gun rounds at the rocks blocking the choke point. The huge concrete blocks shattered under the impact of the tank's direct fire. A Grizzly breaching vehicle moved forward. Under the cover of the mortar smoke, the Grizzly pushed debris off the road with its powerful dozer blade.

The tank fire shifted and the engineers moved forward in their M113 armored personnel carriers, picking their way carefully around the M1A2s that were firing furiously to support their movement. Mackenzie admired the engineers' bravery. Anyone who didn't know that combat engineers have the toughest job on the battlefield was ignorant of war. The sappers attached to Team Steel were tough fighters who were as skillful with explosives as they were with rifles.

Mackenzie had to get through this obstacle. Every second the task force was blocked meant more friendly casualties. He knew that his engineers would prove their skill and bravery today.

7:40 A.M., 6 October, 1st Army Group headquarters bunker, Kaesong, North Korea. Every battle is a gamble, Major General Kang thought, but now the odds were suddenly stacked against him. The enemy was slicing through the North Korean defenses like a clean, sharp knife carving through a melon.

The air inside the command bunker was thick and stale. The gloomy operations room maps forecasted disaster. The Americans had attacked in force in the night. As soon as the attack began, Kang lost communications with most of the brigades of the 815th Mechanized Corps. It appeared that the enemy's technology had secured the invisible "high ground" by jamming all of his FM radio frequencies. His only source of communications with the forward elements was through a few high-frequency radios, wire land lines, and messengers.

The once vigorous and confident chief of staff felt completely drained of energy. He looked knowingly at the new guards who stood at the doorways. Each wore the black band of the People's Militia.

"Comrade General, it is Marshal Kim Seung-Hee," Kang's aide said with a bow, pointing to the remote radio transmitter in front of the map. "He wishes to talk to you immediately."

Kang looked at the militia general standing by his side, the man who now held the power of life and death over his army. General Jong from the People's Militia shook his head.

Kang put the radio transmitter to his lips and pressed the transmit button.

"No, Comrade Marshal. We must withdraw."

"Never, never," Kim shouted back over the transmitter. "Any man who hints of defeat will be shot. Do you hear me?"

Kang smiled a small, bitter smile. Always the resort to death, he thought. Every time a situation goes awry, we shoot people to make it better. "Yes, Comrade Marshal," he responded.

"I want you to give the order to launch all Nodong missiles with chemical weapons at Seoul," Kim Seung-Hee replied curtly. "I still have one nuclear shell left. If I cannot win, then neither will my enemies."

Kang put down the transmitter. The fate of the nation—never rosy—was now clear. The Wolf was ordering the final act. Both North and South Korea would die.

Kim Seung-Hee's deranged will seemed limitless, Kang thought. Just as endless was the supply of eager officers willing to implement their master's orders, at least until now. Their extraordinary devotion to their leader, and their blind obedience to orders, was a sad testimony to their inability to understand the world and the greater issues of morality. The victory of the army, communism, and the state was all that mattered. What did Kim Seung-Hee care if every man, woman, and child in North Korea died? Maybe it was time to consider the future. Kang looked at the militia general.

"Tell him it will be done," the small man said in a cold, heartless tone.

"Comrade Kim Seung-Hee, I will issue the orders," Kang replied into the radio transmitter, shaking his head.

13

GO FOR BROKE

The object of warfare is to dominate a portion of the earth, with its peoples, for causes either just or unjust. It is not to destroy the land and people, unless you have gone wholly mad.

—T. R. FEHRENBACH

8:50 A.M., 6 October, three kilometers southwest of Pochon, South Korea. Team Steel's objective was to breach the rock drop that was blocking the task force. That's exactly what Captain Mackenzie was doing.

His tank, *Conan,* was positioned to the side of a one-lane road right behind the lead platoon. The four tanks to his front, thirty meters apart, formed a tight wedge formation as they fired on an enemy position eight hundred meters away.

Artillery and mortar fire shells crashed into the opening to the rock drop. The white phosphorus smoke shells bursting in billowing clouds like cotton puffs replaced the thinning fog. Within minutes the rock drop was concealed in smoke.

Three combat engineer APCs bypassed the lead platoon to the right and raced forward, firing their .50-caliber machine guns as they moved. Short of the rock drop they lowered their ramps. Sapper teams rushed into the smoke, moved to the center of the rock drop, and placed their charges on the huge cubes of reinforced concrete that obstructed the route. They set and primed their charges, then withdrew to the safety of their APCs. Enemy mortar fire splashed into the wet rice paddies along both sides of the road, a weak response to the task force breaching effort.

"Steel Six, this is Sapper One-Six," a voice came over the company command frequency. "We're blowing it now. Fire in the hole."

The M113s quickly backed up as the fuses to the explosives slowly burned. A North Korean rifleman who craned his head briefly to peer over the rim of the ridge was immediately picked off by a burst of tank machine-gun fire.

"Roger, One-Six. Move forward as soon as she blows," the captain ordered into his radio. He quickly switched the frequency box next to his right hand. "Dragon Six, this is Steel Six. We're blowing the rock drop now. Fire series alpha-charlie-bravo. Over."

"Acknowledged, Steel Six," Rodriguez answered.

A tremendous explosion rocked the ground. Dirt and dust surged skyward as the force of several hundred pounds of explosive detonated in the confined space. The charges pulverized the huge cement blocks that had been halting the task force's advance.

"Sapper One-Six, report," Mackenzie said impatiently.

"It's clear, Steel. Send them forward," came the return message.

The lead platoon needed no coaxing. Charging forward, a plow tank moved rapidly into the billows of white smoke, which blocked the tank from the enemy's view. Machine-gun bullets sparked off the sides of the lead M1A2 as it moved steadily through the constricted area. All the tank's machine guns blazed back at the North Koreans. The loader of the lead tank fired his 7.62mm machine gun to the left while the tank commander fired his .50-caliber to the right. The ear-splitting sound of a 120mm round informed Mackenzie that a main gun had been fired.

Team Steel's tanks plastered the enemy in the northern trench line with fire. The North Korean infantry on the forward slope of the hill had to stand up in their trench to fire their RPGs. Each time a North Korean raised his head above the trench, Steel's machine guns cut down the defender. Unable to be aimed accurately, North Korean AT-3 and AT-4 antitank rockets fell harmlessly short of their intended targets.

The first tank, with its sinister-looking mine plow in the front, entered the rock drop. Three tanks clanked right behind the plow tank and burst into the smoke. Guns were banging all around. A group of ten determined North Koreans with grenades, rifles, and RPGs rushed to the top of the rock drop in a desperate gamble to stop the first tank. A hail of 7.62mm fire from the second and third tanks drilled the attackers off the top while two tanks farther back in the column fired HEAT rounds. The high-explosive shells smashed into the flanks of the rock drop.

Mackenzie waited patiently in *Conan*'s turret, scanning through the fog and smoke with his CITV. He listened to the sound of heavy machine-gun fire and explosions as his lead platoon fought through the enemy.

"We're through, Steel Six, but there's no place to stop," the lead platoon leader announced. "We have to keep going."

"Roger. Don't stop. We're right behind you. Sapper, move through."

Conan surged forward. The enemy suddenly focused on *Conan* and the APCs on the west side of the rock drop, inundating the advancing vehicles in a furious wave of machine-gun fire. Mackenzie ducked inside the turret and locked his hatch in the open protected position. He turned his turret to the enemy trench line and placed the gun in the direction of the enemy's fire. His gunner took the controls and raked the far left ridge with 7.62mm bullets from his coax.

The road on the far side of the rock drop was logjammed with the wreckage of North Korean tanks and vehicles. *Conan* pushed a damaged T62 off the side of the road and into the rice paddy.

"Steel Six, this is Steel One. They've got antitank weapons firing at us from both sides of the road. One of my tanks is hit in the road wheels. He's stuck."

Mackenzie cursed. He had pushed his luck to the limit and far beyond, he thought. Now he was going to push it a little further. His gunner fired toward the left, careful not to hit any of his own vehicles moving in front of him. They raced into the smoke, their tracks crunching the crumbled pieces of masonry that remained of the enemy's obstacle. As Mackenzie exited the smoke, his tank was struck with machine-gun tracers from both sides of the road. The enemy was waiting in ambush.

"Steel Six, this is Red One," the 1st Platoon leader screamed over the Team Steel command frequency. "Combat power is two tanks. My two downed tanks are off to the side of the road, but they can still shoot. I've destroyed four enemy tanks, two Vetts, and a bunch of infantry. We're pushing on."

Mackenzie slewed in his turret to the left, accidentally knocking down a telephone pole in the process. The useless wires fell across the road. The tank behind him churned them up in his tracks.

"Identified tank, left front," Mackenzie's gunner screamed, alerting his tank commander of the latest target. At the same time, Mackenzie identified the flash of an AT-4 antitank missile to his right front.

"Fire and adjust," he announced as he twisted his .50-caliber to fire to the right in the mad hope that a blast of heavy machine-gun fire would at least slow the enemy.

The tank gun fired as Mackenzie got off a quick, twenty-round burst at the enemy antitank position with the .50-caliber machine gun.

"Target," his gunner shouted, announcing the destruction of the enemy tank.

At the same moment, the AT-4 missed *Conan*'s turret and detonated in the rice paddy to Mackenzie's right. His M1A2 rolled on, the turret turning quickly to the right.

"Troops," Mackenzie yelled as he slewed the gun to the far right where the AT-4 had been launched. In front of him an APC from the combat engineer platoon shuddered and exploded with the strike of an RPG round. The APC ruptured in a flash, the left wall collapsing in a blaze of fire. The five combat engineers inside who weren't incinerated in the flames were splattered to bits and pieces.

"Damn," Mackenzie cursed as *Conan* jerked wildly to the left, barely missing the shattered dead vehicle. Dozens of North Korean infantrymen suddenly raced toward the road from the high ground to the right and left. "Identified," the gunner shouted.

The two damaged M1A2s blasted away at the North Koreans with cannon and machine-gun fire. More tanks drove through the rock drop and added their weight to the battle. Machine-gun fire from the advancing tanks tore into the dodging enemy soldiers on the side of the hill, cutting them down like ripe corn at a fall harvest. The M1A2s churned forward, bypassing the two stopped M1A2s, and fired at everything on both sides of the road. Sagger rockets and RPGs fired from both flanks. Most hit the rice paddies, exploding in geysers of muck. Others hit the road embankment. With each miss, enemy positions were identified. The attacking tanks took turns firing at the enemy positions, knocking them out in powerful volleys of 120mm cannon fire.

"One-Six, keep moving. Don't stop," Mackenzie spat out, wondering how much longer their luck would last. "Two-Six, place your lead two tanks forward at the first open space in the road. Plaster both sides of the road with fire. Take the bastards out and cover our move."

"Steel Five, get the eighty-eight to tow one of our damaged tanks with us. Evacuate the crew of the other and abandon one tank."

"Wilco, Steel Six," answered Mackenzie's executive officer, who was positioned in a tank near the rear of the company team column.

American artillery smashed into the trench lines of the North Korean infantry as the American tank fire reached a crescendo. Enemy infantry fell in groups, nailed by artillery fragments or pierced by machine-gun fire. Groups of North Koreans surged forward to counterattack in vain. Each attack was destroyed without pity. It was a massacre. Mackenzie didn't even need to aim. To kill North Koreans he had only to pull the trigger. He could feel the tank bumping as it ran over bodies lying in the road.

"Repeat the series, Dragon Six. The artillery's right on target." Mackenzie's shrill voice was filled with the desire to sweep the enemy away, to stop them from damaging any more of his men. His throat ached. It seemed to be full of nubs and splinters. The smoke from the shells and the burning tanks filled his lungs, making it difficult to breathe.

"Affirmative, Steel Six," Rodriguez answered, the sound of machine-gun fire echoing in the background of his transmission. "Keep moving. Get to the guns."

Firing all the way, the tanks destroyed everything in their path.

The artillery rained down in a deafening barrage on the enemy that tormented Steel's movement along the road. Dual-purpose improved conventional munitions (DPICM) detonated above the enemy trenches and peppered their holes with hundreds of bomblets. With the artillery hammering the North Koreans and the tanks killing everything that moved, the enemy's return fire quickly dwindled.

Mackenzie's entire company team was through the rock drop and moving east. Ringed in flames, obstinate groups of North Korean defenders continued to snipe at the fast-moving tanks. Small pockets of resistance persisted, but there was no coherent defense. Enemy dead lay all over the slopes of the hills flanking the road. Bodies that lay in the road were smashed to red pulp as the rest of the column raced forward. Pillars of smoke from the enemy tanks that had supported their infantry burned oily black from the strikes of shells from 120mm cannons; the black smoke mingled with the white smoke of the phosphorus shells.

Soon the sniping stopped as the few surviving enemy moved off the ridge or hid to avoid the raking fire from the tanks. Groups of NKPA soldiers emerged with their hands up.

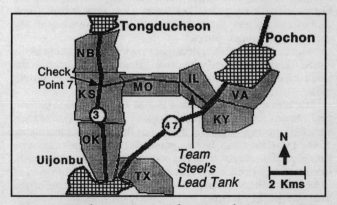

Team Steel Continues the Attack Down ASP

"Continue the attack, Steel," Mackenzie ordered as he switched his radio to the battalion command frequency. "Dragon Six, we've broken through. I'm on Axis Asp in engagement area Illinois, moving unopposed and only half a kilometer from the intersection of Highway 43. Over."

"Good work, Steel. We're right behind you. Dragon Six. Out."

The tanks rumbled down the narrow road. After a few kilometers the road snaked downhill and emptied into the wide Pochon Valley. Mackenzie watched as the lead tank of his column overwhelmed a North Korean roadblock guarded by a section of VTT323 APCs. By the time *Conan* passed the spot a minute later, the two Vetts were flaming wrecks, and the helpless defenders lay sprawled dead on the ground.

Mackenzie smiled a stern, bitter smile. He stopped his tank at the intersection of the secondary road and Highway 43. The highway was a good four-lane road that ran north to Pochon. In front of him he could see the deployed elements of at least ten artillery battalions. His tanks moved into firing lines to engage the enemy howitzers. The 120mm tank cannons struck the enemy's artillery at ranges of two to three kilometers.

"Dragon Six, this is Steel Six," Mackenzie said. "We're on Highway 43. Combat power is ten tanks, one Bradley Stinger fighting vehicle, one Grizzly, and three engineer APCs. I see the enemy artillery group. The enemy guns are still here, south and east of Pochon, sitting in the open like fish in a barrel. My team is continuing to attack."

"Get them, Steel Six," Rodriguez replied, the emotion in his voice filling Mackenzie with pride. "Hold your advance on the southern edge of EA Virginia. I've got artillery coming in right now."

Mackenzie's tanks took up a jagged firing line facing north and blasted the nearest enemy artillery battalion. His M1A2s smashed the enemy guns at a range of three kilometers. Fixing his CITV to the north, he saw hundreds of white spots burst on his thermal display as an eerie, punishing fire fell on the northern portion of Pochon. He recognized the telltale detonation of American MRLS missiles falling on the escape route of the enemy's artillery group.

"Steel, this is Steel Six. Fire at the self-propelled howitzers and the ammunition carriers," Mackenzie shouted. "Leave the towed stuff for our artillery."

Mackenzie's tanks fired in rapid volleys. One enemy howitzer after another fell to the guns of Steel's tanks.

"Steel Six, this is One-One. I've got a bunch of North Koreans surrendering. What do I do with them?"

"One-One, this is Steel Six. Send them south. Let the ROKs handle them. We don't have time for prisoners. As soon as the artillery lifts, we'll move forward and take out everything to the north. Be prepared to move on my order."

"Roger, Steel Six."

Mackenzie watched as enemy ammunition carriers exploded simultaneously under the hammer of MRLS bomblets. The devastating blasts blew apart trucks and jeeps as if they were toys. A string of trucks, towing cannons behind them, tried to escape to the north but were greeted instead by the full force of Mackenzie's ten M1A2s. The trucks were easy targets for the tanks. Not a single truck escaped.

"Dragon Six, this is Steel Six. I'm observing the initial barrage of DPICM. You're right on target. Repeat. I say again, repeat."

"Roger, Steel Six. Renegade has deployed behind you and Bulldog is moving fast. We'll shift artillery in five minutes and rush the bastards with you, Renegade, and Bulldog. I'll call you when we're ready. Dragon Six. Out."

The Pochon Valley shook as more MRLS rockets hammered the enemy artillery positions. Ammunition caches exploded, sending burning shells high into the air. The DPICM submunitions pelted the North Koreans like steel rain.

Suddenly a group of about seven unarmed North Korean soldiers waving a white flag crawled out of a ditch near Mackenzie's tank. Before he could say anything to his crew, the North Koreans seemed to be standing at the right side of the tank. They looked dazed and helpless; they appeared unarmed and had their hands in the air. Several were wounded and were being carried in the arms of their comrades. Most were helmetless.

Pausing for a split second, Mackenzie reached for his pistol, then waved for the prisoners to move to the rear. Bowing their heads, they seemed to understand.

Abruptly one man pulled a pistol from his pocket and fired at the captain.

Mackenzie gasped, covering his face with his right hand. He felt a horrible burning sensation in his right eye as he fell into the turret. He couldn't see anything. He heard his crew shouting. He felt suddenly cold all over. The cold entered his heart. The last thing he discerned was the sound of screams and the bark of *Conan*'s machine guns as his crew slaughtered the North Koreans.

9:10 A.M., 6 October, Marshal Kim Seung-Hee's forward command post, Pochon, South Korea. Chaos. The situation had collapsed before his eyes. Kim Seung-Hee contemplated his next move.

The marshal and his staff huddled in the stone basement headquarters of a well-built building in Pochon University. A security guard captain and fifteen armed escorts from Kim's personal bodyguard stood along the walls of the headquarters. A dozen staff officers and radio operators worked at their posts, updating the fast-moving battle.

Marshal Kim Seung-Hee stood with both hands gripping the edge of the map table. He looked up at the map, saw the red arrows only inches away from their final objectives, and smashed his fists hard against the table. Last night he was master of a victorious army that was about to capture the enemy's capital. Now, in this bleak, tragic morning, he was trying in vain to organize a defense.

The operations map displayed the attack plans for Seoul. In the past few hours, officers had drawn blue lines that depicted the steady movement of an enemy brigade into the heart of Kim's forces. Somehow the enemy had known exactly where to strike. Kim knew that he had been betrayed.

The building that housed Kim's headquarters had once served as a special lecture hall for hundreds of graduate students; it still showed signs of academia. Now, Kim Seung-Hee reflected, it served as an effective bomb shelter. In this setting, he mused, a drama would be played out that would decide the fate of Korea.

The damned Americans, he cursed as he looked at the map. So close. His headaches, stronger now than ever before, were exacerbated by tension and lack of sleep. He reached into his pocket and took three pills, hoping that they would carry him through the next few hours and allow him to be strong enough to pull off a miracle.

"Send in the reserves. Send in every battalion we have left. Stop the Americans," Kim thundered, pounding his fist on the map table.

"Comrade Marshal," a colonel stammered hesitatingly, "there are no more reserves."

"Redirect the 815th Corps," Kim screamed.

"Comrade Marshal, the 815th Corps is under attack," an officer reported. "It took heavy casualties in the forward brigades last night. The 815th can barely defend itself."

"Sir, some of our men are leaving their posts," a colonel announced. "We should consider a withdrawal."

"Colonel So," Kim howled, "all units will stand their ground and defend. Not a step backward. Order my special security detachment to shoot anyone found leaving his post."

"Nam chim," the colonel replied, snapping to attention. He conferred with a lieutenant colonel who was the commander of the local political security detachment. The officer saluted, then rushed up the stairs to do his master's bidding.

Kim Seung-Hee took a long cigarette from his gold cigarette case. The case glittered in the light. He placed it back in his breast pocket. "Do you know where I got this cigarette case?" he asked.

No one answered.

"I took it from an American right before I shot him in the face," Kim shouted. He was getting more agitated with every word. "They can be defeated. We can still win."

"We will counterattack," Colonel So promised in a false boast that no one in the room seemed to believe.

"I want every gun to reorient and fire at the advancing Americans. Every howitzer, every gun," Kim Seung-Hee shouted to his paralyzed and shocked staff. "We must stop them and push them back. Block the roads with every available antitank weapon, gun, and artillery piece. I want every man except my personal staff and the radio operators to the front. Now."

Officers bowed their heads, grabbed their equipment and

weapons, and slipped up the stone stairs to exit the lecture hall. Rapping out orders, Kim's subordinate officers moved the excess men in the headquarters up the stairs and outside to their dubious fate.

"Do we have radio communications with General Kang?" Kim asked, looking at Colonel So.

"Intermittent," the colonel said, appearing distraught. "They come in and out."

"I must know if the chemical strikes have been launched."

"Your orders were clear, Comrade Marshal," So replied, looking nervously at the exit. An officer raced up to the colonel and handed him a message. He read it quickly. "Sir, this message warns us that the enemy has intercepted our command frequency and code. It is signed General Kang, chief of staff, First Army of the People's Militia."

Kim Seung-Hee didn't answer. He grabbed the message and read the title that accompanied the signature. Why sign the letter the People's Militia? Suddenly he understood. Kang had sent him a warning.

Kim's fist tightened around the paper as he crumpled it into a tiny ball. He threw it on the floor and screamed. This was the worst humiliation of all and the one with the most dire consequences. He had been outwitted and betrayed.

He leaned over the map table and gazed at the red arrows, drawn to depict the attack that would isolate Seoul. Several yellow circles displayed the proposed locations of chemical weapons strikes on Seoul. The nuclear weapon was his last chance. He would fire the shell, then fly back to Kaesong. If he bluffed convincingly, the Americans might never know he didn't have any more nukes.

"Has the special shell been delivered to Major Chun?" Kim asked.

"Yes, Comrade Marshal. As you ordered, thirty minutes ago," Colonel So answered.

From his breast pocket Kim took a sealed envelope and the key that activated the ten-kiloton nuclear artillery shell.

"Deliver these orders and this key to Major Chun," Kim shouted, handing the items to a captain of his security guard.

"Immediately, Marshal Kim," the captain said as he saluted and took the envelope in his right hand.

"The helicopters are ready now, Comrade Marshal," So repeated.

Kim ignored his subordinate and held up his hand to stop further interruptions. Somehow he sensed danger. The enemy's strike was too exact, as if they knew his plans. He needed a diversion.

"Colonel So, depart immediately," Marshal Kim ordered coldly as he opened his cigarette case and drew a cigarette from his old war trophy.

"As you command, Comrade Marshal," Colonel So answered, a bewildered look on his face. "But why stay here?"

"Timing, Colonel," Kim said curtly as he eyed his subordinate with a gaze that demanded immediate obedience. "Take the helicopters, all but one, and depart immediately. Call General Kang on the command frequency and return to Kaesong."

"But Comrade Marshal, I should remain with you. I—"

Kim stopped his subordinate in midsentence with a stare and a tense jerk of his head, signaling that So should exit the room.

Colonel So snapped to attention, saluted, and marched out of the building.

9:30 A.M., 6 October, mountain overlooking Pochon, Chorwon Valley, South Korea. "Fifteen howitzers are moving north of the city along Highway 43," Emerson shouted into the transmitter. He coughed several times, cupping his mouth with his hand. "I also see three helicopters taking off from the university. They're flying to the north."

"Roger. We'll have attack helicopters there soon," the voice of Major Lucas promised from the other end of the radio. "Keep sending in reports every five minutes. You're doing great, Emerson."

Emerson coughed again. His cold was getting worse. At least, he reflected with a proud grin, he was evening the score.

Sung-Joo cocked his head. Mixed with the sharp noise of explosions in the valley below and Emerson's conversation over the SINCGARS radio, he thought he heard a noise coming from the path that led to their ledge.

"Affirmative," Emerson said into the radio transmitter, raising the binoculars to his eyes to see the valley below. "I count eight—no, make that ten—MRLs on the eastern edge of Pochon."

Sung-Joo peered down the trail. At the bend in the path where the trail went out of view, he saw something move. The enemy had suddenly arrived to take revenge for yesterday's patrol.

"Communists," Sung-Joo whispered as he crouched low and slithered into a prone firing position. He gently pushed the lever down on the right side of his AK-47 to release the safety. "They come again."

Emerson quickly folded the SINCGARS antenna and dragged the radio back against the cliff.

Sung-Joo waited. A man appeared at the bend in the trail, cautiously moving forward, looking wide eyed to his front. Sung-Joo followed him in his rifle sight. The man crept forward slowly on his hands and knees, motioning back to someone out of view. The man suddenly saw Sung-Joo and reared up to fire.

The crack of the AK-47 sounded two times in rapid succession. The North Korean, struck in the head, fell facedown in the trail.

Several North Koreans sprang up to rush the pair. Sung-Joo and Emerson fired back, killing two and wounding another.

The North Koreans shouted. Sung-Joo could see them squirming on their bellies as they tried to find better firing positions. Sung-Joo fired a few rounds at the closest North Korean, only thirty feet away. The enemy soldier backed off.

The strike of submachine-gun bullets against the rocks sent the ROK lieutenant and the American away from the precipice and back against the ridge. The rounds plugged the dirt in front of them, dancing in a thin line just out of reach. The enemy couldn't get their weapons into good firing angles unless they passed the bend in the trail, something that Sung-Joo was determined to stop. The sound of a Korean voice shouting orders echoed up the slope. A deadly stalemate ensued.

"How many bullets?" Sung-Joo asked.

"Ten. That's all I have," Emerson replied.

Sung-Joo nodded and fixed his attention on the bend in the trail. He unhooked his magazine and stared at the 7.62mm rounds for a second. "I have only nine."

This time five North Koreans tried to rush forward at the

same time. The lead man fired his submachine gun as he moved. Sung-Joo fired again, hitting the leader. The North Korean tumbled off the trail and fell to the valley below. The second man fired. Bullets ripped into the stone wall above Sung-Joo and Emerson. Sung-Joo fired three more rounds and dropped the second attacker. The other three men ran back, out of sight of Sung-Joo's deadly aim.

Emerson inched back against the rock, trying to keep the angry bullets away. Sung-Joo seemed frozen, fixed to his rifle sight, aiming down the trail.

A stick grenade suddenly sailed through the air and landed three feet in front of Sung-Joo, hissing as its fuse burned. Sung-Joo leaped forward and swept the grenade over the cliff with a wild push of his right hand. The grenade detonated just below the rim of the ledge, showering the two defenders with dust.

Two more grenades flew forward. Sung-Joo kicked one down the cliff as the second grenade went off. The blast hurled him against the wall. He sat stunned, bleeding from the mouth and ears.

The world moved in slow motion. His heart was pumping wildly as he gasped for air. He struggled for each breath.

Six North Koreans rushed down the trail. Emerson kneeled in front of Sung-Joo, aimed, and fired his AK-47. Two attackers fell. The rest charged over the bodies of the first two, firing as they ran. Emerson fired and dropped two more, but the North Koreans kept coming.

Sung-Joo looked to his right as a helicopter appeared, hovering like an angel of death. The machine guns lit up with fire as the hill was sprayed with lead. Bullets smashed against the rocks, splattering fragments in all directions. The lieutenant tried to move, but the pain from his wound overtook him and he blacked out.

9:35 A.M., 6 October, 2d Infantry Division headquarters, ten kilometers south of Seoul, South Korea. "Sir, we got him," Lieutenant Colonel Wallace shouted as he read the message. It was a slick piece of work. The information from ROK intelligence sources, confirmed by the report of an observation post overlooking Pochon, had pinpointed the exact location of the enemy commander.

Major Cooper picked up a telephone receiver. "Stallion Six, this is Warrior Two. We have him just south of Pochon. Three HIPs moving north."

General Schmidt walked up to Wallace. "What do we have?"

"Sir, the enemy commander just took off from a landing zone at Pochon University. We have Kiowas from 4-7 Cav already at that location. There are no other aircraft available."

"Any rockets or artillery in range?" Schmidt asked.

"No artillery in range. The MRLS battery is reloading, so we'll have to wait ten to fifteen minutes for rockets," Wallace answered. "By then the HIPs will be out of range."

"What do we know about enemy air defenses?"

"Unknown. Some S-300s must still be operational," Cooper replied. "The Dragon Force is there now, attacking on the ground and killing his howitzers, but the area isn't totally cleared of enemy air defense."

"Sir, we can't hold back now," Wallace interjected.

"Go," Schmidt ordered, nodding to Wallace's comment. "Tell the cavalry to get the bastard."

9:45 A.M., 6 October, north of Pochon, South Korea. The powerful MI-17 HIP helicopters sped north, flying at treetop level. The battlefield below was a smoking graveyard of burning vehicles and dead and dying men.

Colonel So looked out the left side window as the helicopter raced through clouds of black smoke. The HIPs were flying in tight formation, as always. Colonel So's aircraft led the way.

Boom! The helicopter shuddered as the HIP to the left burst into flames. The pilot and copilot ducked. The tangled fuselage of the stricken helicopter fell like a rock. In seconds it had scraped across the ground in a burning mass of twisted debris.

"Pilot," So screamed, "what is happening?"

"Enemy helicopters right behind us," the pilot shouted over the intercom. "They came from nowhere."

"Break formation," So ordered. "Evade them."

The helicopter banked abruptly to the right in a maneuver designed to throw off the attacker. A shower of missiles struck the ground in the original direction of flight, narrowly missing the HIP. The other helicopter banked in the opposite direction.

Colonel So felt his stomach churning as he was forced

against the seat of the aircraft. The engine whined loudly as it strained to exert maximum speed. The HIPs hurtled north, gaining ground and altitude as they ran from their attackers.

"I will try for the eastern hills," the pilot reported. "We are fifteen kilometers north of Pochon."

Colonel So strained to find the American helicopters. He realized that the purpose of his mission was to draw the enemy away from Kim Seung-Hee's helicopter. If Marshal Kim was able to escape, his sacrifice would be a worthy one.

"The Americans are following our every move," Colonel So said as he observed a swirling black object in the sky. "Another enemy helicopter to our right."

"Flares!" the pilot screamed.

The copilot discharged antimissile flares from the tail. The American helicopter fired at the same moment. Colonel So saw the launch of the Stinger missile and a tail of smoke coming right for him. The HIP banked hard to the right, but not in time.

9:50 A.M., 6 October, three kilometers southwest of Pochon, South Korea. "Guidons, guidons, this is Dragon Six. Steel will move north into EA Virginia and attack the guns by fire. Everyone else fall in behind Team Steel. We have an artillery strike hitting the routes in and north of Pochon in fifteen minutes."

Each subordinate commander acknowledged the order and reported his combat power. Team Steel's executive officer, 2d Lt. Mike Reed, answered for the fallen Captain Mackenzie.

Team Steel deployed into engagement area Virginia and rapidly formed a jagged firing line. Immediately Steel's M1A2s engaged enemy howitzers, trucks, and ammo carriers on the eastern side of Pochon. The enemy howitzers, between fifteen hundred and two thousand meters away, were arrayed in open order, with the guns spaced evenly between ammo trucks. It was a tanker's dream—an entire enemy artillery group caught in the open.

Firebreather rumbled forward and rolled up next to *Conan* as the crew carried the body of their beloved captain into an M113 ambulance. Half of the dead officer's face had been shot away, revealing the gray-red pulp of his brain. The medics covered Mackenzie's head with a cloth.

The task force commander looked down from his tank at the

body of the irreplaceable Captain Mackenzie. The scene around the tank clearly explained what had happened. Seven enemy soldiers lay sprawled in gross contortions of death. Several of them still clutched pistols in their dead hands. The white flag covered one of the bodies like a shroud.

Command Sergeant Major Dougan stood in the open back of his armored personnel carrier as it rumbled up behind *Firebreather*. He looked up at his commander.

Rodriguez took off his CVC helmet to hear his sergeant major's report.

"We're cross-leveling ammunition," Dougan said. "Lost five tanks, three Bradleys, and four APCs. I think we can repair most of the tanks. The maintenance officer tells me he'll have one or two back up in a couple of hours. The other three will take depot level support. We evacuated their crews, disabled the guns, and left the tanks for the follow-on forces to retrieve."

"Casualties?" Rodriguez asked.

"We've taken forty-two casualties so far. Sixteen dead and thirty-six wounded. I've got the wounded in APCs. I'll arrange for an air medevac as soon as they can send some birds forward."

Rodriguez nodded and stared down at the APC that contained Mackenzie's body. He thought of Patroclus from the *Iliad* and wished for the vengeance of Achilles.

An explosion rocked the ground as an enemy artillery shell crashed into the ruins of a building three hundred meters to the south. At the same time, a loud volley of tank cannon echoed to the north as Team Steel fired at the North Korean artillery.

"Sir, are you all right?" Dougan asked, arching his eyebrows at his commander. "We've got a lot of guys here to worry about. Their artillery is out in the open, ripe for the plucking. Shouldn't we be pushing north?"

Rodriguez felt dazed from the loss of Mackenzie, but he shook off the hollow, sick, empty feeling, looked up at Dougan, and nodded. The sergeant major always seemed to be at the right spot at the right time. He was taking care of the men, making sure the wounded got medical attention—maintaining the force. He was like Mackenzie—aggressive, proud, and independent. He was doing the kinds of things that only a well-trained veteran soldier could do, something no machine could ever do. What would we do without proud centurions like Dougan? Rodriguez wondered.

"We'll be moving in a few minutes, right after the MRLS is ready for a second strike and the attack helicopters arrive on station," said Rodriguez. "They're on the way."

"Right," Dougan said. He pointed to an open concrete lot to the right of the road. "I'll set up the battalion aid station there."

"How're we doing?" Rodriguez asked his veteran sergeant.

"You're doing fine," Dougan answered, a wide grin on his face. "Just fine. The task force is fighting like banshees. I've seen more dead North Koreans than I can count. We'll have this war over with before sunset."

Rodriguez nodded, hoping the sergeant major was right. He looked at his watch—0954, almost time for the second multiple rocket strike. There was little need to coordinate this fight. The next phase would be the attack north, an old-fashioned cavalry charge right into the cannons of the enemy. But unlike in the days of horse cavalry and bronze cannons, today the tanks held all the advantages.

Dougan's APC turned around and headed back down the road, the way it had come. Rodriguez put his CVC helmet on and checked his IVIS screen.

"Bulldog Six, you'll lead this attack right up Highway 43," Rodriguez ordered over the command frequency. "Renegade, orient to Bulldog's left, Dealer to Bulldog's right. Steel, you stay on the west side of EA Virginia and support by fire until all three companies pass, then refuel and follow in line behind Bulldog."

The team commanders acknowledged their reply as the sky north of Pochon was suddenly lit with the explosions of dozens of American artillery shells. The second rocket salvo scattered fields of DPICM submunitions across the valley, transforming it into an inferno of exploding vehicles. A dozen ammunition trucks and artillery vehicles disintegrated in the first volley. The American artillery smashed a crowded gaggle of enemy vehicles trying to move north along the highway. The exploding bomblets crippled and maimed the North Korean howitzers in a tremendous wave of destruction.

"Dragon Six, this is Dragon FSO." Rodriguez listened to the voice of his artillery officer in the earphones of his CVC helmet. "That's it for our artillery. The coordinated fire line is now one kilometer north of Pochon. Apache Longbows are on their way. They'll attack north of that line. Close air support won't be here for another thirty minutes. You're cleared to attack north."

"Roger, Dragon FSO," Rodriguez acknowledged. The coordinated fire line depicted the area where the enemy could be attacked without any coordination by all types of fires. If he stayed south of that line, he would lessen the chance of being hit by friendly attack helicopters or artillery. "Bulldog Six, attack. Take out his guns."

"Wilco, Dragon Six," the voice of Captain Grey answered. "We'll keep killing them until they go away."

The M1A2s pushed forward relentlessly, firing on the move. A batch of VTT323s fired Sagger missiles at the fast-moving tanks, but every rocket missed and burst harmlessly along the highway. The 120mm cannon took out the enemy APCs in short order. Smoke and flame billowed to the heavens.

A large explosion burst near the center of the enemy artillery group. The tall spire of sparks and flame signaled the destruction of a large ammunition cache. Smaller explosions rippled from one burning enemy ammunition carrier to another as exploding shells showered the ground. Thick clouds of black smoke and raging fires dotted the battlefield.

Kiowa Warrior helicopters, flying off to the east, used their laser designators to pinpoint targets for the artillery. As the American artillery fire came in, more enemy howitzers, personnel carriers, and ammunition vehicles exploded. A salvo of rockets from the Kiowas devastated enemy trucks trying to flee north up the crowded four-lane highway.

A battery of North Korean self-propelled howitzers reoriented their guns to the south and fired directly at the American tanks. Team Bulldog, the task force reserve, rumbled forward and led the attack. Captain Grey's company team dashed to the main highway and turned north. The tanks raced forward eight hundred meters, mud flying from their tracks, and took up firing positions in the open ground amid burning enemy howitzers. Within seconds they plastered the fleeing enemy with cannon and machine-gun fire.

Behind Team Bulldog the rest of the tanks in the task force

moved to positions to fire to the north, adding to the pandemonium of burning trucks and exploding ammunition. The volume of fire was too much for the North Korean artillerymen. They frantically hitched their towed guns to their trucks in a desperate attempt to get out of the killing zone. Self-propelled howitzers turned and drove north, away from the deadly tanks. Panicked drivers started their vehicles and raced about in a futile effort to save their guns.

Then the back door closed on the stunned North Koreans. Like hovering angels of death, American Apache attack helicopters arrived, flying safely out of range along the hills to the east and west of the Pochon Valley. The helicopters launched Hellfire and Longbow guided missiles from six to eight kilometers away and pulverized the North Korean vehicles. The Apaches swept their fire north along the length of Pochon Valley, filling the sky with the black smoke of burning trucks and artillery vehicles.

For the North Koreans it was a complete slaughter. Their defense dissolved. Any thought of turning the guns on the advancing tanks ceased as the Apaches made their deadly attacks. The helicopters worked their way north to finish off the enemy artillery, following the ridges and guided by the fierce explosions. Meanwhile, Rodriguez ordered the task force forward. In a line of blazing tanks, the Dragon Force swept all before them.

As *Firebreather* charged forward behind Team Bulldog, Rodriguez felt the adrenaline run through his veins. The valley seemed consumed in fire and smoke as *Firebreather* passed the shattered remains of the enemy's corps artillery group. Now we've got the bastards, he thought; on to Troy.

10:15 A.M., 6 October, Pochon, South Korea. Kim Seung-Hee tried to consider his next move but couldn't concentrate. Rage filled his mind. His head throbbed with an unrelenting pain that no pills could dampen. He walked out of the command center and looked to the north. He watched the American helicopters race northward as they tried to catch the HIPs. Kim realized that he must get away. Time was running out.

Major Rhee's crew swiftly pulled down the camouflage net that concealed the helicopter. *Wolf 1,* in elaborate Korean characters, was painted on the nose of the HIP. Rhee walked up to the marshal.

"Comrade Marshal, if anyone can outfly the enemy it is I," Rhee said as he saluted. "We will leave in five minutes."

Kim Seung-Hee nodded as he took a last puff on his cigarette. To the north he saw the smoking remains of one of the HIPs, burning from the strike of the American helicopters. He put his gold cigarette case in the pocket of his tunic.

The latest attacks seemed personal. He analyzed the situation, the enemy's interception of his command frequency, and the attack by the American helicopters on his HIPs just as they were to depart. He was too much a student of war to believe that it was all a coincidence. More was at work here. How was the People's Militia involved? He realized that someone had sold out. Someone was working with the fascists to foil his plans. Who could it be?

The sky temporarily cleared of enemy helicopters as the air action moved farther north. Colonel So must have gotten away, Kim thought, throwing away the butt of his dying cigarette. If not, he has at least provided me with an opportunity to flee. Flee. The thought banged in his mind like a sledgehammer. He tightened his fists. "Damn the Americans," he said aloud.

"Comrade Marshal, we are ready," Rhee shouted. The powerful 1,900-horsepower engine of the MI-17 HIP roared slowly to life. The big blades turned faster and faster, kicking up dust.

Kim knew exactly what he would do. First he would fly to 1st Army Group headquarters and gather all available forces for the defense of the motherland. Then he would fire all the remaining Nodong missiles, armed with chemical weapon warheads, at Seoul and Tokyo. The enemy will pay for this humiliation, he vowed.

He walked slowly toward the helicopter, holding his hat in his hand. He stepped up to the door and took one last look at the raging battlefield before climbing inside.

10:20 A.M., 6 October, Pochon, South Korea. The North Koreans rallied on the southern edge of Pochon with infantry, a few tanks, and a hodgepodge of 2S3 howitzers for a final, desperate attempt to stop the Americans. Rodriguez's M1A2s raced forward to meet them, closing the range and driving straight for

the main south-to-north roads. Even with his CVC helmet on
and the whine of *Firebreather*'s engine, Rodriguez could hear
the distinct, loud bang of tank cannons and the rattling of tank
machine guns. The road was strewn with wreckage. A blazing
152mm self-propelled gun lay on the left side of the road, and
items of individual equipment, bodies, and bits of bodies were
scattered about—signs of a defeated army.

Green and red tracers flew wildly in all directions as the
North Koreans continued to fight to defend their positions. The
enemy fired a wave of antitank missiles at the Americans, but
most crashed far behind the American tanks. Rodriguez saw
their line of defense and ordered Team Bulldog to mass fires on
the center of the enemy line where Highway 43 entered the city.
As the tanks closed to within five hundred meters, they were
met by a raging torrent of machine-gun fire. Rodriguez had to
give them credit; the Inmun Gun was fighting hard. Their hero-
ics, however, didn't matter. The M1A2s blasted them with volley after volley at close range and overwhelmed the confused
defenders. The merciless tanks cut down infantry and artillerymen in bunches, leaving nothing but death in their wake.
Lethal, flying metal splashed against armor and tore apart flesh.
Death hung in the air. Suddenly the final North Korean defense
began to break.

"Dragon Six, this is Bulldog Six," Captain Grey reported, his
voice charged with excitement. "We're cutting through them
without a problem. Nothing is stopping us here. We've destroyed at least thirty self-propelled howitzers and more trucks
than I can count. The enemy is running."

"Roger, Bulldog. Be careful if they try to surrender," Rodriguez replied.

"No problem, Dragon Six. Anyone without his hands in the
air dies."

Rodriguez thought he should say something to make sure
that prisoners were not shot out of hand. He knew how difficult
it was for tankers to take prisoners, especially after Mackenzie's death. But if the enemy surrendered, how would he guard
them? If he dismounted precious crewmen, he degraded the
fighting capability of his tanks.

"Bulldog Six, keep moving. Leave POWs for the Renegades

to handle. We'll set up a POW collection point after they stop fighting."

"Roger, Dragon Six. They're running but they haven't dropped their weapons," Grey responded.

A shot from an enemy tank indicated that Grey's response was accurate. Two of his tanks observed the enemy tank and in seconds had reduced it to a smashed, burning hulk.

Rodriguez strained to look ahead from his hatch in the open protected position as he held tightly to the sides of his tank commander's station. The tank moved rapidly, running over pieces of debris in the road. Burning vehicles lined the highway. The M1A2s leading the column had pushed many off the road. They lay at various angles, some on their side, others completely upside down. The fires from nearby enemy vehicles were so intense that Rodriguez could feel the heat through the open space in his hatch.

The whoosh of an RPG sailed past his turret, another indication that Grey was correct. A clump of dismounted enemy soldiers appeared to *Firebreather*'s left front. The enemy was hiding behind an overturned command car. Rodriguez moved the turret to the left and fired a HEAT round. The shell detonated against the belly of the car, which disintegrated into a dozen flaming pieces and took out the enemy RPG team.

The Dragon Force surged on, slowing the pace as the tanks scoured the ground with their machine guns. The noise of the battle was immense and rose to a crescendo pitch.

"Driver, turn left. Follow that two-lane road near the burning vehicle," Rodriguez shouted over his intercom, ordering his driver to move toward the road that led to Pochon University. *Firebreather* churned to the left. *Defiant* and the artillery M113 followed close behind.

Team Bulldog continued north up Highway 43, firing on the move. The North Koreans, gripped by panic, ran away to the east and north. Thick lines of smoke rose into the sky, reaching high above the valley, then floated north like a black blanket. Hundreds of burning armored vehicles—BTRs, self-propelled howitzers, and trucks—lay wrecked in the smoke-filled valley. It was as if some unstoppable force had swept in, killed and crushed everything in sight, then suddenly left.

Rodriguez ordered his driver to slow down as he scanned the

area with his CITV. After a quick look, he saw a hot spot to the northwest. Studying the image in his thermal viewer, he identified a helicopter hovering with a swirl of hot exhaust gases coming from its engines. From the outline of the helicopter he could plainly see that it was an enemy chopper, an HIP. The bird was about to lift off from a field to the northwest. Rodriguez pushed the override button and laid the gun in the direction of the target.

"Gunner, chopper," he screamed. Rodriguez looked into his tank commander's sight. The green numbers at the bottom of the display registered twenty-eight hundred meters.

"Identified," Obrisky shouted.

"Fire."

11:40 A.M., 6 October, south of Pochon, South Korea. A thick pall of smoke hovered over the valley near Pochon. Dozens of trucks and howitzers blazed while others smoldered from the strikes of the enemy missiles. Hundreds of bodies in the earthen-brown uniform of the NKPA lay sprawled along the roads and in the rice paddies. A few of the corpses sat upright, as if manning their artillery pieces with a quiet, deathly discipline.

The army artillery group was disintegrating. Fires raged everywhere, and secondary explosions shook the ground. The enemy's missiles came from nowhere and everywhere. The area north of Pochon was alight with explosions. Aircraft swirled high overhead, out of the range of North Korean air defense weapons, like hungry vultures waiting for the victim to die to devour his flesh. The A-10s and F-16s circled gracefully, lobbing their silver canisters of death at the enemy below from eight thousand feet. American and ROK planes and helicopters had sealed off the escape route home. Blinding showers of fire and steel annihilated the artillery batteries that tried to flee to the north.

A 2S3 howitzer exploded on the far side of Major Chun's firing position. His guns were now under the direct fire of enemy tank cannon more than three thousand meters away. Panic filled the air. Chun could not see his attackers.

"Where the hell is that firing coming from?" he cursed, raising his binoculars to the south.

"Comrade Major, brigade reports that tanks are attacking. We should withdraw if we wish to save the howitzers," a young captain yelled.

"No. Stay in position. The battalion will orient thirty-two hundred mils," the artillery commander shouted, "and fire high explosive, direct fire, at the enemy tanks. Every available man will find an RPG and defend to the left flank of the guns."

"Comrade Major," a captain replied, standing at attention in front of his commander, "we have only ten guns left. There are only six RPGs and about as many rockets. We will not be able to stop the tanks from here."

Major Chun Yong-ho's self-control yielded to a pent-up rage. He took a step toward the captain and struck him across the face. The officer recoiled from the blow, then snapped back to the position of attention. The commander of the 136th North Korean People's Army 152mm self-propelled howitzer battalion knew that his situation was desperate. Such situations required discipline and ruthless determination.

"The Yankees must not get through. Obey my orders immediately," he shouted, pulling his pistol from his holster, "or I will shoot you where you stand."

The officer nodded and rushed back to the howitzers. Men shouted and cursed as the guns were turned. The artillerymen worked in a frenzy to prepare ammunition charges for direct fire.

A jeep rushed into Major Chun's firing position. A captain wearing the dark green uniform of the security bureau—one of Kim Seung-Hee's special police—jumped out of the jeep and rushed up to Chun. The captain ducked as an enemy shell exploded only 150 meters away.

"You have been difficult to find in the confusion. I have urgent orders from Marshal Kim Seung-Hee."

Chun looked at the security captain with disdain. "I expected you much earlier."

The captain glared at Chun and handed him a sealed envelope and the key to activate the nuclear shell. "Do you understand?"

"You are dismissed, Captain. I have work to do," Chun shouted.

The captain spat on the ground in obvious disrespect and ran back to his jeep.

Chun had been specially trained for this mission. He would have to insert the arming key and dial two sequences of numbers into the ringlike analog arming mechanism of the nuclear shell before it could be fired. Without the key or the correct arming sequence, the nuclear shell was just radioactive junk.

Two more of his howitzers exploded. Chun ducked as the shock wave from the explosions pulsed through the air and shook the ground.

"Find that enemy tank and destroy him with direct fire," the major screamed, frantically searching the smoke-filled ground to the south.

Tank fire was destroying his precious howitzers, and he could not see his attackers. He realized that his few surviving howitzers didn't stand a chance in a direct fire fight with enemy tanks. But what could he do? He had his orders. Communications were out except for the field telephone lines with his brigade artillery group commander, who had ordered the guns to fight to the end.

Chun rushed to the only 2S3 howitzer not firing, the one that would launch Kim Seung-Hee's nuclear shell. He stopped outside the howitzer, opened the envelope, and quickly read the coordinates of the target.

"Set the gun at maximum elevation for a range of twenty-eight kilometers," Chun shouted to the firing crew. "Rocket-assisted projectile. Direction three-six-five-zero mils."

The crew parroted his commands. Chun ran to the back of the hull of the self-propelled howitzer. The nuclear shell was sitting on a loading hoist in a special metal canister guarded by two men with AK-47 rifles. The top of the canister was open, exposing the shell and the arming mechanism. Carefully Chun took the key and placed it in the slot. Turning the analog scale on the top of the fuse, he started dialing in the first sequence of numbers listed in the letter.

"I see tanks coming," one of the soldiers howled. "There."

A group of four tanks raced toward them along the high ground to the southwest only three hundred meters away. Another group charged at them from the southeast, coming straight up the highway. They were about five hundred meters away and closing fast.

"Quick, tell the firing officer to volley fire at the tanks along the highway," Chun yelled, still stooped over the shell.

The soldier ran off. Chun finished the first sequence of numbers and the mechanism clicked, signifying that the sequence was correct. He started the second sequence.

The howitzers executed his command, getting off a few feeble shots but missing the advancing tanks. The frenzied crews hand-cranked the turrets to lay their guns on the rapidly approaching tanks. It was a futile attempt. They could not get the fast-moving tanks in their sights. The tanks fired as they moved. Ammunition carriers and guns exploded. Howitzer turrets hurtled through the air. Chun watched helplessly as the enemy tanks devastated his battalion.

Machine-gun fire raked the battalion position as two more howitzers exploded. One howitzer lifted off the ground and turned on its side, belching white-hot flame and sparks as its ammunition exploded.

Suddenly tanks were everywhere. Officers tried to rally their men and fight on, but they were cut down as the machine guns raked the area with short, controlled bursts.

Chun's battalion was being executed as surely as if they were standing in front of a firing squad with their hands tied behind their backs. They were still fighting, but it didn't matter; howitzers were no match for tanks. Chun stood next to the nuclear shell, shouting orders to soldiers who could not obey.

Three rounds smashed him before he heard the sound of the machine guns. One struck him in the shoulder, spinning him to the ground. Another 7.62mm projectile shattered his left leg. The third round hit his jaw, splattering his face with wet, gooey blood. He tried to hold back the blood with his hand, but he couldn't lift his arm. Choking, he turned his head and hawked to clear his throat. He struggled for air but was unable to breathe. His right foot kicked the ground as he fought for breath. Slowly his lungs filled, and he drowned in his own blood.

12:15 P.M., 6 October, Pochon, South Korea. The battle was over. The sound of scattered firing continued in the north as helicopter gunships and attack aircraft picked off the North Koreans as they fled north.

Rodriguez surveyed the battlefield. The sight pierced the soul. The smell was awful—acrid, burning, sickeningly sweet. *Firebreather* and *Defiant* stood silent watch as the battalion commander walked the battlefield with Obrisky. They were looking for survivors.

Blackened, burned-out hulks of North Korean APCs and howitzers sat like mute sentinels to the limits of the advance of the Inmun Gun. One of the howitzers had its turret flipped upside down on top of the hull. The turret of another was still attached; the vehicle commander's hatch was open. A charred object, burned to a crisp and wedged into the opening, had once been a human being.

The bodies of North Korean soldiers lay everywhere. In the haze caused by the smoke, Rodriguez could see the horrific swath of destruction caused by his tanks. Smashed howitzers and armored vehicles smoldered. Corpses lay in pools of reddish brown blood in all fashion of grotesque shapes. Pieces of uniforms and equipment, plastered with shattered human remains, were strewn all over the field.

Rodriguez and Obrisky walked across the smoking battlefield toward the helicopter, their weapons at the ready. They found a line of foxholes dug by North Korean soldiers in the university grounds. The bodies of at least thirty North Koreans, sprawled across the trenches, bore testimony to the fight. The two men walked on as *Firebreather*'s crew covered them with the tank's machine guns.

Off to the east, adding to this macabre scene, was a line of bedraggled North Korean soldiers surrendering to the tankers near the highway. They came from all points of the battlefield, hands on top of their helmetless heads, tired, eyes glazed, beaten. There were hundreds of them.

Billows of black smoke loomed to the north, testifying to the accuracy of the attack helicopters and their newly arrived allies, the U.S. and ROK Air Force.

Rodriguez could see the sun glinting off the attack aircraft heading north at high altitude. The A-10 and F-16 fighter-bombers flew in huge arcs across the sky. The aircraft flew out of range of the enemy's shoulder-fired antiaircraft weapons.

The white smoke trail of an occasional SA-17 shoulder-fired air defense missile indicated that some of the enemy up north were still fighting back. As long as the aircraft remained high overhead, the SA-17s were harmless. With their Maverick missiles and cluster bombs, the A-10s and F-16s rained death upon the retreating enemy with impunity. To Rodriguez's right, in the hills above the line of demarcation that separated his tanks from the fleeing North Koreans, he saw a line of Kiowa Warriors moving north and strafing the enemy infantry.

"War consumes fuel, ammunition, and men like a hungry monster that's never full," Rodriguez said to Obrisky as they walked among the dead.

Obrisky nodded. He and Rodriguez walked across the smoking battlefield, their weapons pointed toward the downed helicopter that smoldered thirty feet in front of them. Rodriguez scanned the wreckage for signs of life. Nothing but the smoking mass of metal, plastic, and wire was visible.

Crack! Crack!

Both men dived to the ground. Another shot kicked up a piece of metal only a few yards in front of them. Obrisky fired a burst of .45-caliber bullets from his submachine gun. Rodriguez could hear the whine of *Firebreather*'s engine cranking up as the crew prepared to rescue their commander.

"Do you see him?" Rodriguez asked.

"No, sir, but he doesn't know that," Obrisky whispered as he fired another burst.

The pistol cracked again. This time Rodriguez saw the flash. "He's over there, next to that wall."

A low, crumbling stone wall divided the open field that had once been a university green.

The loader manning *Firebreather*'s .50-caliber machine gun aimed the heavy weapon toward the wall. Obrisky fired again, hitting the wall near the place the shots had come from, identifying the enemy to the loader on *Firebreather*.

This was all the loader needed. He plastered the wall with fire for almost a minute, then stopped. The battlefield grew silent.

Rodriguez looked at Obrisky. "The fifty must have gotten him. We have to check out that helicopter. I'll go right, you go left. When you get to the wall, cover me with your grease gun and I'll see if anyone's on the other side. Maybe we can take him alive."

"Sir, why don't we just take him out with a 120mm round?" Obrisky questioned. "I can be back with *Firebreather* in a sec. When in doubt, always use the main gun."

The look from Rodriguez ended the conversation. Obrisky shrugged with resignation, then the two men moved out. Rodriguez crawled to the right, his .45-caliber pistol in his right hand, cocked and ready. Obrisky crawled to the left.

Rodriguez reached the wall, hearing only the sound of his breathing. He looked to his right and saw that Obrisky was in position. The wall was only about three feet high. In a quick jump, Rodriguez landed on the other side.

A man sat just to the right against the wall, a pistol in his hand. His left leg was mangled and bloody. White dust from the strike of the .50-caliber bullets hitting the wall covered his bare head and shoulders. His left eye was covered by a black eye patch.

In a feeble gesture the man raised his pistol toward Rodriguez. Rodriguez fired first.

3:50 P.M., 6 October, 820th Command Group, north of Uijonbu. The 820th Corps lay bleeding and dying on the battlefield of Uijonbu. The 815th Corps was smashed too, its survivors fleeing on foot to the north or fighting it out in small, desperate pockets of resistance. It was the end.

General Park staggered to his feet. His bandaged left hand was bleeding. The charred, burning BTR armored car lay on its side. The enemy air forces had returned with a vengeance, destroying everything in the open. Several divisions of fresh South Koreans had attacked in the wake of the tidal wave caused by the Americans.

At first his weary men resisted. The enemy kept coming, attacking with tanks, artillery, and aircraft. His soldiers' ammunition ran out and the enemy air attacks increased. The men, overwhelmed by the power of the enemy's attack, no longer held their lines but gave way. His political officers had gone up and down the trenches, shooting every man who hesitated or broke. Eventually, this no longer worked. Leaflets rained down from the sky, offering safe passage to anyone who surrendered.

The soldiers turned on the political officers. Once these "guardians of the people" were dead, the soldiers surrendered in droves.

The NKPA soldiers had been taught that they would be shot by the Americans and South Koreans if they surrendered. When they found out that this was not true, some wavered. Then the message from higher headquarters came over the radio to stop fighting, and the Inmun Gun's will to fight evaporated.

Park could no longer offer any organized resistance to the enemy. A few fanatics held on, sniping at the ROKs and fighting as they fled to the north. Most of these were gunned down by the advancing ROK battalions. Few, if any, had a chance of making it back to their homes. As far as Park knew, the entire army had been destroyed.

He stood dazed, hatless, his left arm bleeding. The crew of his BTR lay strewn on the ground like so many broken dolls. It had all happened so quickly, a moment in time shimmering in and out. Yesterday we were masters of the battlefield. Now we are the vanquished.

Defeat. The word stuck in his throat. His fate was predictable, inevitable. Vanquished generals had only one fate in North Korea.

"I wonder how it will end," he said to no one, but he knew he would never know. That's the truth, and the hell of it, he thought as he put the pistol to his head and pulled the trigger.

14
TAPS

We can lose the game not only because of the nature of our enemies, but because of our own. We understand we cannot ignore the competition, and realize with frustration that we cannot end it by putting the competitor out of business with a bang, but we will not willingly face that fact that we may walk along the chasm, beset by tigers, for many years to come. . . . If free nations want a certain kind of world, they will have to fight for it, with courage, money, diplomacy—and legions.   —T. R. FEHRENBACH

10:00 A.M., 7 October, 1st Army Group headquarters bunker, Kaesong, North Korea. Major General Kang Sung-Yul, acting commander of 1st Army Group, walked woodenly into the adjoining communications office. The short, People's Militia officer, General Jong, followed him like a guard dog.

Despite the strenuous efforts of Kang's headquarters and the gallant fighting of the soldiers at the front, the flower of the Inmun Gun was vanishing like the morning dew. Some of the few radio messages received were from commanders crying aloud that their men were dying in vain. These reports were full of the names of commanders killed and battalions annihilated. The situation was hopeless. Many units had fought to the last man. Now, faced with futile deaths, many were surrendering. Kang wondered if their sacrifice would have any meaning.

The communications officer stood in silent attention, the telephone receiver in his hand. The telephone was one of the few remaining communications lines still not jammed or disabled by the enemy. The telephone linked the Kaesong Command Center to Pyongyang by fiberoptic cable lines buried deep in the ground.

Kang was pensive, dreading the next few agonizing minutes. He knew the penalty for failure. He could accept responsibility for mistakes, but he dreaded humiliation at the hands of incompetent political officers who knew nothing of the intricacies and friction of war.

He had done everything he could do. His training, experience, and will were not enough to turn the cascading course of events that was unfolding. It had been a closely run thing. The North Korean drive into the heart and psyche of their enemies had inflicted striking casualties and damage to the ROK-U.S. forces. Kang had believed in the strategic plan. He felt that Daring Thrust had been the correct military answer to North Korea's political and economic deadlock. The sabotage of the satellites and the execution of the Paengnyongdo Option had been strokes of operational brilliance. The key to the success of Daring Thrust had always been rapid, unrelenting forward movement toward the enemy's strategic center of gravity—the isolation of Seoul and the threat of annihilation of its population.

The tempo of the attack—speed over time—had meant everything. The tempo had been disrupted and lost. The problem had not been one of the concentration of combat power, or even the movement of combat power, but rather one of movement of the concentrated combat power *in time*. The Inmun Gun had attacked with great velocity but could not accelerate or change course as the situation changed. As the enemy counterattack unfolded, the Inmun Gun could not react fast enough.

A hundred potential outcomes swirled through Kang's tired mind. What if the army had advanced faster? What if Marshal Kim had not insisted on the destruction of Uijonbu? If Kim Seung-Hee had lived, would things have turned out differently?

All these questions were irrelevant now. History had run its course. The invasion had failed; the Heroic Leader was dead. The Inmun Gun, routed and beaten, would never rise again. Some small groups were still fighting their way back north. Thousands had surrendered to the fascists. There were fears about an enemy occupation of North Korea.

A new government had suddenly emerged in Pyongyang. Mao Tse-tung once said, "Political power comes from the barrel of a gun." For North Korea the gun was now in the hands of the People's Militia.

The command bunker was full of soldiers of the People's Militia. People's militiamen, armed with AK-47 assault rifles, guarded every doorway and exit. All of Kang's men had been disarmed. Many had been arrested; a few had been shot.

Kang's communications officer, an army major, looked like a whipped puppy. There were none of the characteristic, proud, formal *"nam chim"* responses anymore. The major's eyes revealed the resignation he felt in his heart. The headquarters reflected the state of the army—defeat.

Kang felt sorry for his somber and depressed staff. They had proposed counterattacks and argued in favor of continuing the battle through guerrilla warfare. He could not blame these young, aggressive staff officers for the debacle that befell them any more than he could permit the agony to continue. Their training had taught them to rely on the offensive and fight to the death against insurmountable odds. It remained for older, wiser heads to apply the medicine needed to cure the critical wounds.

The major handed Kang the telephone.

"This is Major General Kang Sung-Yul, acting commander of 1st Shock Army Group," he said solemnly into the telephone.

"Comrade Kang, it is good to hear your voice again," the new leader of North Korea announced over the telephone's transmitter. "Admiral Bae has been executed. As you know, the People's Militia has taken over control of the military and the country. We will withdraw our forces to areas north of the DMZ and begin direct peace talks with the Republic of Korea."

"I understand," Kang said slowly, trying to place the voice on the other end of the line.

"A man may ruin himself for pride, to save face," the voice of the new leader of North Korea continued, "but he should not jeopardize his country for his own ego or ambition."

Kang stood frozen. The voice was familiar. He suddenly remembered. He was talking to a ghost, an admiral killed in Kim Seung-Hee's coup d'état. How could this be? He cleared his throat. "May I ask, comrade, to whom I am talking?"

"Why my dear general," the voice answered, "I thought you knew. This is Admiral Gung. I am the true successor to Kim

Jong Il and the new leader of the Democratic People's Republic of Korea."

5:30 P.M., 8 October, 1st Brigade headquarters, north of Pochon, South Korea. "Okay, it's official," Colonel Jakes announced with a broad smile. "As of noon tomorrow a cease-fire is in effect."

Everyone in the room grinned as if they had been on death row and the governor had just granted them stays of execution. As the cease-fire order was read, a collective cheer came up from the assembled officers in the brigade command post.

"The North Koreans have agreed to withdraw all their forces back to the prewar DMZ and begin direct negotiations for the reunification of Korea."

"They've surrendered?" Rodriguez asked.

"Well, let's just say a deal was made," the colonel answered. "A faction has taken over the government in Pyongyang that was against the war from the start. They're negotiating the return of what's left of the NKPA and the release of our POWs. There's talk about the disarmament of the north in return for massive economic assistance. As far as we're concerned, the war is over."

"Has every North Korean gotten the word?" Rodriguez asked. If the defense in the Chorwon Valley on 3 October had been a graduation exercise for the Dragon Force, it had received its diploma during the attack on 6 October. Rodriguez didn't want the Dragon Force to pay tuition again.

"Here's a copy of the rules of engagement for the cease-fire," Jakes said as his thin, red-headed intelligence officer, Capt. Audrey Devens, handed out a thick stack of forms. "Some isolated units will probably not get the word. We're rebroadcasting their acceptance of the cease-fire accord on every NKPA command frequency. The message explains the situation and tells the North Koreans where to assemble. That should help."

"We don't expect any major trouble," Jakes said, "but I want everyone on his guard. There's always some bastard who won't quit, and I don't want to take any more casualties."

"Don't worry," Rodriguez replied. "You don't have to tell the Dragon Force to shoot first and ask questions later."

"I know you'll all do the right thing," said Jakes. "Protect your force and keep your sabers sharp. Dismissed."

Rodriguez walked outside, relieved that the fighting was over but unsure of what the future would bring. He walked to his HMMWV. Corporal Finley sat in the driver's seat eagerly waiting for the word from his commander to move out.

As Rodriguez opened the door of the HMMWV, a telephone rang from the backseat. Finley turned around, rummaged through a pile of gear, and retrieved a cellular phone. He handed it to Rodriguez.

"Hello?" Rodriguez answered. "This is Dragon Six."

"Mike?" Alice Hamilton asked. "Mike, is that you?"

10:00 A.M., 9 October, 2d Infantry Division headquarters, ten kilometers south of Seoul, South Korea. Lieutenant Colonel Steve Wallace lay on a cot in the corner of the headquarters building staring at the ceiling. For the past four hours he had slept a sleep of exhaustion. Now, suddenly, he awoke with a start. For a minute, wide awake, he thought the war wasn't over. He felt as if he had forgotten some terrible task.

Slowly he realized that the blood-filled nightmare was over and the cease-fire was in effect. The past week he had survived on nervous energy. Now his body was paying him back for the abuse. His shoulder throbbed. He reached over to a camouflage rucksack and took out a bottle of aspirin. Fumbling with the top, he opened the bottle and swallowed some pills.

The counterattack had gone much better than anyone had dreamed. The 2d Infantry Division's attack penetrated the enemy's defense, disrupted the 815th Corps—which was refueling and preparing to continue the attack—and lunged forward and destroyed the enemy's artillery group. The combined ground, air, and missile attack of the enemy's artillery group and the death of Marshal Kim Seung-Hee had been the decisive stroke. Before dawn on 7 October, seven ROK divisions counterattacked at Uijonbu, drove back the stunned enemy, and marched north. By noon on the eighth, the enemy had asked for an unconditional cease-fire.

"Sir, how are you feeling?" Major Cooper asked as he walked up to Wallace's bunk. The major carried a stack of papers. "I've got the latest intel update for you."

"Jim, I couldn't be better," Wallace said with a cynical smile, sitting up. He stared at the stack of messages that Cooper had laid on his cot. "Especially since you decided to bring me a pile of work."

"Sorry to bother you, but you did ask me to bring this to you the moment it arrived," Cooper said with a sly grin, looking like a fox who knew the location of an unguarded chicken coop.

Wallace held up the papers to the dim fluorescent lights, slowly studying each page. Cooper looked on intently, waiting for a reaction.

Wallace whistled. "You mean to tell me that this guy, Admiral Gung, conducted a countercoup on 4 October?"

"That's what it says," Cooper said with a smile. "And he fed the South Koreans information that helped us launch the counterattack."

"Why? What was his motivation?" Wallace asked.

"Who cares?" Cooper answered. "Maybe he wanted to be king. Maybe he didn't want to live in a North Korea ruled by this Kim Seung-Hee character. Whatever the reason, it's over."

"But I don't get it," Wallace said, scratching his head. "Why didn't Kim Seung-Hee just have him killed?"

"The report says that Kim killed all his rivals, including Kim Jong Il. All except this Admiral Gung character. Gung apparently escaped moments before the massacre of the top leadership. He must have been tipped off by someone who worked for him in the People's Militia. Apparently the battle in the command bunker in Pyongyang was so bloody that the body of a navy captain was identified as Gung's corpse. Obviously they were too busy with events to spend much time worrying about the identification of their victims."

"What about our man on the hill, Private Jamie Emerson?" Wallace asked. "Wasn't he the guy who confirmed Kim Seung-Hee's helicopters?"

"Yes. Let me tell you, sir, that was a close call. Just as they were about to be overrun by a squad of North Koreans, one of our Kiowa Warrior helicopters arrived and saved the day," Cooper answered with a grin as wide as the Mississippi. "They recovered Private Emerson and a ROK lieutenant who was with him. Both of them were wounded, so they were evacuated to a hospital south of Seoul. I just received a report that they'll both be fine. General Schmidt says he's going to recommend them for the Silver Star."

11:00 A.M., 9 October, Seoul, South Korea. The camera was running and the satellite link connected them with the main studios in Atlanta. Paul looked at Alice Hamilton, his left hand counting down the seconds until she would be live on international television.

"Amid the clamor of this horrible war and the specter of nuclear war, a struggle for the leadership of North Korea was taking place in Pyongyang. This coupled with the resolute defense by Republic of Korea and U.S. forces have brought about the cease-fire. Now, the new government in Pyongyang has contacted the United States and the government of South Korea to express its willingness for an unconditional cease-fire and the withdrawal of all North Korean forces from South Korea," Alice Hamilton explained to the camera.

The backdrop of her scene was a gutted, burned-out section of Seoul. The Nodong Scud missiles had hit this area several times in the first few days of the war. Hundreds of people had died in the buildings that stood sagging to the ground behind the reporter.

"In return, Pyongyang has asked that air attacks on its territory cease and the ROK-U.S. alliance make no further hostile moves against the north."

Alice paused, looking down at the ground. Paul kept the camera rolling.

It's all so senseless, she thought. Thousands of civilians had been killed. Large cities in South Korea—Munsan, Tongducheon, Uijonbu, and Seoul—had been devastated. The battle was over, the killing had stopped, but the dying was still going on. The hospitals were full of the sick and wounded. Women, children, and old men had suffered along with the combatants.

Alice composed herself and looked back into the eye of the camera. "A truce, a cease-fire, has been declared. This is the first time that nuclear weapons have been used in combat since Hiroshima and Nagasaki. Luckily for both Koreas, their use was limited to the island of Paengnyongdo in the Yellow Sea."

At that moment an explosion occurred somewhere in the

city. The ground shook. Alice looked nervously to her left. The government had warned of unexploded bombs.

"As you can see, there is still death and destruction occurring here in Seoul in spite of the cease-fire. Dozens of unexploded bombs have been discovered and are being deactivated by South Korean Army units."

Alice paused. The words were becoming more difficult. Mere words couldn't explain how she felt.

"The North Koreans remain unrepentant, with a weakened but potentially deadly capability. No one knows how the new government in Pyongyang will act in the days ahead. So far, in spite of the terrible loss of life on both sides, there is only a cease-fire, no surrender or peace treaty."

She couldn't continue much longer. Too many visions crowded her weary memory. She felt extremely tired and empty. Nodding to Paul, she signaled that this would be her final comment.

"The one hope is that this horrible war will demonstrate that we must not allow it to happen again. More than anything, this brutal, senseless war has taught me that no one is a tourist. No one can remain uncommitted. We cannot allow wrong to prevail. We must be ready to stand up to the tiger and, if he attacks, kill him. We live in a world beset by tigers, each looking for an easy meal. If we want a free, prosperous world, we must have the courage to fight for it. This is Alice Hamilton reporting from the center of a defiant and battered Seoul, South Korea."

9:00 A.M., 10 October, Chorwon Valley, north of Pochon. Between the ridges and low hills lay a long expanse of rice paddies. Every few hundred meters was the sooty, disintegrated hull of a North Korean tank or destroyed armored vehicle. In spite of the wreckage that lay scattered about, the fields seemed haunted with memories of happier times.

The battalion had formed in a schoolyard. The schoolhouse had been smashed and burned in the fighting, but the wide-open dirt yard had gone virtually untouched and was a reasonable substitute for a parade ground. Magpies flew about and cooed from the top of the damaged school building.

The Dragon Force stood in ranks. Major Dave Lucas and three other staff officers were in a line in front of the formation.

Each company was formed in a square, the men in complete battle gear standing behind their company's first sergeants. In front of the task force staff, Command Sergeant Major Dougan, massive and apparently indestructible, was flanked by a color guard that held the flags of the United States and the Republic of Korea and the battalion colors of the 2d Battalion, 72d Armor. Dougan positioned himself in the front center of the formation and saluted.

"Sir, the Dragon Force is formed," Dougan shouted.

"Post," the task force commander replied, returning the salute. Sergeant Major Dougan moved behind the colors. The five company commanders moved forward to the front of their formations, relieving their first sergeants.

An M16 rifle, with its bayonet fixed, was stuck into the ground in front of each company square, a grim and symbolic reminder of lost comrades. A set of boots was placed in front of the rifle. A tanker's CVC helmet rested on the rifle butt.

"You, the American and South Korean KATUSA soldiers of the Dragon Force, are the proud legions of our two nations," Rodriguez said, looking at his soldiers as if they were his own sons. "In a world where courage and determination are often not appreciated, you stood, fought, and saved the day. Today we honor our comrades in arms who fell in battle and purchased this hard-won victory with their lives.

"All of us must die someday. In dying, however, these men lived for something. Their names will not be forgotten by any of us. They were soldiers. The select of their generation, they served when others did not care to. They sought a hard life when others chose safety and leisure. They served their nations on faith, for no amount of pay or honor will make a man kill and stand and be killed. They served on faith in their country, their cause, and their army. But most importantly, they served for their faith in their company, their platoon, their crew, and one another. For in the final analysis, they gave all they had for us, their comrades. For this we salute them and honor their memories."

Command Sergeant Major Dougan's voice boomed. "Present arms."

The soldiers snapped their salute, touching their Kevlar helmets with their right hands. The command sergeant major turned around and with both hands held a sheet of paper listing the slain men. As the bugler played a long, mournful taps, the command sergeant major read off the names of all the soldiers in the unit who had died in battle: "Altman, Charles C., Private First Class; Bradford, Anthony, Major; Collins, Richard M., Specialist; Doan, George, Second Lieutenant," the sergeant major announced.

Rodriguez looked straight ahead. He saw the colors floating gently in the breeze. The notes of the bugler playing taps registered in his heart. At the same time, he felt a pain in his stomach as the roll call of the dead was sounded.

"Elting, George C., Private; Hardee, Nathaniel D., Sergeant First Class; Hernandez, Emilio, Private First Class; Hawthorne, Steve, Second Lieutenant; Kim, Kye-Wan, Corporal, KATUSA; Lee, Hyung-Jung, Private First Class, KATUSA."

A few of the soldiers sobbed in ranks. Rodriguez looked at their eyes. Most stared off into the distance, lost in their own thoughts. All, he felt, were happy to be alive but confused how fate had selected them to survive.

"Nolan, James E., Sergeant; Mackenzie, Kenneth W., Captain; Oh, Kye-Wan, Corporal, KATUSA; Preston, Alexander, Second Lieutenant," Dougan announced, his voice strong and determined.

The names of the fallen continued, all seventy-two of them. The task force had taken serious losses, a full tank company's worth of soldiers, and, as always, a heavy toll of junior leaders.

Rodriguez acknowledged, without much satisfaction, that they had presented the enemy with a much heavier butcher's bill than they had received.

Finally, the last name on the list was read. Command Sergeant Major Dougan executed an about-face. Rodriguez nodded to the chaplain, who said a prayer.

"When our Lord used an example to show the meaning of faith, he used a soldier. In his days the proud legions of Rome held the borders of civilization against the barbarians. One day a centurion, a professional soldier of Rome, sent word to Jesus to plead for a miracle that would save his servant's life. The proud centurion humbled himself to Jesus and said: 'I did not consider myself worthy to come to you, but I know that if you say the word my servant will be healed. I myself am a man under authority, with soldiers under me. I tell this one go and he goes and that one come and he comes.' Jesus was amazed at the faith of this centurion and turned to the crowd and said, 'I tell you, I have not found such great faith in all of Israel.' You are like the centurion.

"This service is for the living as well as our fallen comrades. It is soldiers like you, not just the machines, who made the difference. Without technology, tactics are helpless; without tactics, technology is pointless. Without proud legions, technology and tactics are worthless. Our technology saved friendly lives and helped us to defeat the enemy, but it did not relieve the burden to close with and destroy the foe. You did that. The soldiers who sacrificed their lives for us did that. Each of you is a special breed, a national treasure. You cannot be purchased for any price."

The chaplain folded his notes and walked back behind the formation. The wind blew gently against Rodriguez's face and caused the colors to flutter momentarily. Dougan nodded to his colonel.

"Present," the task force commander shouted, "arms."

The soldiers saluted again. The sergeant in charge of the color guard marched the colors to the flank of the formation and encased them in a green canvas cover.

"Order arms," Rodriguez ordered.

Sergeant Major Dougan turned to Rodriguez and saluted. "Sir, this concludes the ceremony."

Rodriguez returned the sergeant major's salute and replied, "Company commanders, take charge of your companies."

Commands were echoed and the units moved off the field. Dougan and Rodriguez withdrew together, away from the rest.

Rodriguez looked up at a beautiful fall sky with scattered puffy white clouds. The sun was shining and the warmth it generated was welcome. He felt a mysterious fraternity with his men and his past, a fraternity born of smoke, hazard, hardship, and death.

"So what happens now?" Dougan asked. "Will we have peace or just get ready for the next war?"

"What can our past tell us about our future?" Rodriguez said sternly. "That's for our wise politicians to decide. God help them, they'd better not screw it up."

Rodriguez pulled a gold cigarette case from the pocket of his Nomex uniform. The case was old and scratched, but it was now his most cherished possession. He opened the case and carefully read the inscription: "To SFC Robert Rodriguez: When a sergeant gives a soldier an order, it must have the same weight as that of a four-star general. Love, Margarita and Michael Rodriguez."

Tears filled his eyes as he closed his father's cigarette case. He remembered the day when his mother took him to the jeweler's to engrave the gift they had picked out for his father's promotion to sergeant first class. He looked at the mountains in the distance and struggled to control his emotions. Now he understood what his father had understood decades ago. Someone had to make the tough calls. Bad calls kill people; good calls save lives. But even good decisions sometimes can't stop people from getting killed. In spite of the danger, someone has to make the decisions. It had been his father's job and now it was his job.

It was suddenly clear to him why he was who he was, why he had chosen to be a soldier, and why he had been picked to command. He was, as his father had been, a centurion, true to a society that did not understand them but to which they had pledged their absolute loyalty. When so ordered, they went to war; it was as simple as that.

Would the sacrifice of his soldiers and so many others be recognized? Probably not, but that didn't seem to matter much now. Would people still believe that they could live without legions to defend them? Evidently so, because he had met people all his life who believed that; he didn't see that changing. Would misinformed people continue to sneer at people who believed in patriotism? Of course, but Rodriguez considered these people—those who sneered and still lived in the society that defended them—as parasites or idiots or both. He knew that the soldiers who had fallen had given their last, golden moment for something of value, for one another.

Would society be wise enough to allow the centurions to defend the frontier with disciplined, iron-hard legions? That was the toughest question, the one that remained to be answered, because somewhere out there in a world filled with chaos, hatred, and greed, the seeds of other wars were growing, preparing to sprout up and change the order of things. These wars would not be won by push buttons, no matter how high tech war became. It would take soldiers, proud legions, to keep the peace. That was, Rodriguez knew, the nature of the world. It had been and probably always would be, despite the best hopes and wishes of the liberal, peace-loving society for which he fought.

For the first time in his life, Lt. Col. Michael Rodriguez felt at peace with himself. He prayed that it would last.

AFTERWORD

Perhaps some readers may think that various details of warfare found in this novel are fanciful; Task Force 2-72 Armor must seem like something out of science fiction. Anyone who doubts the reality of Dragon Force in combat need only look back to the 1991 Gulf War battle of 73 Easting to understand the awesome combat capability of a well-trained American tank crew and its Abrams main battle tank.

In the early hours of 26 February 1991, a single armored cavalry troop of the 2d Armored Cavalry Squadron (ACR), consisting of only nine M1A1 Abrams tanks and thirteen M3 Bradley cavalry fighting vehicles, ran into a dug-in Iraqi brigade. The Iraqis were primed and ready to defend. The collision took place in a blinding sandstorm. The Iraqis, using older Russian-made T-72 tanks (which had more firepower than those currently in service in the North Korean Army, the T-62) could not see their attackers. The Americans, in spite of the sandstorm, could see the Iraqis clearly in the thermal sights of the Abrams tanks and Bradleys. The result was incredible.

The battle lasted approximately twenty-three minutes. The nine U.S. tanks and thirteen Bradleys destroyed thirty T-72

Iraqi tanks, sixteen BMP infantry fighting vehicles, and thirty-nine trucks, and killed a large number of Iraqi infantry. The Iraqis, members of one of the best-trained Republican Guard units in the Iraqi Army, fought back with all the courage and determination they could muster, but it just didn't matter. The lopsided American victory at the Battle of 73 Easting was the result of several critical factors: superior equipment, superior training, and superior leadership. American tanks and infantry fighting vehicles overmatched their opponents both in firepower, target acquisition (thermal sights), and protection (the M1A1's excellent Chobham armor).

Years of realistic force-on-force maneuvering at the National Training Center and other venues have resulted in an army that is virtually combat proven. The 2d Armored Cavalry Regiment arrived in Saudi Arabia in early December 1990, almost three months prior to the Battle of 73 Easting. Prior to the battle, the cohesive, proud force was forged into hard steel through several weeks of tough, highly focused training.

Lastly, but dramatically essential, the superb leadership of the American armored force made a tremendous difference. The leaders of the 2d ACR did not have to wait for instructions from higher authority to know what to do and when to act. They moved to contact and attacked without hesitation—something the Iraqis, with their highly centralized decision-making process (again, similar to the North Korean Army), could not do. The Iraqis fought back with everything they had—and this was the Tawakalna Division of the Republican Guard, the best-trained and best-armed force in the Iraqi Army—but the Americans killed them until those remaining surrendered.

The United States Army is not looking for a fair fight.

The military forces of the United States train hard in order to put their enemy on the horns of a dilemma, forcing the opponent into situations where his options and actions are irrelevant. America's armed forces did that in Desert Storm and, as long as it maintains a qualitative battlefield superiority, could do so again.

Glossary

alternate position Position given to a weapon, a unit, or an individual to be occupied when the primary position becomes untenable or unsuitable for carrying out its task. The alternate position is located so that the individual can continue to fulfill his original task.

AN/PVS-7 night vision goggles Lightweight, battery-powered, passive night vision device that allows the operator to see in low light (moonlight) levels. The goggles weigh 1.5 pounds and offer clear vision on normal nights out to 150 meters.

APC Armored personnel carrier.

assembly area Area in which a force prepares or regroups for further action.

attack Offensive action characterized by movement supported by fire.

deliberate attack Attack planned and carefully coordinated with all concerned elements based on thorough reconnaissance, evaluation of all available intelligence and relative combat strength, analysis of various courses of action, and other factors affecting the situation. It generally is conducted against a well-organized defense when a hasty attack is not possible or has failed.

frontal attack Offensive maneuver in which the main action is directed against the front of the enemy forces and over the most direct approaches.

hasty attack Offensive operation for which a unit has not made extensive preparations. It is conducted with the resources immediately available in order to maintain momentum or take advantage of the enemy situation.

main attack Principal attack or effort into which the commander places the bulk of the offensive capability at his disposal. An attack directed against the chief objective of the battle.

supporting attack Attack designed to hold the enemy in position, deceive him as to where the main attack is being made, prevent him from reinforcing the elements opposing the main effort, and/or cause him to commit his reserves prematurely at an indecisive location.

attrition (attrit) Reduction of the effectiveness of a force caused by the loss of personnel or material.

avenue of approach Air or ground route of an attacking force of a given size leading to its objective or to key terrain in its path.

axis of advance General route of advance, assigned for the purposes of control, which extends toward the enemy. An axis of advance symbol graphically portrays a commander's intention, such as avoidance of built-up areas or envelopment of an enemy force. It follows terrain for the size of the force assigned to the axis. A commander may maneuver his forces and supporting fires to either side of an axis of advance provided the unit remains oriented on the axis and the objective.

base of fire Fire placed on an enemy force or position to reduce or eliminate the enemy's capability to interfere by fire and/or movement of friendly maneuver elements. It may be provided by a single weapon or a grouping of weapon systems.

block Deny the enemy access to a given area or prevent enemy advance in a given direction. It may be for a specified time. Units may have to retain terrain and accept decisive engagement.

BMNT (before morning nautical twilight) Time between night and sunrise when there is enough light to navigate without night vision devices.

BP (battle position) Defensive location oriented on the most likely enemy avenue of approach from which a unit may defend or attack. The unit can be as large as a battalion task force or as small as a platoon. A unit assigned a BP is located within the general outline of the BP.

BRDM Russian-designed armored car used for reconnaissance and command and control. It is usually armed with a 14.5mm machine gun.

BTR Russian-made armored personnel carrier used by the North Korean Army.

canalize Restrict operations to a narrow zone by use of existing or reinforcing obstacles that may interfere with subsequent operations.

CAS (close air support) Air action against hostile targets that are in close proximity to friendly forces. It requires detailed integration of each air mission with the fire and movement of those forces.

checkpoint Predetermined point on the ground used as a means of coordinating friendly movement. A checkpoint is not used as a reference point in reporting enemy location.

CITV (commander's independent thermal viewer) Sight that allows the tank commander to view targets and areas of interest other than what the gunner is looking at. The tank commander can set the CITV to automatically scan for blind spots or control it from the override control grip. The CITV gives the tank commander the ability to find a target and take control of the engagement, swinging the turret and the gun to his thermal view with the press of a button. Seeing a dangerous target that the gunner has not identified, the tank commander hits the slew/slave button on his override controls and in two seconds the turret moves, the gun is centered precisely on the target, and the tank is ready to fire. Once the tank commander hears that the gun is loaded, the loader shouts "Up" over the intercom, and the round is fired and is on the way to the target.

clear Destroy or force the withdrawal of all enemy forces and reduce any obstacles that may interfere with subsequent operations.

coax (pronounced co-AX) Machine gun mounted in the turret of a tank in a way that its line of fire is parallel (coaxial) to that of the cannon set on the same mounting. In the M1A1, an M240 7.62mm machine gun is mounted coaxially with the M256 120mm cannon. The coax is fired by either the tank gunner (primary) or tank commander (alternate). The coax is fed by an ammunition bin that contains twenty-three hundred 7.62mm rounds.

coil Arrangement of vehicles forming a circle.

commander's guidance Commander's tool to direct the planning process. It should consist of six elements: the restated mission, the initial concept of the operation, the scheme of maneuver, the time plan, the type of order to be prepared, and the rehearsal technique.

company team Team formed by the attachment of one or more nonorganic tank, mechanized infantry, or light infantry platoons to a tank, mechanized infantry, or light infantry company in exchange for or in addition to organic platoons.

concept of operations Graphic, verbal, or written statement in broad outline that gives an overall picture of a commander's assumptions or intent in regard to an operation or a series of operations. It includes at a minimum the scheme of maneuver and a fire support plan. It is described in sufficient detail for the staff and subordinate commanders to understand what they are to do and how to fight the battle without further instructions.

contain Stop, hold, or surround the forces of the enemy or cause the enemy to center activity on a given front and prevent his withdrawing any part of his forces for use elsewhere.

counterattack Attack by part or all of a defending force against an enemy attacking force for such specific purposes as regaining ground lost or cutting off or destroying enemy advance units. The general objective is to regain the initiative and deny to the enemy the attainment of his purpose in attacking. In sustained defensive operations, it is undertaken to restore the battle position and is directed at limited objectives.

cover Natural or artificial protection from enemy observation.

covered approach Any route that offers protection against enemy observation or fire, or an approach made under the protection furnished by other forces or by natural cover.

cross attachment Exchange of subordinate units between units for a temporary period. For example, a tank battalion detaches a tank company that is subsequently attached to a mechanized infantry battalion, and the mechanized infantry battalion detaches a mechanized company that is then attached to the tank battalion.

CVC (crew vehicular communications) helmet Helmet with a microphone and earphones to allow intercom and radio communications. Vehicle crew members wear a CVC helmet in the vehicle to communicate with other crew members and talk over the radio.

dead space Area within the maximum effective range of a weapon, a surveillance device, or an observer that cannot be covered by fire and observation from a given position because of intervening obstacles, the nature of the ground, the characteristics of the trajectory, or the limitations of the pointing capabilities of the systems.

decisive engagement Engagement in which a unit is considered fully committed and cannot maneuver or extricate itself. In the absence of outside assistance, the action must be fought to a conclusion and be either won or lost with the forces at hand.

decisive terrain Key terrain that has an extraordinary impact on the mission. Decisive terrain is rare and will not be present in every mission. To designate terrain as decisive is to recognize that the successful accomplishment of the mission, whether offensive or defensive, depends on seizing or retaining it. The commander designates decisive terrain to communicate its importance in his concept of operations, first to his staff and, later, to subordinate commanders.

defilade Protection from hostile observation and fire provided by an obstacle such as a hill, ridge, or bank. To shield from enemy fire or observation by using natural or artificial obstacles.

defile Narrow passage that tends to constrict the movement of troops.

delay Trade space for time, inflict maximum damage on the enemy force, and preserve the force within the limits established by the issuing commander.

depth Extension of operations in space, time, and resources.

destroy Physically disable or capture an enemy force.

direct fire Fire directed at a target that is visible to the gunner or firing unit.

direction of attack Specific direction or route that the main attack or main body of the force will follow. If used, it is normally at battalion and lower levels. Direction of attack is a more restrictive control measure than axis of advance, and units are not free to maneuver off the assigned route. It is usually associated with infantry units conducting night attacks, or units involved in limited visibility operations, and in counterattacks. (In NATO, referred to as an attack route.)

direction of fire Direction on which a cannon or missile is laid. It represents the direction to the most significant threat in the target area.

displace Leave one position and take another. Forces may be displaced laterally to concentrate combat power in threatened areas.

dominant terrain Terrain that, because of its elevation, proportions, or location, commands a view of and may offer fields of fire over surrounding terrain.

DPICM (dual-purpose improved conventional munitions) Artillery shells that contain submunitions (bomblets) that can damage armored vehicles and devastate unprotected troops.

EA (engagement area) Area in which the commander intends to trap and destroy an enemy force with the massed fire of all available weapons. An engagement area is routinely identified by a target reference point in the center of the trap area or by prominent terrain features around the area. Although an engagement area may also be divided into sectors of fire, it is important to understand that defensive systems are not designed around engagement areas but rather around avenues of approach. Engagement areas and sectors of fire are not intended to restrict fires or cause operations to become static or fixed; they are used only as tools to concentrate fires and to optimize their effects.

economy of force Allocation of minimum-essential combat capability or strength to secondary efforts so that forces may be concentrated in the area where a decision is sought. *A principle of war.*

ETAC (enlisted tactical air control) team In an armored task force, the ETAC consists of two air force personnel, usually sergeants, who operate out of an M113A2 APC equipped with both FM and high-frequency radios. The mission of the ETAC is to control close air support for the task force.

FASCAM (field artillery scatterable minefield) Scatterable minefield, composed of antitank or antipersonnel mines, delivered by artillery.

FEBA (forward edge of the battle area) A term used in the defense to describe the forward limit of the main battle area.

field of fire Area that a weapon or group of weapons may effectively cover with fire from a given location.

fire and movement Simultaneous moving and firing by men and/or vehicles. This technique is used primarily during the assault of enemy positions.

fire support plan Plan on how fire support will be used to support an operation. It should include a portion for each means of fire support involved.

FIST (fire support team) In fire support operations, a team composed of a team chief (field artillery lieutenant) and the necessary additional personnel and equipment required to plan, request, coordinate, and direct fire support efforts for company-sized units.

fix Action taken to prevent the enemy from moving any part of his forces from a specific location within a specific period of time by holding or surrounding him to prevent his withdrawal for use elsewhere.

FRAGO (fragmentary order) Abbreviated form of an operation order used to communicate mission changes to units and inform them of changes in the tactical situation.

front Lateral space occupied by an element measured from the extremity of one flank to the extremity of the other flank. The unit may be extended in a combat formation or occupying a position, depending on the type of operation involved.

frontage Width of the front plus that distance beyond the flanks covered by observation and fire by a unit in combat.

FSO Fire support officer.

gap Any break or breach in the continuity of tactical dispositions or formations beyond effective small-arms coverage; a weak spot in the enemy's defenses.

GLD (ground laser designator) Hand-held device that paints targets with invisible laser light to direct laser-guided munitions with pinpoint accuracy.

GPS (global position satellite system) Signals from three or more Navstar satellites enable receivers on earth to calculate latitude, longitude, and altitude to within about a hundred feet. The concept of the GPS system is simple. With the help of an on-board atomic clock, each satellite in the network continuously broadcasts a signal indicating the time and the spacecraft's exact position. There are twenty-four satellites, including three spares. A GPS receiver uses simultaneous readings from three different satellites to fix the user's longitude and latitude. Reliance on satellites rather than ground stations makes the system more precise than conventional navigation technology. The common GPS receiver in the U.S. Army is the PLGR (pronounced "Plugger").

grid coordinates Set of numbers designating the location of a point in respect to a grid. Coordinates are usually expressed to the nearest hundred, ten, or one meter in a single expression. For example, NK329378 (nearest one hundred meters), NK32943785 (nearest ten meters), or NK3294837853 (nearest one meter). Grid coordinates always consist of pairs of number groups; for instance, NK3945 is read 39 grid line to the right and 45 grid line up. Grid coordinates on a map are always read right, then up.

HMMWV (highly mobile multipurpose wheeled vehicle) Acronym for the three-quarter-ton truck, also known as a Hummer or Humvee.

initiative Setting or changing the terms of battle by action. Initiative implies an offensive spirit in the conduct of all operations.

Inmun Gun North Korean name for the North Korean People's Army.

interdict Prevent or hinder by any means the enemy's use of any area or route.

INTSUM Intelligence summary.

IPB (intelligence preparation of the battlefield) Systematic approach to analyzing the enemy, weather, and terrain in a specific geographic area. It integrates enemy doctrine with the weather and terrain as they relate to the mission and the specific battlefield environment. This is done to determine and evaluate enemy capabilities, vulnerabilities, and probable courses of action.

IVIS (intervehicular information system) Valuable command and control device mounted in all M1A2 tanks. IVIS allows tanks to communicate text and graphics by FM radio digital burst. Operation orders, status reports, and map graphics can be passed instantly at the push of a button between tanks equipped with IVIS. IVIS will portray the location of all friendly tanks equipped with an IVIS and the location of any enemy tanks that an IVIS-equipped tank lazes to. The information that the IVIS system captures from the laser gives the location of the enemy tank. This information can be sent digitally to all other IVIS-equipped tanks to identify the enemy's exact location.

key terrain Any locality or area the seizure, retention, or control of which affords a marked advantage to either combatant.

LC (line of contact) General trace delineating the location where two opposing forces are engaged.

LD (line of departure) Line designated to coordinate the commitment of attacking units or scouting elements at a specified time. A start line.

LD/LC (line of departure is line of contact) Designation of forward friendly positions as the line of departure when opposing forces are in contact.

limit of advance Easily recognized terrain feature beyond which attacking elements will not advance.

LZ Landing zone.

maneuver Movement of forces supported by fire to achieve a position of advantage from which to destroy or threaten destruction of the enemy. *A principle of war.*

mass 1. Concentration of combat power at a decisive time and place. *A principle of war.* 2. Concentrate or bring together fires so as to mass fires of multiple weapons or units. 3. Military formation in which units are spaced at less than normal distances and intervals.

METT-T (mission, enemy, terrain, troops, and time) Factors that must be considered during the planning and execution of a tactical operation.

  mission Who, what, when, where, and why of what is to be accomplished.

  enemy Current information concerning the enemy's strength, location, disposition, activity, equipment, and capability, and a determination as to the enemy's probable course of action.

  terrain (includes weather) Information about vegetation, soil type, hydrology, climatic conditions, and light data that is analyzed to determine the impact of the environment on current and future operations for both enemy and friendly operations.

  troops Quantity, level of training, and psychological state of friendly forces, including the availability of weapons systems and critical equipment.

  time available Time available to plan, prepare, and execute operations for enemy and friendly forces.

minefield Area of ground containing mines laid with or without a pattern.

MOPM Man-portable, 162-pound, suitcase-shaped mine dispenser that ejects seventeen antitank and four antipersonnel mines when executed.

MRLS (multiple rocket launcher system) American multiple rocket launcher that is built on an M2 Bradley chassis. The

MRLS carries twelve rockets per vehicle that can hit targets at a range of thirty kilometers. The rockets carry dual-purpose improved conventional munitions warheads. When the rockets detonate over their targets, the warheads explode and scatter hundreds of bomblets over an area measuring seven hundred by one hundred meters.

nam chim North Korean motto that means attack south.

neutralize Render ineffective or unusable.

NKPA North Korean People's Army.

Nodong missile North Korean version of an improved surface-to-surface missile based on the design of the Russian-made Scud rocket.

objective 1. Physical object of the action taken (for example, a definite terrain feature, the seizure and/or holding of which is essential to the commander's plan, or the destruction of an enemy force without regard to terrain features). 2. *Principle of war* that states that every military operation should be directed toward clearly defined, decisive, and attainable objectives.

offense Combat operation designed primarily to destroy the enemy. Offensive operations may be undertaken to secure key or decisive terrain, deprive the enemy of resources or decisive terrain, deceive and/or divert the enemy, develop intelligence, and hold the enemy in position. An offensive operation includes deliberate attack, hasty attack, movement to contact, exploitation, pursuit, and other limited-objective operations. The offensive is undertaken to seize, retain, and exploit the initiative; as such, it is *a principle of war.*

operation overlay Overlay showing the location, size, and scheme of maneuver/fires of friendly forces involved in an operation. As an exception, it may indicate predicted movements and locations of enemy forces.

OPORD (operation order) Directive issued by a commander to subordinate commanders for effecting the coordinated execution of an operation. It includes tactical movement orders.

orders group Standing group of key personnel requested to be present when a commander at any level issues his concept of the operation and his order.

overwatch 1. Tactical technique in which one element is positioned to support the movement of another element with immediate direct fire. 2. Tactical role of an element positioned to support the movement of another element with immediate direct fire.

passage of lines Passing one unit through the positions of another, as when elements of a covering force withdraw through the forward edge of the main battle area, or when an exploiting force moves through the elements of the force that conducted the initial attack. A passage may be designated as a forward or rearward passage of lines.

PL (phase line) Line used for control and coordination of military operations. It is usually a recognizable terrain feature extending across the zone of action. Units normally report crossing PLs but do not halt unless specifically directed. PLs often are used to prescribe the timing of delay operations.

POS/NAV system Position/navigation sensor unit on the M1A2 Abrams tank that is an inertial navigation sensor unit that remembers where the tank is and where it has gone. It communicates this information to other IVIS-equipped tanks, permitting the commander to see the location of his unit tanks on a digital map screen with a precision of plus or minus seventeen meters. The IVIS system's POS/NAV input can reduce the risk of fratricide by identifying the tanks' exact location.

primary position Place for a weapon, unit, or an individual to fight that provides the best means to accomplish the assigned mission.

priority of fires Direction to a fire support planner to organize and employ fire support means according to the importance of the supported unit's missions.

priority target Target on which the delivery of fires takes precedence over all other fires for the designated firing unit/element. The firing unit/element will prepare, to the extent possible, for the engagement of such targets. A firing unit/element may be assigned only one priority target.

quick combat strength reporting system Color-coded shorthand for reporting combat status of unit: green is 90 to 100 percent, amber is 75 to 89 percent, red is 50 to 74 percent, and black is less than 50 percent.

retain Occupy and hold a terrain feature to ensure that it is free of enemy occupation or use.

reverse slope Position on the ground not exposed to direct fire or observation. It may be a slope that descends away from the enemy.

reverse slope defense Defense area organized on any ground not exposed to direct fire or observation. It may be on a slope that descends away from the enemy.

RPG (rocket-propelled grenade) Russian-designed, shoulder-fired antitank weapon that can destroy most APCs. It can penetrate an M1A tank only if the warhead strikes the rear or the track.

sector Area designated by boundaries within which a unit operates and for which it is responsible. Normally, sectors are used in defensive operations.

secure Gain possession of a position or terrain feature with or without force, and to deploy in a manner that prevents its destruction or loss to enemy action.

seize Gain physical possession of a terrain feature from an enemy force.

SINCGARS (single-channel ground and air radio system) Radio that provides reliable FM radio communications through a frequency-hopping electronic countermeasure system. A common, exact time must be set on each radio to match the automatic frequency-hopping sequence of the other radios on the net.

SOI (signal operating instructions) Pamphlet issued by each unit that contains codes and frequencies for radio operations.

SP (start point) Clearly defined initial control point on a route at which specified elements of a column of ground vehicles or a flight of aircraft come under the control of the commander having responsibility for the movement.

STAFF (smart target activated fire and forget) tank round Round that allows the tanks to fire at targets that are hidden by terrain. A tank could fire a round in the direction of the valley and the round would fly over the trajectory and automatically detonate over the top of an enemy tank or APC. The STAFF round's sensors register any mass of metal that fits its programmed parameters as a tank or an APC. When the STAFF round explodes, submunitions automatically descend toward the target below, aim and fire, and penetrate the thin top armor. In addition, the STAFF round's sensors give priority to moving tanks and APCs. For Korea, this was ideal, making the STAFF round the weapon of choice to silence the ambusher before the lead tank entered the engagement area.

strongpoint Key point in a defensive position, usually strongly fortified and heavily armed with automatic weapons, around which other positions are grouped for protection.

support force Forces charged with providing intense direct overwatching fires to the assault force.

suppression Direct and indirect fires, electronic countermeasures, or smoke brought to bear on enemy personnel, weapons, or equipment to prevent effective fire on friendly forces.

synchronization Arrangement of battlefield activities in time, space, and purpose to produce maximum relative combat power at the decisive point. Synchronization is both a process and a result. Synchronization need not depend on explicit coordination if all forces involved fully understand the commander's intent and have developed and rehearsed well-conceived standard responses to anticipated contingencies.

TAC (tactical command post) In an armored task force, the TAC is usually represented by an M113A2 APC mounted with at least three FM radios.

TACSAT Tactical satellite communications equipment.

target overlay Overlay showing the locations of friendly artillery units, targets, boundaries, and fire support coordination measures.

task organization Temporary grouping of forces designed to accomplish a particular mission. Task organization involves the distribution of available assets to subordinate control headquarters by attachment or by placing assets in direct support or under the operational control of the subordinate.

TC Tank commander.

terrain analysis Process of interpreting a geographic area to determine the effect of the natural and man-made features on military operations.

TOC (tactical operations center) Element within the main command post consisting of those staff activities involved in sustaining current operations and planning future operations. Staff activities are functionally grouped into elements or cells. Units at battalion level and above normally have a TOC.

turret down Position in which an entire vehicle is behind cover but the commander can still observe to the front from the turret hatch or cupola.

T55 Russian-made main battle tank with a 100mm tank cannon.

T62 Russian-made main battle tank with a 115mm tank cannon.

Vee Arrangement of vehicles or personnel in the shape of a V with two elements up front to provide a heavy volume of fire on contact and one element in the rear to overwatch or maneuver. The point of the V is the trail element. A V formation may be used when the leader requires firepower to the front and flanks.

Volcano Truck-mounted mine dispenser system that can launch forty-nine canisters with a five-to-one mix of antitank and antipersonnel mines (960 mines) in less than thirty seconds.

VTT323, or Vett North Korean armored personnel carrier that carries from four to ten passengers. It is armed with a 14.5mm machine gun and an AT-3 Sagger antitank missile or an AT-4 Spandrel antitank missile. The VTT is lightly armored and has five road wheels and a small conical turret. The VTT323 is a licensed copy of the Chinese YW-531 APC.

warning order Preliminary notice of an action or order that is to follow. Usually issued as a brief oral or written message, it is designed to give subordinates time to make necessary plans and preparations.

wedge Formation of vehicles or personnel with one element leading and two elements in the rear to overwatch or maneuver. 1. Permits excellent fire to the front and good fire to each flank, 2. facilitates control, 3. permits sustained effort and provides flank security, 4. lends itself readily to fire and movement, 5. is often used when the enemy situation is vague and contact is imminent.

withdrawal Retrograde operation in which a force in contact with the enemy frees itself for a new mission.

zone Area of responsibility for offensive operations assigned to a unit by the drawing of boundaries.